THE FAMILY PLOT

BREA BROWN

WAYZGOOSE PRESS

Edited by Dorothy Zemach

Cover design by Keri Knutson at alchemybookcovers.com

(Note: An earlier, slightly modified edition of this novel, with the same title, was originally published in 2010, ISBN 978-1535395052.)

CHAPTER ONE

HER ASHES WENT to my mom; her print shop was all mine.

After shaking the hands of what had to be every single Morris resident, my mom, sister, cousins, aunts, and uncles huddled in small groups around the largest room at the Mulligan Funeral Home. The only thing remaining was the huge photo collage of Aunt Velvet with people we didn't know and a few photos of her with us, her family, on her rare visits south to Boston.

In the crook of her arm, Mom cradled the urn containing her baby sister and said, "Well, are we up for a trek to the falls today, or do we save that for some other time?"

My sister, Shelly, wrinkled her nose. "Oh, geez. I thought that was just one of those dramatic things Aunt Vel said to seem interesting. 'Scatter my ashes over the falls.' Seriously, is that even legal?"

Mom sighed. "I don't know. But that's what she wanted."

I held out my hands and wiggled my fingers, as if the object in Mom's arms were a child, not a pot of someone's remains. "Give her here. I'll take care of it in the summer, when it's nice up there."

Without hesitation, Mom thrust the copper jar at me. "Thank you, sweetheart. I knew we could count on you." As soon as her hands were free, she dug out a lipstick and compact from her purse and applied a fresh coat to her plump, newly injected lips.

"I can see you're too broken up about all of this to handle it," I muttered.

She blinked at me while clicking the mirror closed and dropping her cosmetics back into the bowels of her handbag. "I *am* upset. We all are. But Vel didn't want us sniffling into tissues. That wasn't her style. And it would be selfish to wish her still here, suffering like she was."

Nobody knew that better than I did. I'd been Customer of the Year at the rental car company, churning up the road between Boston and Morris every weekend, spending as much time as I could with my aunt. Until this past year, I'd never had to stray far from my cozy apartment near Boston University for anything I needed or wanted. Campus, where I spent most of my time as a communications graduate assistant, was a ten-minute walk away. I hadn't even looked off-campus for romance.

James.

Hm.

I tapped the lid of the urn with my fingernail. This new arrangement wasn't going to be easy on us. But we'd survived a year of my going back and forth nearly every weekend, so maybe it wouldn't be too bad. In fact, this might be a bit more settled. Sure, there would be no more impromptu meet-ups for lunch on the quad, but to be honest, that hadn't been happening for a while. At least now I wouldn't be a moving target. He could come up to visit me on the weekends he didn't have his kids. Or I could go there. Maybe during the week, if business was slower at the print shop then. Surely he could squeeze me in for a lunch or two… or a quickie. Being head of the vocal music department meant he was busy, but summer was right around the corner. Between choir camps, he could have some time for me…

"Earth to Whitney!" my sister said, waving her hand in front of my face.

I blinked, then smiled shakily. "Sorry. I was just thinking about some stuff."

My new life had been official for more than a week, although I was still trying to wrap my head around it. And I didn't know why it was so hard to process. Aunt Vel had told me about her will months before, when she first got sick. She'd told everyone, almost as if she wanted to make sure I couldn't weasel out of my agreement. Like I would. What kind of a jerk went back on a promise to a dying woman?

Okay, if I could have found a way, I might have.

But short of lying and telling everyone the conversation never happened, I couldn't. And no matter how easy it might be to capitalize on my family's long-held opinion of Aunt Vel as being "kooky," I wouldn't do it. I'd obviously meant a lot to her, since she'd left most of her surprisingly considerable estate to me, while pretty much giving the rest of the Faelhaber family a posthumous middle finger.

Not that they cared. After all, at the end of the day, they'd drive back to their normal lives. The new normal for me would be in Morris, a picture-postcard town in southern Maine to which Aunt Vel had escaped and reinvented herself nearly thirty years ago.

There, she'd built a life the rest of her siblings—my mom included—would only have admitted to envying if their lives depended on it. But the truth was, their little screw-up sister had turned out to be the most successful of them all. None of them were business owners, employers, and philanthropists.

None of them held the respect of their entire communities. Not to say they were a bunch of losers. They'd made good lives for themselves, too. But not like Aunt Vel did.

Aunt Vel was a rock star.

"I can't believe you're actually going to live here," Shelly said, looking around the room, as if I were going to take up residence at the funeral home.

"It's temporary," I said for the millionth time with the millionth go-get-'em smile.

I'd promised Aunt Vel I'd give it a go. But my goal was to make sure the business was in decent hands, put in place good managers and advisers, and head back to Boston after a year, tops. Keeping an eye on things from there would be a breeze.

Mom tucked a strand of my hair behind my ear. "It was nice of the university to grant you a leave of absence. I hope you don't lose all that momentum you'd—"

"It'll be fine. I can research and write articles anywhere. And there's always my artwork."

She sniffed. "Yes. That. It'll be a nice hobby to have up here. Lord knows there's nothing else to do. Especially in the winter."

Before I could dwell on her dismissal of my "hobby," which supplemented my income quite nicely, in fact, I felt a tap on my shoulder and whirled, expecting to come face-to-face with one of my uncles or cousins. Instead, I found myself looking up (up, up) into the pleasant features of a stranger.

"Hi," he said, with a shy smile. "Um, I'm Eric. Mulligan."

Considering his last name matched the one on the sign in front of the funeral home, it was less awkward to be approached by him than by the four thousand other inhabitants of this town who'd all felt the need to introduce themselves today.

I smiled back. "Oh, hey. I'm Whitney."

He shook my hand gently and murmured his condolences in a way they must learn at undertakers' school. (Was there such a place? I pictured an ornate Victorian house with a basement full of cadavers, with students wandering the dim, plushly carpeted rooms, speaking in hushed tones.) "Whitney. I'm sorry for your loss."

"Thank you. I—"

Shelly elbowed her way in front of me. "Hello, there. I'm Shelly. Vel's niece."

Eric shook her proffered hand. "Hello, Shelly." He repeated his condolences to her and Mom, and glanced at the urn in my arms. "Anyway. I was a... a friend of your aunt. Well, everyone was. And I wanted to pay my respects."

Mom fluttered her eyelashes at him. "Well, aren't you sweet? And you said you're a Mulligan? So you're..."

He nodded. "Yeah. This is my family's business."

"And you... took care of Aunt Vel?" Shelly asked, glancing meaningfully toward the ashes.

He blushed. "Well, no. I mean, normally, I would have. That's part of what I do, yes, but I... I mean, this time... Well, it's complicated."

He seemed to feel he had to offer us a reason as to why he hadn't attended to her personally, though I couldn't imagine why.

"You see, there was a rush on deaths, so I personally was not the one who— I was already taking care of someone else who happened to pass away around the same time," he said, finishing breathlessly.

"Fascinating!"

"What an interesting job!"

I rolled my eyes at my two fawning kinswomen. "Well, thank you and the rest of the staff for everything," I said, taking control. "Your, um, was that your father?"

"Tall guy? Looks and sounds like James Garner? Charisma up to his eyeballs, none of which I inherited?"

I couldn't speak to charisma, but the son had certainly won in the looks department. *Not that I was looking!* "Uh, yes. That's the one. He did a great job on the eulogy. Very personal."

"Yeah, well…" He broke off, paused, and then muttered something under his breath. I leaned closer to catch what he was saying, but he abruptly trailed off, took a deep breath, and then fixed me with an expectant look, as if waiting for *me* to finish a thought.

To avoid an awkward silence, which, in my expert opinion was worse than any form of spoken word, I rushed on. "I spoke to your sister or cousin or someone on the phone and then again in person yesterday."

"My cousin, Hortense. She does the service planning."

"Yes. And a woman named… Lorna?"

"Lena. My aunt. Hortense's mother and my dad's sister. It's all super-incestuous." As Shelly's eyebrows shot up, he corrected himself hastily, "*Not* that we practice incest. I didn't mean incest. I meant nepotism. We're all about nepotism."

"Well, it *is* a family business, right?"

He cleared his throat. "Yes. It is. All in the family. Except for Jake, in maintenance. He's not related to us. Yet. Horty'll take care of that eventually, though. OhmygoshI'manidiot."

Shelly giggled. "You're hilarious."

"That's why they usually keep me in the basement with the bodies."

This guy was like a case study in social awkwardness. But what was there to be nervous about? If he normally handled the… well, the arrangements, certainly he'd have had to make small talk with family members before. And he'd even known

Aunt Vel. Had they not been friendly, for some reason? Yet he'd called her a friend.

For a few seconds, I forgot I wasn't behind a one-way mirror, observing as an objective researcher. Then, remembering I had to participate in the conversation and try to keep it on track, I cleared my throat and assumed my chirpiest voice, the one I reserved for mean people, large social gatherings, and awkward situations. Shelly claimed I used my "*Legally Blonde* persona" to disarm people and trick them into underestimating my intelligence. In truth, it had nothing to do with my IQ and everything to do with hiding my true feelings. In this case, I just wanted to smooth things over, even though I couldn't figure out why there should be anything to smooth, and put this very handsome man at ease.

"I think we're almost done here. Lena said I could settle up with her tomorrow, after dealing with the lawyer and the bank."

He looked stricken. "Oh, no, I didn't mean … I'm not here to talk about money, and I don't mean to rush you out. I just wanted to introduce myself, express my condolences, and uh… embarrass the heck out of myself. I can embalm a body in no time flat, but my true talent is being awkward, apparently. Sorry for your loss. Again. Bye."

At that, he abruptly turned and sped away, giving us a view of his black suit-covered broad back, neatly trimmed dark hair, and—yeah, I looked—an impressive derriere. When he rounded the corner that led to the offices down the hall, Mom said, "What an odd person."

Shelly sighed. "All the cute ones have issues or baggage. Or in your boyfriend's case, Whit, both."

Her mention of James brought a guilty blush to my cheeks for ogling another man's ass. Especially that man's. You knew it had been a long time when you started eyeing the undertaker.

"Excuse me, but James has been divorced less than two years, so he's allowed to have a few issues. And those 'bags' are his children."

"Hideous brats, both of them. I can't believe you're defending them." Before I could defend *myself* next, Shelly pulled on my sleeve. "C'mon. Let's go back to Aunt Vel's hou — *your* place and start making a dent in all that food people have been dropping off. I'm starving."

Mom waved us away and headed over to a grouping of her siblings. "You two go ahead. Us old folks will catch up to you later."

I twisted the phone cord around my finger until the tip of the digit turned purple while I listened to James give me reason after reason for delaying a visit to see me.

"Anyway, I don't think I can make it up there until the end of the semester, at least. And then I promised the kids I'd take them to the beach our first week of summer vacation."

I swallowed my disappointment at James's announcement, coming so soon after my entire family abandoned me to return to Boston. "Oh. Right. Well, I get it. All that has to come first."

"I know you understand. But it also sucks."

My laugh sounded more like a deflating balloon than an utterance of mirth. "My aunt's dead. Doesn't get much suckier than that."

"Again, I'm sorry about that. And I'm sorry I couldn't make it to the memorial service. It's just... bad timing."

Leave it to James to make my aunt's death sound like an

inconvenience. Still, the intent behind his communication was clear, so I gave him the benefit of the doubt (that's kind of our thing) and said, "The end of term is crazy."

Almost as crazy as talking on a landline telephone in this day and age. Unfortunately, I had yet to find a spot in this house where could I get cell service, and Aunt Vel didn't have a cordless phone. Which was odd, because she was pretty tech savvy for someone of her generation. Her print shop was fully equipped with the latest technology. She'd showed me most of it before she got too sick.

Did that mean I had any idea what I was doing there? Hell no. Fortunately, she had employees who did. Employees who would require paychecks at the end of next week. I hoped I could find the cheat sheet Aunt Vel had typed up for me about the payroll software...

Stretching the long phone cord to its limit, I peeked through the living room's wooden blinds at the print shop, which was dark for the night. Farther down the street, Mulligan Funeral Home shone like a beacon. The parking lot was jammed with cars. No doubt another visitation. Morris, Maine. Population: one fewer. The town was shrinking. I hoped someone else was having a baby.

"You seem far away," James said, with more than a tiny pout in his voice.

"I am. One hundred miles, to be precise."

"Feels like a thousand. It's like a totally different country up there."

"A nice country. Pretty. Especially in the fall."

"Are you trying to get me to relocate?"

I laughed. "Uh... no. But a visit would be nice."

His sigh whistled down the line, piercing my eardrum. I pulled the receiver slightly away from my head and winced.

"You know, Whitney, I've just explained why that's not possible right now, so it's pretty shitty to make me feel bad."

"I— I wasn't—"

"Yes, you were. I'm being pulled in about a hundred different directions, so I don't need the guilt trip from you."

The blood drained from my face. Turning from the window, I plodded over to the couch and collapsed onto it, realizing too late that Aunt Vel's Maine coon cat, Buster, was already occupying the space. He slid out from under me with a yowl and ran from the room. Great. I was pissing off everyone tonight.

"I didn't mean it was your fault. And I'm not trying to pull you in any more directions."

"Well, you are. Listen, I gotta go. We have rehearsal early in the morning, then the spring performance tomorrow night, and we're not even close to being ready. The damn orchestra... Well, you know how it always is."

"It *always* turns out great."

"Only to the untrained ear."

I picked at the fringe on a throw pillow. "I have a long day tomorrow, too. Lawyer, bank, funeral home, figuring out how to run the payroll... and an entire business..."

"I'm sorry I snapped at you."

"It's okay. We're both on edge."

"I miss you, Whit."

"You do?"

"Yeah. Absolutely."

I perked up against the couch's pillows and grinned. "I miss you, too! Maybe I can drive down there one day this week and—"

"Oh, man. This week? Not a good idea. I'll barely have time to breathe. We're hosting state choir competitions for

Class 1A high schools. In between all my usual classes and rehearsals, I'll be overrun by teenagers and teachers."

"Oh, yeah. That's right. I keep forgetting it's that time of year." I laughed at myself. "I don't even know what day it is!"

"Doesn't take long to leave the collegiate calendar behind, does it?"

"No. It doesn't."

"Hang in there, babe."

"Oh, you know me. I will."

"Yeah, you're a trouper. Good night."

"Night."

He hung up without waiting for anything more emotionally declarative, which was just as well.

I scooted farther down the cushions and slouched over on the armrest, laying my head on my arms. The receiver in my hand beeped insistently—just one more thing annoyed at me and letting me know about it. I waited through the fast busy signal until it clicked and stopped. Who would care if the phone were off the hook? Nobody was going to be calling me. Mom and Shelly were on their way back to Boston. And I didn't know anyone well enough here for people to be ringing me up for chats.

That self-pitying woke me up. What the heck? I was a strong, independent woman. I didn't need constant companionship and hand-holding. I could do this. I could do anything! And anyway, this was all temporary. Someday, when this was far behind me, I'd look back and be proud of the way I'd taken care of everything. Because I was going to rock this.

Buster, who had never been particularly interested in making friends with me in all the years I'd known him, jumped onto the couch and rubbed against me. I wrapped one arm around him, careful not to hit him in the head with the phone receiver. He pressed his cold nose to my jawline.

"Oh, Buster. I'm afraid I'm turning into a sad sack!"

I couldn't help but chuckle when he emitted a raspy meow that sounded like the first vocalization he'd made in months.

"Right? Lame! What are we going to do without Aunt Vel, though? Huh?"

Again he answered me, this time with a shorter word.

"I don't know, either. But we have to try, right?"

Apparently bored with the conversation, he jumped down without replying and curled up in the window seat that overlooked the rose bushes next to the front stoop of my new home, a cozy Cape Cod I'd always loved to visit... but had never imagined would be mine.

Buster was right, though. It was okay to be sad, lonely, and lost, but at some point, we had to move forward and—in his case—do the things he'd always done. In my case, I needed to figure out what my new normal was—however temporary it might be—and do it often enough that it felt comfortable.

I dragged myself from the couch and hung up the phone on the kitchen wall.

Now, where was that chocolate pie I'd seen earlier?

CHAPTER TWO

A GOOD NIGHT'S sleep and a bright, crisp morning considerably brightened my outlook. So what if James was too busy doing his thing to hold my hand through mine? Since when had that mattered? We weren't a clingy couple—couldn't be, given our respective hectic schedules. This didn't change anything in that regard.

To be honest, the more I'd thought about it as I got ready for bed last night, the more relieved I was that I was off the hook for at least one thing: vacation with James and his kids. Before Aunt Vel died, James had been forcing the issue, and it wasn't yielding good results... at all. I wasn't sure what his ex had said about me to the kids, but based on some of the things they'd said and how they'd acted the last time we were all together, it wasn't exactly complimentary. At one point, eight-year-old Madeline had glanced at me, then turned to her father with an innocent expression and asked in a loud voice in the middle of dinner, "Daddy, what's a homewrecker?"

For the record, I was *not* one. James and Michelle were already in the middle of their somewhat messy divorce when he and I met, and we weren't anything more than close friends until their divorce was final. But if Michelle wanted to make me the scapegoat, fine. I didn't mind taking partial credit for pulling James away from her toxicity.

And anyway, I didn't know how she could possibly have considered her home "wrecked." She still lived in the beautiful house they'd shared while they were married; Madeline and Michael still went to the same private school; she still drove the same shiny Land Rover that was entirely unnecessary for navigating Boston city streets; and she was still a stay-at-home mom. How had her life changed at all? James had never been at home anyway, which was part of the reason they'd grown apart.

Whatever. I couldn't worry about Michelle or her snot-nosed kids right now. I was sure she was ecstatic about this new arrangement. Out of state, out of mind. As long as James didn't feel that way, everything would be fine.

After feeding Buster, I told him to have a good day, and I popped across the street to the print shop.

Velvet Printing, a square, two-story brick building, took up most of an entire block on the town's main drag. Aunt Vel's house—now mine, I supposed—and a long row of similar, neat, cottage-like homes faced the side of the structure. The front of Velvet opened onto Main Street. Directly next door sat a laundromat and dry cleaner, followed by one of the town's three gas stations, two side-by-side fast food franchises, the locally owned Lobster Shack, a Chinese takeout place, and The Poole Table, the town's only pub. Harrington's, which passed for a "fancy" restaurant, capped off "restaurant row."

On the other side, taking up quite a bit of real estate, sprawled the Mulligan Funeral Home. Lynda's Flowers crouched in Mulligan's shadow, but I suspected Lynda didn't mind since the funerals business alone could bankroll her modest existence. Another gas station occupied the next corner, followed by The Quilting Bee, *the* bank (with Niles Bainbridge, CPA, occupying an office upstairs), a couple of lawyers and bail bondsmen, and then Town Hall and its associated government offices (including the jail and police and fire departments).

The town square, mostly green space, squatted at the far end of Main Street. It filled up each Saturday morning with farmers' market stalls and also featured a fountain and some brick pathways and picnic pavilions. In front of the square, Main made a ninety-degree turn and became another road altogether, one that led out of town, past the cemetery, and eventually to the highway that ran east to Portland, considered to be a big city in these parts.

Back on this side of the street, the newspaper offices occupied the top floor of Velvet, the better to utilize the printing presses below on press day, which was Friday afternoon. (Yes, the local paper ran once a week, folks, and arrived on people's doorsteps on Saturday morning.) On a Monday morning such as this one, only one or two people were stirring up there, planning that Friday's edition.

The print shop's sign was still flipped to "closed," but the front door was unlocked, and when I pushed into the reception area, I could already hear—and smell—the activity in the back.

Here we go!

Bypassing Aunt Vel's office, I headed straight for the noise to say hello to whoever was hard at work. Since communication only occurs if the message is received, I waited for Cath, the shop's lead operator, to turn off the machine and remove her ear protection before saying, "Good morning!"

She offered me more a grunt than a return greeting, which I tried not to take personally, having become somewhat inured to her gruff personality in the past few months of my visits. "Gruff" pretty much summed up everything about Cath, including her appearance. I would never outright ask her age (rude!), and I was guessing she wasn't much older than I was, but she was like the kid at school who was either held back a year or was the same age but didn't go home to milk and cookies and a friendly family so was aging much faster than her peers. She seemed older; harder. How had someone in her late twenties or early thirties become so curmudgeonly before her time? Maybe I didn't want to know.

When she looked me up and down, her barely tolerant blinks told me she didn't approve of my wardrobe choice that morning. Dang it! I'd agonized over it, too. What should the owner of a print shop wear? Aunt Vel had always worn jeans and t-shirts, usually screen printed on-site with the business name and logo on the front, phone number, website, and email address across the back.

It felt weird, though, wearing one of her shirts, even if we were the same size, and jeans weren't my thing on weekdays, so I'd decided to put on something comfortable (for me): a solid peach button-up, fitted cotton shirt with cap sleeves, a cropped denim jacket, a simple, knee-length flowy black skirt, and peep-toe wedges. It was something I wore to kick around Boston with James on the weekend, so I'd thought it would be casual enough for the office but also professional enough for my meetings at the attorney's office, bank, and funeral home later.

"I take it you're not planning to do anything hands-on today," Cath said, looping the headphones around the back of her neck and letting them hang there while she punched some information into the touchscreen on the machine in front of her.

"Uh... Well, I *can*."

"Not dressed like that, you can't. No open-toed shoes allowed back here, for one. And you'll get ink all over your pretty shirt."

Ignoring the sarcasm in her tone, I said only, "I can go change. It'll only take me a minute."

"It's not that important. We don't need the extra hands back here. Actually, we *do*, considering it's our busiest season, but we need hands that know what they're doing, not hands that have to be told every step in the process."

"Right." I laughed nervously. "My hands are definitely more the latter than the former. I'll get there, though! Maybe it's best if I focus on the stuff I need to take care of today, anyway, including payroll."

"You're on your own there. Vel did all that."

"Yeah, I know. She showed me... a while back. I'm sure it'll all come back to me. It seemed pretty easy."

"Don't screw it up. Everyone around here is upset enough as it is. They don't want any headaches come Friday, when they're expecting their paychecks to be in their accounts."

I rocked on my heels and grabbed the lapels of my jacket, like I wasn't worried at all. "No problems on that front. It'll be seamless."

Another grunt, this one sounding decidedly dubious.

"Okay, then! I'll, uh, let you get back to... whatever you're doing."

"Graduation announcements. It's a small senior class this year, thankfully, but as usual, parents waited until the last minute to get their orders in."

"Oh. Right. I bet that's annoying. And, uh... when everyone else gets here, they'll be doing the same?"

"No. Jordy's got wedding announcements and invitations out the wazoo, so Natalie will be helping with those after she's done with the dead sheets."

"Dead sheets?"

She barely contained her annoyance at having to explain. "Funeral home stuff. Service bulletins, mostly."

"Funeral home stuff. 'Dead sheets.' Right." I chuckled. "Clever. I don't remember hearing Aunt Vel call them that."

"Insider shorthand. She probably never mentioned it to you, because you were an outsider."

"Makes sense." I supposed. "And I should expect that email to arrive in Aunt Vel's inbox?"

"It should already be there. Sometimes they forget to copy Natalie, so make sure she gets it."

"Oh. Geez. That could be bad."

"She'll always ask you for it if she doesn't have it by ten, but we don't have time today to wait that long. Eric's awesome about it. The others? Much flakier."

"Okay. Eric: reliable. Everyone else: spotty."

"At best."

I stood there for a few more seconds, mentally putting faces to names. Hortense hadn't seemed like a flake to me when I'd spoken to her on the phone or met her in person. In fact, she' was super-nice. Gentle. But I supposed that went with the territory. You couldn't be boisterous when dealing with grieving loved ones, could you? That would be inappropriate. And I liked her neat, honey-colored French braid. It was so… perfect. I'd kept staring at it as she went over the order of service with us.

Lena, her mom, had been equally friendly and helpful. A small woman with short, graying, wavy hair, she'd brought us tea and told us a touching story about Aunt Vel, who had been one of her friends. I could tell she was heartbroken, too, but she'd remained professional and not overly familiar.

Larry Mulligan, Eric's dad, was also a calming presence, much like a minister. Since Aunt Vel hadn't attended church regularly, he'd stepped up and performed the service, which was beautiful. I hadn't just been saying that to make polite conversation afterward with Eric. You could tell Larry had known the person he was talking about and that her passing would leave a void in his life, too. He choked up a time or two, but not so obviously that it made the rest of us uncomfortable. For some reason, it had made things easier. Misery loves company, right? Unfortunately, the elder Mulligan was nowhere to be found afterward, so I never got the chance to thank him.

In fact, the only "flake" I'd encountered at the funeral home was Eric, who had chosen to come up and speak to us and then seemed totally flustered by it. But according to Cath, he was "awesome." Judging by the dreamy look in her eyes when she said his name, she'd noticed his nice butt a time or two, too. They would make a delightful socially backward couple. She'd grunt and grimace, and he'd spew inappropriate statements. Lovely.

Although I assumed it took more than four people to run the town's only funeral home, I hadn't met anyone else. The memorial service had been on a Sunday, so maybe only the most essential personnel had been on hand. Or maybe the rest of them had been among the mourners. All the faces and names had started to blur together after a while.

Cath cleared her throat, bringing me back to the present. "So?"

My hands dropped to my sides. "Oh. Yeah. Here goes! I'll come back here later to say hi to everyone else when they arrive."

"Goody."

If I were the paranoid sort, I'd have said Cath had a problem with me.

I'd barely gotten my bearings in Aunt Vel's office, careful not to sit idle too long and give myself time to mope too much about how she'd never step foot in it again, when it was time for my meeting at the attorney's office. Since my aunt had added my name to the deeds of her house and business, the title of her car, and all of her bank accounts before she died, I'd been spared the mess of probate. Things went as planned with the attorney and at the bank, so I was ahead of my self-imposed schedule by the time I arrived at the funeral home, checkbook in hand.

Excuse the pun, but the place was as silent as a tomb. In the office, I found Hortense and Lena, but nobody else. Not that it mattered. I didn't require a welcoming committee. My business was with Lena, the bookkeeper.

While she printed the receipt I'd need to present to the life insurance company for reimbursement, Hortense said, "It was a lovely service. You made wonderful choices."

"Thanks! Aunt Vel made it easy. She knew what she wanted."

Understatement of the century. My aunt had not only known what she wanted out of her life (and death), but she'd had some pretty definite ideas for others, too. Namely, me.

"I'm not saying you have to do everything the way I did," she'd said one day, sitting in the recovery area after chemo. "In fact, I'd advise against that. But I do think you're underestimating yourself. Settling."

"Gee, Aunt Vel. Don't hold back."

"I don't have time to beat around the bush, Missy. Time is

of the essence. And I've spent enough precious time trying to figure out a nice way of telling you this: you deserve better."

"What do you mean, 'better'? I have a great job and a great boyfriend. Plus, I'm having a blast with my illustrations. Did I tell you I added posters and coffee mugs to the mix, in addition to the stationery I already sell? My online sales are picking up."

"That's wonderful! And your eyes light up when you talk about your art, so I believe that part. The rest? I'm not so sure."

"Well, I'm sure, and that's all that matters."

"Hmmph. You're too vivacious to be stuck in a dusty library all the time or behind one-way glass, observing research subjects. Academia is for socially backward dullards who get along better with books than people."

"Eat your lunch."

"You mean drink it? I'm sick of protein shakes. And anyway, what's the point?"

"You have to stay strong."

"Why? We're only prolonging the inevitable. And I'm tired." She shivered.

Injecting as much cheer as possible into my voice, I tucked her blanket more tightly around her legs and hips. "Because I'm not ready to say goodbye yet. And you won't be so tired if you get some sustenance."

"I'll drink my shake if you make me a promise."

"Anything," I said, without hesitating.

"After I'm gone, you take a break from Boston and come up here to run the print shop."

"Anything but that."

"Nope. You already promised."

I laughed. "That's dirty!"

"What are you gonna do? Kill me?"

Playfully scowling at her, I pushed her shake closer on the rolling hospital tray.

She took that as a yes and grinned at me while chasing the straw with her tongue. After her first swallow, she said, "You're gonna love it in Morris. And everyone's going to love you, too."

~

The jury was definitely still out on both of those things. Getting used to this place—despite all of its charms—was going to take some time. And I could hardly call what Cath felt for me "love." Then again, there was always a chance for improvement, right? I'd keep lavishing my sunny disposition on her, and soon we'd be best buds. Or at least she'd be able to tolerate me.

As for the other townsfolk, they'd been great. Not a bad one in the bunch to date, that I could think of...

"Hey, guys, one of the hearses has a flat—maybe a slow leak? Horty, can you get Jake on the horn and tell him to meet me in the gar— Oh. Whitney. Hello."

Shaking myself from one of my last memories of my aunt, I turned to see who belonged to the breathless voice, and my pulse quickened. This guy! I couldn't figure out how I felt about him. At all. But manners dictated I reply. "Hey, Eric! How's it going?"

"Uh, fine. You?" Before I could answer, he said, "What am I saying? I'm sure you've been better. Don't mind me. I ask dumb questions."

Hortense smiled tenderly at her cousin. "Take a load off, Eric. I'll call Jake in a second. We don't have any other services today, so there's no rush."

He accepted her invitation and sat in the wing-backed

chair opposite her desk, right next to where I was standing. I stepped aside a few paces.

"Did you get my email this morning?" he asked, his knee bouncing. "I sent it extra early, to be safe. Are you going to have a different email address or keep using Vel's?"

I tried to figure out which question to answer first. "I'll keep the email address the same but change the signature on it."

"Good call. You don't want people thinking they're communicating with the dead. And you got my message okay?"

"I did."

"You never replied, so I wasn't sure. But I didn't worry, because I always copy Natalie, and she sent a thanks, so…"

I scratched the side of my nose. "Do you often have trouble with emails not reaching their destination?"

He cupped his large hands over the ends of the arm rests. "At that place? Oh, yes. The network is horrible, and the spam filter flags more legitimate messages than junk mail."

Lena beamed proudly. "Eric's our technology guru. Helps us out tremendously."

"Took some classes in college," he said with a shrug. "Tried to get Vel to let me help her out, but she said she couldn't afford the fixes, even if I provided the labor for free. Anyway, about the email, it's nice to get a confirmation so I know it got there. We're in big trouble if we don't have bulletins for a service."

"I use read receipts. Or I did… at the university." When he merely stared at me like this was a totally foreign concept, I explained brightly, "That way I know someone opened the email, but they don't have to reply."

"That's kind of impersonal and sneaky."

It was my turn to stare at him.

He sniffed at my blank expression. "Isn't it nicer to send back a quick, 'Got it'?"

I smiled tightly. "Absolutely! Sure. I'll try to remember next time." *Or, more accurately, I'll set up an automatic reply to help me comply with this ridiculous request.*

As Lena handed me my long-awaited receipt, Hortense tilted her head sympathetically and said, "Eric! Give the woman a break. It's her first day. And she's still grieving."

His mouth dropped open, as if he were horrified anyone might interpret his remarks as critical. "Oh! No. I... I'm sorry if it sounded like I was complaining. I'm not. Like I said, Natalie already let me know it got there."

I folded the paper and tucked it into my purse. "Great! Then we're all set."

"I'll be by later to pick up the bulletins. I have a few boxes of business cards and notepads waiting, too."

He stood, and for the second time, I marveled at how big and broad he was—what Aunt Vel would call a tall drink of water. Whatever that meant. On second thought, he struck me as more of a water *tower*.

"Well, I'd better see to that flat tire. And I've got a guy waiting for me downstairs. Not that he's going anywhere, but... you know..."

Hortense snorted.

Lena shook her head and sighed. "What have I told you about saying stuff like that around guests?"

He seemed unaffected by the chastisement. "You mean Whitney? She's one of us now. Right, Whit?"

I gulped. "Oh. Uh... sure!"

"If you're anything like Vel, you're cool and can take a joke. At least, that's what she told me," he said, oblivious to my discomfort.

Good ol' Aunt Vel. Prepping the townsfolk before I ever

arrived. Great. And I couldn't make a liar out of a dead person, either, could I? Wasn't that some sort of social faux pas?

"Yeah, I'm totally cool!" I said. Who would want to admit they weren't cool? Not me!

"Okay, well… See you later."

While I was saying my goodbyes to Hortense and Lena, a short, pudgy, sweaty guy bustled into the office. He nodded politely at me and then turned to Lena. "Mom, how many times do I have to tell you to let me know when we're low on toilet paper in the guest restrooms? Ran out again today in the ladies' room during the Nichols service, and I only know that because Jill was the one to discover it and told me."

Hortense rolled her eyes and muttered to me, "Bobby. My brother." Then louder: "Why was your wife using the guest facilities? Those are for guests."

"For your information, she *was* a guest, Hortense. Mr. Nichols is her best friend's grandfather's brother."

Hortense blinked one eye closed. "So… her best friend's great uncle?"

"Yes. Something like that."

"Still. She could have used the office bathroom."

"She couldn't make it that far. The baby's pushing on her bladder and kicking it all the time."

"What'd she do, then? Drip dry?"

He turned his back on his sister and addressed his mother again. "Anyway. Can we *please* be more diligent with our pre-service inventories?"

Lena patted her son on the arm. "Yes, yes. Calm down, Bobby. You're going to stroke out and not live to see that beautiful son of yours."

"It's completely unprofessional to run out of something as basic as toilet paper and hand soap."

Hortense snorted. "Fortunately, our competitors don't keep well stocked, either." To me, she stage-whispered, "We don't have any competition."

"That's no excuse!" Bobby said, spittle flying from his lips. "People can always go to Portland. It's only forty minutes away."

"Nobody's going to use a funeral home in Portland because we ran out of toilet paper. Pull yourself together and go look at your casket catalogs."

I covered my mouth to keep from giggling at the siblings' exchange while I tried to figure out how to extricate myself from what felt like eavesdropping on a family matter.

Lena inserted herself between her two children. "Bobby, have you met Vel's niece, Whitney?"

He took a deep breath and wiped his palm on the front of his khakis before offering his hand to me to shake. "I paid my respects yesterday, but I'm sure you met a million people."

"Only four thousand or so."

He rolled his eyes. "I'm not surprised. This town..."

"I wish Aunt Vel had been well enough to introduce me to people before... Well. I guess it doesn't matter."

"You'll get to know everyone soon enough," Hortense said. "You've already had some pretty colorful exchanges with Eric."

Bobby groaned. "Oh, Lord. Tell me he didn't say anything too crazy."

Oh, like incest?

"He jokes when he's nervous," Lena explained. "And he felt badly about how your introductions went yesterday afternoon. Came straight here to the office to tell us how horrible it was. Something about bragging about his embalming skills." She winced.

Bobby slapped his hand to the side of his face and shook his head. "You've got to be—"

Hortense cleared her throat. "Guys. I don't think Eric would appreciate us talking about this. He was humiliated." She looked straight at me. "He was."

"It wasn't a big deal. I don't even remember what he said, really. He did seem flustered, though."

"He means well. He just gets carried away sometimes," Lena said. "Drives his father crazy."

Bobby crossed the room to a door, which he opened. "I'm with Larry. The guy's a boob," he announced, and walked through, shutting the door behind him.

Lena sat down behind her desk and riffled through some stacks of paper, looking over the top of her bifocals at the writing on them but saying to the room at large, "Larry doesn't have any patience. But then he was born with all that charm and has never struggled in social settings. I always tell him if he'd spent more time with Eric—you know, after Gayle died... But he was too busy trying not to think about it. He buried himself in his work and didn't leave any room for being a dad. If it weren't for my husband, Hiram, and me, the poor kid would have never eaten anything that didn't come from a box."

Hortense stood. "Let me show you out before Mom turns on her spotlight and starts singing about orphans."

"Well he *was* an orphan! Twice! He's adopted, you know," Lena directed at me. "Larry and Gayle couldn't conceive. Then a friend of a friend of Larry's—or something, I'm not sure about the details—told them about someone who was looking for a private adoption for her unborn baby, so Larry and Gayle brought home newborn Eric a few months later. Sweetest baby ever. So quiet! Big, though."

I blinked at Lena. "Oh, wow. I— I— had no idea. He looks so much like Larry. I assumed—"

"Yeah, funny that, huh? We've always gotten a kick out of it when people forget and mention the 'family resemblance.' Eric usually goes along with it. Doesn't talk much about being adopted, though. It's never been a big deal for him."

"Anyway! That's enough Mulligan Family lore for one day." Hortense rested a gentle hand on my arm and guided me from the room.

I allowed myself to be steered into the hallway and toward the large glass front doors. Once there, she let go of my arm and, blushing, brushed at my jacket sleeve, as if she were worried she'd gotten me dirty or handled me too roughly. "Sorry about that. Eric would kill us if he knew we told you all that stuff."

"It's so— I don't know what it is. Surprising. I had no clue."

"And why should you? You've lived here all of twenty minutes. Plus, Eric probably liked that there was one person who didn't know the whole sad story. He hates being pitied."

"It *is* awful that his mom—your aunt—died when he was young, but as for being adopted, that's not necessarily tragic. It looks like he landed in a pretty nice family." I paused, then revealed, "You know, Aunt Vel was adopted, too."

"Yes. I always assumed that was why she and Eric were so close. Two peas in a pod, those two."

"They were?" *They were?*

"Oh, yeah. They were the best of friends. She took Eric under her wing even more than my mom did. Vel's death has been really hard on him."

For the second time in a short period, I blinked and had to pause to catch my breath as I processed yet another unexpected revelation.

Hortense didn't seem to notice. Instead, she shook her

head and chuckled. "My mom... If she decides she likes some-one, she doesn't hold back. I guess I get that from her, too, but I hope we haven't made you uncomfortable."

"Not at all!"

So, lying was my new thing? Unexpected, but okay...

"And I hope we can trust you not to tell Eric we told you all that stuff. He'd be furious. Well, maybe not furious. That's more Bobby's territory than his. But embarrassed, for sure."

"Don't worry. I'm not going to bring it up, and I can't imagine it coming up in conversation."

"Thanks. He's... Well, he's more of a brother to me than Bobby is. And one of my best friends."

I smiled and touched her arm. "I can tell. My sister Shelly and I are like that. Family is everything."

Hortense grinned and opened the door for me. "You know what, Whitney? I think I'm going to like you. Vel had nothing to worry about."

Before I could ask her what *that* meant, I found myself on the front walk, and it would have been weird to backtrack and force her to explain her statement. I still considered it for a second, but then I shrugged and continued on my way. I was too busy, and I needed to get back to the print shop to figure out how to run the payroll now that I had access to all of Aunt Vel's—*my*—bank accounts.

CHAPTER THREE

IT WASN'T until hours later, when I was finally home after an exhausting, surprisingly emotional day, that I realized I never did see Eric come by to get his bulletins, business cards, and notepads. He must have slipped in and out while I had my head down over my payroll software notes. Mona, the shop's regular front desk clerk, was out on maternity leave, so we were all pulling double duty, listening for the bell on the door. I'm sure Cath had been more than happy to help him with his order. But for some reason, I felt a small pang of regret anyway.

As for this week's payroll... nailed it! Velvet Printing employees would be paid on schedule this Friday. First hurdle: jumped. Next challenge: accounts payable. I spied a bill on Aunt Vel's desk that had a due date of nearly two weeks ago; the day she'd died, in fact. I stared at that date for a long time, trying to convince myself for the millionth time that she was gone. For real. I couldn't seem to get it to sink in.

It felt more like she was on vacation, and I was filling in until she returned. Maybe she was finally seeing Venice. Or London. Or San Francisco. Or Dublin. Or Lisbon. Any of those places we'd watched on the travel shows she'd been so addicted to. Surely she was anywhere but where she actually was.

Any minute now she would breeze through the back door with her luggage, speed-talking her way through her adventures, wildly gesticulating, embellishing the stories like only she could do, holding her enraptured audience until trailing off into a sigh, smiling mischievously and saying, "The rest is between me and Eduardo. Or Teddy, as I took to calling him."

Not that I'd ever filled in for her—because she never did go anywhere. It was a major feat to get her to venture as far as Boston for a weekend. But she could tell a story like nobody else I knew. And she'd dreamed of traveling during her retirement; a retirement that never arrived.

I was exhausted from musing about such gloomy things all day, so I decided to prepare an easy dinner, the first one I'd made since moving here. The chicken curry was bubbling on the stove, and I was pouring myself a glass of wine to celebrate my first successful payroll run as a business owner when I heard a knock on the front door. I looked down at my bare feet and considered not acknowledging my visitor. For about half a second.

Buster beat me to the door, sitting in front of it and meowing at the mail slot, which I noticed as I got closer was open. Two fingers poked through. Then a deep voice said, "Hey, Buster Boy. Is your... aunt... home? Aunt? No. Cousin. That's what she is."

I swung the door open to find Eric crouched on the welcome mat, still frozen in his peeping position. He dropped his hand but remained on one knee, smiling sheepishly up at me. "Oh. You *are* home."

"I am."

He sniffed and looked around my legs. "Am I interrupting dinner?"

"Not yet."

"Oh, good." He rose to his feet and rubbed his neck. "Thing is… I lost track of time with work stuff and didn't get over to the shop in time to pick up my order. I hate bothering you, but I saw your lights on, and… Would you…?"

I leaned against the door frame while I tried to determine if this were one of those moments where a boundary should be set. I'd always sucked at setting boundaries when it came to work. Maybe now was the perfect time to change that. "Is it life or death?" I tilted back a large mouthful of wine.

He tapped his chin with his index finger and looked skyward. "Umm, no. Death only."

The fermented grape juice had two paths to follow my uncontrollable laughter: down or out. Since I didn't want to shower my guest, it went down. Unfortunately, half of it diverted to my windpipe.

While I choked, coughed, and sputtered, he fidgeted help-lessly in front of me. "Oh, gosh. I'm sorry. Just… Put your arms up, or something. I hear that helps. Here, let me hold your glass while you… Yeah. There."

After I could finally breathe again, he handed me back my drink and said, "Shoot. I didn't mean to turn you into a client. We're never that desperate for business."

"It's… it's okay," I said, my voice still catching on every other word and my eyes streaming. "You… you surprised me, that's all. Funny." The way he could casually joke about death caught me off-guard every time. I wasn't sure how I felt about it, but I had to admit it made me laugh. Suddenly remem-bering my dinner, I turned and waved him in after me. "Come in."

He stepped across the threshold and closed the door

behind him. Buster wound between his ankles and meowed, so Eric bent down and picked up the cat, scratching him between the ears. "How you doin', guy? Hanging in there? Not too sad, I hope."

"He seems pretty clingy," I said over my shoulder, as I removed the simmering skillet from the stove. "He must have been lonely when Aunt Vel was in the hospital."

"He was. He's probably glad to have you around."

"Not that I'll be around that much. But at least he has someone to sleep with."

I couldn't be sure, since I was under the whirring vent hood and Eric's still by the front door, but it almost sounded like he said, "Lucky guy."

"What was that?"

He set Buster on the floor and joined me in the kitchen. "Uh, nothing. Oh, wow. That smells amazing."

I swiped at my still-watering eyes. "Chicken curry. You're welcome to have some. I made enough to last me all week, but I'll be sick of it after a few meals."

"Nah. Really? No. I should get my stuff and get out of your hair. This is embarrassing enough, bothering you at home after hours."

"It's not a big deal at all." So much for those boundaries. They were overrated, anyway.

I stirred the simmering chicken one last time and moved it from the hot element to a dormant one, then turned off the stove. I lifted the lid on my pot of rice to check its absorbency. Done. "Let's eat. Then I can walk you across the street to get your stuff."

When he said nothing more, I glanced over my shoulder at him. He flinched when I caught him staring, and said, "I don't know. I feel bad. Like I invited myself to dinner."

"You didn't! You came here to get your stuff. *I* invited *you*.

Would it make you feel better if I said you'd be doing me a favor, letting me eat my food before it gets cold?"

He grinned and sat down at the small table in the center of the kitchen. "That does help." Almost before his butt hit the chair, he hopped up again. "What can I do?"

At my request, but with surprisingly little direction, he set the table with flatware, napkins, and glasses while I served our food. As if he were still that hungry orphan Lena had told me about, I heaped the rice and chicken on his plate, then slid our dinners onto the table while he poured the last drop of iced tea into my glass. His glass remained empty.

I refilled my wineglass and scooted the tea to his side of the table as I sat down. "You drink that. I'll stick with the good stuff."

He smiled. "Are you sure? It's deadly."

"I think I'll be okay, if you stop making death jokes."

"Impossible. It's how I stay moderately sane."

I held the wine bottle aloft, then inquired, "Wine?" before realizing there was no glass to pour into.

"Ah. Um. Thanks, but I don't drink."

"Oh. Okay." I set the bottle down. "You mind if I do?"

"No! Go ahead. I just don't. Can't. Well, can't stop when I do." His cheeks reddened for a second but quickly returned to their normal color.

Another layer to the story... and something else he had in common with Aunt Vel, who had been a recovering alcoholic. When he didn't elaborate further, I assumed he didn't want to talk about it. Unfortunately for him, I always interpreted someone's reticence as a challenge. Which reminded me that I wanted to glean more insight into what Hortense had told me earlier that day, but since I'd promised I wouldn't let on that I'd learned anything from them, I'd have to tease it straight from him. No problem for a communications expert like *moi*.

As he tucked into his chicken and rice, I said, "You sure know your way around my aunt's kitchen. What's that about?"

He stopped mid-chew, his head and fork suspended above his plate, and looked across the table at me. "Mmm?" he said, while keeping his full mouth closed. *Good manners.*

I also recognized a stalling tactic when I saw one. I knew he knew full well what I'd said, so I didn't repeat myself but merely waited for him to finish chewing and swallowing and reply.

Finally, after a long drink of iced tea, he did. "I spent some time here. With Vel."

"Oh, did you now?"

"Not like that! Not that she wasn't— Um… she was just a little old for me. Old*er*. Not old. Too young to die, that's for sure. But that's a stupid thing to say, because there's no such thing as 'too young.' Hell, I prepare much younger people for burial. Heartbreaking. Fortunately, not too often around here. But sometimes. Death spares no one. Sorry. I cursed."

I set my fork on the edge of my plate, placed my elbows on the table, and tented my fingers over my food. "Cursing doesn't bother me."

"Oh. Good. Not that I do it often. But sometimes it slips." The left side of his mouth twitched upward, and my stomach did something that had nothing to do with my dinner.

Disturbed by my reaction to that cute facial tic and its deep resultant dimple, I took my napkin from my lap and wiped nonexistent food from my mouth while I composed myself. Another slug of wine went down my gullet, smoothly this time.

Oblivious to my rogue libido—thank God!—he tucked back into his food. After a few bites, he said, with his eyes on his rice, "Vel and I were friends. And yes, people talked about it. And no, nothing like that was going on. We just, you know, got along. She *liked* my sense of humor—a rarity around here. And she was always full of good advice. She... she looked out for me." He sniffed, then took another bite. "This stuff is spicy."

"Yeah, it is." Going along with his cover seemed the kind thing to do.

"It's delicious."

"Thanks."

I pushed my wine glass away (clearly it wasn't doing me any favors tonight) and said quietly, "She was like a mom to me, too."

His head snapped up, and his red eyes met mine. "Oh? I thought your mother... I met your mom."

I chuckled. "Yeah. I have one still." Flinching at how callous that must have sounded to the twice-orphaned dude across from me, I nevertheless resisted apologizing, keeping up the pretense that I was in the dark about everything. Instead, I explained, "My mom's more like a sister or a friend. Always has been. I love her, but Aunt Vel was definitely the more consistent maternal influence in my life. Mom wanted to be my buddy. Especially after Dad left. She didn't need kids at that point; she needed friends, I guess."

"I see."

"Anyway." I picked up my fork. "I'm familiar with Aunt Vel's motherly advice."

I tried not to let it unnerve me that he was staring at me across the table while I ate. It looked like one of those unfocused things, anyway, that had nothing to do with whatever—or whoever—was in the person's sight line. Perhaps he was remembering something Vel had told him in her no-nonsense, spare-no-feelings way.

Finally, he blinked, sniffed, drained the last of his tea, and remarked, "She was usually right, too."

"Yeah. That was the annoying part about it."

That cute half-smile returned. "I don't know about 'annoying.' It was pretty great to know I could trust her to steer me in the right direction."

"Same here. *Most* of the time."

He wiped his lips. "Most of the time?"

"Like the time she told me I'd look cute with a pixie cut? That was not one of those times." I grinned at the now-harmless memory and flipped my hair over my shoulder.

After he stopped laughing, he said, "She never gave me any fashion advice, so I guess I dodged a bullet. Anyway, I have Horty for that. And Lena for financial advice. I have several advisers."

"People care about you." I tossed my napkin on top of my plate and looked across the table. Not a single grain of rice remained in front of him. Impressive.

"Yeah. Or they think I'm such a spaz that I need someone telling me what to do all the time."

After we each polished off a piece of chocolate pie still left over from one of my neighbor's condolence offerings, he rose and nested his plate on top of mine.

"Let me help you clean up."

"No. Really. Put everything in the sink. It'll take me five minutes to stack the dishwasher before bed."

He obeyed and said down at his feet, "Right. Then I'll get my stuff and be out of your way." He swept his hand toward the arch that led from the kitchen to the entryway. "After you."

I had absolutely no explanation—not an acceptable one, anyway—for the disappointment that seized and shook me as I slid my feet into my wedges by the front door, snagged my keys from my purse, and wrapped a sweater around my shoulders for the quick trip across the street, knowing I'd be making the return trip alone.

~

The ringing phone spurred me to make the second half of that round-trip journey at a trot, the fastest I could go in those silly shoes. Since I hadn't bothered to lock the door when I'd left with Eric, I made it before my caller gave up, but my breathless, "Hello?" elicited a naughty chuckle I could hear well enough to picture as if he were in the room with me.

"Well, hello," James said. "What *are* you doing?"

"Nothing. Running. For the phone. I was… in the street. Across the street."

"How loud is that phone?"

"No, I—" I slid off my shoes. "Never mind. Hey! I didn't expect to hear from you tonight, what with the concert and everything. You're usually so tired after one of those. How did it go? And *don't* tell me 'okay,' then list all these tiny imperfections that nobody—including trained musicians—in the audience noticed."

"Do you want the truth, or do you want me to sugarcoat it?"

"I want you to be content with a job well done."

"It wasn't well done, so I can't be content."

"Oh, now…"

Expecting him to launch into his usual diatribe about off-key sopranos and off-tempo tenors, I was surprised when he more quietly stated, "I'm not content about anything right now."

The bemused smile slid from my face. Paired with this rare, post-concert call, his declaration put me on alert. "What's wrong?"

Silence met my question.

"Hello? Are you there?"

He sighed. "Yes. I'm here. And you're there. And…"

I held my breath, which was dangerous, considering how much I still needed oxygen after my hundred-yard dash.

"Are we being idiots?"

After a few seconds, I gave up trying to make sense of his question and answered it the way I *wanted* to, not with any real honesty. "I— I don't think we are. In what way?"

"Thinking this is going to work. That it has a prayer."

My heart stuttered. "Running Aunt Vel's business, or…?" I couldn't say the other interpretation out loud. But in my head, I most definitely finished the statement with, "*…us?*"

He had no problem voicing it. The one-syllable word hit my ear like a high note from a glockenspiel. Soft at first but piercing the longer it reverberated.

"Say something," he begged, when I let the word echo between us for a while.

"What do you want me to say to that, James?"

"That we're not idiots."

"We're not idiots."

"No, say it like you mean it. Like it's true."

"I've been gone less than a week. And you're already ready to give up because you had a crappy concert?"

"This isn't about the concert. And if something's obvious from the get-go, why continue? When a choir starts off on the wrong note, you don't waste a perfectly good song by letting them go on. You stop them."

The word "waste" sucked from my lungs what little breath I had, but I recovered and continued his stupid metaphor. "Okay, but you don't give up on the song. You start again."

I waited for him to acknowledge I was right and suggest how we could re-start this particular number in the right key.

I needed him to be the pitch pipe. But after a long pause, during which I stared at the hideous wallpaper surrounding the phone, he said, "I wish it weren't falling apart so quickly. But I'm legitimately worried it is. It feels..."

"Hopeless?"

"Yes! You feel it too?"

I shook my head before remembering he couldn't see me. And that was obviously by design. The coward was doing this over the phone so he wouldn't have to witness what this conversation was doing to me. "I— It's only a hundred miles," I finally choked. "That's... that's nothing! The only difference is that I'm not physically there."

"That's a pretty big difference. And it's not only the physical distance. You've been mentally absent for a long time. Now that you've moved up there permanently—"

"It's not permanent; it's temporary!"

"Missing you takes more time and energy than I have. My focus has to be elsewhere."

The thing was, his focus had always been elsewhere. And I'd been okay with that. Because I had my own busy life. I thought I was doing a pretty good job, though, of fitting him —and his ungrateful kids—in. Apparently not.

"I have to go," I whispered.

"Wait! Whitney—"

"No. You've made up your mind."

"But I haven't!"

"Yes, you have. I can tell. You sound exactly like you do when you decide on a program. You know the songs; you know the order. You know which soloists are going to sing which parts. You know. And nobody can change your mind. So." I sniffed and took a deep, restorative breath.

"Whit—"

"I need to go. Please, say goodbye and let's do this like

adults. I don't want to hang up in your ear without some sort of closure."

He cleared his throat and sighed. "Okay. I guess... Well... Bye."

Somehow, I detached and found the strength to repeat his last word before letting the phone fall into its cradle.

CHAPTER FOUR

ONE UNEXPECTED ADVANTAGE to living in Morris: I had no memories of James up here, other than a few terrible phone calls. Also, nobody here knew him. And nobody knew *me* well enough to comment on my zombie-like behavior or appearance.

But I eventually had to 'fess up to Shelly when she accurately accused me of dodging her phone calls. Predictably, she told me I was better off without him and that she'd never liked him *or* his kids—never mind that she'd never met Michael and Madeline.

"I didn't want to, based on what you'd told me!"

I thanked her for her support but ended the conversation as fast as I could.

The trash-talking stage hadn't hit yet. I still missed him. I still remembered what he smelled and tasted like. How his laugh sounded. How he sang like an angel... all the time. In the kitchen. In the shower. Waking me up on lazy Saturday mornings...

I was still expecting him to show up here, to walk into the print shop, to stand in my office doorway with his hat in his hands, to tell me he was lost without me, to reassure me everything would be all right, to kneel before me on one knee and ask me to spend the rest of my life with him.

Never mind that he didn't wear hats, because they looked silly on him. And I didn't know about that last part, either. Fifty years of living in a musical might wear a bit thin. It would have been nice to be asked, though.

Thing was, I'd invested nearly eighteen months of the end of my twenties with him, because I'd thought he could be The One. On paper, we were perfect for each other. We were both in academia—well, I *was* and would be again someday; we adored Boston, especially in the fall; we liked to cook with onions but never eat them, picking them off pizzas and poking around them in dishes; we preferred football to base-ball, if pressed, but could take or leave organized sports alto-gether; we loved early morning runs, followed by hot, sweaty—

The bell on the print shop door rang, startling me from my unfocused stare. For the umpteenth time I imagined it was James, swooping in to beg me to forgive him, aban-doning his high school guests at the university because "I have something more important to do-re-me-fa-so-la-ti-do!"

Of course it wasn't him. He'd never do anything rash and irresponsible. Nor would he be seen dead in… whatever Eric was wearing as he stood in front of me on the other side of the counter. A onesie? No, coveralls of some sort. Made of… paper? Only shinier.

"Hiya," the undertaker said breathlessly, smoothing down his dark, tousled hair. "Windy one out there. Spring is here! Finally."

I managed a flicker of a smile at his small talk and pushed the square box of service bulletins for "June Paul" toward him, its cardboard hissing against the Formica. "Nice of you to make it here before closing… barely."

He grinned and gestured down to his strange get-up. "Close call. I was about to assist on an autopsy when I remembered these were waiting."

My eyes widened in horror as it hit me that he wasn't making a fashion statement in those coveralls. That impervious material served to protect him from… biological castoff.

Taking in my expression, he hastened to say, "We hadn't started yet! I noticed the time right after I prepped, and I rushed right over."

"You couldn't have sent Hortense or Bobby or…" *…anyone who hasn't recently been in the presence of a corpse?*

He shrugged. "Bobby's at Lamaze class with Jill. Horty's with a family. It's my job to do this."

"Why is that? It seems so administrative. Like something they'd do in the office."

"They're busier than I am. Usually. It's been crazy lately. By May, things have generally slowed down in the death department—winter is murder around here—but it's been a rough spring. Not just for Morris, either. We service a pretty big area, miles-wise. Lots of smaller, outlying towns. Plus…"

Smaller towns than Morris? How is that possible? How do you have enough people to run the businesses in a town smaller than this?

"…large elderly population. *And* we're the exclusive funeral home for most of the elder care centers."

His pause to breathe allowed me to inject, "That's quite the goldmine. You must be so proud."

He chuckled. "Keeps us alive. Anyway!" He lifted the bulletins onto his shoulder like a compact boom box. "Better get back. Dad doesn't like to wait. See ya." He turned to leave but stopped at the door and pivoted to face me as I slumped on my elbows to resume moping. "Hey. You all right?"

My spine stiffened. "Yes! Fine."

Closing one eye and raising the eyebrow over the open one, he said, "Because you look a little like the lady hanging out with Dad and me right now."

"Gosh, thanks!" I busied myself by straightening some of the other orders waiting for pickup under the counter—blasted graduation announcements—so he wouldn't see how irrationally hurt I was by his comment.

Too late.

"I'm only kidding. And I shouldn't kid about that. We're doing an autopsy, because… Well, I'm not allowed to say, but it's at the request of law enforcement, so…"

"Yikes!"

"Probably will end up being nothing. Natural causes, that is. But it's sad there's any question, you know?"

"You're talking a lot about it for someone who's not supposed to talk about it." And I hated to admit it, but I was intrigued. At the same time, I didn't want him to get in trouble.

He winced sheepishly. "Yeah. Shutting up now. Anyway, you look… under-rested. Are you sure you're okay?"

"I'm fine! Overworked, because *someone* makes me work late hours, taking his sweet time to come pick up his orders."

"Oops. I think you're talking about me."

"Yes, I'm talking about you! Great deduction. You're a regular Chomsky."

"You mean Shamsky? The baseball player?"

"What? No! Noam Chomsky. The scholar and linguist. And all-around brilliant person."

"Oh. Not familiar with his work, I guess. And I've never

met anyone who drops a name like that in casual conversation."

I blushed at my nerdiness. "He's a hero of mine."

"Obviously. And good for you. It's nothing to be embarrassed about. Personally, I tend to admire adventurers."

I perked up. "Like who?"

He shrugs. "Amelia Earhart, the Wright brothers, Lewis and Clark, Mario and Luigi…"

In spite of my gloomy mood, I laughed. "Get out of here!" I scolded. "Here I thought we were having a normal conversation for once."

He grinned. "Never."

Cath's head poked through the doorway leading to the back. Her glower morphed into a lovesick, dopey smile when she saw our client. She should have stuck to glowering. Smiling made her look like she needed a suppository.

Entering the room, she shifted the jacket draped over her arm to her other hand, as if she didn't know what to do with it or how it had come to be with her. "Oh, hey, Eric."

He mumbled something at the floor.

What's this? Do I sense a bit of a spark between these two? Hey, someone should get laid around here.

"I gotta go," Eric said, pushing through the door for good this time, the bell dinging in his wake.

"What was all that yelling?" Cath demanded, her usually sour expression returning now that her sunshine had left the building.

I continued rearranging boxes of graduation announcements. "Yelling? Nobody was yelling. Eric Mulligan was just being his usual goober self. Listen, we need to keep these alphabetical by last name, or else it's a real hassle to try to find the right ones when people come in to pick them up. By the way, when are they going to do that? Graduation's right around the corner. I would imagine people need to get these mailed out."

"Nobody mails 'em. Most people hand-deliver. And anyway, what's it to you?"

"We're overrun! This mess stresses me out. And I'd like to get paid for these at some point. Why don't we require payment up front?"

"We don't ask people to pay for something they haven't received."

"What if they never come in to get them? Then we've put in the labor and materials for no return."

She shrugged. "I think Vel used to send invoices after ninety days."

"We eat the cost for up to three months?"

"It rarely comes to that. People around here are honest."

"And what if they still don't pay?"

"That's the risk you take, I guess. If they don't pay, it's because they *can't* pay. Vel was okay with doing some *pro bono* work." She sniffed. "Anyway, that's not my area. I make sure the stuff gets done to customers' satisfaction. Vel handled all that gross business stuff."

"Yeah, well, the 'gross business stuff' is my responsibility now, and I say we should charge up front."

Cath stared me down and sucked at her teeth for a few seconds, then said, "Whatever. It's your call. But I'm pretty sure your aunt knew what she was doing. Unlike you." She shrugged on her jacket. "And one more thing: you shouldn't call customers names. It's not Eric's fault you got dumped by your city-slicker boyfriend."

Yanking open the front door, she stepped down to the sidewalk and hunched her shoulders against the wind as she set off for home.

Freakin' small towns.

~

Everyone in this infernal town knew I got dumped. Everyone. I didn't know how, but they did. Communication was my life. Nonverbal cues were my bailiwick. I didn't appreciate these sympathizers' stares everywhere I went. I was a strong, independent woman. Not to mention intelligent. I was a researcher and a respected academic, for heaven's sake! I didn't need their pity.

He was only a guy. A self-absorbed guy, if I was being honest. His interests had always come first. Weekends with the kids or endlessly rehearsing with any of the seven hundred choirs he led? Standard. But if I had to do something on the weekend—like judge a debate or tend to my dying aunt —he'd pout about it. And heaven forbid we ever disagree on what to do when we did have a rare free weekend together. It was no contest—we always did what he wanted to do. Because it was easier than listening to him sigh and whine. What was the point in choosing the activity if the other person made you miserable the whole time?

Ah, the predictable trashing stage had begun sooner than I expected. But that was good. That meant I was getting over him. No, I *was* over him.

That was what I kept telling this economy-sized bottle of Jägermeister. I figured I simply needed to listen to some sad songs, drink this disgusting toilet cleaner, and flush James from my system.

I was well into my self-pitying boozefest, in the middle of a rousing duet with Peter Cetera, when a knocking that didn't go with the beat of the song caught my attention. The doorbell followed.

"I'm not home!" I bellowed, not moving from my half-reclined position on the couch.

The doorbell rang again, this time twice in quick succession.

"Shop's closed!"

A click preceded a squeak, which announced the intrepid intrusion of my uninvited visitor.

I sat up straighter on the couch, sloshing liquor onto my shirt. "Hey! You can't walk in here!"

On the threshold to the living room, Eric averted his eyes. "Are you decent?"

"Yesh! I mean, yesss. But that doesn't matter. Get out!"

He raised both hands in front of his chest and stepped into the room. "Sorry. But I was leaving work, and I glanced over here and saw Vel's car parked in the yard... with the door wide open. And I... I worried that something was wrong."

"Nothing's wrong."

"Okay. Well, it would suck if you killed the car battery."

"Then close its door when you leave. Thanks."

He looked around at the chaos in the room. "Right... Um... Whatcha doin'?"

I drained the alcohol from the glass in my hand and reached toward the floor for the bottle, which I nearly knocked over. After catching the neck of it in the nick of time, I poured myself some more, then turned down the volume on the player docked on the table behind me. "What's it look like? Getting derrrunk."

"Alone?"

Gesturing to the room around us, I said, "Yesh. That's what I am. All alone."

"You're slurring your words."

"Good. That means it's workin'."

"You're going to regret this in the morning."

"Jus' add it to the list."

"The list?"

"Of regrets!"

He leaned against the door frame and crossed his arms over his chest while he smirked across the room at me. "You're in fine form tonight. Were you drunk when you parked the Volvo on the front lawn?"

"Nope. Jusht in a hurry to get tha' way."

"Tsk, tsk. People will talk."

"Don't care."

"And Vel always made you out to be Little Miss Perfect."

"Well, I'm not. Sorry to dishappoint."

He pushed off with his shoulder and stood with his weight on both feet. His hands dropped to his sides. "Who said I was disappointed? I'm actually relieved."

"What's it to you?"

Shrugging, he stared into space, as if thinking about it. "I don't know. I guess it makes you less intimidating."

"Me? Intimidating?" I try to "Pshaw," but it produced more spit than noise. I wiped my chin.

"She also said you were... what was the word? Chipper. This doesn't qualify."

"My favorite aunt died, and I've had to give up everything and everyone and move here based on a shtupid, impulshive promise. And while thish is a lovely place to visit, small-town life isn't for me. Sorry I'm not bringin' the shunshine."

"It's more than that, though. Because the other night, at dinner, you were fine. You even laughed at some of my jokes."

"It was the wine."

"But the past couple of days..."

"Oh, didn't you hear? Everyone elshe knows. I got dumped!"

He pulled his chin back. "You did?"

"Yep. Right after you left the other night. Got the ol' Dear John phone call. Or whatever it is for women. Dear Joan?

Dear Jen? Anyway. Shplitsville. Less than a week into this loverly long-distance relationship—done."

He rubbed his chin. "Wow. Sorry about that."

"Yeah? Well, I'm not. I say, 'Screw 'im!' But not for real. Not anymore. That makes me shad. I'm gonna mish that. A girl has needs, ya know?"

"Ewwwkay. You know, I realize you're past the point of understanding the consequences, but you absolutely should stop drinking now. You don't want to have your stomach pumped. It's not a pleasant experience. For the pumper or the pumpee."

"Whatever."

He approached a card table I'd lugged from the detached garage into the living room. Looking down, he moved aside my discarded pencils and abandoned sketchpad to get to the loose papers underneath. "Tell me about this."

I belched behind my fist after yet another shot. "Oh. You mean, my illu— illushtrations?"

I had tried to work on them earlier, but the paper kept going all wavy. That might have been the Jaeger at work. Nothing decent was going to result from drunk sketching; I'd only have wasted precious materials.

"Yeah. You did these?"

"Mmm-hmm."

"They're"—he flips through a few more—"fantastic."

"Thanksh. My mom calls it my 'art shtuff.' Like, she can't bear to jus' call it 'art.' It's my 'art *shtuff.*'"

"It's good shtuff.'" He continued shifting papers and exploring the drawings, then stopped and cocked a bemused eyebrow. "Well… most of it is." He held up one from tonight. It looked like an unintentional Dali reproduction. "What happened here?" That cursed crooked smile sent warmth down, down, down, to places the liquor couldn't reach.

"Shut up! I was 'spearmenting."

"Do you sell these?"

My lids drooped and my lips seemed to want to move independently from the rest of my mouth, but I finally managed to make myself understandable after a couple of tries.

"Not those. Those're jus' sketches. I draw 'em out firs'; then I reproduce 'em on the 'puter and stick the im'ges on things. Notepads and cal'ndars… and shtuff." That explanation exhausted me, so I collapsed against the sofa cushions. My half-full glass slipped against the pads of my fingers, but my hands were too weak to grip it to prevent a disaster. I didn't care.

I flinched when the tiny tumbler seemed to suddenly defy gravity and rise from my hand altogether. When I opened my eyes—as far as I could open them, which wasn't far—I saw that Eric had arrived in front of me. He set the glass on the trestle table behind me with a clink. Another, louder, heavier clunk could only be the bottle of Jaeger joining the glass. I closed my eyes again and enjoyed the merry-go-round the living room had become.

"Wheee!" I said quietly.

A chuckle arrived close to my ear. This time when I opened my eyes, it was nearly impossible to focus them, but I finally located my visitor leaning over, straightening the pillows behind me. "Hang on a minute, and I'll cover you. And bring you a bowl."

"A bowl? For what?"

"For later. When your stomach decides to tell you how it feels about you."

"Aww… tha's okay. I don't get sick like tha'."

"How often do you drink like this?"

"Never!"

"Yeah. That's what I thought. I'll be right back with that bowl."

Whether he was gone ten seconds, ten minutes, or ten hours, I wouldn't know. I promptly fell asleep (a.k.a. passed out) on the couch, mouth gaping, limbs twitching, room spinning.

The next thing I knew, I was rocketing into a sitting position, and an unholy amount of liquid was shooting from my mouth and nose, like I was recreating a scene from *The Exorcist.*

German liquor is the devil!

I might have said that out loud, because in spite of being splattered by my vomit, Eric laughed as he positioned the mixing bowl under my face. I was almost too horrified to puke anymore. Almost. Somehow I managed to continue, though. For a long time. Forever, it felt like.

When it finally stopped, Eric spent a good thirty minutes —including interruptions for Gag Round Two—cleaning us up, then plunked a large glass of water into my hands and said, "Drink this."

"I can't."

"You can. And you will."

I stared at the couch from my vantage point on the rug in front of the fireplace.

From his position in the doorway, he followed my line of sight. "That thing's a goner."

"No! Aunt Vel's couch!"

"All actions have consequences."

"You jinxed me! I would have been fine, but you put the idea of being sick in my head."

"Is that how it works?"

"Maybe."

Now that I was sober(ish), I had to blame someone else for such horrible decision-making.

"It would have been worse if the bowl hadn't been on standby."

"I'm throwing that thing out with the couch."

He shrugged. "Your call. It's still a perfectly good bowl."

Said the guy who probably put human organs in his cookware, then called it good after giving them a run through the dishwasher.

I rested my forehead against the lip of my glass and groaned. "What time is it?"

"Time for you to go to bed. For real. Upstairs. Close to a toilet."

Realizing I was sounding like a child, I said anyway, "I'm not tired."

He pinched the bridge of his nose. "I am."

"Then go home. I told you to go away, but you ignored me."

"I think I've been thoroughly punished for that," he said, inspecting a splotch of my stomach contents on his shirt.

"Then leave."

"I'm not going to abandon you here in your time of need."

"I don't need anyone... especially not you."

Oh, my gosh. Rude! What's gotten into me? That's right... about a gallon of the hard stuff. Pull it together, Whitney!

Hands on his hips, Eric surveyed the situation without speaking for a moment. "And how are you going to get that stinking couch out of here?"

"Vel has these plastic slider... thingies. Somewhere. She was a strong, independent woman. Like me. You learn how to adapt. Don't worry! I'll be fine!" I tried to smile my rudeness away.

"You can't use sliders to get a couch down porch steps. Or

over the threshold of the front door. Or through the front door, since it'll have to be turned sideways to fit."

"I'll figure it out tomorrow."

"Meanwhile, it sits in here, stinking up the place?"

"I'll be upstairs."

"That'll be a pleasant thing to come down to in the morning, while you're nursing the biggest hangover of your life."

"You don't know anything about my life, okay?" I tried to pull myself together, like a strong, independent woman. "I mean… thanks for your help, but I've got this."

It took me several attempts to rise from the floor. In the process, I spilled water on my hands and heard a sickening rip from the extra-extra-large sleep shirt Eric had found in the dryer for me only minutes ago. The gentleman merely watched me struggle to unpin the shirt from under my knee and eventually make it to my feet. I wiped the liquid from my hand and set the glass on the nearest flat surface, the mantle. Next to Aunt Vel's ashes.

I glared at the urn and groused, "I blame you."

Now that I was up, I realized my sobriety was as much of an illusion as my relationship with James, but I concentrated on walking a straight line to the stairs and only pinballed against the walls and furniture a couple of times. The banister greatly aided my more graceful ascent.

"Good night!" Eric called after me. "I hope you feel better… eventually."

Saying nothing beat the lewd gesture and ungrateful reply that were my strange impulses in this situation. But I couldn't seem to shake the inner bitch I normally kept hidden so well. Eric had made the awful mistake of seeing me at my worst— my *worst* worst.

Why'd he have to go and do that?

CHAPTER FIVE

RELIEF. Not from the nausea, unfortunately, but in pretty much every other respect when I slunk downstairs to face the consequences the next morning. All traces of my indiscretion were gone. The couch was gone, the putrid smell was gone, the bottle of booze and my tumbler were gone, as was the infamous bowl. And so was Eric.

I sagged against the entryway to the living room and inspected the clean, much emptier space. My sketches had been tidied and stacked inside their portfolio. Well, save one that had been placed precisely on top of the folder.

I approached the table and towered over it, studying the drawing that Eric had chosen to leave out. It was the drunken one, the one that was supposed to depict a willowy blonde sitting on a dock, her feet dangling over the water, her weight resting back on her straight arms as she looked out over the lake, at peace with her life. Typically, I'd write something inspirational or motivational in whatever white space remained, but I hadn't gotten that far last night. And my subject didn't look strong and confident at all. She looked like a leaking tube of toothpaste that was about to ooze into nature's sink.

But Eric, having obviously looked through the other drawings to get a feel for the pattern, had written the text for me, albeit in his own block printing: *"You can drink to drown your problems, but problems are damn good swimmers."*

Ha. What a clever guy.

It did bring a slight smile to my face, but smiling made my head pound, so I relaxed those muscles and tucked the picture inside the portfolio with its brothers and sisters.

Since I could recall being shamefully ungrateful last night, I made a mental note to call—or email or something—Eric later to thank him for his help, no matter how unwanted it had been at the time. He was right: having to deal with that sofa this morning would have a nightmare.

Buster mewed at me from across the room.

"Yeah, yeah. You don't have to yell, okay? Where were you last night, anyway? Would it have killed you to knock the bottle over?"

He turned and flicked his tail into the air, showing me his pink butthole as he exited the room.

"Nice. Well, see if I ever intervene again on your catnip binges. I'll leave you to the mercy of practical strangers and see how you like it."

I shuffled into the kitchen after him, intending to brew myself a pot of strong coffee, but I only made it halfway across the room before I had to rest, sinking into one of the chairs at the table. While I was resting my head on my arms and breathing through my mouth, the front door clicked and squeaked. The smell of coffee filtered through the toothpaste-and-alcohol-tinged puffs of air coming from my mouth.

I finally knew what a swoon felt like.

"Oh, there she is!"

All I could do was groan a response.

"You're up and about. That's a good sign!"

"Shhhhhhhhh."

He lowered his voice to just loud enough to be heard over the rustling of paper, but it still sounded like I was in the middle of a construction site. "I got you coffee and a bag of hash browns from Mickey D's."

I lifted my head. "Oh, my gosh. You're an angel."

"That's exactly what Bernadette Usuff said when she woke up as I was about to take her from the nursing home to the funeral home."

The disposable cup froze halfway to my mouth.

He shrugged. "It happens. Well, it happened that one time. And I gave that place what-for, too. I'll be damned if anyone's going to be buried alive on my watch."

"That's… that's… horrifying!"

"You don't have to tell me! Fortunately, it wasn't that close of a call. We hadn't transferred her to the body bag yet. But I about wet myself when she opened her eyes. Here." He reached into the fast food sack and pulled out a disk of pressed, deep-fried potatoes.

"I'm not hungry."

"You'll feel better once you get some salt and grease in that belly. Hangover One Oh One. Now there's a class *I* could definitely teach."

I nibbled at the edges, then took larger and larger bites until the first potato cake was gone. As I was setting aside the empty paper sleeve, Eric handed me another starchy oval. "Keep going."

After a heavenly slug of coffee, I did. Between bites, I asked, "What'd you do with the couch?"

He paused with his lips against the plastic spill guard on his cup, then said, "It's in the backyard. Airing out."

"You were able to clean it?"

Swallowing, he tapped his drink with his fingers and kept his eyes on it as he laughed. "Nyew. Like Mrs. Usuff, it's awaiting transit, but unlike her, there's no hope of resurrection." He looked up at me and gave a half smile.

My shoulders slumped, and I blew air through my slightly parted lips. "Oh. Shoot."

"We can have a funeral for it later, if you'd like, before we haul it off to the dump. You did a number on it."

"And on you."

"Well, I didn't want to mention it, but... yeah. I've been sprayed with worse, though."

My stomach bucked, but I quickly blocked out that mental image and focused on what I needed to say. "I'm so sorry. For barfing on you *and* for being such a jerk when you were only being nice. Evidently, I'm a mean drunk."

He waved off my apology. "What else did I have to do on a Friday night?"

I rubbed my temples while chewing the last bite of my second hash brown. "Next time—not that there'll be a next time, I'm never drinking again, ever—you'll know better. You'll let me deal with the dead car battery and go on with your evening."

He shook his head. "That's not my style. Plus, I promised Vel—" He was suddenly interested in his hands, wrapped around his cup. More specifically, he seemed to be studying his knuckles. I looked at them too, since they were so intriguing to him. They were big, like the rest of his hands, but clean, the skin stretched smoothly across them. He cleared his throat. "Anyway. It wasn't a big deal. Nothing a shower and change of clothes couldn't fix. I hope you're not too embarrassed. We've all been there."

"Really? You've hurled all over someone you know in a professional capacity?"

"Yup." His twinkling eyes met mine. "Fortunately, the guy was too dead to care. And it was only a little bit. On his thigh. Wiped right up, and nobody was the wiser once he had clothes on and was cozy in his casket."

"You're making that up."

"I'm not." He set down his coffee and leaned back in his chair.

"You must be. But I appreciate it. In a weird, sick way, it's making me feel better."

As if satisfied with a day's work, he laced his hands behind his head and grinned. "Good. I'm glad. But I'm telling you the one hundred percent truth. Ask my dad. He was pissed. In my defense, it was my first time. I expect I'll toss my cookies when I lose my virginity, too. If that ever happens." He crossed his fingers near his ears.

What?! Oh, gosh.

He took a bite of hash brown. "Kidding! Your face!" He covered his mouth with the back of his hand to avoid spraying half-chewed food across the table at me.

I chuckled nervously. "Speaking of kidding…" I picked at the corner of one of the paper sleeves. "You do know I don't make a habit of this… right? Binge drinking, that is."

"I'm assuming that's the case, yes."

"Okay. It's just… Well. What you wrote on that sketch of mine…"

His face fell. "Hey, I'm sorry. That was… It was supposed to be a joke to make you laugh. And maybe not feel so embarrassed. It wasn't some veiled attempt at an intervention or something."

I sighed with relief. "Good. Just making sure."

"What a douchey way of sending someone a message,

anyway."

"The messages I put on my illustrations are sincere."

"Yeah, but you don't regurgitate t-shirt slogans."

"Is that what that was?"

He made sheepish eye contact with me. "Maybe. It might have been a meme. I don't remember where I saw it. It's not original, let's just put it that way."

"Do you take anything seriously?"

He considered my question for a second. "Not much. When you do what I do, it puts everything else into perspective, you know?"

"I guess I get that."

He stood. "Well, Bobby and Dad will be here soon to help me get that couch into the back of a truck and haul it off."

My face flamed. "Oh, you don't have to do that!"

More like, *You don't have to tell the whole town I had a drunken accident on an expensive piece of furniture.*

"Already arranged." He stepped closer and rested his hand on my shoulder. "But don't worry. We Mulligans—and Doolans, if you count Bobby—are discreet people. You rest up today and hydrate. Eat a few more hash browns. And Whitney?"

I managed to look up at him despite my mortification. "Yeah?"

He pulled his hand away and jammed it into his pocket. "Your ex is an idiot."

I snorted.

"He is. Maybe it's hard to see that right now, but I hope it doesn't take long for you to realize it."

With that, one of the only serious things he'd said to me since offering his condolences at Aunt Vel's memorial service, he exited through the back door and clomped down the wooden deck stairs that led into the yard.

CHAPTER SIX

CHALKING up James's rejection to low intelligence or explaining it away with poor decision-making skills or emotional deficiency would have made me feel better, for sure. But he didn't suffer from any of those things. He was both highly intelligent and logical; yet at the same time, he was in touch with his feelings. The man cried watching animated movies with his kids, for goodness' sake. (Okay, maybe he was *too* in touch with his feelings.)

Therefore, I couldn't dismiss this breakup as the result of dealing with an emotional, intellectual, or other type of "idiot." A smart, charismatic, evolved guy had chucked me and told me I wasn't worth the effort.

That stung.

So does bile when it comes through your nose. (FYI.)

I didn't have any control over what James—or anyone else —decided. But I could make sure that second thing never happened again.

During a stress-cleaning binge, I threw out the few things I'd brought up here to make me feel closer to James—a selfie of the two of us taken the summer before and one of his t-shirts that still smelled like him—and I deleted from my phone the playlist of songs that reminded me of us. I had a harder time parting with the earrings and necklaces he'd favored as gifts for every occasion (he had excellent taste, and some of them were my favorites), so they went into a drawer for me to deal with later, when I wasn't feeling as raw.

As for what little remained of the hard liquor I'd purchased Friday night, it went into the sink. Aunt Vel had had the right idea by not keeping any of that stuff in her house. Then again, as a recovering alcoholic, her rule had been about more than your average smarts; it had been a necessity. Since I had destroyed her new couch, it was only fair that I poured some of my hard-earned money down the drain.

Moving on was the next thing on my agenda. I allowed myself part of the weekend to sniff t-shirts, gaze at pictures, listen to sad songs, cry a bit, nurse my hurt feelings, and reminisce about the good times before scrubbing everything in sight, but it was a new week in my new life—however temporary that might be—and as much as I wished I didn't care what people in this town thought of me, I did care. And it was a small town. It wasn't going to take long—no matter how discreet certain people were—for it to get around that I was a pathetic, lonely drunk, and "Vel would be so disappointed."

They'd have been right on that score, too. That's what I cared about most. Aunt Vel would have had zero patience with me pining over a guy—especially *that* guy. She'd have said, "I told you so. Now, about this banner for the grocery store…"

So it was time to focus on that banner for the grocery store. I had no clue what I was looking at, but I felt like I should understand these things before blindly passing them on to the appropriate employee. I needed to know who the appropriate employee even was, for one thing. I consulted my cheat sheet, written in Aunt Vel's beautiful cursive, the same "font" I used for my inspirational art, as familiar to me as my own, much messier handwriting.

"Let's see… Banners and large-scale plotting. Dave. Okay." I forwarded the order to him but also rose and left my office to talk face-to-face to him about it. To show I cared. Or something.

At his open office door, I knocked. He looked up from one of the seven huge screens in front of him (okay, it was only four, but dang!) and slid his glasses from his nose to his fore-head, where they stuck as if defying gravity.

"Oh, hey, Whitney!"

"Hey. I, uh, don't mean to bother you, but…"

"Not at all! What's up?"

"I forwarded an order request to you from Harper's." On cue, his computer dinged, which made both of us laugh. "And I'm officially faster than this place's email, which is a problem."

He grimaced. "Yeah. Major headache for Vel, too."

"Anyway. I thought it would be nice if I could get an idea of what happens after I delegate these things. So when you start work on that project—not necessarily now—can you give me a buzz? I'm not going to look over your shoulder, but a quick overview would help me out. Especially when it comes to work flow and load leveling."

He smiled tenderly and scratched at his shaggy gray hair. "I'd be happy to do it now, if you have a minute. Like you said, it won't take but a second."

"Are you sure? I don't mean to make you drop everything."

"I'm not doing anything that critical. C'mon."

Ten minutes later, I had a better idea of—and appreciation for—Dave's job. He was a busy guy. Jobs came in constantly.

Not only from local businesses, either. Mostly, in fact, from Town Hall. Banners for 5K runs and parades and festivals. Requests for print-outs of large-scale plans and drawings. And that was just for Dave's department.

"If Town Hall ever get their own plotters, we're in trouble," he joked. At my wrinkled brow, he added, "Ah, don't worry. Their budget's way too small. And they don't have the space to house something like that. So we get all of their requests. The funeral home and Town Hall alone could keep this place in business forever."

"That's… comforting."

"It is. Neither of those places is going anywhere. People are always going to die, and someone has to run this town."

"Unless too many people die. Then there'll be no town to run."

"Good point!" He chuckled. "But that's not a worry, either. We've had population increases for ten years in a row now. This place is growing, if you can believe it."

That *was* hard to believe, but I kept my snooty, big-city commentary to myself. "That's great. I was wondering, since the funeral home seems to be busy *all the time.*"

Rubbing his eyes, he thought about that for a few seconds. "That's because Larry Mulligan's the county coroner, too."

I shivered. "How does someone get into that line of work?"

"He was elected. Ran unopposed. As for the funerals business? Born into it. His daddy was a funeral director and so was his granddaddy, great granddaddy, great-great granddaddy, and on and on. Now Eric's keeping it going. Doesn't have a choice. Especially around these parts. Only game for miles around."

He clicked around on his screen to minimize and close the files we'd been viewing and went back to the project he'd been working on when I arrived: a banner he was both designing and printing for the start and finish line of the ATV Club's annual Mud Race.

His monologue had made me feel unexpectedly hopeless. Maybe it was the "no choice" part of the spiel. Everyone should have a choice, right? In fact, one of the few choices we tricked ourselves into believing we had in life was our career path. Genetics—in the form of natural aptitude—already dictated plenty in that arena; was it fair when that was the *only* factor?

Plus, in Eric's case, he hadn't been *born* into that life; he'd been assimilated. If he'd been adopted by pretty much anyone else—teacher, chef, doctor, writer, pilot, architect, whatever—his life might not have already been mapped out for him. For some reason, it seemed crueler to force an inherited lifestyle on someone whose blood didn't match, for lack of a better term. Then again, it said a lot about the bonds made through adoption, regardless of genetics. You *were* family, no matter what your birth certificate said, no matter what a bunch of randomly arranged cells and atoms indicated. Family was bigger and stronger than DNA.

Anyway, who could say? Maybe Eric loved being an undertaker. It seemed to suit his awkward personality. I was assuming he was better with dead people than living ones. Maybe I was projecting a dissatisfaction with such a strange career because I'd rather *be* dead than touch a corpse. Or have to deal regularly with grieving friends and family. Or wear paper coveralls.

I blinked myself from my woolgathering and beamed at Dave. "I'll let you get back to it, then. Thanks for the quick lesson."

While I was out walking around, I took a tour of the maze-like halls and poked my head in Natalie's office. "Everything going okay with the daily dead sheets?"

She rolled her eyes, then laughed. "Yes. Finally. Took forever for me to get the email today. Thought maybe it was our system—again. But it was Eric, running behind. Then I had two calls from Hortense about corrections. Seems a certain junior undertaker went overboard with his bios, and he sent them before the families had okayed them. Could have been bad. For Mulligan. I just print what I'm given."

I crossed my arms over my chest. "What do you mean, Eric went 'overboard'?"

"Oh, he likes to spice up the obits, make them more entertaining, and sometimes it gets him in trouble."

"Why is he writing them? Shouldn't he be busy working with the bodies?"

She shrugged. "Says he likes it. Makes for a nice change and brightens his day. And Hortense and Lena hate writing them, so they give him the information, and he does it. He's pretty good. But sometimes too creative."

I remembered the t-shirt slogan he'd written on my sketch Friday night. "What? He makes stuff up?"

"No, no, no! Nothing that bad. He tries to toe the line between fact and commentary when it comes to the more, um, colorful residents who have passed on. But sometimes he doesn't do a very good job of keeping his toes on the 'fact' side. This morning's was a real corker."

I came around Natalie's desk so I could see for myself. After skimming through the usual stuff about birth and marriage dates, military service, and names of survivors for a Mr. Isaac Tremble, I arrived at the first sentence that must have been an issue:

Isaac was a deacon at the First Episcopal Church, where he served loyally and faithfully, often going out of his way to spread the Word, in places as unexpected as The Poole Table, where he was a nightly regular.

I snorted. "Oops. Well? *Was* he good at holding down a barstool?"

"Oh, yes. Not that I would know firsthand, but it was pretty well known that he liked a tipple. Anyway, it gets better. Keep going."

This time, I read aloud. "'In his later years, Mr. Tremble also assumed volunteer enforcement positions, mostly serving to protect his lawn.'" I covered my mouth. "Oh, no."

"Hey, if you want people to say nice things about you when you're gone, be nice."

I shot her a long-suffering look.

She shrugged. "Okay, fine. Let's just say, Eric wasn't one of Mr. Tremble's biggest fans. And this is pretty mild, considering. Mr. Tremble *was* an asshole. Nobody liked him."

"Still, that's extremely unprofessional."

"He got carried away this time, I guess. Or maybe he was in a bad mood. Or showing off. Who knows what goes through that guy's mind half the time?"

"For Aunt Vel's obit, he took the information we provided and wrote something lovely."

"Hortense wrote Vel's. Eric was snowed under that week and didn't have time. And he *was* ticked off that her obit was so—what'd he call it?—'vanilla.'"

"How do you know all this stuff?"

"I'm friends with Hortense. Have been since preschool."

"Right. Of course. But you don't call her 'Horty'?"

"I'd prefer to live. Only Eric's allowed to call her that. Ever."

"Good to know." I sighed. "This small-town stuff. It's so complicated!"

"You'll catch on." Natalie sat back in her chair and twirled her pencil against her knuckles. "Speaking of... A little birdie told me Eric's car was at the funeral home all night Friday."

I shoved my hands in my twill trouser pockets. "And?"

She lifted an eyebrow. "*And* he was seen crossing the street early the next morning. Coming from the direction of *your* house."

"Interesting. Well. There are plenty of houses on that side of the street."

"Only one that belongs to a single woman."

"Hm. Well, *this* single woman went to bed alone that night. And every night since." I widened my eyes. "Oh, my gosh. Do you think he's having an affair with a *married* woman on my street?"

Before she could accuse me of anything further—or of being deliberately obtuse—I stepped into the hallway and threw over my shoulder, "Get back to work and stop gossiping."

Her laughter followed me all the way to my office.

A few hours later, I was tapping my fingers impatiently while I waited for a batch of email invoices to go through. Printing out and walking the messages over to each recipient in town would have been faster. When a few of the missives bounced back, I stifled a groan. There was no way of knowing for sure if the problem was on my end or theirs (although I had a pretty good guess), so I tried to resend the emails. Half of them went, half of them bounced. I tried again. All but one finally found its way.

I stared at the problem child and pressed my lips tightly together. I would have chalked it up to an invalid address, but it was Lena at Mulligan Funeral Home. She was a permanent contact, since there'd been so much correspondence between our two businesses. Obviously, today's issues were an aberration.

"Screw it," I grumbled, hitting the print button on the attached PDF.

One of the few advantages of small town life was that I could walk this across the street. I needed the exercise and fresh air, anyway.

Hand-delivering a bill was a tad more awkward than I'd anticipated, though. Too late, as I was setting the invoice on Lena's desk, and she and Larry were looking at me, both confused and surprised, did I realize that.

Larry, standing at Lena's shoulder, recovered first. "Ms. Faelhaber. Nice to see you. Vel always emailed our statements, but..."

I cleared my throat. "Uh, yeah, well, I tried to do that, several times, but it wouldn't go, and I was on the verge of throwing my computer through the window, so I figured it'd be better to bring it over here."

Lena laughed. "You don't need an excuse to visit us."

"It's not an excuse."

While slitting open the envelope, she peered coyly at me over the top of her reading glasses. "I hear you and Eric have been—what do the young people call it now?—'hanging out.' That's nice. I'm sure both of you can use the company. He's been out of sorts lately, but I believe he's coming around. There's a spring in his step. Can't be a coincidence..." She glanced at the bill, pushed it aside, and gave me her full, penetrating, probing attention.

I blushed, wondering how much they knew. Too much, I was sure. Heck, Larry had helped cart off the ruined couch, and so had Lena's son. Great. I was now Vel's drunk niece. Neither of them seemed worried that I was corrupting Eric, so they must have thought *he* was going to be a good influence on *me*. Dear Lord. He was a nice enough guy, and admittedly easy on the eyes, and he had done me a huge favor last weekend, but I would have been fine without him. Better, in fact, because nobody would have known my shame. And I was sure as heck not taking any life cues from a socially awkward undertaker whose idea of a good time was thinking up new death puns and writing satirical obituaries.

Saying any of that might cause offense, though, so I merely gulped down my chagrin and replied, "I don't think I can take credit for a spring in anyone's step."

"Oh, don't be modest."

"No, really. I… He… I just got out of a relationship, so…"

"Hiram was my rebound guy. And look at us! Nearly forty years later, we're still going strong." She removed her glasses and let them hang from the chain around her neck.

I shifted from foot to foot. "That's wonderful. But—"

"Sis, that's enough," Larry said gruffly. "This is none of our business, and you're embarrassing her."

"I'm not embarrassed. There's nothing to be embarrassed about." I tucked my hair behind my ears and smiled down at her, then up at him, suddenly finding myself in the position of mollifying *them*. Interpersonal communication was so bizarre. "I feel bad, though, that you—or anyone—has the wrong idea. Because he just happened upon me during a vulnerable moment and helped me out."

"With the couch?" she clarified.

I didn't need a mirror to know I was positively purple at this point. "Uh, yeah."

Larry muttered something about finishing later what he and Lena had been doing when I came in, and walked toward his office. "It was bound to happen, though. Buster's older than Methuselah's farts."

"Uh…"

Before I could ask them what was supposedly wrong with the cat and what that had to do with me barfing all over the couch, Eric and Hortense enter the office, in the middle of what sounds like a good-natured argument.

"...but you of all people should be more sensitive to someone who might have had an addiction. Did you have to call him out on that, in his own obit?"

"I didn't! I merely hinted."

"Puh-lease. Anyone who knew the guy— Oh, hey, Whitney!"

Eric's head snapped up. "Whitney."

"Hi, guys." I flashed a hundred-watt smile at them, hoping it would distract from my maroon face.

Dress shoes rasping against the carpet as he skidded to a halt, Eric asked, "Why are you here?"

Hortense snorted. "Geez. Make a girl feel welcome."

"No, I just meant... Uh... What's up?" He glanced nervously at his dad, who sighed, shook his head, and shut himself in his office.

Hortense slid behind her desk and stifled a knowing smile toward her mother, then pretended to be engrossed in something on her computer monitor.

Lena answered for me, "Whitney was delivering this month's invoice."

Eric pulled a face. "Vel emailed those, you know."

"Yeah, I know. The system kept spitting it back at me."

"I can help you update the infrastructure if you—"

"No! You've already, uh, done enough."

Lena chortled. "We were talking about Buster's mishap on the couch last week."

I turned so neither of the Doolans could see my face when I widened my eyes at Eric and repeated, "Yes, Buster's mishap. Was that epic, or what?" *Was it? I need to know.*

He knelt down to tie his already-tied shoe. "Yeah. Well, I knew something was wrong when I saw the car parked in the yard, and when I checked on you and found you cleaning up after the cat…"

"Right!"

Switching to the other foot, he kept his head down while Lena picked up the thread. "Then Eric said the whole thing made *you* sick, poor thing, which I can completely relate to. I could handle my kids' puke, but anyone else's—even an animal's—no way."

"Oh, totally. I lost it." What else could I have said?

"Bobby and Larry said it was bad. Did you take him to the vet? Dr. Judy's wonderful."

"Nah. He recovered pretty quickly. Something he ate, I'm sure. He's fine now."

Eric stood and fidgeted. "Yeah, *he's* fine. We're the ones who'll need therapy. Right, Whitney?"

"Yes. Absolutely."

"And now you know to never share your cookies and milk with him again. Rookie mistake."

"Oh, dear!" Lena muttered.

Great. Now I was not only helpless, I was an idiot, too.

"So, anyway." He jerked his thumb over his shoulder. "I've gotta… go… do some… stuff."

Hortense wrinkled her nose. "I thought you said you were done for the day."

"I was wrong. I mean, I forgot something. And talking about Buster reminded me."

"You've got a sick cat downstairs? Cookies in the oven?"

He laughed nervously. "No! Ew. Anyway."

She snickered. "You're weird."

Without disputing that, he hurried from the room.

As soon as the door to the basement clicked shut, Hortense turned to me and grinned. "Someone's got a crush!"

"That's not it."

"Hey, a guy doesn't clean up barf for just anyone."

To stand here and dispute her theory would be to give more credence to it, so I said goodbye and took my leave, cursing the network issues that had sent me into this situation in the first place. When I got back to my desk, I would have to contact an IT consulting firm to solicit an estimate on those system updates Eric mentioned.

CHAPTER SEVEN

THE PEOPLE of Morris wanted so badly for me to be Vel 2.0. In their minds, I was a single woman who drove an old Volvo, lived alone (with a cat), and owned and operated the print shop, so why not? Unfortunately, we were all finding out it didn't quite work that way.

I didn't fit in. Nobody but Cath had the nerve to come right out and say it to my face, but it was there in the things people didn't say, the details they left out—consciously or subconsciously—so that I was forced to seek clarification. Sometimes it was as simple as asking for a more specific moniker or job title when a first name was dropped. Sometimes I had to dig deeper and receive what felt like a recitation of the person's entire family tree and Morris history. In any case, it was exhausting trying to keep it all straight. I needed a flow chart.

The other day, while I was at Lynda's Flowers selecting a small bouquet of my favorites to cheer myself up (it wasn't pathetic; it was self-care!), I found out that Lynda's husband's sister's granddaughter's best friend's teacher (or something... I tuned out after three degrees of separation) had dated Eric a few years ago, when they were both fresh out of college. Why the florist had thought this was important information for me to have was anyone's guess. Okay, I knew why she thought I'd be interested, but I wasn't. In fact, I'd had to stifle the urge to scream, "I don't care!" Instead, I squeaked out a "That's nice!" between the clenched teeth of my forced smile and paid for my blooms.

Then, as I was making my escape, she stopped me at the door by speaking up again. Anyone else could have claimed ignorance and kept walking, but I knew social cues too well for that trick, and I was, sadly, a slave to them, so I stepped out of the way of any incoming customers and turned, my face open and expectant.

"Larry had high hopes for that relationship, of course. He's the end of the line, you know."

My mask must have slipped, giving away my confusion at why Eric's dad would care, because she elaborated (as people so often have to do for me), "If Eric doesn't have any children to continue the family business…"

"Oh. Right."

"They'll have to change the name to Doolan Funeral Home. It's been Mulligan for generations!"

Not following her logic—I wasn't changing the name of Velvet Printing, after all—I nevertheless made what I hoped were sympathetic noises toward her irrational despair about the fall of a patently patriarchal system I most definitely didn't agree with. Then her more disturbing insinuation hit me: I, as the town's freshest meat, was considered the big hope for continuing the Mulligan line. With Eric. *Well, eff that.*

Of course, I didn't say that out loud. Somehow. But my exit wasn't very graceful, either. Anyone with half a social skill would know I was flustered by her presumption.

I was destined to be a loner here.

So be it. I could fill that role in town. Sounded like it was up for grabs, now that Mr. Tremble had departed. I'd never considered a hermit's life, but if my choices were "recluse" and "heir to a funeral business," well… that was no choice at all. I could do solitude.

In all seriousness, I did need to figure out my place in the community. And finding it didn't have to be that hard. It was all about establishing new routines. So that was what I was now working tirelessly to do.

It started the minute my feet hit the wood floor in the morning and didn't end until my head was resting on the pillow again at night. If I did the same things in the same order every single day, those things would start to feel like the norm, and this place would start to feel like home. People would start to get to know the real me and would learn what to expect from me (i.e., no future funeral directors). In turn, I'd learn their ways, their names, and their relationships with each other. It was already working. Somewhat. At least, the part about me establishing new routines was going according to plan.

On weekdays, I rose before the sun and put on the socks jammed into the shoes next to the bed. Still half-asleep, I switched out whatever clothes I'd fallen asleep in—sometimes the ones I'd worn to work—with the neatly folded sweat-wicking compression tank and cropped running pants next to the shoes. Sneakers in hand, I shuffled to the bathroom, where I brushed my teeth, splashed water on my face, and twisted my hair into a sloppy bun to keep it out of my eyes and off my neck. Then I shoved my feet into my shoes and propped them in turn on the edge of the bathtub to tighten and tie the laces. On my way out the door, I shrugged into the hoodie I still needed in the cool early mornings and slipped my fingers through the handle on my water bottle. I zeroed the activity tracker on my wrist and set out.

Across the street. Past the print shop, past the newspaper, past the funeral home, past dark and shuttered shops and locked stores. Over the railroad tracks. Into the trees and onto the trails that eventually led up to the falls, although I rarely went that far. Not on weekdays, anyway. I was on a strict schedule to return home, brew coffee, shower, dress, primp (not too much, because why bother?), poach and eat my two eggs with a side of yogurt, down my orange juice, gulp my cooled coffee, pour the rest of it into an insulated mug, top it off, and trot across the street to work.

But weekends were another story. I let myself sleep in a bit on Saturday and wait for the sun—or the foggy, gray illumination that passed for sunlight some days—to stroke me awake, like a tender lover. I stretched and blinked in the changing light, then forced myself through the usual routine with promises of a more scenic jogging route and a relaxed pace, followed by a bigger breakfast (including bacon), a leisurely tour of the local farmers' market for fresh food to get me through the coming week, and a day with my drawings.

After only three weeks of this particular routine, I was bored to death.

But that was okay! I was still adjusting, still finding my way, still tweaking the system. Eventually, I'd tune in to all of the local possibilities. Research. That was what it all came down to. And I was damn good at it, when I put my mind to it. Scouting the area, interviewing the locals, and poking around the Internet a bit would surely yield plenty of possibilities for filling my free time.

I also desperately needed a trip to a city—preferably *my* city, but Portland would do—to jolt me out of this rut.

Maybe Shelly could meet up with me here, and we could

continue on to the state capital, or I could drive down to Boston for a girls' day with her. I was plotting that exact excursion, practically sweating with excitement at the prospect, when I heard, "Hi!" from a distance ahead of me.

I ducked slightly to peek through the low-hanging branches on the trail and considered running past when I saw who it was. But that would have been rude. And if there was one thing I wasn't—when sober—it was impolite.

Since my heart wasn't in this run anyway, I slowed to a stop in front of the trailside bench where Eric was sitting with a fat, well-worn paperback (some sci-fi/fantasy-looking thing) and returned his simple yet cheerful greeting.

He grinned. "Oh, you didn't have to stop. I didn't mean to interrupt your workout."

I waved off his concern. "Can't get into a rhythm today, anyway."

"Hung over?"

"No!"

"Because it's Saturday morning, so…"

"Yeah. Well. Not going to repeat that Friday night experience ever again." I kicked at the dirt. "And, uh, you didn't have to lie for me. About the couch."

"Oh, yeah. About that. Sorry. It was just an instinct, to save you from the gossip, but then my family kept asking more questions, so the story got more and more detailed, and—"

"And it turns out I'm a moron who feeds a cat sweets and dairy, then can't stomach cleaning up the mess." I smiled to let him know I wasn't mad.

Looking adorably sheepish, he apologized again.

"It's okay. I guess it's a better story than the real one. And it reminds me, I still don't have a couch."

"Murphin's Flea Market can set you right up."

I wrinkled my nose at the suggestion and instead

wondered if any stores in Portland would deliver this far, but I didn't ask him. I could figure it out for myself later.

"Or not," he said with a laugh, in response to my face-pulling. "Whatever. Minimalist is good, too. Who needs a sofa?" He dog-eared his book, dropped it in his lap, and spread out as much as he could on the bench, his elbows hooked over the back rest and his knees pointing to ten and two o'clock at their furthest positions but moving in and out, like he couldn't sit still.

I wanted to remove my hoodie but all I was wearing underneath was a compression tank that wasn't much more modest than a swimsuit, so I suffered through the rising temperature and merely flapped my top layer to circulate some air under it.

Eric, looking perfectly cool and comfortable in a t-shirt and cargo shorts (paperbacks and cargo shorts? I felt like I'd fallen into a time warp) smirked at me. "Overdressed?"

I propped my foot on the far corner of the bench and stretched my right leg, which had started to tighten since I'd paused. "This time of year is tricky. Cool in the shade"—I gestured around us—"but warm in the sun and if you're active for any length of time."

"It's perfect. Makes for such a nice change after the long, dead winter and cool spring." He closed his eyes and tilted his head back. "Listen to those birds. They're so happy. And alive."

Now that he mentioned it, the birdsong *was* particularly loud this morning, especially out there on the trail. While he communed with nature, I took advantage of the opportunity to study him.

If I hadn't known his background and had never suffered through any of the dozen awkward conversations and inter-actions I'd had so far with him, *and* if he'd never seen me completely wasted or worn my vomit, I would have had the objectivity to admit… he was a fine-looking man. Which was a rarity around here. I'd wonder why he was still single, but his ill-timed jokes and stupid death puns probably didn't help his case.

Was that what had scared away the teacher? I was assuming she was the dumper, because… well. His profession was a pretty tough sell. Who would want to be touched by someone whose hands had been on dead people all day? Then again, he did wear thick gloves on those big, strong, capable-looking mitts when handling corpses.

Maybe *he* was the commitmentphobe. Perhaps he was perfectly happy with life the way it was, resentful of anyone coming along and throwing away his cargo shorts or replacing his paperbacks with an e-reader or reminding him before social outings not to forget his filter.

I stretched my other leg and swallowed a huge slug of room-temperature water.

Yeah. Perhaps he'd be more interested in an *arrangement* than a bona fide relationship. Someone to satisfy certain urges—after a thorough, post-work shower, of course. Someone to rub against him and make him feel alive, like those birds…

Water dribbled from my bottom lip onto my raised thigh, but I barely registered the drool. Instead, I continued wondering what it would feel like to have those hands on my waist, my ribs, my nip—

Without warning, he opened his eyes and caught me gawking. Flustered and immediately on the defensive, I blurted, "Are you stalking me?"

His peaceful expression fled like a squirrel up a tree, to be replaced by one of horror. "No! Who told you that?"

Still embarrassed by my obvious staring, I answered, "Nobody had to tell me. I've noticed you're always around."

"It's a small town."

"Mmm-hmm. But it's weird, because I don't bump into other people nearly as much as I bump into you."

"We travel in the same circles. For work."

"And you show up at my front door and invite yourself into my house and happen to be reading on a bench along the path where I'm running…"

"This is a public greenway! Ask anyone who knows me—I read here all the time. It's where I come to clear the embalming chemicals from my sinuses. And *you* were the one who showed up at my work most recently." He sat forward and rested his elbows on his knees. "You don't really think I'm stalking you, do you?"

"No." I grinned and winked at him, instantly regretting the flirtatious gesture. "But you *are* ubiquitous. It's creepy."

"I'm an undertaker. 'Creepy' goes with the territory. Unfortunately."

"Your weird sense of humor doesn't help."

Oh, balls. Did I say that out loud?

He laughed. "Hey! Some people like my sense of humor."

"Like who?"

"Hortense, for one."

"She's family. She has to." I kept smiling and stuck my tongue out for good measure.

"And Vel. She was one of the only people who got it."

"I *get* it; it's just not funny." His face fell. "Okay, it's funny. You're funny. But I could see where some people wouldn't know how to take you."

"They need to lighten up."

"Maybe. But you could also filter better."

"Uh, look who's talking. Why don't you tell me how you really feel?"

I motioned for him to scoot over and narrow his

manspread. When he did, I sat next to him, stretching my legs straight in front of me, crossed at the ankles. After unstrapping my water bottle and setting it down on the sliver of bench between us, I gripped the front of the seat. "Communication—especially when it fails—fascinates me."

"I must be a dream come true for you, then."

At first, I worried he must have known what I was thinking when he opened his eyes, but it was quickly apparent he was responding innocently to my most recent comment, not any fantasies I might have been having about him. I cleared my throat. "You're an interesting case study, for sure."

His brown eyes sparkled. "Ha. There's your diplomacy, making a comeback." He transferred his hands to his lap and fiddled with the pages of his book. "A case study, huh? That's how you see me? Something to be examined?"

"No. But your communication methods are."

Yeah, that's why I was staring at you. I was thinking about your brain, not your body. Believable? I hoped so.

"Well, let me save you some precious research. I joke because doing what I do for a living is a daily lesson in how short life is, and people who can't laugh aren't worth my limited time on this planet. I tease and make light of things because that's about the only thing that separates me from the people who lie on the slabs and in the drawers at work. Laughing reminds me I'm alive. Making others laugh shows me who I might like to be alive with. Pretty straightforward."

"And Aunt Vel loved to laugh."

"That she did."

"Can I...?" I bent my knees and perched on the edge of the bench, angling myself toward him. He raised his eyebrows expectantly but waited patiently. "I don't know how to say this without sounding like a jerk, but I have a question, something that's been bothering me ever since... well, ever since I found out how close you and my aunt were."

"Spit it out, Professor."

I ignored the inaccuracy of the nickname. "She never talked about you. Ever. Like, not a single mention. Not by name, not by title, not by anonymous anecdote... Nothing."

"Was there a question in there I missed?"

Again, I ignored him. "Not so much as a casual 'I visited with a friend this weekend.'"

"I wouldn't call what we did 'visiting.' That sounds so... Victorian."

"What did you do, then?"

"Finally, there's the question. We mostly hung out. Talked. I helped her around her house when she had computer problems or needed someone tall or someone who had more upper body strength than a newborn."

"She *was* weak in the arms."

He rubbed the back of his neck. "And I told you. She *got* me. And I got her. We had long, deep conversations. I could tell by her forced smile when she was having a rough day. So I'd email a joke to her later. The cornier the better. She loved puns. And she'd do the same for me, although instead of sending me jokes, she'd find quirky stories from around the world about undertakers and cadavers and stuff."

Ew! Aunt Vel!

That must have been written all over my face, because he shrugged and said, "She knew how... dissatisfying... I find my vocation, and was always trying to make it more interesting for me. She knew I felt forced into it."

Ah-ha! I was right!

Stifling my glee regarding my intuition (*I've still got it!*), I adopted a commiserating tone. "Nobody *chooses* to do that, right? It's a family tradition."

He mulled that over a second. "Someone had to be the first one to choose it."

"I don't know. Maybe *it* chooses *you*."

He threw his head back and laughed. "It's a career, not a wizard's wand. Anyway, Vel kept my dad off my back, too, when I was younger. She'd say, 'Larry, you're lucky he isn't the rebellious sort. You should be rewarding his loyalty and sense of duty, not acting like a dick all the time.'" His chuckles took on a more gasping noise, sounding suspiciously like sobs.

I averted my eyes while he composed himself. "She called your dad a dick? To his face?"

"All the time. And worse. She—"

When he stopped abruptly and rose from the bench, I looked up at him.

"I have to go," he said, his lip twitching.

I hopped to my feet and touched his arm. He stared at my hand the whole time as I said, "Hey. I'm sorry. She was your friend, so this must be hard for you." I took a deep breath. "I—I'm just trying to play catch-up here. If you'd been around once or twice when I visited to take care of Aunt Vel or to learn the business, or—"

"You deserved that time alone with her, without some goofball lurking in the background, unsure of what to say or do." He brushed at his eyes and sniffed. Then with a wry smile, he met my gaze. "In case you haven't noticed, group settings aren't my thing. I'm not even good one-on-one with people until I get to know them—and sometimes never, depending on the person. I didn't want to make a sad, difficult time harder... for you or Vel."

I hesitated. "And that was considerate. But now I feel like you're being cheated out of your grief."

He snorted.

"What?"

"You sound like Horty."

"Good! I like your cousin. She's smart. And she cares about you."

"Lots of people care about me. I'm not alone in this world. Only... slightly lonelier in this aspect than in others, because nobody could know—"

Icicles formed then fell through my belly.

He shook his head. "Never mind."

"No. Finish what you were going to say."

"I can't. I promised."

"Who?"

"Myself, okay? I promised myself."

From an academic perspective, this conversation was fascinating. From a social perspective, it was baffling. And maddening.

"Eric—"

He turned and walked away, waving at me with his book. "Have a nice weekend."

Before I could protest his leave-taking or he could get too far, a ringing bicycle bell and crunching mulch heralded the arrival of someone through the low-hanging foliage. Neither of us could have imagined how fast the person was careening down the trail, though, and the bell was hardly sufficient warning... for Eric. I stepped off the path in plenty of time. But he was too close to the blind spot. One second, he was vertical, the next, his head was no longer where it previously had been, roughly sixty-four inches above the ground, but rather *on* the ground. It was still attached to his body, fortunately, but that body had surely felt better. His paperback sailed through the air and landed with a flutter a few yards away.

At the same time, the cyclist flew over her handlebars and landed at my feet with a crash of metal and the thud of a body meeting unforgiving earth.

"Oh, my gosh!" I stared at the two crumpled forms on the trail, unsure which one I should help first. Or *how* to aid them.

Since Eric was conscious and speaking—unintelligibly and rather profanely, but still speaking—I hurried to the prone, unmoving cyclist lying in a heap next to her bike. There was no telling who she was with the back of her helmet facing me. I was worried about moving her, in case she had serious injuries I'd be making worse, but there would be no injuries to worsen—or eventually heal—if she couldn't breathe.

"Roll her over," Eric said through gritted teeth and propped on one elbow.

"Are you okay?" I asked him, kneeling next to the now-groaning cyclist.

He nodded. "Yeah, yeah. Got the wind knocked out of me, that's all. And my ankle's killing me."

"Don't move it. It could be broken."

"If it were broken, I wouldn't be *able* to move it. Can you please turn Cath over before she dies of asphyxiation?"

My head swiveled back to the cyclist. "Cath?" I knelt down next to her and pulled on her shoulder to roll her face-up, then pushed to settle her on her back.

She blinked at me. "You!"

"Me?"

"Yes, you! You made me crash!"

I glanced at Eric for support, but he looked as astounded as I felt.

"*I* made you crash? You mowed down Eric like a... a... mower thingy!"

Words. I couldn't think of anything right now except how irresponsible she was and how galling it was that she'd blame anyone but herself for what happened.

She sat up and straightened her helmet. "He's supposed to be sitting on the bench. He's always sitting on the bench."

"Other people use this trail, too."

"Not at this time on Saturdays. It's always just him—on the bench—and me on my bike."

"Are you seriously accusing me of being at fault, because I dared to run on this public path and upset your precious routine? Do you cycle blindfolded?"

"The branches. The leaves. I always ring my bell through here."

"If you're driving like a bat out of hell, your bell doesn't do a bit of good."

"There's a hill! I was coasting."

"Try using your brakes."

"Ladies, ladies!" Eric shouted, collapsing onto his back and holding his head in both hands.

We stopped arguing and looked over at him.

"Cath, are you okay?" he asked wearily.

She inspected her knees and elbows. "I'm fine. A few scrapes and bumps. I've had worse wrecks. But you—"

"I'm fine. Don't worry about me. Can you ride that bike out of here?"

"Yes, but—"

"Go."

"How are you going to…?"

"I'll figure it out. Go home and clean yourself up."

"If you're sure…"

"I am. I'll be better when I don't have an audience."

"Okay, but what about *her?*" She jerked her head toward me as she lifted her bike from the ground and brushed dirt and wood chips from her skin-tight nylon singlet.

"Whitney's leaving too."

I opened my mouth to protest, but he silenced me with a

pointed look. It was the "shut up and go with it" look, popular with parents, cops, psychiatrists, and others used to dealing with irrational people. Aunt Vel had it mastered, too, and used it often in the presence of my mother.

I smiled shakily at Cath. "Sounds like he has it under control."

"I have my cell phone," he said. "I'll call Bobby if I need help. Neither of you could support me anyway."

"He has a point." I edged away, like I was going to jog toward the falls, as Cath mounted her bike and prepared to pedal it back to town.

"Sorry I hit you," she said to her beloved. "I'm calling Town Hall first thing Monday to have them clear these branches."

He waved from his back. "Good plan. See you around."

When Cath glanced over her shoulder at the top of the hill, I jogged away for real. After a few yards, though, I looped back to the accident scene and stood over Eric.

"What's *your* plan?"

He sighed and closed his eyes. "I need you to call Bobby. Tell him to bring a hearse and park as close to the trailhead as he can get."

"A hearse? I'm sure you're not that bad off."

A long-suffering look was his only reply, but when I made no move to follow his instructions, he asked, "You do have a phone, don't you?"

In the city, the answer would have been a definite "yes," but here? I didn't bother carrying it. When I gave him the disappointing news, he said, "No biggie. Use mine."

"Okay."

"And Bobby will need to bring my dad, too."

"All right. And your phone is in which pocket?" No way was I rooting around near this man's junk in the seventeen or so hidey-holes in those ridiculous shorts.

"Right far-side pocket. Zippered."

I located the device without incident and scrolled through his contacts until I reached Bobby's number. "Got it. How soon do you think he could get here?" I asked, tapping the screen to dial.

"Soon, I hope." Then as if he were talking about something as mundane as being hungry, he declared, "I'm pretty sure I'm concussed."

CHAPTER EIGHT

THE PLACE WAS UNREAL. The Mulligan compound (there was no other word for the sprawling lakefront land that contained five houses, orchards, gardens, tennis courts, pools, and who knew what else?) was a veritable resort—exclusive, mind you—on the outskirts of town. Larry's mansion was more vulgar than impressive, considering there was only one guy rattling around in it, but to each his own. Bobby and Jill had an equally lavish home that was all stone and glass and made me cold just to look at it. Lena and Hiram occupied a massive A-frame log home closer to the water. And Hortense had stuck to the other end of the size spectrum when designing her own place. I wouldn't have classified it as a "tiny house," but it was close. Just enough space for her and her dogs. "Less to clean, maintain, heat, and cool," she told me when I remarked on how cute it was.

Eric's wood-shingled "cottage" was more my speed, with its four bedrooms, three bathrooms, professional-grade kitchen with woodstove, and bright, clean wainscoting-lined sitting areas that transformed into cozy hideouts after sunset.

The wraparound porch and Adirondack chairs near the rocks overlooking the lake were nice touches, too.

Yeah, I could get used to a place like that. Not that I would ever have a chance to. Or would want the chance to. Not this *particular* place, anyway. But a modest-sized house on the lake would be nice. It hadn't been easy going back to Aunt Vel's outdated Cape Cod with the view of the print shop across the street after being here for most of the weekend.

I sighed while staring out at the secluded, rocky backyard and waited for a pot of coffee to brew. Hortense had just left, traversing the pine-studded acres between her house and Eric's to tend her precious pooches.

"You don't mind, do you, Whitney? They tend to chew on things when I leave them alone too long."

Considering Larry was still around, it didn't seem like a big deal at all. I was perfectly willing and able to cook, refresh ice packs, tighten ankle wraps, and keep an eye on the patient's concussion symptoms. I encouraged Hortense to take her time and not worry.

She had whispered on her way out the back door, "Larry's not a natural caregiver, so I'm afraid he won't be much help."

She was right, but I didn't mind. In fact, I was looking forward to the time when he made good on his plans to run into town to oversee a memorial service. Perhaps then I could resurrect the conversation Eric and I had started on the bench. Or not. He was pretty woozy. Mostly I'd been keeping him comfortable and making sure he wasn't about to die of a brain hemorrhage. It was the nicest weekend I'd had in ages.

How sad was that?

Not sure if I'd ever mentioned it before, but I was a strong, independent woman. Difference was, until now, being alone had always been a choice. Companionship was just a phone call or text away in Boston. Here, companionship meant brainstorming new artwork concepts with Buster. That wasn't alone; that was lonely.

Unfortunately, there was no easy solution for it. Every time I spoke to Shelly on the phone, I waited for her to say, "You know what you need? A girls' weekend!" And I had gotten my hopes up when those exact words fell from her lips during our last call. But she quickly followed them up with, "I wish I could too, but work is insane. We have a new Independence Day exhibit going up, and I guess as the curator, I'm supposed to squat and produce some of these items. 'A lathe would look great in that corner!' Oh, would it now? Any ideas where we could get one? Anyone have a Revolutionary War-era lathe sitting in their basement? No? I didn't think so."

Apparently, my big sister had her own stress going on. Fair 'nuff. I couldn't expect her to drop everything and come to my rescue just because I'd done it for her countless times.

Done it for everyone countless times. Who did everyone call when they needed someone? Someone to stay home with his bratty, ungrateful kids when his custody weekend fell on the same weekend as some big choir to-do on campus? Me. Someone to pass her the tissues, pour the wine, and keep the rom-coms playing continuously when she broke up with her latest boy toy? Yours truly. Someone to hold her hand while she was dying? You're lookin' at her. Someone to take over her business in the middle of Nowhere, Maine? One guess who. Someone to toss a beloved family member's ashes over the falls because nobody else wanted to hike up there? You guessed it. (Not that I'd done that yet. But they didn't need to know that.)

Therefore, it was no surprise that my default response following a fluke cycling accident was to spend my whole weekend nursing the victim—a practical stranger—back to health. Nobody even had to ask me; it was reflex.

But that's who I was. I didn't do things out of obligation. I did them because I *wanted* to help. And I didn't do things for anyone hoping to have that person reciprocate someday. But still, it would be nice if they did.

And in Eric's case, if we were keeping score, one might say I already owed him for seeing me through one of the worst nights—and mornings—of my life, thanks to the demon drink, then covering for me and blaming the cat for the ruined furniture. Yeah. That was my motivation. We'd go with that.

Anyway, I was sure as soon as things settled down at work for Shelly, she'd save me from this bleak existence. It would be when it was convenient for her and on her terms, but beggars can't be choosers, right?

Right.

When I delivered the mugs and coffee carafe to Eric's living room, I found him dozing on the couch and Larry standing on the room's threshold, jingling the keys in his pocket.

"I hate to do this to you, but I need to go set up for that memorial."

I set the tray on the coffee table and followed him to the front door, so we could talk without disturbing Eric. "Don't worry about it!" I chirped.

"I was hoping Hortense would be back by now."

"I told her not to rush. I have it under control."

Brow furrowed, he rubbed his neck, and for the umpteenth time that weekend, I marveled at the similar mannerisms and physical resemblance between him and his son, despite the absence of a biological link. Nurture was sometimes as powerful as nature. Perhaps there was a research paper in that: *The Role of Nonverbal Communication Mirroring in Adopted Families as a Form of Subconscious Assimila-*

tion. (The title might need some work.)

Larry startled me from my brainstorming by saying, "I feel bad that you're spending your whole weekend on this. You were so nice to wait with us at the hospital, and now this is your second day here, taking care of him. You've really gone above and beyond." While his tone was grateful, it also held a tinge of suspicion, like he wasn't quite sure why a mere acquaintance would be willing to do all that. "If you'd like to leave and salvage what's left of your Sunday evening, I'd understand. I can text my niece to get back here or see if my sister and brother-in-law have returned from Portland."

"Hortense just left, though. And it's not necessary to pull Lena and Hiram away from their anniversary weekend. I have nothing better to do."

When all else fails, tell the part of the truth you can tell, no matter how embarrassing it is.

"If you're sure…"

"I wouldn't be here if I wasn't sure. And to be honest, I feel somewhat responsible."

He snorted and waved off my claim while reaching for the door handle. "I know my son, and I'm sure this was another instance of him being lost in his own thoughts, not paying attention to his surroundings."

The impatience and implied criticism hit an unexpected nerve. "That wasn't the case at all. Cath came out of nowhere. He would have heard her sooner, maybe, if I hadn't been talking to him."

"Having a conversation with someone at the time of an accident hardly makes you responsible."

"Still. It wasn't his fault, either. And he helped me so much when… Buster was sick." In spite of my best efforts, I blushed. "This is the least I can do."

"Buster. Right." Oddly enough, instead of looking more

skeptical, for which my paranoid, guilty conscience was on alert, he seemed relieved by the reminder. "We appreciate it, then. And I suppose we shouldn't expect anything less from a relative of Vel."

Before I could ask him what *his* relationship to my aunt was, he ducked his head and pulled open the front door, hurrying down the steps to his car in the driveway.

I stared after his taillights in the golden evening light.

When I returned to the living room, I was surprised to see Eric sitting up, his foot propped on a pillow-stacked ottoman.

"We didn't wake you, did we?" I asked.

He shook his head, then winced at the resultant pain. "Ow. No, I wasn't sleeping. Head hurts too bad."

I bustled to his side and handed over the large plastic cup he'd been given at the hospital. Checking the time, I shook two painkillers from the prescription bottle on the end table and gave those to him as well. "Here. I'll top off your water after you take these."

"Thanks."

When I came back from the kitchen with a fresh jug of ice water, he bobbed his head toward his phone on the coffee table. "You mind shootin' a quick message to Natalie to let her know not to expect anything from me tomorrow, since we don't have any services?"

"Sure."

"Then I promise to stop treating you like a secretary."

"It's okay. It feels good to be useful."

Too good.

As soon as the email from "Eric" was on its way to Natalie, I smiled brightly at him. "Done. How's the ankle feeling?"

"It's fine. I think it's hogging all the painkillers. That's why my head hurts so much. Is that a thing?"

I shrugged. "Sounds logical to me. You'd know more about it than I would."

"Huh? Why?"

"I'm sure you've taken more science classes than I have. Biology and anatomy, specifically."

"Dead people don't get headaches. In fact, that's one of death's biggest draws: no more pain."

"Right. Anyway. I guess my answer is, 'I don't know,' then. Your guess is as good as mine."

He grunted.

"Relax. Keep drinking that water."

After several long sips through the wide, bendy straw, he set down the mug. "I could use something stronger than water."

"Oh."

"Sorry. I don't mean to make you uncomfortable."

"You're not. I wish you felt better. And that I could do something to help... that."

"Even if I didn't have a problem with alcohol, mixing it with prescription painkillers isn't a good idea. I do know that much."

"True."

He stared at his foot, which drew my attention to it. "Do you need more ice for your ankle?"

Wiggling his toes as if to evaluate the pain, he dropped his head to the back of the couch and rested his eyes. "I guess it couldn't hurt."

Grateful for the escape, I grabbed the spent ice pack from the footrest. In the kitchen, I took my time pouring out the water and icy slivers and replacing them with fresh, dry cubes from the bottom drawer freezer.

Alcohol addiction was hardly a new topic for me, so I wasn't sure why Eric's openness about his struggle with sobriety was such a conversation killer. It must have had something to do with the humiliation of him so recently taking care of me in my own drunken state. After all, I'd listened to or been a part of numerous conversations about alcoholism since I was a child and had overheard the adults in my family talk about Aunt Vel when she wasn't around.

Unfortunately, those eavesdropping sessions had spawned a lifelong preoccupation with my own alcohol usage. Although I wasn't related to my aunt by blood, I still had my share of boozers in my bloodline. Didn't we all? So any time I got to the point that I craved a drink or found that I'd fallen into the habit of having one or two glasses of wine every single night, alone, I worried I was sliding down that slippery slope into addiction. Better to be paranoid than to be in denial, though.

Aunt Vel had never made me feel guilty about partaking, but I hadn't drunk in front of her out of respect. And when I shared with her my worries about any latent addiction, she'd laughed. "The first sign you're *not* an addict is that you suspect something *could* become a problem for you. When you're a drunk, you tell yourself it's not a problem, and you have everything under control. At the same time, you're consumed by the lie that you can't function without it. Is that how you feel?"

I shook my head, and she patted my knee. "Then have a glass of wine with your dinner and stop obsessing. When you replace your morning coffee with booze, *then* you can worry."

I wondered how Eric had come to the realization he had a drinking problem. Had it required a family intervention, or had it been less dramatic, a personal awareness after one too many hangovers or blanked-out nights? I would have asked, but this didn't seem like the right time to be nosy. Then again, he didn't shy from the topic. Maybe talking about it helped; de-stigmatizes the issue. Communication could be a balm, after all.

But by the time I made it back to the living room, the painkillers had kicked in and he was asleep again, complete with snoring. I draped the ice bag over his ankle and cover him with a nearby throw.

To resist the temptation of staring at him (for the purpose of assessing his symptoms, of course), I poured myself a cup of coffee and pulled up a book on my phone. Curling into an overstuffed chair, I sat and read, waiting for Hortense to return so I could make my way home.

After all, there was a cat there who needed me.

CHAPTER NINE

"I HEARD the 911 call came from her... but on *his* phone. What do you think *that* means?"

"By itself? Not much. But connect that with Juanita seeing him leave her house in the middle of the night a couple of weeks ago, and it definitely adds to the evidence there's something going on between them."

"First Vel, now Whitney? He definitely has a thing for the Faelhaber women."

"Maybe he's a gold digger."

"The Mulligans have plenty of their own money."

"Yeah, money made on dead people. Maybe he's looking to... diversify."

I cleared my throat outside the tiny break room to notify Jordy and Natalie of my presence, then entered as if I haven't been eavesdropping on their Monday morning water-cooler gossip.

I smiled at them while dispensing coffee from the pump-top decanter. "Morning, guys! How was your weekend?"

Jordy nudged Natalie, who answered, "Fine! Great. Uneventful. And yours?"

I shrugged. "Pretty typical. Except for that part when I had to call an ambulance for Eric Mulligan on Saturday. But I'm sure you've already heard all about that from Cath."

"Cath? What does she have to do with it?" Jordy asked, frowning.

"She's the one who ran over him with her bike! I just happened to be there. Thank goodness." I blended powdered creamer into my mug with a plastic stir stick.

Natalie's mouth dropped open. She rested her hands on her hips. "I just saw Cath, who didn't say a word about that. Not even after I told her—" Two spots bloomed on her cheekbones. "Er... never mind. She acted like nothing was different."

"Maybe she's embarrassed about being a menace on the trails. Granted, visibility on that part of the path is bad, but then all the more reason to be careful and take it slow." I licked the stir stick and pitched it into the trash can at the end of the counter. "Anywho. It was pretty wild, and I didn't have my cell phone with me, so I used Eric's. He wanted me to call his cousin and dad, but concussions are no joke. And it all happened so fast. I wasn't sure if he'd hit his head on a tree root or what. There was no way I was going to risk it."

"He's fine, though, right?" Jordy asked, no doubt trying to get the inside scoop and some juicy tidbit about *how* I'd know about Eric's condition.

"Last I heard, yeah. Hortense says he tweaked his ankle and had a bump on his head but passed all of the tests to rule out anything serious. Should be back to work today. You got the dead sheets, right?" I said to Natalie.

She shook her head. "He sent an email last night saying not to expect any."

"There you go, then." I test-sipped my hot coffee and pretended I didn't notice the knowing look pass between the two co-workers when I said, "Welp, gotta scoot. Big conference call first thing this morning with some IT folks to see what we can do about this place's sloth-like network. Toodles!"

The "toodles" was a bit much, but I hoped it spoke to my nothing-to-hide attitude and covered my lies. If it weren't for their ridiculous addiction to gossip-mongering, I wouldn't have had to be dishonest. Helping a guy I witnessed being injured in an accident was nothing to be ashamed of. I was simply nipping their salacious tongue-wagging in the bud. Sounded like everyone was already borderline obsessed with Eric and Aunt Vel's relationship—whatever it was—but they weren't going to transfer that obsession to him and me. If it took a few white lies or lies of omission to redirect their attention elsewhere, so be it.

I was too busy to feel guilty about it anyway. Running a business was all-consuming, and today it included whipping our sorry IT network into shape.

"Vel, Vel, Vel," I muttered at the audit results on the screen in front of me, which made me wonder if talking to dead people was as bad as talking to cats. But seriously. Maintenance was about more than keeping the floors clean, the walls painted, the exterior brick and wood power-washed, and all things physical shiny. The infrastructure had to remain strong, too, or you were screwed.

The sorry condition of the network wasn't the only thing on my mind, either. Later, I had bank statements to pore over and an accordion file of receipts to dig through. Aunt Vel had withdrawn fifty thousand dollars from her personal savings account a couple of months before she died, but she hadn't bought any big ticket items or used it for medical bills, and everything she owned was paid off, including the business, so I could only assume she'd bought something for Velvet

Printing with that cash. I was no financial expert, but something told me her CPA—and possibly the IRS—was going to wonder what the heck that was all about when tax time rolled around. It surely wasn't going to be as easy as finding one receipt for that exact amount, either, so I was rounding up all the receipts for business purchases made with cash, hoping they'd add up to fifty grand.

Why she hadn't written checks or used her company credit card was another mystery. And why dip into her personal savings? Who knew what went through someone's mind, especially at the end of her life? Unfortunately, I was going to be expected to figure it out.

There had to be a reasonable explanation somewhere. I simply had to find it.

Good thing I had nothing but time to do so.

Staying at the print shop after hours to go through those receipts might have been a mistake. At least if I'd dragged the bulging brown file across the street, I'd have had food.

For the millionth time, I checked the adding machine printout to make sure I'd entered the figures correctly (I had), then muttered some obscenities and pulled at my hair when the total didn't come close to 50K. I pushed back from the desk until the rolling chair hit the metal filing cabinets behind me. Closing my eyes, I rubbed my temples.

"I give up," I said aloud, at first hating how it sounded and felt, but then experiencing a foreign relief at the admission. It was like taking off my bra at the end of the day. I hadn't realized how truly uncomfortable I'd been while crunching these numbers over and over again until I decided I wasn't going to do it anymore. I'd cart that file and all of Aunt Vel's bank statements to her CPA, Niles, if I had to, and say it right to his face, too.

"I give up," I repeated, louder. "I give up! I GIVE UP! I GIVE UP!!"

Crinkling plastic and a clearing throat startled me from my chant. My eyes flew open, and my fists fell from my head to my sides, colliding with the metal behind me. "Gaaaaaaaaaaaaaah!"

The tall silhouette in the office doorway slowly gained features as my eyes adjusted.

"Oh, my gosh!" I leaned forward, picked up the first thing my hands grasped on the desk—a ballpoint pen—and hurled it at the person.

Eric flinched as it bounced off his chest.

"Ow! What the hell?"

"No, *you* what the hell?!" It might not have sounded like anything a verbal adult would utter, but it perfectly conveyed my meaning, which he understood. And that's all that matters in communication—as long as you don't care what the other person thinks of your intelligence. Or lack thereof.

"I came here to give you these and say thank you for taking care of me last weekend." He held out the flowers I finally noticed, their cellophane wrapper the source of one of the sounds that had scared the crap out of me.

"You can't sneak up on me like that!"

"I wasn't sneaking up on you. The bell rang on the front door. I walked normally down the hall. My shoes squeaked on the floor. The plastic wrap on these flowers is like fake thunder. I cleared my throat. What more did you need?"

I clenched and unclenched my fists to still my shaking hands but didn't reply.

"I guess your yelling drowned out everything. Sorry." He

thought about that for a second. "Hey. Why am *I* apologizing?"

"Because you're a creeper?" Having recovered from my scare, I could deliver the question with a rueful chuckle.

He grinned back. "We've already discussed this. I can't change my DNA."

"Yeah, but you're not—"

He waited.

"Uh… never mind."

Not only was I not supposed to know that he didn't have any undertaker DNA, but my experience with Aunt Vel had taught me that adoption is a personal issue and not something to be joked about without the person's permission. Not everyone's story had a happy ending. Eric's kind of didn't. After all, the woman who'd adopted him hadn't live long enough afterward for him to clearly remember her. And while it seemed like most of the Mulligan/Doolan clan had accepted him as one of their own, it was hard to tell looking in from the outside. Anyone could fake it for a weekend when a guy was laid up, hurt, right?

The thing was, some of Larry's interactions with his son, plus his quickness to blame the bike accident on Eric's propensity for daydreaming, pointed to a general air of disapproval. And I couldn't stop thinking of Bobby's remarks that day at the funeral home: *"I'm with Larry. The guy's a boob."* Without the first sentence, I'd have taken that as a typical older cousin in a tight-knit family expressing frustration with someone of a different personality type than his. But the "I'm with Larry" part bugged me. It indicated a long-time collusion between uncle and nephew.

But what did I know? I was a communications scholar, not a psychologist.

I'd had to keep reminding myself of that the last weekend,

too, or there were several occasions I would have said to the Mulligan patriarch, *"Do you really think your son's a boob? Because I get it. He is boob-ish at times, but... do you say that out loud to people? Have you called Eric that to his face? Not cool, man. Not cool."*

Instead, I kept my promise to Hortense and my mouth shut on the topic of Mulligan family history. It was none of my business. I was naturally fascinated by the power of words and their effect on people, but those particular people weren't research subjects (technically), so I needed to rein in my academic curiosity.

I snapped back to reality and gestured to the bouquet of lilacs and leafy ferns. "Those are gorgeous. Thanks! But you didn't have to."

"I wanted to." He moved to set the blooms on the desk but couldn't find a clear space for them, so he shifted awkwardly on his feet, turning in half-circles, looking for an available surface. Finally, he settled on a stretch of credenza on the wall by the door.

As he made his way to the middle of the room, I noticed his limp. "You should get off that ankle." He waved off my concern, but I went on. "I didn't spend all weekend keeping your big foot wrapped tight and refreshing your ice packs so you could walk around on it too much too soon and hurt yourself."

"Fine, fine. Bossy. Just like Vel." He pulled up a chair and took a load off. "What are you doing here so late? By the way, you should lock the front door when you're working alone. Being from the city, it must seem like everyone around here is harmless, but..."

I stretched and yawned, then rolled my watery eyes. "Yeah, I told Cath to lock up when she left, but... shocking that she didn't. She's probably hoping the one suspected serial killer in town—every town has one, right?—will happen to walk by one of these nights and pounce on the easy kill." Realizing that an undertaker would be the prime suspect for local serial killer, I averted my eyes from his. "Anyway."

He laughed. "Cath doesn't like anyone, so don't take it personally."

"She likes *you*."

He reddened and pinched at the side seam of his black trousers. "Whatever."

"She does! The only person besides Aunt Vel I've heard her say anything nice about is you. My first day here, she said you were 'awesome' about getting the dead sheets to us."

"I love that you guys call them 'dead sheets.' I wish I could refer to them that way."

"I don't think that would be prudent."

"Yeah, I know. Vel told me it might sound irreverent. I already get in enough trouble with the obits."

"So Aunt Vel called them dead sheets around you? I thought— Cath told me— Well, I guess you're more of an insider than I was."

He shrugged. "I guess."

"It *is* kind of disrespectful."

"Every industry has its own lingo. It's no worse than when we call overweight people 'three-man lifts.'"

To prevent cracking up at the insensitive terminology, I refocused on the mess on my desk and scooted forward, using my feet like pedals against the floor and pulling myself flush with the surface by gripping under the center drawer. "Anyway, if only my aunt had confined her creativity to inappropriate shorthand and didn't let it spill over into her accounting practices…"

Eric chuckled. "Oh. *That's* why you're here."

I gathered the receipts into a haphazard pile and shoved

them into the accordion file. "Yep. But as I'm sure you heard, I give up."

"Aw, come on, now. You'll get the hang of it."

"I don't give up altogether. I give up trying to figure out what she spent fifty thousand dollars on a couple of months before she died."

That revelation met with silence. I looked up from the ribbon of adding machine paper I'd torn off the spool and saw a slightly paler companion, his mouth frozen in the shape of an unspoken *Oh*.

I pointed at him. "This is *not* grist for the gossip mill, either. Don't make me regret saying anything to you."

"No, I—"

"I helped you to the bathroom last weekend. You owe me."

Some of the color returned to his cheeks, but he ran his hand through his hair and dragged his knuckles across his suddenly sweaty upper lip. "Um. Wow. Fifty K, huh? That's... that's a decent chunk of change. Still... she could have done any number of things with it. More than one thing, maybe."

"She didn't put it into this place's network, that's for sure."

He winced. "No. It's in a sorry state. You know how that goes, though. It's hard to keep everything in tip-top shape. When you have to make the choice between fixing or replacing a machine you use every day to stay in business and upgrading something that's inconveniently slow, you choose the machinery every time."

"It wasn't a machine, either, though. In any case, I'm going to hand over the mystery of the missing money to Niles tomorrow." Holding up the curly paper, I folded it lengthwise to flatten it before securing it to the inside of the accordion file with a paper clip.

"N-Niles? Bainbridge?"

"Yeah. He's ... or was... her CPA."

"He's everyone's CPA. But, uh, hang on. We can figure this out. Before you ask him to look into it, let me think about it for a night or two."

Receipts tucked away, I tapped the bottom of the file against the desk to settle them all the way down, then stood. "Why? It's not your problem."

He rose too, rocking on his feet and wincing when his ankle reminded him they were in a fight. "Maybe she had a secret drug habit."

"Not funny."

"Yes, it is. Because... you know... irony. Miss Clean Livin.'"

"Lot of good it did her."

Leaning forward, he snatched a tissue from the box on my desk and mopped his brow and lip. "It could be as simple as her paying off some debt when she found out she was sick, so you wouldn't have to deal with it."

I shook my head. "Everything's been paid off for forever. Which has always struck me as weird, come to mention it, because according to all the stories, she came to this place with nothing, yet she became a homeowner and started a business practically the day she landed here."

"Back then, things were cheaper."

"I guess. But still..."

"Grants, maybe? Charitable donations?" He snapped his fingers. "That's it! I bet she donated that money to charity. You know... a way of giving back. Maybe the same charity that helped her out when she moved here."

"Which was?"

"I don't know. That was a super-long time ago. I was a baby."

My shoulders sagged. "I wish she'd gotten a receipt! She should get credit on her taxes, if nothing else."

"Vel wouldn't want credit. That might be why she used cash, and you can't find a receipt."

Still not convinced, I nevertheless relaxed my face (Mom always called me "bulldog" when I got worked up about something and warned of premature wrinkles) and assumed a casual, breezy tone. "Oh, well. For now, I'm going to leave it to Niles and not worry about it, and I suggest you do the same. Forget I said anything."

He swept up the flowers behind him and stepped forward to hand them to me, but my arms were full of the receipts file. "I'll trade you," he offered. When I hesitated, he urged, "Listen. What if… what if… Vel didn't want anyone to know?"

I sighed. "Just forget it. It's okay. Niles will figure it out."

"No. Hear me out."

His uncharacteristic seriousness, coupled with his over-productive sweat glands, convinced me to heed his plea. Rewinding to his question, I replied with some of my own. "Why? What would she have to hide?"

"I'm speaking hypothetically. Isn't it better to forget about that money altogether? It's obvious she didn't keep a record of what she did with it. We should respect that."

"*I* could get in trouble, though, if the IRS finds out. I have to at least try to find out where it went."

"You know, honestly, the IRS doesn't care. You can withdraw your entire life savings and it won't even be red-flagged. Now, if you make any large deposits, they want to know where that came from so they know how to tax it. But money that's yours and you're simply getting around to using for whatever? In most cases, they've already taken their piece of it. If she'd drained her 401K or some other pre-tax account, that'd be a different story."

I stared at him for a second and watched him squirm. "You sure know a lot about this."

"I own a business. It's my job to know."

His jab at my inexperience seemed unintentional, so I let it slide. "I thought that was Lena's expertise."

"I took some classes in college. Shit, what is this, the third degree? I'm only trying to help!"

I widened my eyes at his outburst.

"Sorry," he muttered, tossing the soggy tissue in the trash.

"Are you okay?"

"Yeah. I'm just... I guess your frustration is contagious or something."

"I *have* been sweating it," I said. "Since I saw that withdrawal amount on her bank statement, I've had nightmares about government accountants barging in and hauling me off to federal prison."

"That's not going to happen."

"Well, I'm going to ask Niles, to be sure."

He blocked my way to the door when I stepped around the desk. "What if I can promise you it had nothing to do with the business?"

I tried to swallow, but my mouth was suddenly drier than my sex life. My lips stuck to my teeth when I squinted at him and asked, "What do you know?"

"Will you please take these flowers?"

"I'm not sure I want to accept them."

"But they're your favorites. Lynda told me."

"The creep factor is so high right now, I'm about to throw an entire desk's worth of office supplies at you and make a run for the door." It came out like a joke, but my pulse knew I was totally serious.

He backed off and slumped into a chair again, then waved toward the file. "You're not going to find anything in there. Neither is Niles. Vel and I made sure of it."

CHAPTER TEN

"AUNT VEL GAVE some bizarro undertaker fifty thousand dollars before she died? But why?" Shelly demanded two hours later when I relayed the incredible story to her on the phone. I'd discovered I got decent cell reception in one place: bed. For best results, I placed the phone on the unoccupied pillow next to me and moved as little as possible.

Draining the last of the water in my glass, I set it on the bedside table. "Out of the goodness of her heart, apparently. Seed money for a new life."

"But he doesn't need her money. He's already rich."

"Rich? I don't know about that. Not by today's standards. Well off? Comfortable? Yes."

"Whatever you want to call it, he's not busking on Main Street with an open guitar case."

"No, but all of his money is tied up in the family business. His house, his car, his... everything."

"And?"

"He hates that life. But he's stuck there. He's never been allowed to pursue what he *wants* to do."

"Wah-wah!"

"I'm merely explaining to you the story he gave me."

"You don't believe him."

"What makes you say that?"

"You called his explanation a 'story.'"

Yeah. I did, didn't I?

I sighed and tried to verbalize what I'd been thinking since I found out about Aunt Vel's strange gift. "It strikes me as odd that I had to drag it out of him, that's all. When I first mentioned the mysterious withdrawn money, and I said the specific amount, you should have seen his face. He *knew* I was talking about the cash Aunt Vel had given him. Yet he threw out all these other explanations and lectured me about tax code before trying to convince me she donated it to charity. Then, when I was still determined to figure out which charity, exactly, he tried to get me to drop it altogether, saying he was sure Aunt Vel wouldn't want us to know."

Shelly gasped. "Do you think he killed her? Like, poisoned her with mind-controlling chemicals from his creepy undertaker basement, and after he got the money from her, turned to fatal poisons?"

"What?! No!" I seriously considered the possibility for a second. "No. He— he loved her."

"Ew."

"Like a mother!" I backed up and told her more of Eric's history.

When I finished, she said, "Sounds like the making of a sociopath to me. I'd go to the cops if I were you."

"I'm not going to the cop—singular. This is Morris, remember?" She snorted, so I defended my decision. "He hasn't done anything with the money. Says he won't do anything with it. He's worried about depositing it, because he doesn't want to have to explain where it came from. Even offered to give it back to me."

"Oh, he's good. You should totally call his bluff and see what he does. Wait, though, until I can be there. I'll hide in a different room, so he doesn't know I'm there. You ask for the money back, and before he can fly into a murderous rage, I'll run in and tase him. Or something. Whatever you do, don't accept any food or drinks from that whack job."

I giggled at the idea, then sobered slightly when I realized I already had. More than once. Before my imagination could run too wild and I started exhibiting strange symptoms, I scolded, "Shelly! You've been watching too many *Diagnosis: Murder* reruns."

"What can I say? I love Dick Van Dyke." She paused, then asked, "Do you ever feel weird when you're around him?"

"Dick Van Dyke?"

"No! Eric!"

I blushed, glad she wasn't there to see me. Because of course I felt weird around him. All the time. It was like maggots invaded my innards when he walked into a room. Yes, maggots. Because I was largely repulsed by this silly crush I had on him, and I was finding it harder and harder to chalk it up to good old-fashioned, desperate horniness.

Now, though, I had to face the possibility that something sinister—or at the very least, perverted—had occurred between him and Aunt Vel. I was having a hard time believing it, but all evidence was pointing there.

Instead of answering her stupid question, I snapped, "Eric's not a murderer. He didn't poison Aunt Vel. She had cancer."

"Drinking formaldehyde will do that to you."

"Bone cancer? I don't think so, you nitwit."

"Okay, okay. Let's say he's telling the truth about generous Aunt Vel wanting to help him start a new life away from dead people, herself included. What would this new life entail?"

I shook my head, though she couldn't see me. "He didn't say."

"And you didn't ask?"

"No. I was… I was too shocked by the whole thing to think of any questions. And he—" I stopped, unable to continue.

"Are you *crying?*"

"I'm sorry. I'm— It's— Sometimes life is so sad!"

"Oh, hell. Don't cry. Unless you're upset about the money, which I kind of am. *I* didn't get fifty thousand dollars from Aunt Vel, and I'm related to her! I got her vinyl collection and some china. Ugly china, at that. You got a business, a car, and a house. It's like you won the damn Showcase Showdown on *The Price is Right*. Mom and her brothers and sisters didn't get fifty thou between them! They'll be super-pissed when they find out."

"You can't tell them!"

"What do you mean, I can't tell them? This is a big deal."

"If Aunt Vel had wanted them to know, this would have been in her will. She specifically gave Eric this money—all cash—before she made the last version of her will so that nobody would know."

"Why all the secrecy? If she wanted to play Mommy Warbucks to some local guy, that was her call."

"I don't know. I couldn't get a decent answer about that from Eric, either. He kept saying she didn't want the whole town to know."

"Which suggests this was something a bit more shameful than a good deed for a person she loved like a son."

My stomach flipped. "Stop it. It wasn't like that."

"Sounds like it to me. And I say good for Aunt Vel! He's pretty hot, if you can get past that socially awkward mortician vibe."

I ground my fists into my eyes. "I can attest; this town is

gossip crazy. It makes sense that Aunt Vel would want to be careful. Heck, look at all of the crackpot theories *you're* coming up with. She didn't want Eric to start his new life under so much suspicion. Rumors about affairs or murder or sex for money or any of that!"

"Oooh. Sex for money. I hadn't thought of that one. She was paying him for years of services rendered."

"Stop. You're making me regret telling you. And I needed to tell someone."

"Why do you care? You should be relieved. You know where the missing money went, so you can move on to other things."

I dropped my hands, then brought one back up to my mouth and chewed on my nails. "I don't know. Something still... He was so vague. And maybe it's because it has to be some big secret. He said Aunt Vel would be okay with *me* knowing, and *he* was okay with me knowing, as long as I didn't tell anyone else, especially his family. He seemed mighty ashamed and... and... guilty. And he must have said a thousand times, 'You can have it back. All of it. I don't want it.'"

Shelly snickered. "This is sounding more and more like sex money." Before I could yell at her again for being a perv, she said, "Anyway. It's late. After you get some sleep, you'll feel better. Now that you've had a chance to think more about it, you'll have some questions for him the next time you see him. Maybe he'll have perfectly reasonable answers."

I grunted something I hoped sounds agreeable so she wouldn't worry as much as I was... or spill the beans to our mother.

After we hung up, though, and I turned off the lamp, I couldn't sleep. Shelly would have no problem, because she hadn't seen the tortured look in his liquid brown eyes when he'd said, "I didn't want the money. But I knew it would hurt Vel's feelings if I rejected it. She wanted me to have it. She... she told me it was her dying wish that I do something with it that made me happy... because I deserved it. Because I made *her* happy."

Oh, I bet he did. Those hands... those long, strong limbs...

Ew. Now, thanks to my sister, everything sounded sexual.

But I hadn't told her everything. She had no idea that one of the last things he said to me before leaving me to puzzle over this baffling development had been, "Whatever I do, though, it won't change anything that's happened in the past thirty years. It won't make a damn bit of difference."

That made no sense at all, coming from a man who hadn't even been alive that long.

I woke minutes before my alarm with rock-hard nipples, a throbbing yingyang, and damp panties. A sound from my throat that could best be described as a primal moan roused me. The strongest emotion I felt upon waking was disappointment that my dream wasn't reality, followed by deeper regret that I'd woken before...

Anyway!

Flashes of the dream danced behind my eyes while I rubbed the last sleep from them. Arms. Legs. Face. Oh, gosh. It had been... *him.* I groaned for a different reason and buried my face in my pillow.

This was dire. I was fantasizing about the local undertaker, who might or might not be the serial killer I'd been ironically joking about with him, and he might (or might not) have been having intimate relations with my aunt, for which she'd felt beholden to pay him before she passed away— which was less than two months ago.

In my defense, Eric had been very much on my mind when I finally drifted to sleep long after midnight. But in the interest of full disclosure, I had to admit I'd been having steamy dreams about him for a while, ever since he'd taken care of my drunk—then hungover—ass. I was pretty sure that made me all the more pathetic, though.

On a somewhat related note (stay with me), I'd plucked a nose hair yesterday morning after my post-run shower. A nose hair! Not a dainty little thing, either. Not a mostly-invisible-only-there-to-prevent-foreign-bodies-and-germs-from-entering-my-system sort of nose hair. No. A manly nose hair. A what-the-heck-is-that-oh-my-gosh-it's-a-man-whisker-growing-from-my-nostril-how-long-has-that-been-there-and-has-anyone-else-seen-it-get-it-out-now nose hair.

I was hideous, and I was going to die alone. Like Aunt Vel.

Not that Aunt Vel had been hideous… or alone. She might have been schtupping the nicest piece of ass I'd encountered so far in this town, in fact. And she'd been old enough to be his mom. Maybe I should have started looking more closely at the high schoolers who came in to pick up their graduation announcements. They were my sexual future. Not the popular kids, though. They'd want nothing to do with the old print shop lady. *"Have you seen her nose hair?"*

Sick. Sick. Sick.

This morning, both Eric's bouquet of spring blooms and Aunt Vel's ashes seemed to be judging me from their perches on the mantle. After Eric had made his hasty, emotional exit from the print shop, it seemed petty and cruel to reject his thank-you bouquet. I'd locked up on auto-pilot and come home, put the flowers in water, and placed them in the least personal space I could find.

Truth was, I was rattled. And my conversation with Shelly had made things worse, not better. Now I had to worry she'd tell our mother about Aunt Vel's little donation to Eric's self-improvement cause. And I kept thinking something depraved might have happened between my aunt and the undertaker.

Worse than that, though, was the disappointment. Because if Aunt Vel *had* been getting a piece of that, it definitely meant I wouldn't be. Ever. I might have had some strange sexual cravings heretofore uncovered, but I still had limits. Contrary to what the townsfolk thought, I wouldn't be following in my aunt's footsteps in every aspect of her life here. That was just gross.

Unable to face what was left of my predecessor with those shameful thoughts swirling, I turned my back to the dormant fireplace and guzzled the rest of my coffee. I escaped from the living room and placed my now-empty mug in the dishwasher. Buster, knowing that "click" meant it was breakfast time, appeared from wherever he'd been hiding while I was getting ready and rubbed against my legs, depositing long gray hairs on my black tights.

"Yeah, yeah. I'm gettin' there," I told him, reaching into the cabinet for his canned food. "But you might not want to rub against me like that. I'm highly volatile and in desperate need of physical attention. Who knows what might set me off? If I'm having sex dreams about the undertaker, animals can't be far off."

He yowled at me in his old-cat voice that cut in and out first thing in the morning.

"You're right. It is gross. I'm sorry I told you that. You shouldn't be burdened with that information. And anyway, you're safe. I've decided to take a vow of celibacy. My libido is obviously broken." I plopped a blob of wet food into his dish, broke it up with a fork, and watched him chow down for a few seconds. Blinking out of my unfocused stare, I said, "Looks like our talk hasn't dulled your appetite, so I guess we're all good! Have a lovely day, Buster."

My side of the conversation received nary a peripheral glance from the ravenous feline as I deposited the fork into the dishwasher. I poured the remaining contents of the sad, four-cup coffeemaker (which we all know makes only two decent-sized cups of java... enough for lonely singletons) into a thermal mug and headed out the door.

~

We had a full staff at Velvet for the first time since my arrival. Mona had returned from maternity leave that week, so we no longer had to rotate shifts at the counter. She cried a bit now and then because she was hormonal and missed her newborn son, but everyone in town knew her situation, so they'd been gentle. And customers made a point to patiently look at the five thousand pictures she had of Sam on her phone. He was an adorable munchkin, so it wasn't a huge imposition.

Today, though, I wasn't in the mood to coo over digital images or listen to her sniffles. Hence my closed office door. I also didn't want to paste on a smile while I dealt with petty workplace problems, technical troubleshooting, or customers. Definitely not customers. One in particular.

The closed office door was more for everyone else's benefit than mine, anyway. (That was my story, and I was stickin' to it.) I hadn't been in this foul a mood since James dumped me. I thought I had problems then... What I wouldn't have given for merely a bit of bruised ego right now! My pride had gotten over that eventually.

Now, though... Now...

I focused my attention on the email in front of me, the one

from the IT consultant about the drop-off and delivery portal I wanted to set up to streamline our operations. It was ridiculous that every online order from every customer had to go through me, then to the appropriate employee... if the system was working correctly. The regulars knew whom to carbon copy, based on years of the same operations. But businesses and individuals who used us more sporadically didn't. And, frankly, it wasn't our customers' responsibility to keep track of that, nor should they be dictating our workflow.

Furthermore, if we were to operate most efficiently, it shouldn't always be the same person who did the same jobs. Sometimes poor Dave was so bogged down with Town Hall work he couldn't see straight, and certainly didn't have time for other projects. Other times, he'd be left idle if that was his only source of work. Everything ran in cycles and spurts, which was why everyone should needed to be well-versed in each facet of the business.

What we needed was a central location for incoming orders to arrive, a place that all designers and printers could access, where the customer filled out an electronic form, uploaded their file—if they already had one—or described what they want designed. Then, whoever was available to do the job could grab it and go.

That was how it worked at the copy shop I used on campus. If I needed thirty photocopies of a four-page exam, double-sided, stapled, and ready to go by Friday, I uploaded the file to the shop's server and BAM! Exams were delivered to my desk by Thursday afternoon. There was no need to know which employee had printed and collated the tests; that information was irrelevant... unless something went wrong. And even then, I, as the customer, didn't need to know, as long as the shop corrected it before my deadline.

Velvet's improved interface wouldn't require any training

on the part of the customer, either. Uploading a job to the portal would be exactly like attaching a file to an email. On our side of it, the jobs would queue up, and the program would sort them by deadline or, in case of no specified deadline, by date ordered. And for those who preferred the old-old-fashioned way, they could call or come by, and one of us would enter the information into the portal for them.

Being the only shop in town, this change was long overdue, but I could understand why Aunt Vel had kept putting it off. Hiring a professional—or a team of them—to make the improvements, with little to no interruption in service, had netted an eye-watering figure. These guys weren't shy when it came to putting a price tag on their worth. Of course, in addition to designing and installing the best system for our needs, they'd also have to beef up our network, which included an upgrade to our email (yes!) and access to an online backup server system for our archived files.

It was way over my head, of course. In theory, I understood it, but in practice... someone else was going to have to do it.

All I had to do was sign the agreement attached to this email and send it back to initiate the work. The business needed it, the employees needed it, *I* needed it. The sooner this place ran itself, the sooner I could get back to my real life back in Boston.

But that price quote...

Maybe I'd been a bit too hasty turning down Eric's offer to return the money Aunt Vel had given him. Fifty thousand dollars would solve all of my problems right now. Well, the financial ones, anyway. And those upgrades would only require a small percentage of that amount, a drop in the bucket. But I'd already bent over so far backward to honor each of my aunt's dying wishes. If she'd wanted Eric to benefit from her generosity, so be it. Even if it was at the expense of the business she worked so hard to build. Even if it did inconvenience her favorite niece. Inconveniencing me seemed to be another one of her dying wishes anyway.

There was nothing else to do but work with what I'd been given, which was plenty. Niles Bainbridge, Accountant Extraordinaire, and I were going to have to crunch some more numbers before I committed to the IT consultants' proposal, though. Would this upgrade pay for itself—as they claimed—fast enough? Things were tight right now. Not like "I-can't-make-payroll-this-week" tight, but more like "Let's-explore-cheaper-coffee-options-and-possibly-switch-to-single-ply-toilet-paper" tight.

Before it came to that, I'd pawn that useless jewelry from James. That would keep us in two-ply t.p. for a while. And how rewarding every wipe would be!

I laughed out loud at the thought. Everything was going to be fine. With a smile and a straightening of my spine, I forwarded the IT quote to Niles with a request for him to meet with me later to discuss Velvet's options for funding the project. The trusty accountant would know what to do, and we'd be up and running in no time!

CHAPTER ELEVEN

WELL. That wasn't the news I'd been hoping to hear. Niles knew it, too, and he seemed legitimately sorry to have been the one to tell me, "You don't have the capital to make changes like that to the business right now. Your operating costs would bankrupt you."

Oh. I see.

"How about just the network upgrade?"

He quickly punched some numbers into his loud, old-fashioned adding machine. "Nope. Neither." Squaring his shoulders, he looked me in the eyes, like a parent standing firm on a decision. "It's not happening. Not this year or next year. *Maybe* the year after next." On an inhalation, he shifted his focus to some papers on his desk blotter, peering at the text through the bifocals on the end of his long nose. "Now, if you'll okay some more aggressive investment ventures, and they pay off..."

"But if they fail?"

He plunked his glasses down on top of the papers. "You'll be in worse shape than you are now and will have to wait that much longer to make these improvements."

I smiled, stood, and shook his hand. "Glad I checked!" I chirped, tamping down the hysteria right below the surface as I said a quick goodbye.

Seconds later, I found myself on the sidewalk, where I closed my eyes against the dropping sun. After a brief deliberation, I headed across the street toward the infamous Poole Table, Mr. Tremble's former stomping grounds, according to Eric's nixed obit. Outside the bar, I paused, peering down Main Street to the sprawling funeral home. It occurred to me I could stop in and see if Hortense were around, but the chances of running into *him* were too great, and anyway, while I didn't want to be alone with the cat just yet, I also wasn't in the mood to be "on" for a companion. The companionship of others who didn't expect conversation from me was what I craved.

All talking ceased as I push into the dim pub. The sudden silence was such a cliché that I have to stifle a giggle while I waved and said, "Hiya." Most people got the hint and immediately went back to their drinks and discussions, but a few of the patrons watched me the entire distance to the bar, where I pulled up a stool and lightly slapped the shiny wooden surface in front of me.

Before I could place my order for a large glass of pinot noir, the grizzled guy next to me said, "That's Shorty's stool."

I immediately hopped down. "Oops! Sorry. Didn't realize someone was sitting there."

"He ain't."

"Right. Not right now. But coming back from... wherever."

"I hope not, little lady. He's dead. But that seat's retired."

Somehow I managed to keep a straight face when I said, "Of course. As it should be. I'm sure Shorty was... a great friend."

"He was a bastard. Slept with my sister."

"And mine," said a guy farther down the bar, his eyes glued to the baseball game on the wall-mounted television.

"Slept with my wife!" chimed in yet another old codger.

"Oh, geez. Shorty got around."

"Sure did," Old Dude #1 confirmed with a nod and a smack of his lips against his loose dentures. "And he'd be the type to stick around from beyond the grave. That stool's cursed."

And a breeding ground for sexually transmitted diseases, if nothing else.

"I'll sit over here then," I said, pulling up the seat at the far end of the bar, a few chairs down. "Is this one reserved for any other dead people?"

All three guys shook their heads like *I* was the crazy one for asking.

"Excellent!"

The bartender finished his transaction across the room and approached, wiping the bar's surface as he went. "What can I get ya, Ms. Faelhaber?"

I'd never been there, much less seen this particular person, but of course he knew my name. Whatever. Wine. In my belly.

After I put in my order, I said, "Thanks…"

"Ernie. Ernie Poole." He flipped the damp towel over his shoulder and offered me a hand to shake.

"Ah. The 'Poole' in The Poole Table."

"The one and only."

"Cute."

"My wife's idea."

I dropped his hand. If that was his subtle way of telling me he was taken, I was going to need a bigger glass of wine. Maybe he should bring the bottle.

No.

One glass. That was it. That was all I needed to recover

from my meeting with Niles. And I didn't *need* it. But I did want it.

While I sipped my drink, Ernie washed and wiped glasses and left me to my thoughts. The old guys occasionally tossed a comment or two my way, as if they felt it was impolite to ignore me, but they clearly wished I'd do them all a favor and remove myself. To reward their efforts and reassure them I wasn't here to cramp their style, I kept my responses short, and I certainly didn't initiate any topics of conversation.

And when they started to grouse about the country "goin' to Hell in a handbasket," I pretended to be engrossed with my phone so they didn't solicit my opinion. From what they'd been saying, they definitely didn't want to hear it, and I wasn't in the mood to set anyone straight with a feminist rant. Sometimes you had to pick your battles. Plus, in this instance, I preferred to save myself the frustration and let nature cull the herd.

In any case, they were probably only saying half of these things to elicit a response from me or get me to leave, and I wasn't going to give them the satisfaction. Surely they couldn't see my flared nostrils, pursed lips, clenched jaw, and jiggling foot in the poor lighting. And if they could, maybe they assumed something on my phone had me peeved. I focused on relaxing my facial muscles while I looked up funny cat videos to distract me from my unavoidable eavesdropping.

When I thought I couldn't take another minute more of my fellow patrons' sexist, misogynist discourse, the air changed in the bar, and everyone fell silent again as someone entered.

Ah, good. It wasn't just me.

The newcomer blinked into the relative gloom of the establishment, allowing his eyes to adjust from the sunny outdoors. I shrank behind my wineglass, which was suddenly not nearly large enough. Eric spotted me and limped in my direction. As he approached, I notice the white gift bag with red polka dots in his hand. He plopped it into my lap as he lowered himself onto the stool next to me, placing himself at a ninety-degree angle to me. That was when I realized those weren't polka dots; they were little red hearts.

I tried to ignore the implication—and its resultant pulse increase—and instead said, "I thought you didn't drink."

"I don't. Of course, by this time tomorrow, it will be all over town that I've fallen off the wagon, and 'Isn't it a shame Larry's son is such a disappointment, but what can you expect from those Irish?'"

"But are you even Ir—" My spine straightened as I reeled in the end of my original question and substituted instead, "Are you falling off the wagon?"

Whew. Close one.

"No. I'm here strictly to see you."

"Oh, well, you didn't have to go to that trouble. And if this is about hanging out with you while you were hurt, you already got me flowers, so you didn't have to—" I broke the tape holding the top of the gift bag shut, but he quickly engulfed my hand in his.

Surprised by the intimate contact, I looked up at him, then at the others near us, but they'd long since tuned back into the ball game. The Sox were down by one in the ninth with the bases loaded and one out. Eric's supposed soon-to-be-historical sobriety was peanuts, comparatively.

Under his breath, he said, "Don't open it now."

I thrust the bag into his lap. "Oh, geez. What's in there?" I gulped and whispered, "Lingerie?"

"Huh? No! Why would I—"

"I don't know! Why can't I look in it right now? And why is it in a bag covered in hearts?"

He tapped the sack against my knee, but I refused to take it, so he plunked it on the bar, next to my wineglass. "That's the only bag I had, for some reason. And I just don't want you looking at it right now or drawing any attention to it with your reaction."

"Why—"

"It's the money," he hissed.

"The mon—"

He reached over and clapped a hand over my mouth. "Shush. Play it cool."

"All of it?" I muffled against his hand.

"Yeah. All fifty smackeroos."

I wrenched my face from his grip. "Eric, that's—"

"It's what I've wanted to do ever since she gave it to me. It belongs to you, to your family, to your business."

The business. Oh, gosh. Yes! Yes, yes, yes! But...

"No," I said out loud, surprising both of us.

"What?"

I slid the sack on its flat bottom until it was resting in front of him once more. "Aunt Vel wanted *you* to have it."

"But I don't want it."

"Why?"

"I don't need it, for one. And it doesn't feel right."

"Why?"

His jaw tightened, but he didn't say anything.

I listed toward him, closing the small gap between us and whispering, "Did you *do* something... shameful... to... to earn that money?"

He cocked an eyebrow. "Shameful? Like what?"

I wiggled my brows at him.

Realization dawned in his eyes. His cheeks flushed, then all color drained from his face. "NO!"

Not even a successful sacrifice fly to advance the runners could hold the fans' attention.

I smiled sheepishly at the nosy patrons. "He was hoping for a grand slam, I guess," I said.

Eric rubbed the back of his neck and waited for everyone to look away. When the others cheered at a borderline strike the ump had decided to call a ball, he said quickly, "How many times do I have to tell you, it wasn't like that with Vel and me?"

"You keep saying that, but then you tell me something else to make me wonder again, and... I'm sorry." Since he looked truly hurt by my refusal to believe him, I felt the need to repeat, "I'm sorry."

"Just take the damn money."

"No."

He muttered another obscenity under his breath, followed by something that sounded like "Faelhaber women," snatched the bag from the counter, and swung his leg over the stool, knocking it loudly against the bar in the process.

"Hey, where are you going?" I asked as he eased to the door while trying to avoid putting too much weight on his injured ankle.

Old Dude #1 swayed on his perch and sneered at Eric. "Pretty lady reject your present?"

"How can you leave now? The Sox are about to win it!" I threw out desperately.

Old Dude #2 shook his head. "And you call yourself a fan."

"Actually, I don't," Eric replied. "Bunch of greedy meat-heads with 'roid rage, managed by corporate money-grubbers."

"Hey, hey!"

"And the longer I sit in this place, the more I want to drink," he said to me. "So goodnight."

"Eric wait—"

But he didn't. He pushed through the pub door and stepped into the gloaming.

I flung some bills on the bar and rushed after him.

In the funeral home parking lot, his car chirped unlocked. To catch up to him, I'd practically had to run, which was no easy feat in my slingback heels. My shins burned from holding my shoes on with my toes while jogging. Fortunately, it wasn't a long distance, and he hobbled much more slowly than he would normally walk, but I was still out of breath from the effort.

"Hey!" I bellowed at his back.

He stopped but didn't turn to face me. The heart-covered sack hung alongside his thigh, the rope handles looped around his fingers.

"Why are you always running away from me?" I demanded.

No response.

"It's like nobody taught you how to properly end a conversation. And your 'flight' response has a hair trigger." I pinched my sides in my hands.

When he still said nothing, I kicked off my shoes and bent over to hook the straps through the first and second fingers of my left hand. The blacktop beneath me now sat in the shade of the building, but residual heat from earlier in the day radiated through my soles. The disparity between our heights was more dramatic now as I came within reach of him.

Tentatively, I rested the tips of my fingers, then my palm, against his shoulder blade. It was the first time I'd touched him more intimately than to shake hands, and although I'd imagined what that would feel like (unfortunately), the reality caught me off guard. That he was solid and warm was no surprise. What was more disconcerting was the zing that traveled all the way up my arm to my chest during the contact.

"Hey," I said, more softly this time. "I can't help you if you don't tell me the whole story."

His back shook against my hand, and although he didn't make a sound, it was obvious he was crying. Full-out weeping.

Horror. That was my initial reaction, I'm ashamed to say. Until I met James, I hadn't had much experience in the grown-men-crying department, and it was still not the most comfortable thing for me to witness. I understood it was supposedly okay and that I should support every person's right to show their emotions, regardless of sex or gender, but most of the men in my life were the type who would rather die than cry in front of someone else. They'd fake hysterical blindness and go into permanent seclusion before weeping openly. And the females in my family had followed suit. We were too tough for hysterical breakdowns. We chose sarcasm. Or in my case, forced jollity.

"C'mon… It can't be *that* bad."

Sure, it can! A dozen or so horrible possibilities immediately sprang to mind. My instinct was to start naming the most outlandish of the bunch to get him to laugh, but… what if one of them ended up being true? So I said nothing. For possibly the first time in my life, words failed me.

While I was trying to figure out if standing back there and touching his back was a supportive enough response, he whirled and, without warning or asking permission, wrapped me in a bear hug, smashing my face to his chest and jabbing me in the back with the bottom corner of the gift bag.

With some difficulty, I turned my head so I could breathe. His body heat sent waves of clean scent up my nose. Soap, laundry detergent, and deodorant... and maybe some last vestiges of lotion from that morning's shave. Mix in some sun-warmed skin and a tiny bit of sweat, and you had about as close to the smell of "sex" as you could get while standing in an open parking lot, for the entire town to see.

As soon as the shock of what was happening wore off, that last thing sank in. Not that I cared.

Okay, I cared.

There was nothing sexual about the embrace, but it was still intimate; something that should be private. The man was a mess. A wet, hot, solid, strong, great-smelling mess.

Snap out of it, Whitney!

Right.

Returning his hug gave me a mechanism for steering him while I forced us into a crab-like limp-walk to move our display behind one of the SUVs, where it wasn't so public. Eric barely seemed to notice as he continued to sob into my hair. I backed him up to the space between the back door and the tailgate, against the windowless panel that normally shielded a body in transport from view.

"Shh... It's okay," I murmured, registering the start of a crick in my neck. I giggled inappropriately, now on the edge of hysteria. "Geez. *Is* it that bad? Is this money your share of a bank heist, or something? If so, you guys screwed the pooch. Fifty thou isn't that much."

"I'm s-sorry. I just m-miss her s-so m-much!"

I wiggled my shoulders to leverage a bit more space so I could look up into his miserable, blotchy, tear-soaked face. Should I be relieved or terrified that he wasn't denying one of the worst-case scenarios? What if it was worse than that? Murder?

Stifling my inner Jessica Fletcher, I tried to focus on the blubbering possible psychopath in front of me. If nothing else,

I needed to calm him down so he didn't slip into some homicidal fugue state and kill me for coming too close to the truth.

"Listen... I miss her, too. But maybe not as much as you do."

He shook his head. "No. I'm sure you do. But you're allowed to show it whenever you want."

"And you aren't?"

"Of course not."

Without thinking about how intimate it was, I reached up with my shoeless hand and swiped the tears from his cheeks. "Why not? You were friends."

He let go of me and dropped the bag at our feet with a rustling thud before taking over his own tear-wiping. His huge paddle-hands acted as skin-covered wiper blades. "She was more than my friend."

I KNEW IT!

"She was... she was... my *mom*."

Oh, that old line again.

I rolled my eyes internally but maintained a passive expression as I waited for Oedipus Rex to continue. But he didn't. He merely stared at me, waiting for a reaction that never came.

"Well?" he prompted. "There. I said it. Aren't you going to say anything?"

"What am I supposed to say to that? Your birth mom gave you up, your adopted mom died, and your dad couldn't find his parenting ass with both hands, so you found a new mom in Vel. I already know all this stuff."

He shook his head. "No, it's—"

"Sorry. Hortense already told me you were adopted a long time ago but said it wasn't something you liked to discuss, so I've pretended not to know."

"But—"

"Not that it's some huge deal. Aunt Vel was adopted, too. That's probably why she took such an interest in you, initially. She could relate."

"No, that's—"

"But I can see where in a town like this, something like being adopted defines you, especially when you're adopted by one of the town's most important families and forced to take up a birthright that wasn't part of your birth at all. It makes sense that you'd seek out someone like Aunt Vel as a stand-in for your birth mother, a—"

"Vel *was* my birth mother!"

I stopped, swallowed, blinked. "Excusemewhat?"

He gripped my shoulders in both hands and locked eyes with me. "Vel. Was. My. Biological. Mother."

"I heard you. But that's— that's impossible. Because… because…" Patiently, he waited for my supposedly ironclad reason. But I didn't have one. All I had was, stupidly, "Because Aunt Vel never had any kids!"

"That you knew of."

"Sh-she would have told me!" I shrugged from his grip and backed away. "And you— you're not… You're too tall to be her son!"

He chuckled through his tapering tears. "Ah. Yes. Well… that's where Dad's genes kicked in. Larry's a big dude."

"Larry? Your biological father is also named Larry? That's a… a… freaky coincidence."

Eric rolled his eyes and released a huge breath. "Same Larry. C'mon, Whitney. You're smart. Put it together."

My jaw nearly came unhinged this time. "Your adopted father is your biological father?"

"Yep."

"You *do* have undertaker DNA?"

Frowning, he closed one eye. "Is that a thing?"

I blushed. "I mean… you *are* the undertaker's son?"

"'Fraid so. Always would have been, anyway, legally."

"Good point."

After a moment, he continued. "Listen. I wanted to tell you. I wanted to tell your whole family when they were here. But I've been keeping this a secret for almost thirty years. I don't even know how to tell the truth about it. I don't know where to begin."

"I think you've just figured it out."

He swallowed. "My dad… I promised both him and Vel I'd never tell anyone."

"Nobody? Ever?"

He shook his head. "Never."

"That's not fair, though."

Shaking his head, he looked off toward the funeral home. "You think I don't know that? I'm tired of keeping a secret for the sake of everyone else. I deserve to be acknowledged. But I won't do it at someone else's expense."

I pinched the bridge of my nose and studied my now-filthy feet. "Nobody else knows? Not even anyone in your family?"

"Especially not my family. Nobody. Well… except Larry, me, and now you."

Searching his face, I scoffed at that improbability.

"It's true. Why would I lie about that?"

Instead of trying to figure out the answer to his question on the fly, I asked one of my own. "How the *hell* did Larry and my aunt keep a secret that huge in *this* town, where you can't fart without an exposé showing up in the paper about it?"

"Maybe it was too… *out there*… for people to consider?"

It was out there, all right. It was way out there.

"Wait. What came first, your birth or Aunt Vel moving here?" My brain was so overloaded, I couldn't possibly do the math.

"Me. She and Dad... they had an affair in Boston. Then Dad pretended he'd heard about a 'friend' whose unmarried sister-in-law—or something equally untraceable—got pregnant and was giving the baby up for adoption. After Gayle died, Dad begged Vel to come here, to help him out. To be closer to me. And him."

My knees suddenly didn't want to hold me anymore. I staggered forward, hoping to hit the SUV before the pavement.

Eric's arms worked equally well.

"I'm sorry, Whitney."

For the second time in a short period, I found myself talking into his chest. "So, you're my cousin?"

"Sort of. But not really."

"Yes, really. You're my aunt's son, so..."

"But she wasn't your aunt by blood."

"*Excuse me?*" I pushed away from him and stabbed into his face with my dagger eyes. "She was every bit my aunt by law and in my heart. That makes you my cousin."

Hands up, he backed away a step. "Fair enough. I guess. Fine. You're my... cousin."

Hang on.

Wait for it...

Oh, gosh.

Flashes of sexual, orgasm-inducing dreams taunted me. I'd lived in this backwater a month, and already... incestuous thoughts.

"I don't feel so great."

"Please don't puke on me again."

I leaned against the SUV, then slid to the ground. Staring at my knock knees, I breathed through my nose and silently count backward from a hundred.

When I reached fifty, Eric sat next to me, wincing as he

took the weight off his sore ankle, and said, "I'm sorry it came out this way. I— I've been going back and forth on telling you, then trying to figure out when and how, and... I'm sorry."

"Why didn't *she* tell me? In a letter—to be opened upon death—or whatever. Didn't I *deserve* to know? From her? Hadn't I earned that trust?"

He covered his face and scrubbed his palms up and down it, raking his fingers through the front of his sweaty hair. "I don't know. Maybe she was worried about those of us still living. Or maybe—more likely—she didn't want to burden yet another person, especially one she cared so much about, with the secret."

"Why keep it a secret then? You three could have been a family!"

"No, we couldn't have. Not here." He grabbed my hand, resting on the pavement between us. Threading his fingers through mine, he said quietly, "It... it was complicated. And now... it's a moot point."

"I hate their moot point. And I'd like to go on record as saying their stupid solution was... stupid. And not a solution at all. I... I don't get it! If you guys are so good at lying and keeping secrets, why not tell a half-lie so you could live some semblance of a normal life? Why not pretend like she and Larry fell in love a few years after she moved here? And you're her stepson? And you all lived happily ever after?"

Instead of answering right away, he sighed and squeezed my knuckles between his. Then he said, "That wouldn't have worked, because... It just wouldn't have."

There was obviously more to the story, but honestly, I didn't know if I had the capacity to hear any more of this depressing tale. Letting that part go—for the time being—I asked, "When did they tell you?"

He swallowed loudly. "I don't remember not knowing, so I

must have been little. Too little to question it. Too little to be taken seriously if I repeated it to anyone."

"But when you got older, you could have told anyone at any time, and the whole town would have known in a matter of hours."

"I didn't, though. Once I was old enough to know the full story, it was just as important to me that nobody know."

"Why, though?"

He rubbed his thumb along a healing scrape on his elbow. "Shame, I guess. My origins were shameful, the result of an extramarital affair. I've always respected their wishes to keep that from everyone."

"Because you're loyal."

"Or cowardly."

I pulled my hand away and rested it in my lap. The queasiness had subsided, but that sick pit of betrayal was still marinating in red wine.

He flattened his mussed hair and stood with some effort, then offered me a hand up, but I scrambled to my feet without assistance. Now that we were related, it was creeping me out that every time he touched me, I got all tingly. I was definitely going to need therapy when I returned to civilization.

Most of the evidence of his emotional breakdown was gone when he straightened from picking up the bag of cash and shot me a crooked half-smile. "Friends?"

"Cousins."

"Well…"

"Yeah. I get it. I won't tell anyone."

He shrugged. "That's your choice."

"Are you ever going to tell anyone else?"

"Don't plan on it."

I squared my shoulders resolutely. "Then neither will I."

CHAPTER TWELVE

GOOD NEWS: nearly two weeks later, I was no longer having sex dreams about my cousin. Bad news: I was now having nightmares that featured a white gift bag with tiny red hearts.

Last night's variation: the bag blew down the middle of Main Street, and all of the money spilled from it and flew high into the air, beyond my reach, while everyone in town stood on the sidewalks lining both sides of the street, watching me chase down the cash. In those stupid slingbacks. Eric was one of the bystanders, and he was pointing and laughing the hardest.

Not good. Not good at all.

The psychological strain... of everything... was showing, too. I longed for the days when I agonized over a rogue nose hair that could easily be plucked with a bit of eye watering and a shiver of revulsion at the follicular anomaly's mere existence. After a fortnight of restless sleep plagued by tormenting dreams, I had more zits than I ever did as a teenager; my skin and hair looked and felt oily, no matter how often I showered; I had dark circles under my eyes; and my spine was about to take on a permanent curvature from my slumped posture. Worst of all, stringing together coherent sentences sometimes required more energy than I had.

Thanks to such persistent sleep deprivation, my waking hours seemed as equally surreal as the ones in my dreams each night, so I was starting to have a hard time telling them apart.

That's why it had taken me a minute to react to what was happening when I bumped into Hortense at the farmers' market that morning, and she'd pulled me aside and said without preamble, "That's it; you and Eric are going out tonight."

"Huh?" I looked down at my canvas tote, half-expecting it to have transformed into the red-heart gift bag, which would soon fall from my grip and fly over the stalls, money pouring from it and fluttering in the wind.

"Listen. I get that you're still recovering from your breakup with that guy from your old job—"

"It's technically still my current job. I'm on a sabbatical... of sorts."

"Whatever. I heard Eric brought you flowers, then tried to give you something else, and you rejected it. You're scared. You're gun-shy. But Eric's a great guy. And he's devastated. You should see him. He looks worse than you do, if you can believe it. No offense. Girl, are you drinking enough water? Anyway, he came on a little strong, maybe; he's out of practice. But he likes you so much. I can tell by the way he smiles and his eyes light up when he talks about you."

"Hortense, it's—"

"Please. Spare me the lame excuses. And don't become old before your time, like me, spending your weekends researching your family tree and watching period dramas on BBC. If nothing else, you need to get laid. It'll clear that skin right up." She winked and nudged me.

Oh, Lord. This was happening. This was real life, and my half-cousin (sort of?) was trying to convince me to date and sleep with my cousin-cousin (sort of). In the middle of a crowded (for this town, anyway) farmers' market. I just wanted some sugar snap peas. And maybe some tomatoes and spinach for a nice salad...

While I was freaking out, Hortense had continued talking, but now she stopped and said, "Okay?"

Desperate to catch up, I reflexively repeated her last word, more as a conversational placeholder than as a statement of agreement.

She smiled proudly and patted my shoulder. "Great. He'll stop by around six o'clock to pick you up. Sorry it's so early, but I need him to run a quick, uh, errand for me in Portland before you head to the restaurant and theater. But I've heard good things about the movie. You'll have a great time!"

Before I could protest, object, throw myself to the ground and fake a seizure, or anything that might detain her and slow down what I feared was happening, she was gone with a jaunty wave and a "See ya!"

Noooooooooooooooooo!

Fresh produce was going to have to wait for some other time. I needed to get somewhere private and call a certain "cousin" of mine.

Unfortunately, Eric didn't agree that going on a date was a horrible idea.

"We're friends, right?" he asked, when I finally got in touch with him on the phone later.

I immediately responded affirmatively, but were we? Didn't friends talk? Didn't friends make eye contact when they encountered each other? We'd done little of either since his big revelation in the funeral home parking lot.

"Anyway," he continued, "It'll be the perfect red herring. Nobody will ever suspect the truth if they think we're, you know, hanging out."

"'Hanging out'? Why does everyone keep calling it that? Is that a small-town, repressed way of saying 'sleeping together'?"

"No! Hanging out. Dating."

"Listen, I'm willing to keep our big family secret, but I'm not willing to perpetuate the con you and your dad and my aunt have been pulling on this town for decades."

"It's not a con."

"It is, though. And I'm also not going to pretend to be your girlfriend."

"Fine. You don't have to pretend anything. People are going to believe what they want to believe. We might as well benefit from it. I don't know about you, but I could use an evening away from this place. Let's go and have a good time and not think too much about everything."

I wonder what "everything" entailed for him. Because in addition to the shocking truth he'd dropped on me two weeks ago, "everything" also included much more for me. It included loneliness. And disappointment. And money worries. Throw in some guilt and shame for good measure, and that about summed it up. I wasn't sure how going to see a movie with the person who was at the root of most of that "everything" was going to solve anything.

What I needed was some time with my sister. Or better yet, to go back to my real life. Since Shelly was too busy for me (and I'd worry about blurting the truth every minute I was with her), and the other thing wasn't possible right now, thanks to my dumb-ass promise to Aunt Vel, I'd settle for a

Saturday night in my pajamas with Buster. Now, *there* was a good companion. No baggage there. Although I was sure he'd seen his fair share of interesting comings and goings through his mom's back door. If cats could talk…

What finally settled it for me, though, was when Eric said, "C'mon… Please? For me? I'll throw in dinner at any place you like, and we don't have to talk about serious stuff."

"Okay."

"Yes!"

"But I have one other stipulation."

He sighed. "Yes?"

"I don't want to see *that* movie."

"Oh. Okay. It's… Horty assumed you'd want to see a romantic comedy."

"That would be a reasonable assumption if this were a date. Which it's not."

"Right. What else did you have in mind?"

"Anything. As long as it's not too sad. Or romantic."

"Fine. We'll decide when we get there. I'll pick you up at six."

And that was how I ended up riding high in the passenger seat of one of Mulligan's big black SUVs, heading east toward Portland with my newly minted cousin… and a dead man… on a Saturday evening.

At first, I hadn't realized we had a stiff companion. I figured the "errand" Hortense had mentioned at the farmers' market simply afforded Eric the luxury of using the business's gas to get us to and from Portland. I would never have gotten into the vehicle had I known we had the ultimate third wheel tagging along in the back.

It wasn't until we were well on our way, traveling at speed down the highway, that Eric said, "I'm really sorry about this. So embarrassing. It'll only take a second, though, to drop this guy at the airport. Then we can get on with our evening."

My smile wobbled. "What guy? Are we picking up someone else?"

"No. He's already back there." Eric jabbed his thumb over his shoulder.

Since the SUV had no backseat, and the only people who rode "back there" didn't have a pulse, I was almost afraid to turn and look through the window separating us from the cargo area. I did, though, only to see what you'd expect to see in the back of a mortuary vehicle. I wasn't shocked to find the casket, but I *was* plenty freaked out.

"Uh... there's... there's a dead person in there?"

"Yeah. We don't typically put live people in coffins. It's bad manners. We've had complaints."

"B—but... that coffin isn't empty?"

"No. I have to get it on a plane to Detroit. Mr. Jepsen's visitation is tomorrow."

"And Mr. Jepsen?"

"Try not to think about it. In fact, I try not to think of them as people at all, once they're... no longer burdened by this earthly life."

"How else do you think of them?"

"As cargo."

"Isn't that a bit cold and impersonal?"

"Not really. I understand people mean a lot to their loved ones, but the soul that made them a person is no longer present. Bodies are merely... vessels."

"Well, I don't want to be in this car anymore with Mr. Jepsen's *vessel*."

"Let's talk about something else. You want to listen to the radio?"

"I feel like we should get Mr. Jepsen's vote."

"He's not picky."

Normally, I'd have laughed it off and turned on the sunshine, but weeks of lost sleep had rendered me incapable of chirping my way through life when I wasn't feeling it. "Actually, I'd... I'd like you to turn around and take me home."

"No can do."

"What do you mean? You can't hold me against my will! You can't kidnap me and take me on this morbid road trip with you and your dead buddy."

"I'm not kidnapping you. But I don't have time to take you back. I have to make the transfer at the airport in less than an hour."

My inner problem-solver engaged. "Okay. No biggie. Pull over and let me out. I'll walk back. I'm a strong—"

"Independent woman," he finished. With a glance over at me, his grin faded as he realized I was serious. "No way! I'm not letting you walk along the interstate for twenty miles back to Morris."

"It's not about you 'letting' me do anything." It was, though, and we both knew it. He was driving. We were going seventy miles per hour. What was I going to do? Open the door and hop out?

Still, I hoped he realized he wasn't the boss of me.

I giggled at my immature thought.

"What?"

I shook my head as I laughed harder at myself.

"Seriously. What?"

Leaning forward, I slapped the dashboard as my chortles gave way to full-blown guffaws.

"Okay, now you're messing with me," he said, propping his

elbow against the window, resting his cheek against his fist, and staring through the windshield. "I'm ignoring you."

I caught my breath and wiped the tears gathering under my lids. "Sorry. But only you would pick someone up for a date—"

"You said it wasn't a date."

"You're right. Only you would pick someone up for a casual, friendly, non-romantic outing with a dead person in the trunk."

"He's not in the trunk! Plus I'm sure a few mobsters have done it."

"Excellent. Eric Mulligan and mobsters: social skills galore."

"Shut up." He laughed and slapped in my direction, his fingers skimming off my shoulder. "It's part of my job, okay?"

"Yeah, yeah. But I had no idea when Hortense mentioned she had an errand for you to run that she meant... corpse delivery."

"I wasn't pleased about that detail, trust me. And I almost called and rescheduled after I did find out."

"Giving *me* the option to reschedule would have been nice."

"And you would have jumped at the out, right?"

I blushed in the shade on my side of the car. "Not necessarily. I don't know. Maybe."

He wasn't buying any of it. "You've been avoiding me ever since I told you Vel was my mom."

Rather than deny what we both knew was true, I said, "And you thought forcing me to ride in the car with you and a stiff would improve things?"

With a huge sigh, he overtook a semi, then glided back to the right lane. "This life warps you, all right? You forget that normal people aren't comfortable around corpses. And the thing is, I'm tired of this stupid job dictating what I can and can't do, preventing me from making friends or having normal relationships."

"I don't think it's the job," I muttered.

"When Horty casually dropped that I'd have to take Alfred Jepsen to the airport before anything else, it was almost a deal-breaker. I had my finger on the screen of my phone to call you, but I thought, 'Screw it. I'm not going to let this ruin my night like it's ruined my life.'"

Ruined. Strong, hopeless, melodramatic word for a grown man to use. I'd have called him on it if I'd thought he was overreacting, but... it wasn't nice to make light of something that distressed him. Plus, knowing what I now knew, he might have been justified in thinking that.

Instead, I said, "You hate it, don't you?"

He pondered that for a second. "I hate that I don't have a choice. That I was never given a choice. Every day, I feel like I'm in one of those." He gestured to the casket behind us.

Something told me Shelly would love to pick this guy's brain and figure out the secret to rendering me speechless, because he had a knack for it. All I could manage was to listen to his words echoing in the car while I studied the ergonomic design of the door handle.

He cleared his throat. "But you understand what I'm saying. You're in Morris against your will, too. People do what they feel they *should* do, not what they want to do, every single day. It's immature and pointless to whine about it. Some days, though, it's harder to suck it up." He glanced over at me and smiled. "And we're not supposed to be talking about stuff like this tonight. We're supposed to be having fun."

"Tell that to the guy in the back."

Eric laughed so hard he swerved and clipped the rumble

strip on the highway shoulder. The vibration tickled me through my seat.

Yeah. The rumble strip sent that jolt through my panties. We'll go with that.

After gently correcting his road position, he said, "Alfred was a great guy. Everyone loved him. He and his wife, Iris, moved to Morris when they retired. Always loved the area, although they didn't have any family nearby. They honeymooned here back in the forties and promised they'd come back when they were old and gray. Iris died a couple of years ago. And at the time of her memorial, before *she* was transported to Detroit for burial, Alfred told me, 'Eric, I expect you'll be pumpin' me full of those chemicals before too long and shipping my carcass back to Mo Town. Life ain't worth livin' without my girl.'"

I blinked the sting from my eyes, partly touched by the romantic story but also selfishly jealous I'd never had that with anyone. Before I could dwell too long on that depressing thought, I asked, "Is it... Isn't it hard to... do what you do, when you knew the person in life? When you had conversations like that one? Isn't it hard to see them, once so full of life, lifeless, cold, and naked on a steel table in front of you?"

"Sometimes. Sometimes it makes it easier, though. To keep the happy memories in mind. And remember that a body's death is only a stage in the journey."

"So, you're religious?"

"No. I'm a person of faith."

"That's what I meant."

"But they're not the same thing. Not to me, anyway."

"You believe there's *something* after death, though?"

"Yes. I have to believe that."

"You believe it because you *have to*, or you believe it because you know it to be true, based on facts?"

"Screw the facts. Faith isn't about knowing. It's about trusting, in spite of not knowing."

I considered that for a few silent minutes. As an academic, what he'd said was a foreign concept to me. Beliefs were based on facts. If you believed something to be true but weren't sure, you took steps to prove—or disprove—your hypothesis, then adjusted your original thinking accordingly. You didn't say, for example, "Some people, after years of knowing each other, can communicate nonverbally with one another as effectively as they do verbally," and call it good, simply because you *needed* to believe that. You read scholarly texts on the topic to see what others had already discovered. You ran studies. You interviewed test subjects. And if your results weren't conclusive, you admitted as much. You didn't say, "I can't prove it, but it's true." If you still didn't know, but you felt strongly enough about it, you might keep working to prove it. After a while, though, if the facts weren't there to support your hypothesis, you had to accept that you might have been wrong.

But maybe intellectualizing something didn't necessarily make it better (another theory that couldn't be proved). Maybe some situations called for less thinking and more feeling, more intuition. Maybe certainty was overrated.

Eric interrupted my musing with a nervous cough that startled me as effectively as a gunshot would. "I didn't— I mean, Dad and I didn't—" He took a deep breath and started over. "When Vel died, we were—I hate to use the word, 'lucky,' but... It just so happened that several others passed away around the same time, so... In cases like that, we often send out calls to other professionals in the area to help out. A semi-retired guy from Gorham prepared her for us. And it didn't raise any eyebrows that someone else did it, because that's standard procedure for busy times."

"Is it against the law or some undertaking code of ethics to prepare the body of a relative?"

He shook his head. "Nope. In fact, many wouldn't have it any other way. They see it as a final act of love. Wouldn't trust their loved one to anyone else, but…"

"That's not you or Larry?"

Scratching his chin made it appear he was thinking about it, but I could see he was trying to maintain his composure enough to answer, so I rushed ahead with my next question to relieve him. "What would you have done if she'd been the only person at the funeral home that weekend?"

He sniffed, blinked, and smiled sheepishly. "Dad and I were going to fake food poisoning."

"Elegantly simple."

"We thought so. Glad it didn't come to that, though."

"So this other mortician…?"

"Yeah. Charlie came down, and we casually assigned Vel to him, like it was some random thing, and tried to act like everything was business as usual."

"That must have been hard."

"I don't remember much of that week, other than dying for a drink, so… Yeah. It wasn't easy. But life rarely is, right?"

"Right."

"And you've had your share of difficulty this summer."

"I guess so…"

"Let's get Alfred on the plane to his reunion with Iris and have the fun evening we both need and deserve. Please."

Quietly, I said, "Okay." Because I *did* need a break from Morris and grieving and thinking.

∾

"Eff me, I love Jack Black!" Eric said a couple of hours later, as we climbed back into the SUV after the movie.

"Me too. The rubber face, the willingness to look and act ridiculous... The shape of his body alone is comical."

"Right? He's like this hilarious bowling ball."

"But he jumps around like a kid."

"Which is impressive but looks crazy."

Eric started the SUV in the cinema parking lot but almost immediately turned it off again and swiveled sideways to face me. Reflexively, like the good little communicator I am, I mirrored his pose, assuming we were going to continue talking about our mutual love for the comedic actor.

Instead, he said, still smiling, "This has been the best night I've had... maybe ever."

The sincerity with which he said it sucked the wind from my chest and the grin from my face. "Ever?" I checked. "It was just dinner and a movie. And a dead guy hand-off."

He shrugged and transferred his eyes to the console between us. "Yeah, well... I do that last thing often enough, but..."

Regretting that I'd minimized his happiness, I reached over and placed my hand, palm up, on the spot where his eyes were resting. He looked down at it, then up at me. When I smiled and nodded, he wrapped my hand in his.

"I had a great time, too," I said. "It felt good to laugh. And talk about... nothing important."

Because we had. After dropping off Alfred at the airport, it was like we'd made a silent pact to pretend we were two different people, people with no cares at all, people whose biggest questions in life were, "Where should we eat, and which movie should we see?" We were great pretenders.

Now, a few of the real-world worries I'd been carrying around for the past couple of months crept back in. The most immediate was how nice it felt to have my hand nestled in his. Better than "nice," if I was being honest. I looked at him, but he was smiling down at our linked hands. Then, as if reading my mind, he said, "I've missed having someone around who gets me. Vel said you and I would make good friends, once we were allowed to meet, but I wasn't sure. The way she described you—and then what I observed, myself—made you seem…"

I waited, but he never finished.

Instead, he let go of my hand, squared up to the steering wheel, and gripped it in both hands at the five- and seven-o'clock positions, his eyes down. "Anyway. I'm well aware you could have spent your evening any other number of ways, but—"

"I'm glad I came."

"Nobody says no to Horty." He shot an uncertain smile at me.

I grinned back. "Uh, I could. Easily. If I wanted to. But I needed this. And she wasn't the one who convinced me to do this. You did. Twice. It takes a special person to keep me from walking home after I've discovered a body in the back of the vehicle I'm riding in. You can be a persuasive man, Eric Mulligan. Anyone else, and I'd still be walking."

He chuckled. "Not in those shoes."

I slid one of the kitten heels off my foot (it was killing me, anyway) and held it up in front of me, examining it. "Ah, yes. Well, I'm not saying I wouldn't have immediately regretted it, but I still would have jumped out of the vehicle before thinking of the consequences… or the blisters."

"You're stubborn. Like Vel."

"Independent. Strong."

He nodded solemnly. "That she was."

I faced forward, reached back, and pulled the seatbelt

across my chest, fastening it with a loud click in the silent vehicle. "Let's go home, Cuz."

"Man, I don't want to," he said, more resigned than plaintive.

"Me neither, but… we'll do this again. Soon."

"Next week?" He leaned forward to turn the key in the ignition but looked at me in the process. The hope in his eyes saddened me at first. Then my tummy flipped when I thought, *Why not?*

After I said those exact words, he sighed. "Well, someone could die, and I'd have to work."

"The nerve of some people."

"But we could work around that, I guess. Do a Sunday afternoon matinee. Or something."

"Let's play it by ear."

"But commit to it."

"Okay." I dropped my shoe into the floorboard but didn't put it back on. Instead, I slipped my other foot from its mate and wiggled my toes. "Weekend movie. Every weekend. Barring a rush on deaths."

He laughed and shifted into reverse, checking his mirrors and over his shoulder as he backed from the parking space. "It's a date. Er… a deal."

CHAPTER THIRTEEN

YOU COULDN'T GO to Portland nearly every weekend with a guy and convince the townspeople in a place the size of Morris that you weren't a couple, especially when you couldn't tell them the most definitive reason you weren't a couple. Therefore, according to everyone in town, Eric and I were going to be heading down the aisle any day now.

Of course, we would have been the most chaste nearly thirty-year-olds in the world outside of Amish country, but it didn't seem to bother anyone that they'd never seen us kiss or hold hands or hug—other than that time in the funeral home parking lot. But even that instance had been written into "our" story as "the chapter where the girl rejects the boy before coming to her senses and realizing she's in love with the boy."

Ha.

Because that was ludicrous.

If they only knew.

They couldn't, though. I'd promised.

Therefore, as much as I was against perpetuating this

decades-long lie on the citizens of Morris, the fact that I wasn't willing to expose it had made me an accomplice.

It wasn't bothering me as much as it probably should have. I didn't have a stake in that town or those people, so I didn't feel bad letting them believe what they wanted to believe. And they desperately wanted to believe their oddball junior undertaker had finally found his matching headstone.

Most of them, that was. At least one—one I worked with every day—wasn't as taken with the concept. In fact, due to some of the murderous looks I'd caught from Cath, it would be best to never be alone at Velvet with her. Unfortunately, that was an impossibility, considering the nature of our respective roles and schedules—today being a perfect example.

It was a Saturday, but we were both here. Her, because she obviously had no life and thought inhaling ink fumes only five days a week wasn't enough. Me, because... Well, same, more or less. But I owned this place. And I wasn't working. Well, I was, but not on *that* business.

Eric was busy at work, so we couldn't go to the movies that day. It would be nice if people could die earlier in the week, but nobody had asked me. That meant I was at loose ends for the first time in a while.

I was using this time to figure out how to combine Velvet's operations with my artwork and save myself money by having my print runs done there, at wholesale. I simply needed to write up the plan and the contract to make the merger official.

I could draft it all at home, but the walls were closing in on me. And Buster and I needed some time away from each other. His random grousing was getting on my nerves. I had a feeling he wasn't too thrilled with my frequent grunts of frustration, either, as I tried to write up the contract based on a template I found on the Internet.

It wasn't that it was a complicated plan. Technically, it wasn't my plan at all. Aunt Vel had offered multiple times to be my printer, but I didn't have massive print runs, so the print-on-demand online service I used had been working fine for my purposes and afforded me the independence I'd craved in the early stages of my fledgling side business. Now that this shop was mine, though, it was almost irresponsible to keep the two entities separate.

Last weekend, when I'd mentioned it to Eric on the way home from Portland, he was shocked I hadn't been printing my stuff at Velvet from the beginning. "I assumed…"

"I didn't want it to seem like I was taking advantage."

"Well, you would have paid her, of course."

"But she would have cut me some crazy deal that wouldn't have even covered materials not to mention labor."

He frowned and tilted his head from side to side. "Mmm… Possibly."

"Definitely. You knew her."

"Still. She wouldn't have had it any other way."

"That's why I didn't let her do it. Can you imagine how much *more* Cath would hate me if I had gone along with Aunt Vel's plan? She'd think I was an entitled leech."

"Who cares? That girl has a screw loose. Always has."

I giggled. "When I first moved here, I thought you and she were… you know."

He looked across the dark car at me, and I wiggled my eyebrows.

"What?! Good God, no!"

Laughing, I put up my hands in surrender. "Sorry. It seemed like there was something—a tension—between you."

"'Tension' is right. She makes me uneasy."

"She lurves you, Eric."

"Gross."

"Oh, I don't know. She's not physically unattractive."

"It has nothing to do with her looks. Her personality is awful."

"Prolonged unrequited love warps a person."

"I hope not," he muttered, then attempted a smile and a lighter tone. "Anyway, she's had a crush on me since kindergarten."

"I can't imagine knowing someone—other than my sister —that long, much less crushing on them."

"I've known a ton of people that long. Unfortunately, the normal ones have all left, leaving only us weirdos. And the old folks relentlessly try to pair us up. Those of us who aren't related, anyway. Like it's a good idea for someone like Cath and someone like me to reproduce? Please. At least now that you're around, and we're hanging out, people have stopped harassing me about that."

I pushed playfully on his shoulder. "Glad I could help. But think about it. Nobody says you have to marry the woman. Just, you know… satisfy each other's physical needs."

"Not you, too! I'd rather never get laid for the rest of my life."

I laughed to cover my relief at his vehemence. "I'm only kidding. I wish someone would stick it to her, though. Or, more romantically, sweep her off her feet. If nothing else, it would give her something to do other than lurk around the shop 24/7."

"You're the boss; tell her to go home."

I snorted. "Right."

Now, though, I was tempted. Because I wanted to do a test run of one of my posters, to see if I could do it myself and save that much more on labor. But I couldn't with Cath there.

Then again, I couldn't do it without her—or someone—to show me how. I'd be especially lost on the more complicated jobs, like coffee mugs and note pads and t-shirts. I could possibly have asked Natalie, but she was always so busy. And apparently, she had a life, so she wasn't there on the weekends or late in the evening.

On second thought, I had to admit, Eric was right. As uncomfortable as the reality made and as much as she hated it too, Cath *was* my employee. She had to do what I told her. If I wanted her to go home, she had to go home. If I needed her to train me on the machines, she had to do it. There was no reason to be afraid of someone who worked for *me*. And this... this... uneasiness between us because of something that wasn't even *true* was ridiculous.

I tossed my pen on top of my desk and sprang from my chair, striding out to the work floor, where she was... I didn't know what she was doing. Cleaning?

She draped an ink-smudged dust rag over her shoulder and faced me when I said her name to her back. "What's up?"

Hmm. Well, that was better than the "Go away, you man-stealing whore" I'd been half expecting, so I took it as encouragement and answered, "Not much. I'm glad you're here."

"Yeah?" Her raised eyebrow made it clear she knew my pants could use a fire extinguisher right now.

"Yeah! I was hoping you could show me a few things."

"Like what things?"

"Like... how to operate some of this stuff." I gestured to the computers and machines around us.

"Why?"

I shrugged and chuckled nervously. "Why not?"

"Because you have people who work here who know how to do it. You don't have to know."

Shifting my weight from one foot to the other, I placed my

hands on my hips. "I *want* to know, though. Aunt Vel could operate every machine in here."

"That was different."

"Why?"

"Because she started this place. She was interested in graphic design and printing, back before it was all computers and automated machines, back when you had to set the type and roll the ink. Whereas you…" She looked me up and down. "You're only here out of obligation. Nobody will think less of you, you know, if you run the place and don't understand how it all works."

Right. I was merely a clueless figurehead, huh? *Huh-uh. No way.*

I set my jaw and said through clenched teeth, "Show me how to print something."

She snorted and rolled her eyes. "What am I supposed to do, produce a job out of thin air for you?"

After cramming my hand into my jeans pocket, I pulled out a flash drive. "Here. Print something from this."

She eyed the device pinched between my thumb and forefinger. "What's that?"

"Some stuff I made." I averted my eyes and sidled up to the machine I suspected we'd be using.

Still, she didn't move.

I sighed. "Listen. I can ask Dave or Natalie or Jordy to help me during business hours, but then I'll be in the way while you're trying to get out paying jobs, so don't you agree this is better?"

When she mumbled something that sounds like an affirmation, I tried to build on my momentum. "I'll buy you lunch. At Harrington's."

"Make it The Lobster Shack and you have a deal."

"Whatever you want."

She snatched the drive from my grip. "Fine."

"Pick any of the files in the 'Posters' folder on that. We'll start there."

It wasn't until the lobster rolls had been devoured that Cath said, from the other side of the small high-top table, "You know, you caught on quicker than I thought you would, back at the shop."

I smiled down at the root beer foam sticking to the sides of my stein. "If I didn't know better, I'd say there was a compliment hidden in that statement. Along with the insult, of course."

She sat back in her chair and squinted. "You're catching on to a lot of things."

Sighing, I pushed my glass to the side and leaned over the table, bracing my weight on my elbows. "Listen, Cath. Eric Mulligan and I are just friends."

"I wasn't talking about Eric."

"Right."

"I wasn't. I was speaking in general. You're getting the hang of things around here. With the business, with the townspeople…"

"Including Eric."

"Yeah, he lives here."

"Okay. But we're not… We're not *dating*. Or anything else."

"None of my concern."

"But I think it is. And I want you to know, I'm not your competition."

She shifted in her chair and made a move to hop down. "Well, thanks for lunch."

"Wait!"

She did, but angled herself closer to me in her seat and practically growled, "What do you want from me?"

"I want... I want us to get along."

"I already have friends, and I don't need another one."

"I'm not saying we have to be friends. But I am your—" Her eyes widen, so I pulled back the "boss" card at the last second. "We spend a ton of time together. And I... I respect your knowledge and skills."

"Man, now I know I've arrived. Big City Girl respects me."

I reeled at the contempt in her tone. "What did I ever do to you to make you hate me so much?"

She chuckled mirthlessly. "Hmm. Let's see. You have a great business—not to mention a house and a car and a bunch of other assets—dropped in your lap, but you treat all of it like some huge imposition, something that's keeping you from your glamorous life in Boston. Everyone loved your aunt, which she deserved, but that means you've been hailed as a princess from the minute you arrived in town. Not because you've earned it, but because you're smart and pretty and confident, and people respond to that. And yeah, since you've figured it out, I might as well admit it: it sucks that you were single all of five minutes before you laid claim to one of maybe five decent guys in this town. And he's followed you around like a lovesick puppy from Day One."

Since I couldn't do anything about the other beefs she had with me, I seized the one that wasn't an actual issue. "You know, Cath, it's such a cliché to despise another woman because of a guy. And I've told you, I haven't 'laid claim' to anyone."

"Whatever. If you're not interested in Eric in that way, maybe you should stop leading him on to inflate your ego."

I pulled my chin back and blinked at her. "Excuse me?"

"You heard me. Back off the guy and give the rest of us a chance."

"You've known each other since kindergarten. Is that not a long enough chance? Don't you think, if he were interested, he would have asked you out long before I ever swanned in here and monopolized his attention, or whatever the hell you're accusing me of doing?"

She gulped. I'd landed some hard blows, but now I was on a roll and couldn't stop, despite knowing I should.

"He and I are friends. Period. The fact that he wants nothing to do with you has nothing to do with me."

Now she did stand. I made a point not to shrink away as she crowded my personal space. "He's in love with you. If you can't see that, I take back everything I said about you being smart." Pivoting on her toes, she stalked away from our table, leaving me to suffer alone under the other diners' scrutiny.

Screw her! And everyone else in this stupid town, for that matter. Including Eric. And Hortense. And anyone who either won't believe the truth or is doing their damnedest to conceal it.

I didn't consider myself some goody-two-shoes Pollyanna who spouted maxims like, "Honesty is the best policy," and never took into account the grays of the world, but shit! We'd come to a point where honesty couldn't *be* a policy at all... because nobody trusted it. People *wanted* to be lied to. There was some perverse comfort in fabrication. Even when it made them miserable. Because then, they could be the persecuted.

Sadly, I'd experienced the aching, hurts-so-good satisfaction in victimhood before. But that was a truth *I'd* rather not face.

I stared into nothingness for a while before dropping my napkin on my plate and signaling for the check.

CHAPTER FOURTEEN

I WAS A MEAN GIRL. For real! I'd laughed about Cath behind her back with Eric, then taunted her with hurtful facts she surely already knew and didn't need rubbed in her face.

But I'd fed her lobster rolls first, so... that must have made it better?

No.

That made it worse.

It was like fattening a calf, then stroking it and whispering sweet nothings into its trusting face before slaughtering it for dinner.

Veal is gross.

I was gross.

And I was so horrible, I couldn't muster the courage to apologize to the woman.

Not that she'd given me much opportunity. She'd made sure to be busy all week, running the loud presses nearly non-stop for eight hours each day, then leaving at five on the dot. None of her usual early mornings, either. I guess she'd finally decided I didn't deserve the one hundred and ten percent she always gave Aunt Vel. And fair enough. I'd never asked for that, anyway.

Emailing an apology to her seemed cheap. Since it had been almost a week, though, I didn't have much choice. That morning, I'd shot a simple, *"Hey, I'm sorry about what I said at lunch last weekend. It was a lousy way to show my appreciation for all your help and hard work."*

And snark. And bitchiness. And backhanded compliments. And thinly veiled insults.

But it was only fair that I not keep score about those things, after all, since I wasn't going to come clean about all of my sins against her.

In any case, she hadn't replied. Whatever. I'd sent the message for selfish reasons, to assuage my guilt. That type of "apology" didn't require—or deserve—a response.

When the entrance bell rang at close to five o'clock, Mona said, "Hey, Eric! Well, look at you! Fresh haircut and nice duds. You and Whitney have a date tonight?"

Oh, gosh. Why did I feel like slamming my office door, locking it, and hiding under my desk? And why was Eric there, all dressed up? We didn't have plans until tomorrow, and our usual movie in Portland definitely didn't require fancy clothes.

Before he could answer and end all the suspense, the bell rang again.

"Hiya, Eric," came the voice of the newspaper editor, Bret. "Lookin' good. You didn't have to get so dressed up to help us with tonight's deadline."

Eric chuckled nervously. "Oh, you wouldn't want my help."

"Are you kidding? Your obits are some of the best content each week. Speaking of... awesome job on Elma Ourbach. Everyone's so sad to see her go, but your tribute was really touching." Bret's voice approached my door as he traveled from the lobby toward the back. "Anyway. Have a nice weekend!"

"Yeah. You, too."

The enthusiastic journalist peeked through my door on his way past. "Hi, Whitney!" And he was gone, surely to find Cath for any last-minute additions or changes before she did the paper's weekly print run.

I closed my eyes and cursed his alerting everyone to my presence in my office. Hiding was now out of the question.

"Go on back," I heard Mona say, followed shortly by Eric's appearance at my door.

He grinned and knocked. True to Mona's spoiler alert, he was sporting a tan line around his ears and neck where hair used to be, immaculate shoes, pressed pants, a crisp blue dress shirt, and a shiny navy tie.

"Hi!" I said, wishing I looked busier.

"Hey. TGIF, right?"

Faking it hard, I smiled. "Yeah! New clothes?"

"Is it that obvious?" He looked down at himself, then back up, wincing.

"Only because I've never seen you wear that."

"Everyone's made a point to say something today, though."

"Slow news day, I guess."

"Must be. Anyway, I wanted to pop by and make sure we're still on for tomorrow night."

"It's usually not up to me."

"We have a visitation tonight and a service in the morning, but as long as nobody pops their clogs between now and then, I'm free and clear."

"Great. See you at the usual time, then." For lack of anything better to do, I picked up my cell phone and check for fresh texts—of which there were none. Shelly had a new boyfriend, Dominic, some guy she met at the Independence

Day exhibit unveiling, so she'd been an absentee sister-friend. Although she still hadn't answered the message I sent her earlier today, I dispatch another one, to give my fingers something to do.

Standing sideways in the doorway, Eric wrapped his hand around its frame and leans into it in a standing push-up. "Uh... are you okay?"

"Fine." Tap, tap, tap.

"Are you sure? We don't have to go to the movies tomorrow, if you're sick of that. I haven't checked what's playing."

It was true we'd already seen everything we really wanted to see (and a few things we didn't want to see, when we ran out of interesting options), but the movies had become secondary. In fact, I usually dozed huddled under the jacket I draped over myself in the frigid auditorium. Our outings were more about the company... and getting away from Morris. The talks we had in the car and at dinner were the main attractions— er, events. The movie was merely something to do to fill some of the time, to rest our voices and provide us with discussion fodder (if I stayed awake).

I glanced up from my phone. "That new one came out last weekend when we couldn't go. Some post-apocalyptic something-or-other."

He groaned, then made a barfing noise. "I hate those."

"Me, too. They stress me out."

"We'll skip it, then."

"It's the only one playing we haven't seen."

"Poo."

"'Poo'?" I lifted an eyebrow and tried not to laugh.

He chuckled and pushed away from the door frame. "I guess we'll have to figure out something else to do then. Mini golf? Go-carts?"

"Uhh..." I tapped out yet another text to my sister. *Answer my dang messages, you twit. You were my sister before you were that guy's—*

"Or maybe the library or a bookstore? You must miss that atmosphere. Books and journals and... scholarly things."

"Well..."

"There are a few county fairs within driving distance, too. Good people-watching, if nothing else. Or... I'm not a huge fan of shopping, but The Maine Mall, maybe? And we still haven't checked out Old Port, as many times as you've said you'd like to. Tons to do there, especially in the middle of summer, and it's cool by the water."

"Eric, I—"

Before I could respond to any of his suggestions, Cath appeared in the doorway behind him. He half-turned and flinched.

"Oh, geez. Cath. I... I didn't realize..." He shoved his hands in his pockets and slid sideways to get past her into the hall. "I'll, uh, call you later, Whitney, and uh, we'll firm up plans."

"But—"

"See ya."

I wanted to collapse on the desk and bang my head on top of it, but with Cath still standing at the threshold to my office, I flashed her a tight smile and eased my phone away without sending that latest text to Shelly. "What's up?"

"Number Three is on the fritz again. Maintenance is working on it, but they say it's going to be at least a couple of hours before it's up and running."

"Oh, no."

"Yeah. It's going to be a late night. So much for your big date."

"I don't—" I stopped and sighed. "Tell me what I need to do."

She looked like asking me for anything landed in distant

last place on her list of wants, after oral surgery without anesthesia. "It's going to be all hands on deck to get the paper to customers on time."

Great.

Buster was going to have to do without my charming company tonight.

~

"A couple of hours" ended up being nine hours. Nine. Hours. We didn't even *start* printing until two in the morning. Fortunately, the paper wasn't much more than a glorified pamphlet. And it had a circulation of barely three thousand, plus the couple hundred stacked in machines outside of Town Hall, gas stations, fast food places, and the grocery store. Still. The sun was peeking over the horizon when I finally dragged myself home and collapsed, fully clothed, into bed.

My morning run time came and went. I slept. My sister answered both texts I'd sent the day before. I slept. Buster yowled next to the bed, demanding food. I threw a pillow at him, then felt bad and got up to feed him and refresh his water. Straight back to bed I went... and slept. The buzzing and chiming of my cell phone on the nightstand was barely a blip in my dreams. The louder landline phone downstairs filtered more insistently into my consciousness. Not enough to fully stir me, though. The doorbell and loud knocking on the front door below the bedroom window roused me more completely, but my brain didn't register what they meant. At first.

I bolted upright in bed when I heard Eric shouting my name. "Whitney!" BANG, BANG, BANG! DING DONG!

Scrambling for the head of the bed, I kicked the covers free of my denim-clad legs. I pushed the curtains and blinds aside and poked my head between the plastic slats and the window, hanging onto the headboard for balance. Eric backed off the small front stoop and peered up at my window, his phone clamped to his ear. The landline trills again.

I shoved the window open and pressed my forehead against the screen. "What the heck?" I shouted down.

He shaded his eyes with his free hand. "There you are!"

"Uh… yeah… Where else would I be?"

"That's just it; I didn't know. I've been trying to get ahold of you for hours." He lowered his phone and jabbed at its screen, plunging the house into silence once more, mid-ring. Again, his hand rose to his forehead. He squinted at me. "Are you sick?"

"What? No! I— I didn't get home until after six o'clock."

He tilted his head, obviously confused.

"A.M. As in"—I checked the time on the alarm clock —"seven hours ago."

"Oh. Oh! What— I didn't realize… I'm sorry I woke you. I'll, uh…" He spun in the yard, then faced me again, then turned away. Finally, he lined me up in his peripheral vision and said, "You can call me later."

"Eric, wait!"

He pocketed his phone.

"I'm up now. Use your key and come in. Wait for me downstairs. I'm going to take a quick shower."

"I don't have a key, though."

"Yes, you do. I've seen it." And he'd never use it without my permission, which was why I hadn't made a big deal about it.

He rubbed his neck.

"Please, save me the trip downstairs and use it," I implored.

He stepped up to the front door, and the key scraped in the lock. I closed the window, fixed the blinds and curtains, and jogged to the house's only bathroom across the hall.

Ten minutes later, I trotted downstairs, led by my nose.

"You are a saint," I said, upon entering the kitchen.

He laughed and tucked his rolled-up necktie in his pocket. "It's only coffee," he said, undoing the first two buttons on his dress shirt.

"'Only coffee.' That's like saying, 'It's only oxygen.'"

"Rough night?" His tone was casual as he propped his hip against the counter.

I bought some time by pouring two large cups of hot, dark brown liquid and slid one toward him. "You could say that. Jordy's a machine, though. Who knew?" After shutting off the coffeemaker, I set the nearly empty carafe onto the cooling burner, under the filter basket, and turned to face a choking Eric.

"Jordy?!"

"Yes. The guy doesn't quit."

He swiped his hand under his chin to mop up the dripping liquid before it hit his shirt.

I tossed him a towel, which he caught with one hand. "He seems so easygoing. But back the guy into a corner and give him a deadline, and he's all business. Really take-charge." I wiggled my eyebrows and sip, closing my eyes to the taste and savoring the heat as it traveled to my core and penetrated through the ceramic mug to my palms.

"I— I had no idea."

"Me neither. It was quite unexpected." I opened my eyes and pressed the hot mug to the dull ache in my sinuses.

"No, I mean... I had no idea you... and Jordy... and..." He set down his drink and wrung the towel in his hands. "Not that it's any of my business. But I thought... I *assumed* you weren't—" His cheeks and forehead were blazing red, but the other areas of his face glistened grayly.

"Are you okay? What's wrong with you?"

"Me? Nothing. I... I'm fine." He dropped the towel onto the counter behind him. "Taken by surprise, that's all. Like I said, I didn't realize you had plans last night, much less with Jordy. You didn't mention it when we talked."

"I didn't know until after you left."

"Oh. I see. Last-minute. Spontaneous."

"That's how those things tend to work."

"Those things. Yes. Well. I— I wouldn't know. That is, I don't have much experience with... that type of arrangement."

"Oh, come on. You're no stranger to the unexpected duty call."

"Hmm." He chuckled, despite still looking sick and unamused. "The term is 'booty call.'"

"Excuse me?" I laughed. "No, that's something else entirely."

"I guess I'm not familiar with the new lingo, then."

"It's not new ling—" I set my cup next to his and rested my elbow in one hand, my cheek in the other. "I'm so confused."

"About?"

"Your reaction to this. It's not a big deal. Not something I anticipated or thought about when I took over the business, but... New town, new life, new me, right?"

"I... Yes. I suppose so. And I shouldn't be grilling you about it. It's your business."

"Yes... Velvet *is* my business."

"So is what you do outside of Velvet. Although, I would caution you against rolling in the ink after hours with the people on your payroll. That could get messy. I'd imagine. Of course, that's not something *I* have to worry about, since... Well, you know. I'm related to all of my co-workers. And our clientele... I'm not into that. I can't afford to be too picky, but the one requirement I do have in a sexual partner is a pulse. Weird that way, I guess." He took a deep breath. "'Duty call,' huh? That's cold. Makes it sound like a chore. If you're not that into it, why do it?"

I reached behind me, turned on the water, seized the sprayer, extended the hose, and took a quick shot at him. It hit him in the chest, so I squeezed the trigger again and aim higher, misting his face.

He blinked and raised his hands. "Hey!"

"Shut up."

"What are you do—"

Another spray deflected off his palms and dribbled onto the floor.

"Stop it!"

"First, you have to promise to shut up for a minute so I can figure out what the heck you're talking about, then compare it to what I'm talking about. And if you're talking about what I think you are—which is most definitely *not* what I'm talking about—then I'm going to come over there and kick your ass."

He cowered behind his dripping hands. "Okay."

I holstered the sprayer. He fumbled for the towel behind him and mopped his face and hands, then dabbed at the front of his dress shirt before unbuttoning it, sliding his arms from it and then removing it altogether.

I look away from his white t-shirt-covered chest and tousled my shower-damp hair while collecting my thoughts. Finally, I said, "I'm not 'rolling in the ink,' or whatever you called it, with Jordy. Or doing anything with him that you could do with dead people, if you were disturbed... and so inclined. Unless they make it a habit to resurrect and stay up all night getting a small-town newspaper to press."

He smiled sheepishly, and his face returned to a normal

shade. "Oh. Ooooh. Right. No, they don't. Sounds like an interesting new show, though. *The Walking Deadline*, perhaps?"

I laughed. "Yeah. I feel about that great today after being up all night with Jordy. And Cath. And Dave. And Natalie. And the maintenance guys. And the editor of the paper."

"Bret's a good guy."

"He is. Although if I never have to help him print another newspaper, that will be too soon."

"Why did you have to last night?"

My coffee regained my attention. After a few long, luxurious swallows, I replied, "Because the machine we use broke down right before print time. And it took until about two a.m. to get it back up and running again. Then the paper had to go through the folding thingy, and the machine that inserts the store fliers, and the stacker, and the bundler..."

"Your grasp of the industry's terminology is stunning."

I scowled. "Don't make me get the sprayer out again."

"How can you not know what half of the machines inside the business you own are called?"

"You mean, their model names? Like the Nimbus 2000?"

"Pretty sure that's the name of a flying broomstick."

I set my mug into the stainless steel sink with a clunk and eye the sprayer, contemplating another surprise attack. "Yeah? So? Maybe that's what I call it."

"It's cute. You're cute."

"Ha!"

"You are. Even when you're in unfamiliar territory, you don't let that get you down. Don't know the name of a machine you own? Who cares? Call it the Nimbus 2000 and move on."

In spite of myself, I laughed at his characterization. Because it was pretty accurate. "I'll figure it all out eventually."

"Of course you will."

"It's not worth stressing about it or beating myself up about it until then. I have to prioritize. Learning how things work and keeping the business in business are my main concerns. I'll learn as I go."

"And you'll be great."

I blushed and picked at a cat hair on my t-shirt. "I doubt it. But 'great' isn't necessary. I have other interests that may lead to greatness."

"Must be nice."

"It is." In order to end this squirm-worthy examination of me, I jumped on the opening to shift the focus to him. Snatching the towel from him, I dropped it onto the floor and used my foot to move it back and forth and soak up the tiny puddle at his feet.

"Listen, Eric. Of all people, I understand you feel a certain obligation to your dad and your family to do what you do for a living, but that doesn't mean you have to give up every dream you've ever had."

"You sound like Vel."

"Well, then, she was right." Curling my toes around the cloth, I kicked my leg up to place it within arm's reach, caught it, and tossed it toward the sink.

"The thing is..." He stopped and took a deep breath, staring down at his shiny shoes as if inspecting the droplets still lingering there. "The thing is... I... I don't remember what or who I dreamed of being, before I was informed I wasn't allowed to consider any career I wanted. I don't know myself well enough." He looked up and smiled sadly at me. "Pretty pathetic, huh?"

I shook my head. "No. That makes sense."

"I wish it made sense to me."

"But maybe—hear me out—you should give yourself

permission to think about it now. To pursue, in your free time, the things that make you happy."

"Wouldn't that make the rest of life miserable in comparison?"

I shrugged. "Maybe it could. But in my experience, it makes the rest of life livable. Gives me something to look forward to. Gives me a reason to get out of bed."

"That's a good way of looking at it."

"So? Will you at least think about it?"

He nodded and grinned. "Yeah. I will. I might need someone to bounce ideas off, though."

I turned and rinsed my mug, then nestled it into the dishwasher and reached behind me for his cup. "I bet Cath is available."

He laughed while handing the empty mug to me. I stuck out my tongue over my shoulder.

"Maybe instead of going to Portland tonight," he said, sobering, "we could just hang out and talk?"

I'm not sure if the suggestion itself or the topic of discussion was responsible for the worry on his face. Either way, I wanted to erase it, so I immediately shot him a comforting smile and said, "Sure!"

His shoulders relaxed. "Great. I'll, uh, grab some lobster and scallops and fire up the grill tonight. See you around... eight?"

His mug slipped through my wet fingers and I cringed, waiting for the crash on the tile floor, but the dishwasher rack saved it from a shattered death. Righting the cup, I swallowed and clarified, "At your place?"

"Yeah. If that's okay."

It was true the thought of schlepping to Portland that night, as exhausted as I was, didn't appeal to me, when we could just as easily talk in the (extreme) privacy and comfort of his house. Pushing aside any nebulous reservations I might have had, I focused on putting him at ease for what might be a difficult conversation for him.

"Sounds great! What do you want me to bring?"

He flipepd his shirt over his shoulder, using his index finger as a hook. "An open mind. And maybe a cattle prod. I might need it."

CHAPTER FIFTEEN

I ARRIVED PROMPTLY at the designated time, bearing an assorted cheese tray and a bottle of sparkling grape juice. No cattle prod. But my mind was open. I was ready to help Eric brainstorm how to fill his nights and days away from the dead.

Since I could already smell the grill, I bypassed the front door and followed the wrap-around porch to the back, careful not to turn my ankle when I stepped down to the flagstones in my black ballet flats.

His back was to me as he moved the seafood around on the grates, ensuring an even cook. Looked like he was still wearing the same white t-shirt he'd left my house in, but he'd exchanged his dress pants and shoes for khaki shorts and flip flops. The ropey muscles in his forearms protruded when he squeezed lemon halves over the lobster tails and skewered scallops. The hot grill sizzled.

I licked some moisture onto my lips, cleared my throat, and trilled, "Hellooo!"

He pivoted at the waist, waving the drained lemon halves at me. "Hey, there. Oh, geez. Watch your step."

Pitching the spent fruit into a nearby trashcan, he turned and met me halfway across the back patio, relieving me of my offerings. When he kissed my cheek, I got a good whiff of his freshly shaven face. And citrus.

"'Make your patio look like your house is rising out of the rocks,' the architect said. 'It'll look amazing,' he said. And possibly kill any intruders lurking around where they shouldn't be. Or sprain the ankle of every invited guest."

I laughed. "It's okay. It does look cool."

"Nice to look at, not so great to navigate."

"Isn't that how most things in life are?"

He ogled me (most definitely for laughs, which I readily provided) before answering, "Yes" and setting the cheese plate and grape juice on the umbrellaed table, already set for two.

I approached the grill and peered down at it. "Oh, wow. This looks and smells..." My growling stomach finished my sentence.

He stood next to me, taking up the tongs and poking at the white meats. "We're almost ready. If you'll hold that platter..."

I did, and we worked together to transfer the food to the table. He disappeared inside for a few seconds to grab coleslaw from the fridge and cornbread from the oven. I poured iced tea into tumblers and grape juice into goblets.

By the time he got back, and we dug into our dinners, my nervousness had subsided somewhat. What was there to be anxious about? It was a casual meal at a friend's house. And this was hardly my first time here. Still... with the sun sinking lower and lower over the lake in front of us, it felt different somehow. More romantic, definitely, than when I'd spent the weekend helping someone I barely knew recover from an injury.

I must have been be picking up on Eric's mood. Despite his brave talking at my place earlier, he'd led the conversation everywhere but where he'd said it would go when he planned this evening. And that was fine. We didn't have to follow an agenda. But it was obvious he was avoiding any talk of his interests. Maybe he hadn't had time to think about it much after he finished shopping for food and went home to start cooking. Looked like he'd also spent a fair number of minutes grooming. Which was hilarious.

By contrast, I'd barely put any thought or effort at all into my appearance. Sure, I'd showered again, because the one I'd taken that morning (er... afternoon, technically) was rushed, and I spent the rest of the day doing some light housework, including refreshing Buster's litter box, so I felt grimy. I'd only worn this breezy skirt because I was afraid I was becoming a frump, always wearing jeans and t-shirts, the unofficial dress code of this town. My simple fitted tee and sloppy ponytail conveyed an appropriate amount of *laissez faire*, I hoped. And my makeup... I definitely skimped there. It was only Eric, after all. A tiny bit of blush and lip gloss to ensure I didn't look sickly. Oh, and mascara, because my skimpy lashes didn't show up otherwise, and have you ever talked to someone with no eyelashes? It's disconcerting. I didn't want that to be a distraction. As for my legs... I only shaved them because of the skirt, and I would have done that, regardless, even if I'd been spending the evening alone. This girl had standards that had nothing to do with someone else's opinion, no matter how handsome and funny and sweet and...

Eric stopped in the middle of telling me about how the rocks around his house were a combination of existing boulders plus a few specifically trucked in as part of the construction and landscaping. "I'm sorry. I'm rambling."

"What? No. I was wondered if you'd built the house around all of this or if it was imported."

"You're nice, but it's not that interesting. You have that

glassy-eyed stare I get when Bobby rants about everyone being careless and wasteful with our office-supply usage, and I trace back the last time I saw my pen and wonder if it's going to be buried with—or in—someone." At my horrified reaction, he waved his hand. "Just kidding. I mean, I have worried about that once or twice, but it's never happened... that I know of. You're about as faraway as all those lost pens, though."

I blushed. "I'm still tired from last night. Can't pull all-nighters like I used to."

"If you want to go home, I—"

"No!" I laughed breezily to cover that word's unintended intensity. "I just got here. I'll get my second wind after a while. The food... I'm so full. It was all so good. You're a great cook!"

"Thanks. I like to eat good food, and I'm the only one here to cook it. How about I go make some coffee, and we'll walk down to the chairs?" he suggested. He was referring, of course, to the Adirondacks perched under some pines on the grassy hill of his front yard. They sat by yet another grouping of rocks overlooking the lake.

"That sounds nice," I said. "I'll clear the dishes."

Ignoring his objections, I did exactly that, more to keep busy than because I was dying to be helpful. I couldn't sit out here and continue to think (fret) while he puttered around making coffee and looking so freaking adorably domestic. Returning order to the back patio, I hoped, would return order to my runaway thoughts as well. By the time the table had been cleared, it would be clear in my mind that this shouldn't feel any different than the times we'd talked in the car on the way to and from Portland. Or at dinner before the movies. Or across my desk when he dropped by to pick up the dead sheets or the funeral home's stationery orders.

It did, though.

I blamed lobster and loneliness.

Thank goodness there weren't any oysters.

Closer to the water, it was remarkably cooler. As the sun provided less and less heat on its descent into the water, I huddled over my cooling coffee mug and wished I'd grabbed my sweater or denim jacket on the way out the door. But it had been warm—approaching hot—then, and I hadn't foreseen hanging out by the shoreline so long into the evening. If anything, I'd thought the mosquitoes would chase us indoors. But the pests seemed to understand this place was special. Or —more likely—the Mulligans had some high-tech, expensive thingamajiggy hidden somewhere that drove them away.

Despite the goose bumps on my arms and legs, I was hesitant to move or go indoors. It was safe out here. We were in our separate chairs, content to look out over the water at the occasional passing boat, most of the time not saying anything.

Eric didn't seem bothered by the temperature or the silence. He was the most placid I'd ever seen him. Not a twitch of a toe, not a fidget of a finger, not a bounce of a knee. He stared at the lake with a Mona Lisa smile that made me wonder what the heck he was thinking, but there was no way I was asking that stupid question. For one thing, I wouldn't want to break the spell. For another, I'd probably be disappointed by the no-doubt irreverent answer.

After several minutes, he looked over at me and asked, "What?"

"What?"

"You're staring at me."

Busted.

I tried to laugh off his accusation. "Whatever."

"I'm not imagining it."

"I'm waiting for you to... talk."

He smiled sheepishly. "Yes. We're gathered here this evening to discuss my lack of a personality. I almost forgot."

"Personality is something you're definitely not lacking."

"Correction: my lack of a *good* personality."

"I like your personality. It takes some getting used to, that's all."

He tossed his head back and laughed, capping it off with a groan. "Ohhh... that's almost worse."

"It's not. It's just... different."

"Whitney."

I met his eyes, which sparkled in the reflection of the sun off the water. "What?"

"You can be honest. I can take it. I have pretty thick skin. And I know I'm... odd."

"Show me someone who's not a bit odd, and I'll show you someone who's boring and not worth getting to know." Before he could object and accuse me of being too diplomatic, I continued, "And I'm glad I got to know you."

He rubbed his chin. "Yeah... see, that's the thing. It seems like all we ever talk about is me. Especially since you found out about... everything."

"It's a fascinating topic. Does it make you uncomfortable?"

He shook his head. "Nah. But it would be nice to talk about something else once in a while."

"We do! All the time."

"Okay, let me rephrase that: it'd be nice to talk about *you* once in a while."

I crossed my eyes and stuck out my tongue, fake-retching. "Me? Ha! I'm one of those ultra-normal boring people."

"But, see, that's unique and interesting for a weirdo like

me. I want to hear how the other half lives. You know, the half who successfully interacts with living people every day."

I sat up straighter in my chair. Suddenly, I was no longer chilly. In fact, sweat was forming on the back of my neck when I asked, "What do you want to know, then?"

He scooted his chair closer to mine and sat forward so he was literally on the edge of his seat, his knee grazing mine. "Well. Since you asked…"

At the risk of sounding like a hysterical hyena, I cackled at his talk show host act. "I can't imagine there's anything you don't already know."

"Let me worry about the questions. I have quite a few, in fact." He tapped his lips with his index finger.

"Before you get too excited, I reserve the right to not answer. Like, I'm not copping to any of my most embarrassing sex fails or what color panties I'm wearing or anything like that." His raised eyebrows indicated those questions weren't on the list anyway, so I cleared my throat. "But go ahead."

"I was thinking more along the lines of, 'What was a typical day like for you in Boston?' but now you've piqued my interest on the sex fails. For one thing, the 'most embarrassing' part indicates there are enough to rank them, so…"

I blushed, hoping the sunset would camouflage it as I chose to address his original question. "A typical day before my whole world was turned upside down? Uh, let me try to remember. It seems like forever ago." I flapped my ponytail near the base of my skull to allow the cool breeze to dry the flop sweat. "Gosh."

"It doesn't have to be a minute-by-minute account. Let's start with… How is your apartment different from Vel's house? And what's happened to it now that you've moved here?"

"My apartment…" I stared wistfully at the water as I remembered it. "I'm subletting it to a fellow graduate student while I'm here."

"Furniture included?"

"Yep. I have a couch there and everything."

"Nice. That would be one big difference, then."

"I miss my apartment. And not just the couch. It's… it's all mine, you know? I still feel like I'm visiting Aunt Vel's. In fact, I stay in the guest room, because… Well, it would seem weird to sleep in her bed."

"Move your bedroom furniture up here and get rid of her stuff or put it in storage."

I shrugged. "I dunno. That feels wrong, too. I… I don't want to change anything. And since I don't know how long I'll be here…"

"You're still planning to go back to Boston as soon as possible?"

"Yes! I think so. I don't know."

He frowned.

"I feel like… like I'm in limbo. Permanent Purgatory, or something."

"Let's hope the same can't be said for Vel." Immediately, he winced. "Sorry. The death jokes… They're a reflex."

"It's okay. They're funny."

"You think so? I always got the impression they annoyed you."

"Maybe at first. But they're part of you. And… I like you."

He grinned. "Oh. Okay. Next question…"

"Wait."

He held the breath he'd inhaled.

"Before you continue this bizarre interview, can I ask you something kind of… personal?"

His exhalation moved my bangs. "I suppose. But I don't

have *any* embarrassing sex fails, much less a top ten list. And I don't remember what color my underwear is today, although I only own black or dark gray. For some reason, I gravitate toward mourning colors. Like it's ingrained, or something."

I bit the inside of my cheek to give the appearance of long-suffering during his underwear monologue. That was better than revealing my true thoughts and feelings. When he finally stopped rambling, I asked, "Did you ever call her 'Mom'?"

His cheeky expression faded, and his eyes sank to his lap. "No. Well... maybe once or twice, but not regularly. I— I was always afraid I'd slip up and call her that in front of someone else, so I never let myself get in the habit of thinking of her that way."

"That makes sense. But in a way, it sucks."

"It bothered me more when I was a kid. Every kid wants a mom, like all the 'normal' kids." He looked up. "But then, after a while, it would have felt more awkward to call her anything but her nickname. Because it became synonymous with 'mother' to me. Like, when you call her 'Aunt Vel,' it always takes me a second to reconcile it in my brain. It would be like me calling *your* mother 'Aunt Mom.' It's almost contradictory. Like, which one is it?"

"I guess that *would* be odd."

"Odd. There's that word again. Pretty much sums up my whole life, right?"

"That's not your fault, though. Anyway, speaking of unconventional mother-child relationships, you're talking to someone who felt compelled to take her mother's maiden name in a show of solidarity when her parents divorced. I get 'non-traditional.'" I paused. "But... don't you ever— Were you ever *mad* at your parents for, well, for everything?"

"Only constantly from the age of about ten to... still waiting. Hang on; that's not accurate. There were about six years in my late teens, early twenties when I was too drunk all the time to be angry. That was the draw of being perpetually wasted. One of the draws. The other was that I was never hungover. Because I never got to that level of sobriety."

"Wow."

"Messed up, right?"

"How'd you break the cycle?"

He turned his head sideways and squinted. "We're supposed to be talking about *you*."

"Yeah, but I'm boring. Do you really want to discuss the ins and outs of subletting and how much of an instant failure I was at a long-distance relationship with one of the most self-absorbed men on the planet?"

"Maybe not the first part, but that second thing sounds pretty interesting."

"It's not. Subletting is a more exciting topic."

"Hm. I sense you don't want to talk about it."

"For a guy who hangs out with dead people so much, you're super-perceptive."

"Why, thank you. And for a communications expert, you're super-sarcastic." He flicked my knee and smiled.

I smiled back. "So, you don't want to talk about your recovery, and I don't want to talk about… that guy." I rubbed my arms. "What's left?"

He drummed his fingers on the arms of his chair while he pondered that. Finally, he said, "You know, it's okay to make changes to Vel's house. Nobody would fault you. In fact, the only person who'd potentially care would be me, and for what it's worth, I'm okay with it. It might be easier if it didn't look so much like the place where I spent half my childhood. Like she's about to come home at any minute and fix me a snack."

"Modifying it to suit my style feels like putting down roots, though."

"And you don't want that."

"No. Well, maybe. Well... no."

He sighed, then brightens. "Okay, but if you *were* to make changes, any changes you wanted, what would they be? Hypothetically. For fun."

Tucking my hands in my armpits, I shivered and said, "Sounds like you're fishing for something specific."

"I have a whole list of things I hate about that place, the first being its location. She could see the dang shop from her couch, may it rest in peace."

I laughed and said through chattering teeth, "I'm sorry I killed the sofa!"

"I'm not. It was heinous."

"It was brand new!"

"New couches can be ugly, too. And hers was. It deserved to be barfed on." He looked around us at the dusk. "Wow. It got dark fast. And you're freezing. Let's go inside." With one hand, he grabbed both our empty coffee mugs by their handles; with the other, he moved his chair to its original place. Waving me up, he said, "C'mon."

As we hiked up the hill, I decide to humor him. "You asked me how my apartment is different from Vel's place."

"Yes?"

"The answer is, in nearly every way."

"Aha! You *do* hate her house!"

"No! I liked it when it was *her* house. It fit her. You know, quirky, kitschy, cluttered, and scattered."

"Then your apartment must be sleek and modern."

"Not in a sterile way. And I have my own hoarding issues —books and art supplies."

"To each her own."

"Exactly. But at my place, I don't have to be in bed to make or receive calls on my cell phone."

"Right? I hope you have an unlimited data plan. Everything in her house is 'roaming.'" He held open a door for me, and I passed into the sun room.

"Roaming? I'd kill for roaming. I don't get any service at all on the entire first floor. Extremely frustrating." Inside, away from the water and out of the wind, the hair settled flat on my arms, and my shoulders relaxed. "It feels good in here."

"Are you sure? I can start a fire."

"It's the middle of summer!"

"Who cares what the calendar says? If you're cold, you're cold."

"I'm fine now. Thanks."

He didn't argue, but as soon as I sat on the couch in the living room, he tossed a blanket at me, the same throw he'd slept under while recovering from Cath's bike attack. Then he continued toward the kitchen. "I'll be right back. Think of more ways you can improve Vel's house. It needs a serious makeover."

By the time he returned, I'd folded the blanket into a neat square and set it on the other half of the love seat. No need to get too comfortable here. Instead, I stayed on topic. "The plumbing is loud. Very loud."

Lowering himself to the cushion next to me, he said, "When I was a kid, I thought there was a ghost in the walls."

"Me, too! I hate the radiators and the boiler."

"The whole HVAC system needs an overhaul."

"I feel horrible bad-mouthing the place," I said, biting my thumbnail.

He waved off my guilt. "Whatever. It's a cute house. But it needs some major updating. One word: wallpaper."

I groaned. "It's hideous."

"I'm pretty sure that stuff was up when she bought the

place. She couldn't be bothered to strip it. 'I'm hardly ever home, anyway. What's the point?' The point is, it's god-awful!"

"And carpeting in the bathroom? So gross."

He gagged theatrically. "As a guy, I can't fathom making that choice. Or sticking with the former owner's choice, in her case."

"Right? Someone else's pee is on that carpet.

"You know it. Lots of it. Trust me; I pre-clean before the service drops by every other week, so I know how quickly stuff... builds up."

"Me too!" I said for the second time.

"You regularly miss the toilet?"

When I recover from laughing, I slapped his arm. "No! I clean the night before the cleaners come. Or I did. In Boston."

"You had a housekeeping service? Swanky!"

"It was included in the rent. Personally, I'd rather do it myself. I don't like someone else seeing my dirt. Plus, cleaning is a great stress reliever. I like it," I said quietly, like I was admitting something shameful.

Eric snorted. "I don't. I don't even care that I have the time to do it; I gladly fork over the dough every other week and let someone else have at it. Except for around the toilets. I draw the line at making someone else mop that up. It's bad enough they have to sweep up my hair."

"You *are* hairy."

"Yeah, but I wasn't shivering out by the lake, was I?"

"This conversation is... weird."

He sounded delighted when he said, "Totally weird!" Then he rested his chin on his knuckles. "What else?"

"'What else,' what?"

"What else would you change at Vel's?"

I produced a trumpet noise through my lips that made him chuckle. Then I said, "I don't know. We could be here all night. Like you said, it has great bones, but it needs an overhaul. That kitchen…"

"I'm a fan of old-*looking* things, but I want them to work like new. Like the wood stove in my kitchen. Rustic-looking, but it's actually state-of-the-art. Saves me money on gas and electricity, too."

"But you have to chop wood. That's kind of a pain."

"I don't mind it. Gives me something to do on weekends."

"About that…"

He leaned forward and pressed his finger against my lips. "Shh… Let's not. It's been such a nice evening. Let's not ruin it by trying to figure out how to fix me."

If I'd been able to speak, I would have told him I didn't think he needed fixing at all. I'd have said he bore no resemblance to Aunt Vel's outdated house or his high-maintenance wood stove or tripping hazard of a back patio. But with him sitting so close to me that I could feel the heat from his body, and his warm finger resting on my lips, I was absolutely speechless. Mostly aghast at my racing heart and tumultuous insides.

He dropped his hand and backed off, leaning against the couch's arm behind him. "Sorry." His hands fell into his lap. "I — I was trying to be funny, but that came off… creepy."

"No, it—"

"Yes, it did. I recognize 'horror' when I see it."

I rolled my eyes and tried to laugh. "It's not a big deal." My eyes flicked to the clock on the mantle.

"Now you're going to leave. I've ruined it by telling you not to ruin it."

"It's not about that. I promise. I'm tired."

"Yeah." His lips tightened. "Tired. Of my awkwardness."

I sighed and, at great risk to my own psychological comfort, kissed his cheek on my way up from the sofa.

"There," I said lightly over my shoulder while walking toward the front door. "Convinced?"

He laughed. "Not at all. But thanks for playing. I'll, uh... see you around."

"Thanks for dinner."

And the raging case of the horny heebie-jeebies.

CHAPTER SIXTEEN

NOT THAT I'D ever doubted it, but Aunt Vel had been a smart cookie. Her system of distributing all electronic orders after funneling them through her one email address had been an effort to level the workload without an expensive system she couldn't afford. And it had likely worked well in the early days of email, when that wasn't everyone's preferred method of communication, but the majority of our current orders came in that way now, so it quickly bogged down while the person in charge of the landing zone sorted through it. Or died. Or took over without knowing what she was doing. I was getting better at it, but it was still a clunky system. What if I were on vacation? What if I got sick?

What if I didn't want to get out of bed because I was freaked out by certain feelings for a certain person?

Ahem.

Hypothetically, of course. I'd never been a hide-in-bed kinda gal. No, I was a distract-yourself-with-complex-work-problems kinda gal.

Anyway, I might not have had the funds to develop an

online order form and upload portal, but I *could* make things more efficient with the system we did have.

"So… we *all* have to log into that email address? Several times a day?" Cath asked in the break room, where I'd called the graphic designers and print technicians to announce the change.

Handing out business cards with the email account login information, I confirmed, "Exactly."

"But that was Vel's account."

"And now it's all of ours. Think of it as, simply, an inbox. It's a generic address, not her name, so it works well for these purposes."

"Except only one person at a time can use it, right?" Dave checked.

I wasn't going to let anyone derail me. "That's one of the drawbacks, yes. But nobody should be in there for long periods of time anyway. And if you're ever locked out, shoot an IM to the group. We'll get used to going in and out of there quickly. Log in, check for jobs, claim a job, mark it as yours, forward it to your individual email, and log back out."

Natalie held up the business card I'd handed her and flipped it to the backside, where there was a colored square next to each of their names. "And we use these label colors on the messages to show that we've claimed a job?"

"That's right."

"I'm orange?" Cath said under her breath. "I hate orange."

I ignored her. "This cuts out the middle man—me—and will significantly streamline things."

Cath pocketed the card. "Yes. Less work for you. Meanwhile, the rest of us have one more thing to monitor."

"You were already checking your own email regularly for forwarded messages; this is no different than that."

"It's another password to remember."

Dave snorted. "The password is 'VelvetPrint,' Cath. How hard is that to remember? Stop being so difficult." To me, he said, "I like it. And you said there's a dedicated folder for finished jobs, where we can drag the messages after we've delivered the final product?"

I beamed at him. Finally someone was getting it. "Yes, exactly. That means the main inbox is for in-progress or unclaimed jobs only. I'll be going in there regularly to make sure jobs are being claimed and to sort out administrative stuff. I've already set up a few filters to automatically forward things to an account I've set up for billing and correspondence with vendors. Eventually, those messages will bypass the main inbox altogether. In the meantime, ignore them."

Jordy and Natalie glanced at each other, then shot me wobbly smiles I supposed were meant to encourage but only made me feel less sure. "I'm not claiming this is going to be perfect, guys, especially at first. But it's better than what we're currently doing. And it's the best solution I can think of that doesn't cost us anything. As long as we're all diligent about marking jobs as claimed and communicating with each other when issues arise, it'll be a decent system until I can afford a more modern upgrade."

Cath rolled her eyes. "Are we done? I have a ton of work to do. And another email account to babysit, apparently."

I cleared my throat. "That's all I have. If anyone has questions, or if you notice something's not working smoothly with this, let me know. We'll keep fine-tuning until we get it right. It's hard to anticipate every possible hicc—"

Everyone watched, agog, as Cath left in the middle of my sentence. Blinking and smiling tightly at the remaining few, I finished lamely, "…hiccup. I'll leave you to it. I know you're all busy."

Natalie and Jordy departed, arguing happily on their way

down the hall to their offices about whose color would get "credit" for their many joint efforts. Dave moved toward the door too, but paused to pat my arm. "You're doing good, kid."

"Ha!"

"You are. Don't mind Cath. She doesn't like change, unless it's her idea. And none of these recent changes have been her idea. Least of all her hero dying."

I swallowed loudly. "Hero? I— I had no idea. Everyone loved Aunt Vel, so I assumed..."

"She'll be okay. We all handle grief differently and go through its stages at our own pace. Something tells me she'll be stuck on 'anger' for a while. Ride it out." With a final pat, he exited the break room, whistling as he ambled back to his office.

As I walked the opposite way to discuss some front desk procedural changes with Mona, Cath bellowed from the work floor behind me, "I'M ALREADY LOCKED OUT!"

I stopped in my tracks, closed my eyes, and sighed. Pivoting on my heel, I headed toward my own office to make sure I wasn't the culprit before helping the angry bear troubleshoot the system.

"Ride it out," I whispered to myself.

"You're avoiding me."

The motion sensor activated the porch light and illuminated the large figure on the front stoop.

I gasped and pressed my hand to my chest. My keys jangled to the concrete walk. "Oh, my! You— What the... blazes are you doing? Trying to kill me?"

He leaned forward, snagged the keys from the sidewalk, and held them out to me. "No. I—"

I snatched them from his fingers. "You're weird."

"I'm pretty sure we've already established that several times."

"Waiting for someone on their front porch in the dark is a whole new level of weird."

"It wasn't dark when I started waiting."

"It's ten o'clock! How long have you been out here?"

"A couple of hours."

"A couple of—" I pushed past him and unlocked the front door. "Get in here," I demanded when he still remained outside after I'd entered the house. "People are probably having a field day with your behavior."

"I don't care."

"Well, I do!"

He strode into the entryway and picked up Buster, who acted like we were his favorite rock stars.

"Hey, Buster Boy," Eric crooned. "Is someone working all the time?"

"Save the passive-aggressive lecture. It's one late night."

"You haven't been home before dark once this week."

"What are you, stalking me?"

"We work right across the street from each other. I notice things."

"And now you've graduated from noticing things to loitering on my doorstep?"

"I wanted to make sure you're okay. You haven't been at your desk when I've dropped by Velvet this week, and I've been busy, too, at the funeral home, handling some of the administrative stuff Bobby usually does. It's come at a decent time, though, in the middle of summer. We've been relatively death-free."

Now that my heart rate had slowed to normal, and Eric had provided a semi-reasonable explanation for his creepy behavior, I attempted to recover my usual cheer. "That's great!" I dropped my keys on the table next to the front door and slipped off my shoes, tucking them under the table, although that gave Eric an even greater height advantage. "How are Jill and—what's the baby's name again? Nicholas?"

"They're fine."

"I haven't had a chance to talk to the proud grandma. How's Lena enjoying her new role? What's the little dude look like?"

"Lena's over the moon, of course. And Nicholas looks like a baby. They all look the same to me. Blobby and alien and all..." He blinked and pursed his lips, clicking them wetly together. While I laughed at his impersonation, he returned his features to their normal positions. "Like newborn kittens, only not as cute. Because they're bald and have those creepy, wrinkly hands."

"Maybe at first, but—"

"Horty dragged me with her to the hospital to visit them, practically right after he was pulled from Jill's body. Good Lord, he was fresh." He stuck out his tongue and gagged. "I haven't seen him since. Haven't wanted to. But I've made sure I've had plenty to do anytime someone mentions a visit to Bobby's house. No thanks."

"I hope you do a better job of hiding your true feelings around everyone else. People can be a bit sensitive about their offspring, you know?"

"Yeah, yeah. I've kept my mouth closed and head down. Stop trying to change the subject, though. Something's not right with you."

"Shelly's been telling me that my whole life."

"Your replies to my texts have been curt."

"How can a text be curt? You ask me how I'm doing, I say, 'Fine,' or 'Busy.'"

"That's curt."

"I'm sorry I haven't had the thumb stamina to text back a dissertation on how fine and busy I am." I hung up my purse and led the way into the kitchen, where I fed the cat before considering my own dinner. Buster rewarded me with a hiss when I didn't move away from the dish fast enough after Eric set him down on the floor.

"Whoa. He's pissed at you."

"Well, I'm not too thrilled with him, either. He clawed the crap out of my favorite suede booties the other day."

"Another late night at the office?"

"That doesn't make it okay for him to be a jerk!"

"He's a cat. He doesn't need a reason."

"Exactly. It had nothing to do with my schedule."

"What's keeping you there so much, anyway?"

"Just… stuff. Trying to do a better job of knowing how things work and what things are called." And doing some preliminary print runs of my artwork.

"But you're okay?"

I uncorked a mostly empty bottle of wine with my teeth and drank directly from it. "Yes," I said, after a few swallows.

"You don't seem okay. You seem… pissy. Almost as pissy as Buster."

"I'm not a ray of sunshine after being ambushed on my dark front porch after a long-ass day? Where are my manners?"

"I don't know. I'd suggest we look for them under the couch, but…"

I flipped him the bird.

"When are you going to replace that thing, anyway? And holy cow. If your manners *were* anywhere close, they'd be pretty easy to spot in here. This place is freaking spotless! Do I smell bleach?"

"I cleaned. So sue me."

"So you don't have time to text me more than one word replies, but you have time to give this entire house a deep clean? That makes perfect sense. I don't—"

"What's it to you all of a sudden? Why don't you just go home, Eric?"

His smile faded. I'd have felt guilty if I hadn't been feeling so many other, stronger things. Resentment, frustration, restlessness, loneliness, exhaustion, homesickness, and sadness, to name a few. They overpowered the guilt. Well, almost.

"I'm sorry," I said with a sigh, draining the last of the wine and dropping the bottle in the glass recycling bin by the back door.

"Need a hug?" he asked, opening his arms.

I stared at a spot on his chest, one I knew felt pretty damn good, but I shook my head and turned my back to him. "Nope. I'm good. Just tired. And bitchy."

I heard his hands slap against his legs as he dropped his arms. "Okay, then. Well. I, uh… We're okay, though, right?"

"Mmm-hmm," I managed through clamped lips as I gripped the edge of the sink and stared out the window into the side yard.

"I'll leave you alone, then. Sorry if I came on too strong. I… Well, you know how I am." He stepped up behind me and gave my upper arms a quick, brotherly squeeze, then crossed the kitchen to the back door, saying goodbye and "Be good" to Buster on his way out.

The door clicked, and Buster emitted a belated half-meow before resuming his crunching.

When Eric's head passed by the kitchen window in front of me, I ducked down so he couldn't see my face. After a few seconds, I straightened to my full height again. A quick peek revealed he had already made it to the street, with his back to me, so I felt safe watching him go. Safe from him catching me, anyway. Not safe in any other way, though. Particularly mentally.

Eric was right: I had been avoiding him—big-time—since the whole finger-to-the-lips thing on his couch. I didn't know what to do about how that had made me feel. How *he* made me feel. How he *couldn't* make me feel that way.

In addition to dodging him and making everything around me spotless, I'd spent the majority of that week justifying and explaining my reactions to him. Of course I liked the guy. He was funny and warm and quirky… like Aunt Vel. Now that I knew the truth, it was obvious he was her son. I didn't know how the people who were around both of them every day, side-by-side, had never seen it.

And I'd loved Aunt Vel, so it stood to reason that I would… love… him, too. In a cousinly way. Of course. Those other rogue emotions were simply amplified by the surreal nature of my entire existence there. Loneliness, stress, and—yes— horniness were conspiring against me, and I was projecting my reactions to those things onto him, because he was the only person I regularly confided in. I was grateful to him for being a good friend. It was easy to get carried away and inter- pret gratitude and friendship as something more.

And I was sure that was all it was on his part, too. I should have never let Cath get into my head. She'd been screwing with me when she'd said at The Lobster Shack that Eric was in love with me. He was not. Of course! He was equally aware of how inappropriate that would be and, given what he'd known the whole time, wouldn't have allowed himself to go there.

But suppose he did. Or didn't have any control over it (as I didn't seem to have). If he were in love with me, I would know. Wouldn't I?

Ah, who was I kidding? The only thing I knew was that I didn't know anything.

Oh, and I knew one other thing: I had to get out of this town.

As Eric drove from my view, I slumped with my forearms on the edge of the sink, my eyes burning with tears I refused to shed. If only this house weren't already so stinkin' clean...

CHAPTER SEVENTEEN

"I'M sick of your excuses, Shell. I need my sister, and I need her now."

"Well, sorry. Your sister is too busy getting laid."

"Nice. Real nice."

"Oh, it is. Trust me. Not to rub it in, of course."

I clenched my teeth.

"And anyway, the highway goes both ways. Sounds like you need to get away from there more than I need to get away from here. Come down to Boston for a weekend."

"And stay where? My apartment is occupied, remember? Sounds like yours is, too."

"Hmm... yes," she replied, without a hint of regret. "You can always crash at Mom's."

I'd have laughed along with her, but I was having a hard time finding humor in anything right then. "I can't come down there anyway."

"Oh, yes. Busy and important business owner now. You almost let me forget for two seconds."

"What's your problem?"

"What's *your* problem? Wait. Don't answer that. I already

know. You're so stressed out by this massive gift bequeathed to you by your favorite aunt. And you need to get laid."

"Not everything is about sex, Shelly. Geez."

"Oh, so it's more of the second thing than the first thing."

"No. It's neither of those things. I miss my best friend and sister, and she's suddenly MIA in my time of need."

"Buh-ruther. Since when have you needed *me* for anything?"

"Since right now. Since... since..." My voice cracked, but I quickly pulled it together and muttered, "Stupid cell phone reception. You're cutting out. I have to go."

"Call me back on the landline!"

"No, it's late, anyway." I leaned to the side so the phone actually did cut out a few times. "Have fun this weekend with Dom. I'm sure I'll get to meet him *someday*. Hopefully before you're married."

"Whit!"

I tossed the phone onto the foot of the bed, where it dropped the call, then pulled my knees to my chest and rested my forehead against them.

I will not cry. I will not cry.

The bar of chocolate I'd put in the bedside table drawer around this time last month called to me. That was it. I was hormonal. And overwhelmed. And lonely. But I was also—yes —a strong, independent woman. With chocolate.

I reached over and pulled the candy from the nightstand, unwrapping and breaking off the next row of deliciousness along the scores. This was the good stuff, too. Not that fake-tasting, chemical-laden crap from a few states over. This was Swiss, melt-in-your-mouth, take-all-your-cares-away, better-than-any-sex-Shell's-having heaven.

While chewing, I stared down at my feet. Ugh. The patch job I'd done on my pedicure a couple of weeks ago looked terrible after several morning runs and consecutive days in closed-toed heels. I traded the chocolate bar for the clippers, polish remover, and cotton balls also stashed in the nightstand drawer, then chose an autumnal color to match my mood.

And why not? The bite of fall was already in the air each morning when I raced the sunrise. Folks had traded their BoSox hats for Pats jerseys. Bruins gear would join the fray in a few weeks. It made me more homesick than ever, seeing all that Boston apparel. This stupid state didn't even have its own professional teams; it had to poach ours. It stole everything.

I sniffled while stripping my toes of their summery turquoise paint—or what was left of it. Then I tossed the stained cotton balls on the floor, in the general direction of the wastepaper basket next to the dresser. As I was trimming my nails, collecting the clippings in my left hand, the lit-up screen of my cell phone caught my attention. I stared at it for a second, shocked I was able to get a call all the way down there at the end of the bed. Figuring it was my sister, calling to apologize for being such an insensitive, sex-starved jerk, I continued with my foot grooming and let it go to voice mail.

A few seconds later, the landline downstairs rang. I froze.

There was only one person who called that phone. He was as sweet as that chocolate bar in my nightstand and cared about me, even when I was a complete bitch to him. When he didn't get an answer on my cell phone, he called the landline, because he knew how crappy the service was in this house—in this town—and he wasn't going to let a stupid black hole in cell reception stop him from getting in touch.

The phone downstairs stopped after the fifth ring. Sighing, I stared at my now-dark mobile phone, then at my feet, then back at the phone.

In general, I prided myself on being a fairly straight

shooter. I didn't play games. And while I sometimes might have said one thing while thinking another, what I said was what I wanted to be the truth, and by voicing it, I was making a promise to myself to make it true. I wasn't being duplicitous; I was trying to drown out an uglier side of myself. So when I'd told Eric last night before he left that everything was fine between us, I meant it. At least, I wanted it to be true, and it was my way of vowing that it *would* be true... in time.

Because what was the alternative? He was my only friend here. I couldn't let some inappropriate, rogue hormones get in the way of that, could I? No. I could not, and I would not.

Before I could think too much about it, I nudged my cell phone closer with my foot, tapped the device to wake it up, and dialed the last known caller before activating the speaker phone.

He answered after only a ring and a half. "Hey! I just called you."

"I couldn't reach the phone."

"On the toilet?"

"No!"

"It happens. Nothing to be embarrassed about. Everybody poops."

"If you must know, I'm trimming my toenails."

"You should have stuck with the toilet cover story. Not as gross."

"What's up?"

"Nothing. What's up with you—other than shaving down your talons?"

I bit my lower lip to keep from laughing but failed.

"Ah! There she is!" he said, the gloat loud in his voice.

"Like I went anywhere."

"You've been in a funk for weeks."

"A lot on my mind."

"Tell me about it, then."

I deliberated for a second but decided against confiding anything, including the stuff I *could* talk about to him. The last thing I wanted was to be a downer. Instead, I continued clipping and said, "Nah. It's not worth dwelling on it. I'm a strong, independent woman, and I don't need—"

"What you need is to stop saying that over and over again like some kind of self-help mantra. If you truly believed it, you wouldn't have to say it all the time."

"I don't say it 'all the time.'"

"Yes, you do."

"Whatever." *Click... click... click.* "Anyway, maybe if I say it enough, I *will* believe it. Or better yet, I'll be it. Like Aunt Vel."

He sighed. "She might have put on a good front for you, but she also knew when to admit she needed support from friends and family. If you want to be strong, you have to admit when you're not."

Click... click... click.

"You also have to stop doing that while we're talking, or I'm going to barf."

"You drain bodily fluids from dead people and inject them with chemicals. But *this* grosses you out?"

"Yes. The sound… And then when one goes flying…"

"I'm catching them in my hand."

"That might be even more disgusting, somehow."

"Did you call for any particular reason, or…?"

"I can't remember now, I'm so totally wigged out."

"Would you like me to call you back?"

"No, I'd like you to take a break from *that* and talk to me."

"Well, aren't you demanding?"

He laughed. "I'm sorry. But seriously."

"Fine, fine. I'm finished now anyway." I set the clippers next to me on the bed. "Proceed." Looking down at the crescents of dead cells in my hand, I decide it *was* gross to be holding them, so I took them to the waste can, dropping them in as quietly as possible, along with the stray cotton I retrieved from the floor before the acetone-soaked balls left marks on the wood.

By the time I got back to bed, he was well into the original purpose of his call, how he'd thought long and hard about what he enjoyed doing and how to parlay that into a hobby— or a career. Then he stopped.

I checked to make sure we hadn't been cut off, and when I saw we were still connected, I moved the phone closer to the "hot zone" on the bed to be sure. As I rested it on one of the pillows, I said, "And?"

"This is the part where I might chicken out and not tell you, because I don't want you to laugh at me."

"Oh, c'mon. Give me some credit." Nevertheless, I steeled myself to think of sad or serious things, just in case, so I wouldn't hurt his feelings.

He sucked in a huge breath, then said, "I'd like to go to clown school."

Must. Not. Laugh.

War refugees.

Car wrecks.

Sick babies.

Cancer.

Terrorism.

Big, strapping Eric in a clown suit and face makeup, fumbling with balloon animals.

No, no, no! Climate change!

"You're trying not to laugh, aren't you?"

"Nope." But I could barely choke it out, because now Eric the Clown was stomping around my brain in his big, red, floppy shoes.

"I guess it's okay, because clowns are supposed to make people laugh. And…"

I held my breath, waiting for him to finish his permission for me to lose it.

"…I'm totally messing with you."

"OhthankGod!"

We laughed together, then he said, "But I had you going, huh?"

"I… I wanted to be supportive, but… oh, geez. Although the world does need clowns, so…"

"Does it? Does the world really need clowns?"

"Umm… maybe?"

"Not sure about that. They mostly freak people out."

"Spoken like a true Stephen King fan."

"Oh, gosh! That book traumatized me. But anyway…"

I scooted down on the pillow behind me and positioned my head closer to the one next to me that was holding the phone. "You would make a great clown, though, since you don't know how to be serious about anything."

"Okay, okay. I wanted to see how you'd react to something outlandish. You know, to determine if I could trust you with the truth."

"How'd I do?"

"Meh. I could tell you wanted to laugh at my dream."

"It wasn't your real dream!"

"But you didn't know that."

Before I could defend myself further, an image of what he must look like right now while teasing me—the drawing up of the lower lip, the crinkling of the chin, the twinkling of the eyes, the dimple in his left cheek—brought me up short. I took a deep breath. "Are you going to tell me the real answer, or what?"

He blew out a breath. "I'm not feeling it now. Maybe tomorrow? Come over and hang out?"

My heart stuttered in and out of rhythm (maybe I should get that checked out?), so I didn't respond right away.

"You could bring your art supplies and do your thing while I do mine."

"This 'thing' of yours is an indoor activity, then, I take it?"

"Most definitely. But we could set you up by the lake, if you want. Or if you're not in the mood to do that... Since it's supposed to be such a gorgeous day, we could take Vel's ashes up to the falls and... give her her final send-off."

I pictured the urn still on the mantle downstairs, and the old, familiar guilt punched me in the gut. "I do need to do that."

"Yes. *We* do."

"Is it wrong and selfish that I'm not ready?"

"No."

"Oh, good."

"Vel doesn't care. It was only a suggestion. We have a bit more time. Of course, if you wait too much longer, we'll have to hold off until spring. They close the trail in the late fall and winter. Icy and dangerous. Doesn't stop idiots from going up there. Every year, someone bites it."

"Yikes."

"'Yikes' is right. But that's not going to be you. Not if I can help it. I'd have to process your body, which isn't as great as it sounds. It would be horrible. Traumatic."

"Well, let's not think about it. I promise not to go up there in the winter. But... does it have to be tomorrow?"

"Nope."

"Okay."

"Does that mean you'll come over here and hang out, though?"

I sighed, not because I didn't want to, but because I *did* want to. A Saturday at Eric's sounded appealing… too appealing. So I tried to talk myself out of it. "I don't know. I leave Buster every day."

"He's a cat. That's what he prefers. In fact, the other day, he told me he loves how you guys don't have one of those suffocating relationships where you expect him to cuddle you all the time. He loves his Buster time."

I giggled in spite of—or maybe due to—my nerves.

His cheeky smile came through the phone loud and clear. "What do you say? I need an answer. Because if you're coming over, I need enough notice to clean the pee from around the toilets. It's Sharon's off-week."

"And you say I'm gross."

CHAPTER EIGHTEEN

SEEING the work area Eric had prepared for me went a long way toward dispelling the many doubts I'd had about spending my entire Saturday with him. As soon as I arrived at his house, he ushered me through to the sun room like a proud child who wanted to show his parents his clean room, and swept his arm toward the setup.

By the wall of windows, to take advantage of the natural light, sat a black metal easel. Next to the easel, he'd placed the table that normally rested in the middle of the room for dining or whatever else you did when you had access to a beautiful space like this that overlooked the sloping yard, rocks, and lake. Situated in front of the easel was a tall, padded swivel chair.

"It's not elaborate, but considering you're using a card table and a folding chair at Vel's, I figured it would be some-what of an improvement," he explained.

"It's very nice," was all I could manage—inadequate for sure—without gushing and throwing myself into his arms. For a platonic hug, of course.

Fortunately, he seemed fine with my subdued reaction and

nodded with satisfaction. "Excellent." He set down the portfolio and plastic tote of supplies he'd carried in for me. "Before you get started, though, I have coffee and pastries. Gotta have fuel, right?"

I followed him through the living room and up the steps into the kitchen, all vestiges of dread now gone. I was eager to get started, inspired by that room and that view. Ideas, images, and specific hues and their names flitted through my head, where I filed them away for later.

I hadn't felt a thrill like that in months. Sure, I'd still been working on my illustrations, but it was more out of habit than an overwhelming desire to create. This burbling brew of intellect and emotion was producing a giddiness that prompted an overwhelming urge to hop on Eric's back for a playful piggyback ride to the coffeemaker.

I resisted, though. Because... weird.

Instead, I drank my coffee and picked at, then ate, the flaky pastry I'd selected from the bakery box on the butcher block. After our strangely silent but comfortable breakfast, I sat back in my chair and said, "Now you have to tell me how *you're* going to be passing the time today."

"I thought you'd never ask."

"I didn't realize you needed a written invitation. I would have printed one up at Velvet before coming over."

"I could tell you were over there thinking about... stuff that artists think about. I didn't want to interrupt."

"Well, I'm completely focused on you now."

And I was. For the second time since he'd met me on the gravel driveway, I noticed how eager and happy he looked. His eyes were bright, his hair was neatly combed and still damp from the shower, and his face shone clean and smooth around his seemingly permanent smile. I'd seen him this groomed before, of course, in a suit and tie for a funeral. But although he was dressed much more casually today, barefoot and in jeans and a t-shirt, covered by an unbuttoned flannel shirt to keep out the early morning chill, he looked more pulled-together than I'd ever seen him. Anticipatory. Ready. At yet the same time, he was completely relaxed and at peace.

Leaning toward me, he said, "Video games."

"Video games," I repeated, trying to catch up and wondering how I was suddenly so lost and behind in a conversation that had only just begun.

"Video games."

When he simply grinned proudly at me, I said, "Okay. Um, care to elaborate? You're going to play video games today? Like, all day? Not that there's anything wrong with that." I sat up and scooted toward the front of my chair so I could rest my elbows on the table, like he was doing. A millimeter of wood peeked between our knuckles as our loose fists faced off on the surface.

If he had noticed how close our hands now were, he gave no indication. "Yes. That's Phase One."

"Phase One?"

"Uh-huh. Phase One is to rediscover my love for video games. Playing them, mostly."

"And Phase Two is?"

"Studying them. Figuring out why my favorite ones are so addictive. Paying attention to the writing and world-building. Then Phase Three is developing my own."

"Oh!" I said, catching his enthusiasm. "That's cool. Like, writing the code, though? I had no idea you—"

"Yeah. The code, the story, the dialogue... All of it."

"Don't they usually have massive teams of people who contribute to one game?"

He shrugged. "Yeah. Sometimes. And I can't do everything. Artwork and animation aren't my thing. But I figure I can get it far enough along, concept-wise, to pitch it to a company that might be interested in buying it."

"Wow. That's... that's really... ambitious."

"It's only for fun."

"And you already have an idea?"

Flopping backward, he said, "I have so many ideas! But first I need to reacquaint myself with the process; get a better grip on modern gaming. I majored in mortuary science in college..."

"Obviously," I said, barely holding back the snicker.

"...and although I minored in information technology, I had to take mostly practical classes. I did sneak in a couple of coding and game design courses, too, but all of that technology is outdated—probably was before I even had my diploma. I'll have to get caught up on where the industry is now." He laced his fingers together and rested his palms against his belly. "Easier said than done, right? But it'll be fun. And interesting. And fun. Did I mention 'fun'? I haven't done something like this, just for me, just for fun, in... well, ever."

"I'd say you're overdue, then."

"Tell me about it. So? What do you think?"

"I think you're a dark horse." He tilted his head and scrunched his eyebrows together, so I explained, "When I suggested you find something to do, solely for yourself, you were at such a loss. You didn't want to talk about it. You didn't seem like you *could* talk about it. You said you had no idea."

He looked down at his hands. "I didn't know. Which was embarrassing. I bitch and moan about the funeral home, but when someone asks me what I'd rather do, I have no clue. And it was terrifying to face that, that I could be so clueless about myself, that I could have, um, buried my interests and personality so far down that I couldn't answer such a basic question to save my life. Like, what sort of loser allows that to happen?" He looked up and smiled, but it faltered.

Blinking away sympathetic (annoying) tears, I swallowed and answered, "Not a loser. An amazing, selfless guy."

He slapped his hands onto his knees and pushed against them as he stood. "Well, this 'amazing, selfless guy' has some gaming to do. And I know someone else who could brush some cobwebs off her passion, too."

I stood and grinned across the corner of the table at him. "Why the heck are we hanging around here, then?"

Maybe it was bizarre that I'd accepted an invitation to someone else's house so that we could spend the majority of our time together *not* together, pursuing completely separate interests, in completely separate parts of the house, and only surfacing once in a while to eat or hydrate or... do what you needed to do after you'd eaten and hydrated. But it seemed perfectly normal and natural and right. It was the first time I'd ever been totally at ease around Eric. Maybe because I hadn't been around him the whole time.

When I took up residence in the sun room, he retreated to one of his spare bedrooms, where he'd set up a gaming computer he'd bought in Portland last week. I checked it out during one of my breaks, and it was impressive. He hadn't gone about this half-assed. He showed me the game he was trying first—some medieval, multi-player, interactive experience that looked complicated (and interesting, if you're into that)—but I didn't linger. Watching someone else play video games was the epitome of boring to me. Plus, I didn't want to make him self-conscious.

We broke at noon for sandwiches and chips, but both of us

were still foggy, in our own worlds. My world included whimsical boats on a sparkling lake and the back of a long-haired, brown-skinned woman holding a straw hat at her side as she watched the watercraft float by. His world featured medieval knights and hooded mercenaries. And possibly some scantily clad damsels in distress, if I had to guess. Back to "work" we both went after exchanging sheepish smiles and admitting we didn't want to lose our respective mojos.

Hours later, I hopped down from my stool, having finished my third large-scale sketch, to stretch my stiff back and shoulder muscles. My stomach growled to remind me it had been a long time since lunch. Outside the windows, the light had turned gray with a golden edge. At some point, the over-head light in this room had come on automatically, either on a timer or activated by motion sensor. I barely registered it. I cared more about deciding what color to make my latest empowered woman's dress and shoes. (Russet to match the leaves on the tree above her.)

Since Eric was nowhere to be seen or heard, I packed up my supplies and slid my sketches into my portfolio, zipping it closed. I carried my stuff out to my car, then slipped back into the house. I didn't want to interrupt my host, who was obviously enjoying himself, so I took advantage of this rare opportunity to explore (a.k.a., "snoop") without him around.

Unfortunately, there wasn't not much to see down there. He'd explained in the past that he didn't keep pictures of Vel in the public parts of his house. "Not that I entertain people... ever. But I do have a housekeeper. And Horty hangs out here sometimes. When I'm expecting anyone, I try to remember to put the pictures in my room in a dresser drawer. Just in case."

"Wow. You're dedicated to keeping your parents' secret," I said.

He shrugged. "You do what you have to do, I guess."

I guess. The more I learned about Vel's secret life, the more I wanted to know. At the same time, the more I learned, the angrier I got on Eric's behalf. He'd been robbed of not only a normal childhood but of the public acknowledgment of his own mother's love and affection.

That's effed up, Aunt Vel.

I said that out loud to her urn after Eric revealed to me on the phone—in a heartbreaking, matter-of-fact fashion—that the only family vacation he'd ever gone on was with the Doolans. "We went to Hilton Head for Fourth of July. It was cool. Except for the part where I got stung in the privates by a jellyfish and Bobby laughed at me and called me Jelly Junk throughout the rest of high school. Still calls me that every once in a while, in fact. But whatever. I'd totally do the same to him. And it's funny now."

If that was what he needed to believe, then who was I to argue otherwise? I hung up and gave Aunt Vel's ashes an earful, though.

A framed picture from that vacation rested on an end table in Eric's living room. I studied it now: Jelly Junk, Hortense, and Bobby standing with their arms around each other, hair salty-wet, bare, tan teenagers' shoulders sandy, the ocean ebbing and flowing behind them.

That was Eric's best summer vacation memory. Being a fifth wheel on his cousins' trip and earning a humiliating nickname in one of the most painful of ways.

Aunt Vel and Larry had been so selfish, so determined to keep their stupid affair—an affair that everyone would eventually have gotten over and forgotten all about—secret that they put it above their own son's happiness. That wasn't the Aunt Vel I knew. It, frankly, baffled. Like the person I knew hadn't been her at all.

"She wasn't selfish," Eric defended her once, on the way

home from Portland. "She was protecting me from the unbearable scrutiny this town would have inflicted on all of us if the truth came out. Gayle was a local sweetheart. Homecoming Queen and everything. And dying young only made her more of a saint in their eyes."

"Then Larry and Aunt Vel should have moved away from here, moved you to a place where nobody knew you or Gayle or anything about the marvelous Mulligans."

"My dad's livelihood is here. And so was Vel's."

"Only because he brought her here. They have dead people and print shops all over the world, you know?"

"Vel didn't want that. She loved this town. That might be hard for someone like you to believe, but..." He said it kiddingly but with finality, a way of neatly closing the discussion. Not a huge fan of conflict, I let it go, but I'd thought a lot about it since then.

The fact was, Larry could have made a living off the dead anywhere. There was no danger of an undertaker's line of work disappearing due to technology or downturns in the economy. Their job security was as tight as it came. Becoming more in demand, no doubt, since it wasn't exactly the most popular choice of professions, yet there were more people than ever in this world... and we all had to die sometime.

They could have settled in a sleepy town in... in... Wyoming. Somewhere, anywhere, they could have provided their only son with a normal life. (Well, normal-ish, since, let's face it, as long as your dad was a mortician, your life wasn't going to be exactly normal.)

Perhaps then Eric would have been allowed to be and do whatever he wanted. He wouldn't have had to get a degree in mortuary science from... I peered at the only other photo down here, one of him in his cap and gown next to Larry, both of them squinting into the sun beside a brick pillar with a green-and-white sign. Mount Ida College.

I wondered if Aunt Vel had taken that picture, or if she had been there at all. Wouldn't have wanted to clue anyone in to the truth, would she? But to miss seeing your only child graduate from college? That would suck, even if he were receiving a diploma in a field he wasn't exactly thrilled about. It was still a major accomplishment and milestone.

Wait a second.

Mount Ida College. That… that was in Boston!

I picked up the framed photo to look more closely at it. Quickly, I did the math to figure out what year that would have been. Seven, eight years ago? I'd still been an undergrad at BU.

I recalled one of the rare times Aunt Vel had torn herself away from her business and left it in someone else's capable hands—most likely Dave's, at that time—to come down for a visit. A short one. Like a long weekend. We'd met for lunch on Sunday, before she had to head back here.

The details were fuzzy. It had been a while ago. And, honestly, I probably hadn't been the best company, as it was the end of the spring semester, and I was tired from "studying for finals." But I did recall that time. She'd seemed amused by my exhaustion, wistful, as if she were remembering her younger days. Then I'd asked her why she hadn't come back to Boston to live, move her business south, where her family was, and she'd said something about people needing her in Maine and "family" being a fluid term.

At the time, I'd dismissed it as Aunt Vel being Aunt Vel. I'd also attributed her explanation to the usual apathy toward siblings to whom she was never close. It made sense she had friends in Morris she loved like family.

Or *were* family.

"Man," I muttered, still staring at Eric's graduation picture but focusing my attention on Larry, puffed up and proud of the young life he was railroading and ruining. I was sure he didn't see it that way, but I did. He'd sacrificed his son's happiness to save his precious reputation. "Disgusting."

"Well, I wouldn't go that far," a voice right behind me said.

I flinched and fumbled with the framed photo, juggling it in startle-numbed fingers. Before it could tumble to the floor, Eric caught it and returned it safely to its original spot, opposite the matching end table holding the Hilton Head snapshot.

"I was—"

"At least I'd grown out of my gawky phase by then. Oh, yeah... you should have been around for that. Add frequent drunkenness to the equation and you get some interesting stuff. You think I'm awkward now?"

"No, I don't."

"Yes, you do." He smiled gently. "Because I am. I just spent thirteen hours playing—and beating, I'd like to add—a video game set in the fourteenth century. I half-expected to come down here and have you serve me some stew and pour me some mead. Then I'd call you wench and sexually harass you, because that's my right as a white, heterosexual man."

Suddenly, I realized how close we were, close enough that I could see the stubble on his face and smell his laundry detergent. But I was pinned in by the table and the sofa, so until he moved, there was no way to put any distance between us.

I stared down at the picture. "I was, uh, thinking about... what your college classes must have been like. All those bodies..."

"I grew up around dead folks, so by then it wasn't as big of a deal. Granted, I'd never touched or manipulated one, much less someone I'd known when they were alive, but... It was easy to spot those of us in the program who were there because that's what our families had been doing since forever." His eyes trailed down to my lips, which I had to concentrate not to reflexively lick. "Nothing fazed us. We gave the cadavers names and acted like what we were learning to do was as normal as learning how to... to..."

"Balance an equation or diagram a sentence?"

"Exactly. Or something like that."

"Mount Ida, huh? Private. Fancy."

"Willing to take my dad's money, ignore my abysmal SAT scores, and overlook the obvious fact that a middle-aged man had written my entrance essay. 'We'll take good care of him, Mr. Mulligan. Make that check out to... Actually, let's set up automatic withdrawals to make things easier for you.'"

Looking at him now and going from memory, I said, "You don't look all that happy in that picture."

"I was hungover as hell." He chuckled, but his eyes remained sad. "Dad and Vel were cramping my style with their visit."

"So she *was* there? How'd that work? How did you guys explain that to the rest of the family?"

He cleared his throat and stepped back, sliding one hand in his pocket. "Did I mention I was weird?"

"Maybe a few times."

"Well, when you're slightly off-kilter, you can make requests that might raise eyebrows, but nobody calls you on them. They've learned it's easier to go with it and chalk it up to the person's usual eccentricities. I invited the whole town to my college graduation. Hardly anyone took me up on it, of course. But a few non-family members did. Vel blended in with them. And since she had family in the city, nobody thought twice about it; it gave her the opportunity to catch up with people for the weekend."

"We were her... *cover*?"

"Not really. She legitimately wanted to see you guys."

"I'm sure."

"But it was also convenient."

I shook my head and looked up at the ceiling. "Wow. Everything. Everything was a lie."

"No, it wasn't. She loved you."

"Because she was allowed to treat me like family in public. She got her mothering fix."

"Maybe," he conceded. "But that didn't make her love for you any less real."

I dropped my head, then raised my shoulders up to my ears and smiled ruefully, waving toward the graduation picture again. "Anyway. I wasn't calling *you* disgusting."

"I didn't think you were." He moved toward the kitchen but held me where I was with a raised hand. "Relax. I'm going to throw a couple pizzas in the oven and grab some drinks for us. Then I want to hear all about your afternoon."

"There's not much to tell," I said to his retreating back.

"Show me, then."

He was no longer in the room for me to argue with, but I remained immobile for a while, debating whether to comply. Vanity eventually won out.

It had been a long time since someone close to me had shown any interest in my "art stuff." Not since Aunt Vel passed away, in fact. I suppose this was technically the second time Eric had seen my work, but the first time I'd been too... indisposed... to care much. Now, I chewed my bottom lip while his eyes roamed the three illustrations, spread out, side-by-side, propped against the back of the sofa.

When he said nothing for several seconds, I explained,

"These are rough. Mock-ups, if you will. I'll add some shading here." I pointed to a spot next to my boat-watching beauty. "Give it some dimension and depth."

He rubbed his chin, then turned a slow, sheepish smile my way. "I can barely draw stick people, so… these are fantastic."

I blushed. "Whatever. They're doodles."

"Please. False modesty is so gross."

"It's not false modesty!"

He wrapped an arm around my shoulder and pulled me to his side. "I like these. A lot. But I couldn't tell you why they're good or how they could be better or any of that. My appreciation is purely instinctual."

Relieved he didn't feel the need to critique simply for the sake of providing input, I wrapped my arms around his waist and hugged him back. "That's cool. 'I like them' is music to an artist's ears." I let go of him and leaned forward to gather the pages.

He stopped me with a gentle hand to my lower back. "Leave them. For a while. They're… soothing."

"Where are we going to sit?"

He plopped down on the floor in front of the fireplace, still facing the sofa, with the coffee table between him and the drawings. One knee up, he propped his elbow on it. "You should be used to this. Pizza will be ready in a few, anyway."

"All right."

I came to join him on the floor, but I'd been staring at the drawings all day, so they didn't hold my attention as well as they once did. Suddenly wiped out, I reclined against the rug, my spine popping as its vertebrae fell into line. I closed my eyes against the sensation and inhaled the scent of baking dough and garlicky tomato sauce wafting from the kitchen. My stomach gurgled.

"Keep it down over there," Eric said. "Your art is speaking to me."

"What's it saying? Because I still need to figure out what words of inspiration to put with each of those."

I waited, keeping my eyes shut, despite the real risk of falling asleep like this with my feet crossed at the ankles and my hands resting on my abdomen. I suspected I looked like the one of the people Eric regularly hung out with in the Mulligan basement. But I didn't care. This felt good.

After several minutes, his voice startled me from a warm doze.

"Boat girl."

"Yes?"

"She's a weekender. So... not something as trite as 'TGIF,' or whatever, but something deeper. Like, 'Weekends are for watching.' Oh, God, no. Don't use that. That's horrible."

I giggled toward the ceiling.

"Hang on, hang on. I'm still thinking." Silence; then, "'Let your worries set sail.'"

"Not bad."

"Or how about just, 'Float on'?"

"I like that better. Simple, short, sweet. Open to interpretation."

"Float on," he repeated softly.

I do believe I will.

CHAPTER NINETEEN

SIX WEEKS LATER, the leaves were slightly more orange, red, and yellow, and the skies were much grayer, but life felt lighter, somehow. I'd spent my Saturday at home, cleaning, baking pumpkin bars, and cuddling with Buster, then at Velvet, marketing the completed and finalized art I'd been neglecting in my push to produce new pieces. However, I'd promised Eric I would come by his place after dinner to make sure he was still alive. "I've heard stories about these people who play video games for hours on end and... and die!" he'd said to me on the phone earlier.

I'd laughed at his horrified tone. "Set a timer and make yourself get up and walk around, use the bathroom, get a drink of water."

"It would be easier if you were here to remind me."

"Sorry. You're going to have to attempt functioning by yourself. I have other stuff to do."

"Do it here."

"I've been there every weekend. I need some alone time."

"You're sick of me."

He said it kiddingly, so I played along. "Yes. I'm absolutely sick of you and your awesome house and your awesome food and your hilarious suggestions for my artwork text."

"I still think, 'Have some cheese with your whine' and 'Say it, don't spray it' were winners."

"Close runners-up."

"Then come by for dinner. You have to eat. And you said my food was awesome."

"Are you going to want to cook, though?"

"I busted out the slow cooker. Single man's best friend."

"I see." When he told me the stuffed peppers would be ready at seven, I couldn't resist. I loved stuffed peppers. Something told me he already knew that. Something told me he knew many things I'd never told him, things someone *else* had told him about me.

It was merely a theory I had, based on a few uncanny instances of intuition on his part: delivering my favorite flowers after I'd nursed him through his collision injuries (Lynda, my ass); maintaining a healthy (or unhealthy, depending on how you looked at it) stock of my favorite frozen treats at his house; mentioning my favorite movie genre before all others when listing our options; personalizing the streaming music to suggest and play my favorite songs and artists... It couldn't all be coincidence. Two people as different as we were couldn't have *that* much in common. Could we? Or was it that we weren't as different as I thought?

Either way, I wasn't complaining. As far as I could tell, Aunt Vel hadn't told him anything too personal. Seemed like the things he knew all fell under the heading "Creature Comforts"; things she might have guessed I'd need or want after she was gone: good music, funny movies, delicious food, pretty flowers. Surely, she hadn't given him advice on how to woo his own cousin. That would have been... unseemly.

Then again, who knew what had been going through that

woman's mind? I'd finally admitted to myself that I had no clue, and I hadn't known her half as well as I'd thought I did.

And that was part of why I'd kept my distance this weekend. Sure, I legitimately had things to do other than watch the boats go by and scratch graphite onto flattened, bleached wood pulp. But one of those things was to take a step back after realizing how easily he and I had fallen into this comfortable routine and how much I looked forward to it during the week. Because that couldn't be good.

Last week I'd prayed for someone to die on Thursday or Friday so Eric would be busy this weekend and force me to spend some time alone. I didn't want to have to make the difficult decision myself. But Morris's population was holding steady—growing, in fact, since I'd heard the shop clerk at Lynda's, Monique, had *finally* had that overdue baby. Which reminded me... I needed to drop by the print I'd made and framed for her daughter's nursery.

Anyway. Where was I? Oh, yes. Stuffed peppers. They were amazing. As was the company at dinner, although Eric had talked about first-person shooter games for a ridiculously long time when I first arrived. The subject matter might not have been the most interesting, but his delivery was typically hilarious, complete with sound effects, so it didn't matter what he was talking about. Seeing him so animated and passionate about something was definitely the bright spot in my day.

But as he placed the last dish in the dishwasher, and I deposited into the trash can the disposable cleaning wipe I'd used on the table and counters, I forced myself to turn to my host and say, "Well, thanks for the food. It was marvelous, as always. But I have to be going."

His crestfallen expression almost made me say, "Just kidding," but I held steady.

Must be strong.

"Why? You just got here."

Good question. I chose the answer meant for him, not me. "Because I'm tired."

"Then stay here and relax."

"And the weather's supposed to be nice tomorrow."

"Yes?"

I fingered the edge of the butcher block and mumbled, "I was wondering if you'd be up for a hike."

"A hike?" He rubbed his chin, considering it. "I guess I could use some exercise and fresh air."

Raising my eyes and widening them, I tried to channel some of the enthusiasm he'd showed during our dinner conversation. "Yeah! And... you, know... Maybe we could..."

He held his breath, his lips parted.

"...take care of Aunt Vel's ashes," I finished.

After a brief deflation, during which he exhaled and inhaled again, he smiled encouragingly. "Ah. A hike. To the falls. With the ashes. Right. Of course."

Suddenly self-conscious, I babbled, "I guess it's time. I don't know. It seems like it's expected. Mom keeps asking me if I've done it. If she wants it done so friggin' bad, why doesn't she trade her Manolos for sneakers and go up there her own damn self?"

"Fair question. Did you ask her that?"

"No. Like a cornered teenager, I lied and said it was done. So now I have to do it."

He cocked an eyebrow and raised one side of his mouth. "How's she going to know? It's not like she's coming for a visit anytime soon. Right?"

"No," I grumbled, voicing part of what I'd been fretting about all day during my vigorous scrubbing and other solitary tasks. "Nobody wants to come up here and visit me. It's like

I've been banished from the family, sent up here to take care of this remote, unwanted part of the empire. Out of sight, out of mind."

"That's not true."

"Isn't it? That's how everyone treated Aunt Vel, too. And now I've taken up the torch. Only it's more like a... a... match that keeps burning my fingers, and I have to continuously light a new one off the old one."

He stepped around the island, and I walked into his chest. While he hugged me, he said, "You're so broody all of a sudden. What's up with that?"

My instinct was to pull back and laugh at myself. With anyone else, I would have. But his embrace disarmed me. I pressed my forehead against the front of his shirt and said to his breastbone, "I told you, I'm tired."

"You were fine at dinner and during cleanup. Then it was like someone flipped a switch. Where is that pesky switch, anyway?" He ran his hands up and down my back, then around to my sides, his fingers scurrying, pausing here and there, pretending to search for my "brood button" but mostly only managing to tickle me.

"Stop it!" I said between giggles, but I didn't attempt to escape.

He continued, muttering under his breath. "Not there. Nope. It's gotta be here somewhere, though."

A brush against my ribs sent me flinching forward. "You're going to make me pee."

"Well, that would be nasty... but funny." He repeated the motion to recreate the original reaction and test my bladder control. Only this time, when I spasmed, his pinkie grazed my nipple, which responded spectacularly and obviously.

Both of us froze.

He cleared his throat. "Uh, I'm sorry. I—"

"No, it's... It's okay."

I should have stepped back. I should have taken several steps back. I should have stepped all the way to the front door, collected my jacket and purse, then stepped on the gas in my car to take me home. Well, not my car. And not my home. But the closest things I had to them.

I didn't do any of those things. Instead, I stared at the pulse in Eric's throat and listened to my own blood whooshing in my ears, mimicking the dishwasher behind me. The roar intensified when he swallowed hard, his Adam's apple bobbing before my eyes, and nudged the same spot again with his knuckle so both it and its twin stood up, begging to be recognized through my bra and soft cotton tee. I closed my eyes and focused on the delightful tingling there and much lower.

His audible breathing stirred my hair as a warmth engulfed my entire left breast when he placed his palm against it. I tilted my head back and sighed. Newly formed whiskers teased against my chin as he tentatively, hesitantly brushed his mouth close to—but not yet fully against—mine. I parted my lips slightly, a not-so-subtle invitation he readily accepted.

And all I could think for the next several seconds was how much I wanted this, how much I needed this, how much I'd craved any physical contact that could remind me someone cared about me and wanted me, too. This would definitely do.

He transferred his hand from my breast to the small of my back, pulling me closer to him. I rested my forearms on his shoulders and my hands in the back of his hair, standing on my tiptoes to intensify the kiss, to smash my lips against his, to thrust my tongue into his mouth. He backed me against the dishwasher. Its steam dampened my shirt, which clung to my lower back and butt.

Now that he'd gotten the idea how deeply I wanted him to

kiss me, I let go of his head and ran my hands between his shirt and chest, marveling at how warm and soft he felt against my palms, yet how firm he was when I pressed harder.

But then… then… my brain caught up to everything else. And it shot a series of pesky reminders to the rest of me, the loudest of which was one word: "Cousin."

With a sound that was a cross between a whimper and a moan, I wrenched my lips from his and gasped, "Oh, God."

He mistook it for an exclamation of rapture and tried to chase down my mouth again, but I pulled my head back farther and gasped, "This is wrong!"

His blinked accelerated, from lazy to rapid, as he stared down into my face. "Huh?" he finally grunted.

"This… We're… We can't do this."

"We can. We are."

"But we shouldn't."

My hands reappeared from under his shirt and flew to my hair, which I raked with my fingers as I ducked away from him to the other side of the kitchen. "We… We're family. Cousins."

He rolled his eyes and did his own hasty hair pat-down but didn't attempt to adjust or hide any other evidence of our impulsive kiss—or his arousal. I looked away, at a rogue grain of rice on the kitchen tiles.

"No, we're not," he said.

"Legally."

"Not even legally."

"But—"

"There's no such thing as an adopted aunt. She wasn't related to you by blood."

"But in my mind—"

He groaned. "Whitney, I love you for your mind, but I wish it would shut the fuck up for once."

In spite of my misery, I laughed. "Me, too." The hopeless-ness of the situation quickly stifled my rueful chuckles and made me want to cry. Or puke. Or both. "I have to go," I said, already halfway to the door.

If he followed, he reconsidered before catching up to me.

Good. That was really for the best.

CHAPTER TWENTY

LOGICALLY, I understood that Eric and I weren't technically related. We shared no DNA whatsoever. But there was still a familial connection, one I couldn't ignore, no matter how much I might have wanted to. And I was disturbed by how much I did want to.

It didn't help that he wasn't as conflicted as I was. Maybe it was because he had a more logical, scientific mind. Maybe he pictured our genetic material running parallel, never inter-secting, and that was good enough for him. But I saw other things, things that reminded me so much of my aunt that they sometimes made breathing difficult. Like the way his eyes sparkled when he was teasing me. Or the forced patience in his voice when he was trying to persuade me to see things his way, followed by the sarcastic chuckle when I stubbornly continued to state my case. She was family. And he was a part of her. My deductive reasoning couldn't get past that.

A few more kisses like the one in his kitchen, though, and I wouldn't have any brain cells left with which to reason. He had nearly short-circuited my motherboard.

Thinking about it now, I lay in bed while the rest of the

day marched obliviously on without me. My hand reenacts the contact with my breast, but it's not the same. Until I remember how he tasted.

A moan, equal parts frustration and lust, escaped my lips. I buried my hand under my pillow and clamped my eyes shut more tightly, as if I could get away from my own thoughts that way.

"Stupid, idiotic, horny, dumb moron," I grumbled to myself. "Pull yourself together."

While I was plotting what huge cleaning job I could tackle to keep my mind off things (power-washing the back deck sounded sufficiently consuming), the doorbell rang. I wish I could say I was surprised. But it was past ten o'clock, and I hadn't expected to be left alone after last night's disaster. I'd hoped, but I hadn't expected it.

Well, I wasn't answering the door. Screw that. Screw *him*.

Wait!

Strike that.

Not. Gonna. Do. That.

I was going to ignore him, though. I was going to stay in this warm cocoon until he went away. Maybe I could be a hide-in-bed kinda gal, after all. Time to see how that strategy worked.

I was so exhausted from my fitful, nightmare-filled sleep that I actually dozed off between knocks and phone trills and bells and buzzes. Therefore, I was shocked to be awakened by the smell of coffee and a loud "GET UP!" coming from the foot of my bed.

Despite recognizing the voice, I quaked under the covers, more from shock than from any actual fear for my safety. With the quilt over my head, I shouted back, "GET OUT!"

"No. I brought coffee."

"You can't fix everything with coffee."

"Yes, you can. Take it from a drunk: coffee fixes everything."

"You need to leave. And set your key by the front door." I flipped the covers back to reveal only my head. "I can't believe you let yourself in, uninvited!"

"I was worried about you."

"Bullshit. You're here to bully me."

He laughed and set the paper cup with the emblazoned curvy "M" on my nightstand, where it steamed provocatively. Like the dishwasher against my lower back last night.

I blushed.

Eric sipped his hot beverage as if he didn't have a care in the world other than a burnt tongue (which he received, judging by his wince). I waited for him to either leave or refute my accusation. Preferably the former.

Finally, after staring me down for a few seconds, he smiled indulgently and said, "C'mon, Whitney. It would be a shame for us to deny each other the awesomeness that is our friend-ship because we got a little carried away one time. So, no, I'm not here to bully you or to try to convince you to pull back those covers and invite me in there with you, as amazing as that looks."

"Excuse me?"

"I said I'm *not* going to ask for that."

"You'd be disappointed anyway."

"I figured. I came here to apologize."

"This is an interesting start."

"I brought coffee!" He waved at my untouched cup. "You know you want it."

I did. Badly. Among other things. Still. That was why he had to leave me alone. There was obviously something seri-ously wrong with me. I was like one of those trashy people on daytime TV. You know, the ones who have their babies' DNA test results read in front of a studio audience, then participate in hair-pulling fights with their cousins… to compete for the affection of… their cousins? The only thing saving me from that scenario was that Hortense wouldn't fight me for Eric. Because she was normal and didn't have sexual feelings for her family members.

In response to his clever double-speak, I glared at him and said, "You're having way too much fun with this."

He drew himself up and assumed a snooty tone. "On the contrary, m'lady. But one must laugh at one's misfortunes, or one will sink into the depths of despair. Or worse, the depths of a bottle."

I pointed at him. "Don't put that on me. Don't threaten me with your lost sobriety if I don't… whatever."

He rolled his eyes. "I'm not. It was only an example. Sheesh. Listen." At the windows not blocked by my bed, he pulled open the curtains. Glorious suns streamed into the room, illuminating dancing dust motes. He sneezed but didn't let it distract him. Nor did he wait for my courtesy blessing. "It's a beautiful day out there. One of the last ones like it before the rain and the snow… and the dead people… take over. Winter is coming, you know?" He wiggled his eyebrows at me.

"You've been playing too many medieval video games and binge-watching too many shows."

"Shows? Sweetheart, I've read every single one of those books. Twice."

"Nerd."

He stuck out his tongue.

Oh. That tongue…

I squirmed under the blankets and wished I had a rubber band on my wrist I could snap every time I thought something depraved like that.

"Anyway," Eric continued. "Winter *is* coming. Which is why we need to go on that hike, like we planned, and scatter Vel's ashes, like she wanted."

Vel. I was hardly feeling receptive to her wishes right then. Look at the mess she'd gotten me into. Yes, <u>she</u>. This wasn't about my hormones or strange sexual proclivities. This is about her keeping a secret from *me,* her favorite niece, and railroading me into coming here, then briefing her love child with information about me so that he knew exactly what to do and say to make me his best friend.

What she couldn't have predicted was how vulnerable I'd be, on the heels of my breakup with James, and how—like a dummy—I'd start to have big-time feelings for her big galoot of a son. Of course, this could all have been avoided if she'd only confided in me.

"I have a son. He's tall, dark, and handsome, but slightly damaged and somewhat odd, thanks to his father and me and our selfish deception. Good thing he's not your type at all. Because he's off-limits, being that he's your cousin. Anyway. I hope you'll be the best of friends. But nothing more. Oh, and here's the deed to... everything."

"Gee, thanks, Aunt Vel! And thanks for the heads up, too. You're right. I'm not at all into the tall, solid, rugged-yet-boyishly handsome type with the great sense of humor. Oh, wait... Yes, I am. Because my artistically gifted boyfriend is going to dump my ass when I have to move away from him to run your print shop, and frankly, it gets old when a guy sings everything to you. Life isn't a musical. I longed for a conversation that didn't involve three-part harmony... all sung by the same person at different times. So Eric makes for a great change. Also, I'm so horny and lonely right now, the only 'type' I have is 'warm' and 'breathing.' He ticks those boxes and so many more. But thanks for warning me about the ground rules so I'll never allow myself to go there. Whew."

"What do you say?" Eric asked now, backlit by the window.

"Go away."

He sighed. "Hey. I'm sorry, okay? I'm sorry. I— It was an accident." When I raised a skeptical eyebrow, he explained, "The nipple... thing."

At the mere mention of the n-word, both of mine contracted against my flannel pajama top. I nearly spontaneously combusted. Then he'd have two sets of ashes to scatter over the falls.

He continued, "It was an innocent brush-up. At first. But then... it was so... responsive."

Yanking the covers an inch or two higher, to make sure I wasn't revealing my breasts' treachery, I snapped, "Okay, enough."

"No, really. I—" He cleared his throat, and the sparkled returned to his eyes as he struggled to maintain a straight face. "'Boing!' None of the nude bodies I've seen lately do that. I'd almost forgotten—"

"You're sick."

"I'm only trying to show you that this is a comedy, not a tragedy."

My sex life was most definitely a tragedy.

Huffing like an indignant asthmatic, I pointed a finger at him. Not the finger I wanted to point toward the ceiling, but my index finger. "There were parts of you that were doing some boinging of their own, you know. It wasn't just me."

He laughed, which splashed his drink on his hand. Hissing, he transferred the cup to his other fist so he could wipe the hot liquid onto his jeans. "I didn't say it was. In fact, I'm taking full responsibility. It was my house, and I'm the one who kept poking the... headlamp, like the curious caveman I am. And I kissed you first. You were only being polite, right? Not wanting to hurt my feelings."

If I weren't so miserable, I'd have laughed. I'd hardly call shoving my tongue down his throat and grinding against him "polite," but... yeah. We'd go with that.

"And I'm sorry I put you in that position," he continued, saving me from lying. "You're too good a friend to lose over a silly misunderstanding."

My eyes filled. "It's just..."

He stepped up to the end of the bed and grabbed my foot through the quilt. "You don't have to explain anything. It was dumb. Let's forget it happened."

"You're okay with that?"

Bringing his chin back, he pulled his mouth sideways. "Uh, yeah! Why wouldn't I be?"

Because Cath said you're in love with me. And I was getting used to the idea, as impossible as it is. Being loved is nice.

I shook my head. "No reason."

"Then let's not waste any more time on this. Let's go hiking. Some fresh air and exercise will put everything into perspective."

Sitting more fully against the headboard, I reached for the bedside table. "Coffee first."

He crossed to the dresser and leaned his hip against it. With his lips to the rim of his cup, he said, "I thought that went without saying."

CHAPTER TWENTY-ONE

THIS MIGHT HAVE BEEN A MISTAKE. Or ill-conceived, at best. It was all fine and dandy to say, "Let's be best friends and forget last night's nipple joust," but it was another to implement said plan, mere hours after the event. In theory, it shouldn't have been that big of a deal. You said, "Get over it," and you did so. But when you added a bunch of other factors —like, oh, for instance, feelings into the mix, it wasn't that simple at all.

For example, despite knowing my way to the falls (there was a clearly marked trail with signposts the entire way), I'd unthinkingly let Eric take the lead in our single-file caravan up the narrow path. Therefore, I'd been treated for the past fifteen minutes to the backside view of a sexy lumberjack in his boots, jeans, thermal Henley, and puffy vest.

Now, to distract myself from the perfect butt a few inches lower, I glared between his shoulders at the small backpack that contained Aunt Vel's urn.

Why'd you and Larry have to make such a hot kid, anyway? Your wit and sensitivity plus Larry's traditional good looks equals trouble. Why couldn't he be a troll with the personality of a card-

board box? Then his social awkwardness would be much more resistible. And he'd probably already be married to Cath with several unibrowed babies, and I wouldn't be in this mess. But no, you had to produce a decent human being. Thanks for nothing, jerkface.

Of course, if you were still alive, you'd point out that I've always had a knack for wanting what I can't have. Like that time there were two identically wrapped presents under the tree at Christmas, but after Shelly and I tore open the paper to reveal similar—but not identical—dolls, I took one look at the one Shelly got and wanted it. Not because it was cuter, but because it was not the one in my hand, so by default it must be better. Sure, I was six. But that dumb impulse has followed me into adulthood. You were always so good at talking me down from those insecurities. In fact, you were the one that Christmas who pulled me aside and listed all the ways the doll I chose was better than Shelly's. As a newly single parent, Mom was too exasperated with me to attempt mediation. But you... you knew exactly what to say to diffuse the situation.

You're not here to diffuse this one. You're the cause of it. (You are. Don't try to reason with me. You produced that man; therefore, you're the root of the problem. It's science.)

And if you were here, you'd also find it hilarious that after years of criticizing every boyfriend I've ever had, you happened to make the perfect one for me. You always said, "You need someone less like you. Less in his head, less uptight. It may be a cliché, but opposites do attract." And I always thought, 'What would you know about it, Miss Permanently Single?' But you were my favorite aunt (Lord knows why), and I idolized you and took to heart every single thing you ever told me. I didn't know how to fix that particular problem, though. I was around academics like myself all day. Where was I supposed to meet this funny, quirky, nurturing, out-of-his-head, amazing person? Oh, that's right... In Morris, Maine. Barf. I hope you're proud of yourself. Way to prove your point in the most annoying—and disgusting—of ways.

"You doing okay back there?" Eric tossed over his shoulder, glancing to check for himself.

It *was* somewhat challenging to keep up with his long strides, but Miss Morning Runner was hardly willing to admit that, so I simply puffed out a "Yep!" while wondering what the big rush was. Why were we hurtling up the trail at such breakneck speed?

"We're almost there."

"Yep!"

"You want to stop and rest before this last hill?"

"Nope."

"Ewwwkay…"

Oh, he gets that *from you, too. Awesome. That "I'm-giving-you-a-chance-to-make-a-face-saving-choice-here"* Ewwwkay *that always made me second-guess myself and change my mind. Well, not this time. I've got this. I'm strong. I'm independent. I'm…*

…running out of oxygen, and my legs are screaming. But I'd pass out before I admitted I couldn't keep up with Lumbersexual of the Year up there. It was only a hill.

By the time the terrain finally leveled off, my legs were jelly, and I wanted to lie down in the drifted leaves on the side of the path and die to the soundtrack of the rushing water in the distance. But I returned Eric's cheeky grin when he stomped to a stop and adopted a wide-legged stance with his hands on his hips. I'd have asked him where his blue ox was, but I didn't have enough breath to say anything.

He was out of breath, too, but he wiped his forehead on his sleeve and said, "Whew! I forgot how intense that final incline is. Deceptive, because it's not steep, but it goes on forever."

Still light-headed, I said nothing while I struggled to replenish my oxygen levels without gasping and letting on how much trouble I was having.

Chest heaving, he waved a hand toward me. "Not a

problem for you, though. Look at you. You're a cardiovascular marvel. I'm a big oaf who plays video games on the weekend."

Right. Loping along on flat pavement or level trails didn't prepare you for this, but if he wanted to be impressed, I'd let him.

He slid the backpack down his arms and held it out to me. "I gotta take a whiz. Too much coffee this morning."

Somehow, I managed to fuel my arm muscles with enough oxygen to take the pack from him and hold it next to my leg by its nylon loop. He tromped off into the trees, and as soon as he was out of earshot, I dropped the bag to the ground by my feet, widened my legs, and bent over with my hands on my knees, wheezing at the ground.

"Fuhhhhhh," I muttered, cursing my pride while my head pulsated and my lungs strained against my ribs. I stared at the zipper in the backpack and focused on recovering without hyperventilating.

Oh, my gosh. Your son almost killed me. You always told me I was too proud for my own good. What's it like to be right all the time? I wouldn't know. Because I'm always wrong.

Gosh, I miss you.

We'd laugh about this if she were here. After I could breathe again, that was. We'd laugh, and she'd chide me for being a stubborn idiot, but she'd say it in a way that made it obvious she loved me for it, that she admired me, that she accepted me. Then she'd make me drink some water and rest. And while she waited for me to recover from my latest stupid decision, she'd act like nothing was wrong and tell me a story —usually about me as a kid—to distract me from my pain. Then she'd pat my hand and kiss my forehead and say, "Don't tell anyone, but you're my favorite. Always have been."

That never got old. Ever. In fact, it became more and more important the older I got. Because when you're a kid, you don't question being loved. As you age and become your own person, however, not everything you do and say is cute or endearing. That unconditional love is no longer a given. I knew my mom loved me, because she was my mom and she had to. Aunt Vel loved me because of me, because she wanted to, because she chose to.

I staggered to the nearest embankment and plopped onto it, barely registering the dampness of the leaves soaking through the seat of my jeans.

When Eric got back, he found me sobbing into my knees with my hands over my face.

Rushing to my side, he slid on the rotting foliage and sat down hard next to me. He pulled on the wrist closest to him. "What's wrong? What happened?"

I shook my head while struggling to keep my face covered. The combination of tears and continued breathlessness made it impossible for me to explain myself, even if I wanted to.

Eventually, he gave up trying to figure out why I was crying and concentrated on consoling me. "Hey." He wrapped his arm around my shoulders and squeezed me to his side. "It's okay." A quick kiss landed on my hair, near the top of my head. "She's not in there. They're only ashes."

I nodded so he'd think his pep talk was hitting the mark. He didn't need the extra burden of my grief. If he wanted to believe I was upset about dumping Aunt Vel's biological remains over the side of a bridge, fine. It was easier than explaining everything else. Maybe he needed to say these things to himself, anyway.

He retrieved one of the water bottles from a mesh pocket on the side of the backpack and wordlessly nudged my knee with it. I took it from him, pulled on the top to open it, and sipped.

Looking toward the bridge still farther up the trail, he said,

"You know, I was surprised when Vel said she wanted to have her ashes scattered here. But she was adamant. She said, 'I go up there all the time to think.' I had no idea. She wasn't exactly the outdoorsy type."

I snorted at that understatement.

"But maybe that's why she came here. Because nobody would think to look for her up here. Anyway, when I said I never knew this was her favorite spot, she said, 'You don't know everything about me, you know.' It was a throwaway statement, to her, but it leveled me. Because she was right. I… I… viewed everything about her life in relation to *me*, like a child typically does with his parents. But after she said that, and since she's died, I've thought much more about her life… her situation… from the point of view of an adult. It's been eye-opening."

Since I'd had a similar experience in the wake of finding out about her secret family, I sniffled and nodded. "Yeah."

"She was younger than we are now when she had me. Much younger. And… I don't know. Maybe you say, 'Well, things were different then; people of her generation were more mature, more responsible, less selfish and entitled. But I don't know if that's necessarily true, for one thing. And for another, no matter who you are or when it happens, it must be terrifying to find yourself unexpectedly pregnant. And for her in particular."

"How did she and Larry meet, anyway?" I asked through my sniffles.

He smiled sadly. "The story goes—and keep in mind, I've heard a few versions of varying detail and accuracy over the years, depending on my age at the time of the telling—that she would take her breaks from her job as a print setter on a bench in a park. And that park and bench sat right across the street from a hotel—a nice one—where she'd watch the 'rich' strangers come and go and imagine what their lives were like."

He picked at a leaf next to his leg. "She'd sit there after work, too, delaying the time she'd have to go home to her drunk husband, a guy who couldn't hold down a job because he was so hammered all the time. Since she was already in recovery, hanging out in a bar to avoid home was out of the question, so there she sat. And one day, a tall, handsome stranger crossed the street and sat down next to her." He laughed at his wry description. "Well. Handsome enough. And sober. I'm guessing her standards were pretty low."

Before I could weigh in on my opinion of Larry's—and by association, Eric's—attractiveness, Eric rushed on, "Anyway, the first encounter, they didn't talk about anything more than the weather. The second day, he got up the nerve to ask her name and what she did for a living, using the ink stains on her hands as an icebreaker. He reciprocated and revealed his unusual vocation—plus his reason for being there, at the undertakers' convention—which she found fascinating and wasn't at all put off by. Unlike *some* people."

"Sorry, but it's creepy and weird."

"I totally agree! I'm just saying… she thought it was interesting and asked him so many questions that he missed dinner and half the evening presentation he was supposed to attend. He suggested meeting in the hotel lobby the next evening, presumably because it was a more comfortable place to talk, but… C'mon."

I chuckled. "Larry's got moves."

"Well, she was no dummy. She wanted to see for herself what it was like in that fancy hotel. And she knew what he had in mind and was just as interested in that, too, wedding rings on both of their fingers be damned."

"Hm."

He pulled his head back. "Are you judging?"

I winced. "A little. It's a personal rule of mine not to sleep with someone else's spouse."

"Good rule. Has it ever been tested?" When I shook my head, he said, "I don't think Dad and Vel made it a habit to have affairs with married strangers."

"And if they did... none of my business."

He looks away from me and stared off into the distance, toward the water we could hear but still couldn't see. "Of course, they didn't stay in the lobby. Vel followed the out-of-towner up to his room, and..." He clears his throat. "At this point in the story, no matter how old I was, they spared me the details. Thank God."

I giggled.

"But while she was sick, Vel told me more about what both of them were dealing with in their 'real lives' at the time. Larry Mulligan, small-town big shot married to a local sweetheart, who seemingly had it all, couldn't seem to give his wife the one thing she wanted most: a child. Velvet Faelhaber, black sheep and family screw-up, married the first guy who ever told her he loved her—probably to get her to sleep with him—because she was in such a hurry to leave childhood behind. During the hours Larry and Vel were together that week, none of that mattered. They could pretend reality didn't exist." He sighed. "For those hours, Vel was a vivacious career woman, an artisan, who took pride in a job she did for the love of it, not to support a failed dream she was too proud to let go of. For those hours, Larry didn't feel like he might as well be just another body on a slab, seeing that he already felt like he was there most days." He swiped at his eyes with the back of his hand, but his voice remained steady as he continues, "When they were together, they were doing what *they* wanted to do, not what everyone else needed them to do."

I wiped my eyes on my sleeve but tried not to make any other movements or sounds for fear of interrupting the story I'd been dying to hear.

"But at the end of the week, Larry went back to the saintly Gayle, and Vel went back to her harmless but useless husband, because those were the lives they'd originally chosen, the lives they felt duty-bound to see through. They promised to see each other again the next year—same time, same conference, same place—because one week a year is better than nothing, right? And they weren't hurting anyone as long as nobody knew. Only..." He raised his hands and wiggled his fingers. "Surprise! Looks like Larry was more reproductively compatible with Vel than with the lovely Gayle. And that's when things got a lot more complicated."

I swallowed thickly, actually feeling the panic Aunt Vel must have experienced when she'd figured out what was happening. She was already taking care of a person who couldn't seem to take care of himself and struggling every day to stay sober. Now she had to add a baby to the equation? How was she going to manage?

My heart thundered, as if I were the one faced with that predicament, right here, right now.

Eric seemed to sense my distress, because he patted my knee. "We all know it worked out okay. Dad and Vel were quite the dynamic duo. Nobody but me knows that, which is sort of a shame. But when those two got together, no problem was ever too big. In their first big challenge, Vel had no money and no time for a baby, yet she also wanted to die at the thought of giving up—or worse—the result of one of the best times in her life, to date; Larry had no luck giving his wife the baby she so desperately wanted. So he told Gayle about this 'friend' of his, whose sister found herself unexpectedly pregnant and wanted to give the baby up for adoption...

to a nice, Christian couple who couldn't have their own kids." He let out a noisy breath. "The irony is pretty awesome, you have to admit."

Awesomely sad, but... whatever.

"Gayle—sweet, sweet Gayle—jumped all over it. Not only would she be starting the family she wanted, but she'd be doing her Christian duty to help others less fortunate and in need. She couldn't sign those papers fast enough. Meanwhile, Larry was a hero to two women. What a guy."

He dropped my hand and rubbed his palms on his knees. "Anyway, there's a price for everything eventually. And my dad paid big. I had just turned two when Gayle got her diagnosis. Ovarian cancer. She died less than six months later. Big funeral, big, public grieving period for Dad, big single-parent responsibilities."

He snapped a twig with the toe of his boot as he shifted his legs to stop his subtle slide against the silky leaves under us. "Too big. He broke down and told Vel he couldn't do it alone, that he needed her. Her husband had left her at the first sign of her pregnancy—even drunks know something's up when you can't get it up to save your life but your wife manages to find herself knocked up, anyway—and she rarely talked to her family. Managed to hide her pregnancy from them altogether, in fact. But that estrangement meant nothing was holding her in Boston other than her job. Dad begged her to move to Morris, although the romance had fizzled between them by then, and their yearly meet-ups were no longer hook-ups but sad, short family reunions for the three of us. Thank God I can't remember that!"

My breath hitched in my chest at that unexpected detail. "Wait. What? I thought— Are you saying Aunt Vel and Larry weren't still...?"

He shook his head, the corners of his mouth pulling downward. "Nah. Too much baggage, too much stress, too much guilt."

So much for that happily-ever-after nugget. "Damn. At least if they'd stayed together and had been in love, it would have been..."

"Worth it?" he asked with a bemused smile. "Uh... hello. I'm right here."

I blushed. "Sorry. You know what I'm saying, though. From their point of view, outside of their love for you, obviously."

"It all worked out okay. The way it was supposed to work out. Vel got to be a mother to me and see me grow up, but she maintained her independence, and I didn't have to suffer—publicly, anyway—for their sins."

He stood and brushed the dirt and damp from his butt, then offered me his hand. "There you have it."

With his help, I pulled myself to my feet, stomping my still-fatigued but working legs. "Thanks for the depressing fairy tale, Mulligan."

"Right? Hey, at least I'm not one of only two living people who know it now. You, Dad, and I can distribute the depression between three of us."

"Goody." Without thinking, I hugged him. It was quick, though, and my tone was light when I backed off and said, "I'm glad you told me. That must have been a heavy burden, especially for a kid."

When I stepped away from him, he shrugged and cleared his throat, busying himself with donning his backpack and adjusting its straps. "I keep reminding myself it's not my story. I had a bit part in it, but none of it was my fault."

"No, it wasn't. We're all accountable for our own lives."

"So, better not eff it up like they did, right?"

"You're not effing it up."

He chewed the inside of his cheek and looked off toward the bridge again. When he appeared to be about to refute my statement, he instead held the deep breath he'd inhaled, then released it and said, "C'mon. Let's go violate some clean water ordinances."

CHAPTER TWENTY-TWO

THE WIND WHIPPED my hair into my mouth and eyes. First it blew north, then it blew south. It was like me on any given day: fickle. But fierce. And acting like it knew what it was doing but getting nowhere and making a chaotic mess of everything it touched.

Now that we were here on the bridge, we'd have to squat down and slowly pour the ashes into the water below, instead of tossing them. Eric squinted against the gales as he pulled the urn from the backpack. He held the small container out to me with both hands and said, "We don't have to do this today, if you're not ready."

"No, I'm ready." I wrapped my hands around the jar, but he didn't let go, so my palms rested on the cold metal, but my fingers overlapped his knuckles.

"Screw everyone else. They asked you to do this, so you do it on your own time."

I pulled slightly so he'd get the hint to let go. "I'm not doing it for them or me; I'm doing it for Aunt Vel. This is what she wanted."

"When she was alive. She doesn't give a shit now." He held firm to the container.

Meeting his eyes, I said, "If *you're* not ready, just say so. You don't have to pin it on me."

"Me? I'm not the one who was crying in the leaves. As far as I'm concerned, the stuff in this urn is no more Vel than a pile of her toenail clippings would be."

"Considering your opinion of toenail clippings, that's pretty sad."

"It's true. It's waste. So pitch it over; I don't care. But I want to make sure you're ready."

I bit my lip. The wind had died down, so now would be the perfect time, but...

"Would we really be breaking laws by doing this? Is... is it... unsanitary... to put her ashes in the water?"

"Technically? Yes."

"Oh. I... I didn't think about that."

"It's like peeing in a lake."

"First toenails, now urine? Stop comparing her to biological waste."

He sighed. "Fine. Sorry. But it's true."

"Peeing in a lake is wrong."

"Everyone does it."

"No, they don't. And if everyone did, that would be a huge problem."

"That's why water goes through a treatment plant before it comes out of your tap."

My hands remaining on top of his, I looked down at the flowing falls and gulped. "This is Morris's water supply?"

"Yes. Part of it." He laughed. "Do you know how anything works, or is life a series of magical events for you? 'When I push up on this lever, it makes water from nothing!' 'When I turn on this switch, the fairy inside the bulb wakes up and shoots beams of light from her wand to illuminate the room!'"

"Shut up. I know how stuff works. Sort of. But I never put two and two together that the town's water came from... here."

"Not just Morris, either. Several communities downstream."

"Oh, gosh."

"It's not going to hurt anything. Sure, there are laws for a reason, because you can't have companies dumping waste into the river willy-nilly, but the concentration of ashes in the water would be crazy-tiny. Like point-oh-oh-oh-oh-one part per billion... or something. I don't know. I'm not an environmental scientist."

"I was more concerned about my aunt's ashes going through a treatment plant, like fish poop."

He looked toward his forehead to follow my logic, then muttered, "*You* can compare her to fish poop, but..."

"I'm not saying she *is* fish poop. I'm saying her ashes will be treated no better than that."

"You are the queen of semantics." Unscrewing the lid from the jar, he said, "C'mon. Stop fretting about the details. I'm sure Vel considered all of this when she made her decision, and she didn't mind being... processed. Because it's not her."

Without warning, he let go. The urn slipped sideways in my hands, its contents dumping onto my shoes in a narrow stream. Before I could react and right the container, the wind kicked up again, blowing directly at me, and the powdery rivulet turned into a mist that coated my hands, arms, face, and hair.

"Oh, my gosh!" I gasped, squeezing my eyes shut and inhaling my aunt's remains while simultaneously attempting to straighten the jar and stop the spillage.

Eric's laughter floated on the wind.

"It's not funny!" I screamed.

He relieved me of the urn, but since my hands were covered in ash, they were still useless to me. I sputtered and spit against the fine grit.

"Oh, gosh! Help me!"

Still laughing, he said, "Hang on." I heard the threads on the lid scraping against the top of the container, then the zipper closing on the backpack.

"Get them off me, get them off me, get them off me," I chanted as a whimper, holding back my irrational urge to cry.

His voice was closer to me when he said, "Hold out your hands. I'll pour water on them to rinse them off. Then we'll deal with your face."

"Do it already!"

The cold liquid drenched my hands. I rubbed them together to slough off the residue more quickly.

"There you go," he crooned. "Now… uh…"

"Get it off my face!" I said over and over, ejecting saliva like an out-of-control camel.

"It's hard to think with you spitting on me."

"It's in my mouth!"

"Here." A familiar shape and texture hit my palms and told me I now had possession of the nearly empty water bottle. I swigged, swished, and spat; I heard a zipper, then rustling nylon. There was more splashing.

"What are you do—"

"Don't worry about it. I'm going to get your face clean. Finish off that water."

I did, tapping every last drop into my mouth and swallowing. The bottle disappeared from my hand.

Within seconds, a wet, soft, textured cloth swiped over my lips first, then my eyes. I grabbed at it and took over the job myself, scrubbing furiously against my whole face. Cheeks, then forehead, then cheeks again, then nose, then eyes, then more nose, then the inside of my mouth and nostrils. Then I started all over again, mostly concentrating on my eyes.

"I think you got it all," he said at last. "Can I have my shirt back?"

My lids flew open. I took in the dark green thermal shirt in my hands, then transferred my attention to my companion. My shirtless companion. He smiled sheepishly and cupped his hands over his nipples. "It's the only thing I could think to give you."

He had given me the shirt off his back. Literally.

I looked down at it, wet and streaked with ash and makeup. And snot and saliva. Lamely, I held it out to him, snapping it open. He stared at it for a few seconds, then shrugged and took it. I tried not to stare at his broad, hairy chest as he pulled the filthy garment over his head. The chilly breeze pressed it against his skin, and he hissed quietly through his teeth while quickly sliding his vest up his arms and over his shoulders and zipping it. "Nobody will ever know," he said, patting his front.

"You're going to freeze!"

"Bah." He holstered both empty water bottles and shouldered the backpack. "It's not that bad. It's not as windy on the trail. And it's only fifteen minutes back to town."

Looking down at my dusty clothes, I stomped my foot to both clear the mound of ashes from my shoe and express my displeasure at how this had turned out. All of it. Everything.

On his way past me to get back to the path, he patted my shoulder, stirring up a cloud of Aunt Vel. After a subtle cough, he said, "It's going to be all right."

I looked up and smiled bravely at him, suspecting I looked more insane than optimistic. "Yeah. I'm sure it will be."

"Let's go." He took my hand and led me from the bridge.

~

But what if it *wasn't* going to be all right?

That question plagued me when I stepped into the shower and stood under the water after saying goodbye to Eric downstairs.

What if, twenty or thirty years from now, someone else was illegally dumping my ashes somewhere after I'd died too young, having only done the things I felt obligated to do, not the things I truly wanted to do? And who would that person be, anyway? Probably my sister. Because I had no one else. I never would, either, if I stayed here. I'd take up Aunt Vel's baton as the strong, independent woman who was too strong and independent to let anyone love her the way she deserved to be loved. Because let's face it: the only candidate I'd be remotely interested in getting that close to was disqualified. Sort of.

No, not *sort of.* Completely!

Letting myself think otherwise was a muddy, leaf-covered slope that I couldn't begin to navigate without falling flat on my ass.

The only solution, I realized as I rinsed the shampoo from my hair, was to get Velvet Printing into as good a working order as I could and… then what? Sell it? Ask around the family to see if anyone else wanted it? (I already knew what the resounding answer to that would be.) The next step was beyond me, and it was driving me insane.

As recently as a couple of weeks ago, my future had still been in Boston. But now that future—or at least my place at the university—was drifting from my grasp, too. I'd had to give up my fall assistantship, and I couldn't give them any answer about the spring semester, either. That had been an uncomfortable conversation with the graduate affairs director. It was apparent she couldn't understand my indecision. To her, this distracting little family matter of mine shouldn't have taken any time at all to sort out, if I truly knew what I wanted, which—in her mind—should be to come back to the university and resume my doctorate studies and teaching duties.

And I did want that. Perhaps. But perhaps not. The more I thought about it, I wouldn't be returning to the same life I'd had, no matter what. And if I couldn't pick up exactly where I'd left off, was heading back to Boston as attractive a proposition as it seemed before? No. It was not. It sounded almost as lonely as the life I was leading here. Only... worse. Because at least here...

No. He couldn't be the deciding factor.

I slumped against the tile wall as I admitted to myself that he *was*, no matter how much he shouldn't be.

What was happening to me?

SNAP! CRUNCH!

"Agggh!"

One minute I was in my head, the next I was in... the wall?

Cursing, I removed my shoulder from the now-broken tiles, cutting myself in the process. "What the...?" I hissed and pulled on my arm to draw the laceration into better view. "Aw, hell." It wasn't a serious cut, but it was a cut nonetheless. From jagged grout. Around a now-gaping hole in the shower wall.

I quickly turned off the taps to prevent any more water dripping into the gap and soaking the drywall. Of course, there was no need to be careful, because the wall had clearly already rotted. That tile was just waiting for someone to put some weight on it so it could get its ultimate revenge for the undetected decay that had been plaguing it for who knew how long.

Eff you, wall.

I dried off and wrapped myself in towels, then stared at the body-shaped hole.

Now what?

Seemed like that was all I ever asked lately. And I never had an answer.

CHAPTER TWENTY-THREE

MY REFLEX, of course, after I'd dressed both my wound and my body, was to call Eric. But his voice mail picked up, so I left him a message explaining the situation. When ten minutes passed with no reply, I kicked myself for bothering him at all and figured he was playing video games and wouldn't surface for hours. And when he did, he'd probably decide he'd had enough of me for one day.

So I called the first local handyman I found online.

But Titus Jeems of A-1 Repairs said, "It's Sunday, Miss Faelhaber," like that was the reason the shower wall had collapsed in on itself, and it would be fine once Monday rolled around.

When I realized he meant he wouldn't come out to look at it because it was the Lord's Day (or, more likely, because of the Pats game I could hear in the background), I sighed and asked him to come over the next day. But that was a no-go, too.

"I have a backlog like you wouldn't believe. Can't get to you until... say"—fingertips met stubble—"two weeks from Wednesday?"

"What?!"

"At the earliest."

"But... but... It's the only shower in the house. And it looks like an archaeological site from ancient Greece."

"Sorry. First come, first served."

"Never mind, then!" I said, pulling back the statement from "snappy" with my cheer. "I'll call someone else."

He laughed as I put down the phone in his ear. Satisfyingly, too, since I was using the landline attached to the kitchen wall. *Take that, Titus!*

I moved on to the next guy on the list, a Homer Garrity. He had no problem coming out today and could get to work on it right away. *HA!* Now there was a man who understood the meaning of the word "service."

I was smugly awaiting Homer's arrival when Eric, in mid-laugh, called me back about twenty minutes later.

"Why does everyone think this is funny?"

"You're having quite the day," he said, catching his breath. "Whatever you do, don't call Homer Garrity. It'll be tempting, because I'm sure Titus Jeems has a waiting list a mile long, but—"

"I don't have time for waiting lists."

"He's worth the wait."

"But this Homer guy won't make me wait. As long as he's relatively competent and can get my shower back in working order..."

"Oh, hell. You already called him, didn't you?"

My silence was all the answer he needed to get him wheezing again at my expense. "Oh, Whitney... Call him back and cancel. Then call Titus and get on his—"

The ringing doorbell drowned out his last word.

With pursed lips, I stared at the wall in front of me. "Gotta go. Homer's here."

"Wait!"

"It'll be fine. Who cares if he's not the best? I just need it fixed."

"No, seriously. He's a letch. Don't let him in."

"I can't leave the guy on the front stoop! I'm the one who called *him*."

"Go to the door and tell him it's not as big of a deal as you thought, and you can fix it yourself."

"But I can't. And I can't go weeks without a shower."

"You can shower at my house."

"That's not feasible."

"I'm begging you, Whitney. Don't let that guy in. I'll— I'll fix it for you. Please." He wasn't laughing anymore. And now I was a bit scared of who—or what—was waiting on the other side of the solid wood door.

I stared at it down the breezeway. "O—Okay."

"Open the door, laugh at how silly you are, and apologize for calling him out on a Sunday, but tell him you changed your mind. And stay on the phone with me while you do it. The cord will reach."

I clenched my teeth. "Fine. Hang on."

I headed for the front door, despite hating the whole time that I was following someone else's orders, and opened it. To be greeted by a wizened, bearded dude who could have been an extra in a Tolkien adaptation.

"Keep the storm door between you," Eric said.

I hissed, "Shut up," at him, then deliver my ditzy lines, which amounted to, "I'm a girl and don't know what I want until a man tells me."

Homer sneered and muttered something but eventually shrugged his shoulders and shuffled back to his beat-up pickup truck at the curb. As soon as his taillights rounded the corner to take him down Main Street, I said into the phone,

"Now that I've turned Gimli away, you have to fix my shower. You promised."

"What do I look like? A handyman?"

Before I could reach through the phone to strangle him, he said, "But I saw Jake's truck at Horty's—all night, if you know what I mean. I'll pop over there and see if he's available to come by and take a look. We'll figure it out. Anything's better than Homer Garrity."

∾

An hour later, when Jake declared, "This is a gut job," Eric grasped my upper arms from behind and said through my groans, "Hey, hey. No biggie, right? You said yourself that you'd like to change a few things about this place. Now you know where to start."

Jake turned from the tub area and grinned at the two of us, likely thinking what a cute couple we made—irrational, impulsive me and calm, logical Eric.

When I asked, "How long's that going to take? And what's it going to cost?" Jake raised his hands.

"Oh, no. That's way over my head. You'll need to hire a contractor, maybe a master plumber. It's one thing to cut out a piece of drywall, replace it, and re-tile a section of wall. But you've got mildew on your studs. I don't do structural work."

Eric squeezed my arms, then moved his hands up to my shoulders and kneaded them. "Did you hear that? You have mildew on your studs."

"Yeah! Thanks! Got it!" I threw an elbow to get him to back off.

He let go of me but remained standing right behind me. "Okay, well… It's not the end of the world, right?"

I turned and glared hard enough to bring a lesser man to his knees.

Determined to push me to murder, he indicated the hole. "So, you went through that? What were you doing in there, anyway?" He stepped over the side of the tub and crouched down until his own meaty shoulder lined up with the breach. He leaned sideways, then exchanged a knowing look with Jake, who snickered.

"Oh… I see…"

I blushed. "No. It wasn't like that. I was… I was thinking!"

"That's what I call it too, sometimes." Eric straightened his knees and stretched to his full height. In a choked voice with his eyes pinched shut, he said, "I'm thinking… so… hard… about… Reese Witherspoon."

Jake nodded. "Yeah, that's a good one. I'm partial to redheads, myself. Emma Stone. Good material."

Neither Eric nor I pointed out that Hortense wasn't a redhead. Eric was too busy laughing at his own filthy antics; I was too busy trying not to laugh… or cry… or become aroused.

"Okay!" I spun and left the bathroom, calling over my shoulder, "That's that, I guess. I'll phone Titus in the morning and tell him to put me on his list."

The two guys followed me into the hall and down the stairs. Jake, ever the cheerful bearer of bad news, said, "Oh, Titus can't do a remodel like that either."

"Of course he can't," I grumbled, practically throwing the teakettle onto the stove burner.

Eric, back to his normal self, ran his hand through his hair and cleared his throat. "You'll have to get someone from Portland. I can recommend the guy who did my place."

Although I was sure I couldn't afford his "guy," I said, "Thanks," not wanting to appear ungrateful for the help.

Jake shuffled from foot to foot. "Well, sorry I couldn't be more help, but… I guess…"

Eric pushed on the younger man's back. "Go back to… whatever."

"We were watching a movie," Jake said with a grin, on his way out the back door. "See you tomorrow."

After he'd gone, Eric muttered, "I've called it that before, too," then glanced at me and blushed. "Anyway."

"Tea?" I asked, lifting the metal box with Aunt Vel's assortment of leaves in baggies.

He shook his head, but I continued to root through the box for my own while the kettle popped on the stove behind me. Maybe a hot cup of lemongrass would help purge the persistent fantasies brought on by Eric's constant allusions to sex. Perhaps in a fantasy world of its own, that would work.

While I packed a metal strainer with the aromatic dried flakes, Eric stood at the threshold to the kitchen and said, "I'm sorry, Whitney."

At first, since I was so fixated on it, I assumed he was talking about his childish behavior, starting with his accusation about what had caused the wall to cave. When I ungraciously remained silent, he said, "It sucks that Jake couldn't give you better news or fix it himself."

I waved him off. "Whatever. It's not your fault."

"I still feel your pain, though."

The kettle whistled. I snatched it off the element and poured the scalding water over the strainer in the mug. "Do you? I don't think you do," I said quietly, maybe so quietly that he didn't hear me. At least, after it was out, I hoped he hadn't heard me.

Of course, I was not that lucky.

"Yeah, I do. You can't catch a break."

Tears stung my eyes and nose. "Don't be nice to me, okay?"

"What?"

Dunking the metal ball up and down in the hot water, I sniffed. "I already feel sorry enough for myself; I don't need you pitying me, too."

"I don't pity you. I'm merely empathi—"

"Well, don't. I'll find a way to pay for that. And bathe. And keep Velvet going. And return to my old life—which is now unrecognizable." Leaving my mug on the stove, I whirled and practically collided with a wall of man. I kept an inch or two of air between us but stared at his chest, a chest covered by a clean t-shirt marking him as a Foo Fighters fan. Knowing him, though, he was wearing it as a joke. Everything was a joke to him.

Which reminded me... I was mad at him.

I edged past him and stood at the end of the counter. "Apparently, this is all hilarious to you."

"What? Where do you get *that*?"

"With your snide remarks about how the wall must have given way while I was... you know..."

He snorted. "I don't really think that! If I did, I wouldn't joke about it. And even if that *is* how it happened—"

"It's not!"

"Fine, fine! But *if* it was, who cares?"

"If it was, it would be none of your business and definitely not something for you to laugh about with your equally immature buddy."

"Jake's hardly my buddy. He's a co-worker who happens to be boinking my cousin."

"Boinking? I rest my case about your maturity."

"Hey, I never claimed to be mature! And upstairs, I was *trying* to lighten the mood, to get you to laugh, because I could tell you were freaking out."

"So you thought humiliating me would make everything better?"

"I was making fun of myself more than you. Nobody thinks you busted out the wall masturbating in the shower."

"Good. Because I didn't."

"Great. Do you feel better now that the record's been set straight?"

Rather than answer, I mulishly stared him down.

He showed his exasperation by throwing up his hands and rolling his eyes. "Whatever. You know what? I'm gonna head home. That offer of showering at my place is an open one, if you need it at any time in the next few weeks. Just call first, so you don't catch me… thinking about Reese Witherspoon. And I'll text you the details for my builder. Have a great rest of your day."

He moved toward me, then decided to exit through the back door when he realized he'd have to walk past me to go through the front.

With the slamming back door still echoing, I snatched my tea from the stove and dumped it into the sink, then stormed upstairs and heaved myself into bed.

I give up on this day.

CHAPTER TWENTY-FOUR

MOLD, not mildew. That's what was on my studs. I had moldy studs. And not just in the bathroom, either. Everywhere.

"It's a miracle you haven't been sick," the expensive Portland contractor said from behind his protective mask.

"I haven't lived here long," I muttered, thinking about Aunt Vel and how sick *she* had been. But mold doesn't cause bone cancer, right?

I was making a mental note to Google that later when Studly Do-Right said, "Well, you won't be living here while we tear all this out, either."

"W-what?"

"Pack up your stuff and the cat, ma'am. I have to alert the Health Department of this. They'll have a vacate notice up by the end of the day."

That was how I'd ended up, cat in hand, on Eric's front porch, one week after falling through my shower wall.

He swung the door open and waved us in. "Get your moldy butts in here."

"It won't be for long… I hope," I said, not at all sure that was the truth.

"Who cares?"

"I do!"

"Well, I don't." He hoisted the cat with one arm and one of my rolling suitcases with the other and led us inside. "And neither does Buster. Do you, buddy?"

Buster rasped his answer, then leapt from Eric's arms to scope out the best place to sun himself. Eric smiled down at me. "It's not the end of the world, right?"

I drew myself up with what I hoped looked like determination and resolve. "Of course not."

"You're worried about the cost, but don't be." He led me up the stairs, lugging both of my huge cases behind him.

I shook my head at how simple he made it sound but focused on his back when I asked, "Do you think that house killed Aunt Vel?"

He stopped at the top of the stairs and turned to face me. His huge grin made me backpedal.

"Is it stupid to think that?"

"Stupid?"

"Yeah."

"Maybe."

"The house is toxic! And, from the looks of things, has been for a long time!"

He tilted his head and blinked, swallowing as if he was choking back laughter.

"It's not funny! I stayed there. I *live* there now."

He let go of the handles of my suitcases and transferred his palms to my shoulders. "Whitney?"

"Yes?"

"I want you to take a deep breath and repeat after me."

I inhaled.

"Everyone."

"Everyone."

"Dies."

"Dies. I know that! But not everyone dies of cancer in their fifties."

"Not everyone works in a print shop around chemicals all day, every day, either."

"Or lives in a house riddled with mold."

"Or gets their water from a stream where people dump human remains."

You did not *just say that!* I clenched my jaw to resist laughing.

"Go on. Let it out. You know you want to."

My eyes watered. "No, I do not. I want to have a serious conversation with you about the biohazard that is my home and was your mom's home for decades." I stomped my foot.

He looked down at it, then back at my face. "I'm supposed to take *that* seriously?" he asked, gesturing toward my leg.

Reaching around him, I took control of my suitcases and marched down the hallway toward the only bedroom not currently in use for sleeping or gaming.

He followed, doggedly attempting to employ logic on me. "Whitney, I'm serious now. Do you honestly think Vel died because she had mold in her walls?"

"Maybe. I haven't researched it or anything. It's just something I've been thinking since packing up all of my clothes and all of Buster's stuff and finding myself displaced... again, with nowhere to go, because it's frickin' fall, and every hotel, motel, and B&B within a six-hundred-mile radius is jammed full of people who have never seen a decaying leaf before, apparently." I dropped both cases flat on the floor between the foot of the bed and the dresser and unzipped the one holding my casual clothes and... delicates.

Eric leaned in the doorway and watched while I stuffed

the clothes haphazardly into drawers. "What do you mean, you have nowhere to go? You're here, aren't you?"

I halted with a pair of my rattiest underpants in my hands. My arms fell limply to my sides as shame and embarrassment caught up to me. "Oh, my gosh. Yes. I'm so sorry. And I truly appreciate this. I do. I didn't mean to be rude."

I flapped the panties in the air in front of me, hoping to dry the rogue tears of frustration that had popped through my ducts. When that didn't work, I pressed the undergarment to my face. "I don't know what's wrong with me. I used to be such an optimist, such a cheerful person. Ask anyone who knows me—or used to know me. Nothing got me down; not for long, anyway. Then I moved here, and..." I uncovered my face and slung the underwear into the drawer with its friends. Resuming my unpacking, this time at a less frantic pace, I chuckled nervously. "It must be the clean air up here. Or something. Or maybe mold causes nerve damage and mental health problems. Surely printing chemicals could, right?"

"Are you going to be okay?"

I blinked and smiled at him on my way to the suitcase for another handful of socks and panties. "Of course. Yes. I'm sorry. I'm just stretched a little thin, maybe. I guess the past few months have shown me how easy I've had it my whole life. Because toss some adversity my way and I'm a basket case. Who knew?" I dumped the clothes and bent over for more. "I always perceived myself as so capable... Definitely not like my mom. More like Aunt Vel. But after a small taste of her life, I'm collapsing like a... a... something collapsible. Words. I can't think of them right now."

Scrambling to fit the remainder of the suitcase's contents into my arms, I sniffed back dripping snot and burning tears while bobbing up and down like a deranged bird pecking at the ground as I kept losing bundles of socks and balls of bikini briefs.

Eric's legs came into view, then his hands as he retrieved the latest flurry of undergarments to hit the floor. Somehow he managed to hold everything in one hand while resting the other on my back, keeping me from straightening too quickly and bumping heads with him. When I did rise to my full height, his palm stays between my shoulder blades. The flat-out alarm I saw in his eyes was mortifying.

"I'm okay," I hastened to reassure him, piling on a grin for good measure.

He smiled back, but like one did in the face of insanity. "I don't think you are."

"Yeah, I am. I'm just hormonal or something. Look out! There's a woman under your roof now. We're... zany."

He pulled me to the side of the bed and pressed me to a sitting position there. When I was seated, he relieved me of the clothes in my hands, adding them to the ones already in his, and threw them in the general direction of the dresser. "There." He sat next to me, mirroring my slumped posture and straight legs. "I'm not sure I would have been able to concentrate with a handful of your lingerie."

In spite of my misery, I rolled by eyes. "Sorry about that."

He patted my knee. "They're nice undies. Now. Are you gonna cut the crap and be real for a second? You're not okay. And that's... okay. Okay?"

I nodded but twisted my mouth to the side to suppress my tears.

"A weaker person would have taken to bed with her smelling salts a long time ago. Or something. You lost someone you loved... a lot."

"So did you."

"I'm not finished. Then you were forced into running a

business you had little interest in running. It cost you your boyfriend—which was no big loss, in my opinion, but I'm sure it's not that simple to you. You're dealing with financial stress, your house is condemned, and… and you ate some of your aunt's ashes. On top of all that, your family's practically abandoned you through all this. Where *is* everyone, anyway? I'd say you've had a shitty go of it lately."

"Can you please stop enumerating how awful everything is? It's not helping."

He wrapped an arm around my shoulders. "I'm sorry. I guess my point is, if you want to throw a temper tantrum, you should. I get it. You don't have to put on this brave front. I can take a pinch of 'crazy,' but… but this manic smiling thing you've got going on is freaking me out. And I'm an undertaker. We have a pretty high freak out threshold."

Too weary to remain upright any longer, I listed against his shoulder, intending for it to be for only a second. But that second turned into several seconds, then a minute. Or two. My throat ached with pent-up tears. I'd already cried once in front of him. I didn't want to do it again. But I did let my face fall into something more natural and un-Joker-like. After all, when the mortician's creeped out by the grin, it needs to go.

Finally, when I was sure I could talk again without losing it, I said, "I guess I just… I thought life up here would be simpler. But it's about three hundred times harder—and more complicated—than my life was before."

"You miss Boston."

I considered that for a second, then answered honestly—and surprisingly, "No. I don't. I miss my sister. And sometimes my mom. But only when I think too much about it. I miss my apartment a little. I miss my couch a lot."

"And your job?"

"I miss not being the boss of everything. But I don't necessarily miss the work. Or my colleagues. To be honest, they were all a bunch of snooty bullshitters."

He laughed, which made me laugh too. "Nice."

"It's true. And I was one of them. I don't miss being that person."

"Morris is growing on you, then? Is that what you're saying? No. I don't believe it."

"There are worse places in the world."

"High, high praise."

I pushed myself upright before getting too comfortable against him. He put both hands back in his lap and cracked his knuckles one by one with his thumbs. "If you want to invite your sister to visit while you're stuck here with me, you can. There's plenty of room. And I want you to feel at home here."

"Oh, gosh. That's nice, but... that's okay."

"No, I mean it. It sounds like you could use some time with someone who knows you better than anyone here does. Someone who doesn't need to drag everything out of you. Someone who can take one look at you and know, 'Day-um. Whitney's about to lose it. Better get her a pumpkin spice latte, stat.'"

I wrinkled my nose.

"Or whatever your crutch of choice is."

"Bleach."

"A bit caustic for my taste, but... um..."

"Stress-cleaning, dork. Remember?"

He slapped both hands against his cheeks and dropped his jaw. "Ermagerd. Have you come to the right place, or what?"

"Show me to your cleaning supplies."

He tucked a piece of hair behind my ear. "You got it. Just, uh, stay away from my bathroom. Nobody needs to see that."

❧

While scrubbing the already immaculate, rarely used shower in the bathroom attached to Eric's guest room, I mulled his offer of having Shelly come visit. And by the time I'd finish the tub and moved on to the toilet, I couldn't think of a single reason why she shouldn't. Talking face-to-face with my sister was long overdue. I needed someone to reason with me, to convince me that my latest impulse—to chuck everything in Boston and move here permanently—was madness, a type of fever brought on by ingesting human remains.

Having her there would be fun, too. She'd love Eric's house. And I could show her the modest but nice plans I had for Aunt Vel's house, once the walls were back up. Bye-bye, wallpaper! See ya, bathroom carpet! Hello, subway tile! How you doin', laminate floor? Okay, so it wouldn't be as fancy as Eric's heated wood floors, but it would still look nice. And it would be cleanable. (That was the key.)

I could also show her what I'd done at the print shop to streamline operations and introduce her to the people I saw every single day. She could get to know Eric and Hortense, our quasi-cousins. Of course, she wouldn't be allowed to know that… unless Eric decided to tell her. And I'd advise against that, since keeping secrets wasn't Shelly's strong suit. But she could still meet everyone.

In my mind, her visit was a *fait accompli*, so my disappointment was crushing when she had excuse after excuse for not making it up here anytime before Christmas. And by then, the weather would play a huge factor. "But you'll be at Uncle Kevin's, right? For Thanksgiving? That's only a month or so away."

I quickly and brightly answered affirmatively, although I had no idea at all if that was going to be possible. Sobbing most unattractively in her ear was seconds from happening if I didn't hang up that instant.

After I disconnected, I stared at the device in my hand for a while, then seriously considered throwing it into the sparkling toilet in front of me. The trouble it would be to replace the device, however, wouldn't be worth it.

I was still staring into the toilet fifteen full minutes later when Eric poked his head into the room to check on me. He sidled up to me and looked with trepidation into the bowl.

"What are we looking at?" he whispered.

"My life," I whispered back.

He steered me by the shoulders from the room. "Enough bleach. Let's go take a walk. Fresh air. That's what you need."

Around the lake we went, kicking through the leaves, saying nothing for the longest time, until the crisp breeze and warm sun had chased the last vestiges of doom, gloom, and bleach fumes from my head. Now, as we lay on the sloping front lawn on a bed of pine needles, staring up at the brilliant blue sky peeking through the branches overhead, I said, "Shelly won't be visiting."

"Ah."

"But you know, that's okay. Because I'm busy. And it's not a good time."

"I see."

"I don't even have a house to entertain her in. It was nice of you to offer to host both of us, but that probably wouldn't have worked. She doesn't know you. It would have felt weird."

He twirled a pine needle between his thumb and forefinger, then flicked it at my face. I blinked and shook my head to rid my cheek of the fragrant stem.

"Screw her," he said finally, after a pause.

"What?"

"I said, 'Scuh-rew. Uh-her.'"

"I'm pretty sure Dom has that taken care of. Which might

be part of the reason she doesn't want to spend a precious weekend up here."

He snorted. "Well, double screw her, then."

"I don't know what that means, but okay."

He laughed at himself. "Seriously, though. If she thinks she's going to bring her boyfriend up here and rub our noses in it that she's getting some and we're not, forget that, too."

"What's this 'we' business?" I asked through my giggles.

"You're getting some?"

"No! But I don't know. It sounded funny, like you and me against her."

"That's obviously the way it is, isn't it?"

"Uh…"

He propped himself on his elbow and turned onto his side, looking down into my face. "The way I see it, she's jealous of us."

"Still not following, Delusional Dude."

"She doesn't want to come up here and be the third wheel. She won't know any of our awesome inside jokes."

"Such as?"

"We have them. We don't realize it, because nobody's ever around us who isn't normally around us, so we don't think of them as inside jokes; they're just jokes, because we're already on the inside."

"Did you drink—a lot—while I was cleaning?"

He collapsed onto his back, then clutched my hand and patted the top of it. "No."

"Your theory is crap."

"I'm reaching, okay? I'm desperately trying to come up with an explanation—any explanation—for your family abandoning you the way they have."

I swallowed the sudden lump in my throat. "Oh. That. Well, everyone's busy. We all have our own lives. And down there… I don't know. This place seems so far removed, you know?"

"Forget that. You had your own busy life, too. And you dropped everything."

"I had to, though. I couldn't stay there and run Velvet the way it deserves to be run."

"Before that! When Vel was sick. You were here. All the time. I've been meaning to thank you for that."

I turned my head the same time he turned his, and looked into his eyes. "You're welcome. I did it for her, though."

On his side again, he rested his head on his hand and looked down at me. "She laughed about that more than once."

"I didn't realize it was funny."

"Well, you know, she had me. And Larry."

"I *didn't* know that, though."

"Right. You didn't know about us, so you assumed she had nobody up here to look after her, and you stepped up, without being asked."

"You don't wait for family to ask. Only a jerk does that."

He raised his eyebrows as we both thought of the other people in my family—her siblings, specifically—who had never considered doing what I had done.

I waved off his praise. "Ah, well. In their defense, I didn't give anyone time to step forward. I just did it. She was my Aunt Vel. She would have done it for me." When he didn't agree right away, I checked, "Right?"

He smiled sadly. "If it had been convenient for her."

"Hm. Yes." Chuckling ruefully, I turned my attention back to the patch of sky above me and away from his probing gaze that made me want to pull him on top of me and kiss him until both of our mouths cried out for mercy.

"Maybe she and Shelly had more in common than I thought."

CHAPTER TWENTY-FIVE

AND LIKE THAT, my life in Boston was no more. All it took was a couple of emails, with a more formal resignation letter and withdrawal form to follow via certified mail on Monday, and a few phone calls. Done. Without Shelly or Mom there to convince me otherwise, I couldn't muster the nostalgia for my old life that was required to make hanging onto it worth the energy.

That whole era didn't even seem like my life. When I recalled the way things had been before Aunt Vel got sick, it felt like I was watching a movie shot from the point of view of the main character. It was a movie I'd seen several times, so it was familiar to me, but I still felt removed from the action. It didn't seem like *I* was the one living that life.

This was my life now: morning runs and weekend art marathons, the sharp tang of chemicals in my nostrils, jeans and boots more days than not (especially now that the weather was getting cooler), budget spreadsheets, payroll software, and people who depended on me to show up every day to tell them what to do—or at least sit in this office and wait until they needed to be told something, which was admittedly rare. The point was, I feel *engaged* in that life. And not only with my brain. I felt physically alive.

I was sure I had in Boston, too, at the university. Or with James. But the past few months had been so vivid, so uncomfortable, in a way. Even during the dullest of times, I'd felt like I was strapped into a roller coaster, hanging onto the safety bar in front of me, not sure if I were about to go down a huge hill or spiral into a corkscrew or be turned all the way upside down in a series of dizzying, disorienting loops. And man, I loved a good roller coaster. That beat going to the movies any day.

Therefore, I'd made my choice. No more straddling my old life and the new one. In what might have been the most impulsive decision of my life, I chose Maine. And I wasn't bringing anything up from Boston. Well, I would be sending for my couch and my bedroom furniture. But my renter was buying everything else from me and officially taking over my lease.

After ending the call with her, I sat in my office, the rest of the building around me buzzing with Saturday silence, and stared at one of my framed illustrated prints I'd hung there to make the room feel more like mine. *You can do this.* Yes, I could. I had. I did. I would.

The final thing I needed to do was look at the upcoming vacation schedule for everyone at the shop. I didn't want to get too excited too early, but it looked like I might be able to take Friday and the weekend after Thanksgiving to travel to Boston as a bona fide visitor. I was definitely on the apex of a huge hill, judging by the weightlessness of my insides.

Or maybe that sensation was due to something—or someone—else.

Eric had had a funeral and a visitation today, so after rattling around his empty house with Buster for a few hours, thinking about cutting ties with my old life, I'd come here to do it. As soon as I was sure the current home renovation across the street wasn't going to render me homeless, I composed and sent the emails to the university and picked up the phone to make this my new normal.

Of course, it wasn't normal to be cohabiting with my secret, technically-but-not-biological cousin, whom I also happened to be inappropriately attracted to. It was also extremely abnormal to have an entire town watching said living arrangement with knowing and, in most cases, approving eyes, thinking they knew *exactly* what was going on, while they really didn't have a clue. At all.

I'm sure they would have been shocked, for example, to know that half the time when I went to bed each night, Eric was still up, talking to disembodied voices from all over the world on that silly gaming headset of his. I would fall asleep alone, in my flannel jammies and fuzzy socks, to the oddly comforting murmur of his voice through the wall and an occasional profane yet quickly stifled outburst. Hours later, he'd crawl to his own bed.

Or not. One day not too long ago, when he'd had no funerals or visitations scheduled, I woke to find him still wearing the same clothes and playing the same game he'd been playing when I'd retired seven hours earlier. He blinked sheepishly when I asked if he'd been up all night, then seeing I was up, gave himself permission to yell as loudly as he wanted at his opponent, wherever that person was. I simply closed the door on the room and continued down the stairs to take my morning jog.

And then just this morning, I'd been startled from a deep, lazy slumber by blaring screamo music coming from the first floor. I wrapped my pillow around my head, but it was quickly apparent sleep was over for the day, so I bundled up in my cold-weather running gear and stumbled downstairs, where I blinked against both the sun and the noise. My hands over my ears, I approached the kitchen, from where two voices were emanating. The gravelly one belonged to the lead "singer" of the horrid band; the other, I assumed, was Eric's, "singing" along.

I was about to yell a "Good morning!" as soon as I got to the threshold of the room, but the sight before me rendered me speechless. Eric, in boxer briefs and a plain white t-shirt, was standing at the island with his back to the doorway, gripping a bowl in one hand and whisking its contents with the other. Occasionally, he'd flip up the whisk and sing into his "microphone," hips thrusting forward, muscles standing out in his hairy legs, like an intense rocker putting everything into his performance.

I transferred my hands from my ears to my mouth and slid back around the edge of the entry, poking my head around the frame just enough to peek at him.

Whisk, whisk, whisk... "[SOMETHING UNINTELLIGIBLE BUT LOUD AND ANGRY], I DON'T KNOW THIS PART AT ALL... BABE!" If I hadn't recently emptied my bladder, there would have been a puddle in the hallway. As it was, I produced plenty of liquid from my eyes as I watched and silently laughed at the vision. Not that I had to be quiet. There was no way he could hear me above that insane racket... and his own growling.

Finally the song ended, and before the next one started playing, I wiped my face and entered the room, clapping slowly.

The high-pitched screech Eric emitted when he whirled away from the counter was even funnier than his musical performance, but my belly laughter was drowned out by the first chords of the next song. He dropped the whisk into the bowl and fumbled with his phone, silencing the noise, then dropped the device with a clatter against the butcher block.

"Whitney! I... I... I didn't think you'd be back so soon."

"I haven't gone anywhere yet. I was sleeping when I thought I heard a murder in progress down here."

I'd never seen a man's entire body blush before. Well, the parts not covered were blushing, anyway; I assumed the rest...

He waved in the general direction of the bowl behind him. "Uh, I was... I thought you were jogging."

"I get that now. And I thought you had a funeral... for something or someone other than your vocal chords."

"Not until this afternoon. I was whipping up some breakfast for when you got back."

I peered around him at the eggs so well beaten that, if they hadn't included yolks, would have been meringue. "Uh-huh."

"I'm sorry. If I'd known you were still in the house, I—"

"Wouldn't have performed your super-exclusive concert? That would have been a pity."

He laughed at himself and poured the eggs into a glass casserole dish already full of diced ham, veggies, and cheese. "Don't hate," he said.

"No hate at all. In fact, if those guys all sang in their underwear, they'd be a heck of a lot less scary."

He slid the dish into the preheated oven, set the timer, and brushed past me. "I'll, uh, get dressed then. See you after your run?"

Now, remembering that performance, I giggled. Then I blushed. Then I closed my eyes and allowed myself to think more about the sexiness of someone goofing off, presumably alone and for their own fun.

I didn't have long to indulge in my daydream, since he was going to be here any minute to see if there was anything he could do to optimize the network until I could afford a more permanent solution. Like he'd said the other day, "Kinda defeats the purpose of email when you can walk to someone's office and have an entire conversation before one message about the topic can be exchanged."

The bell over the door to the reception area rang. Speak of the closet rock star...

I opened one eye and winced, waiting for the lecture about the unlocked door that was sure to accompany Eric's stomping feet. I gathered my defenses while waiting for him to appear in the doorway. Maybe I could distract him with my big news about permanently moving to Morris.

As soon as I saw his murderous expression, however, I realized the apology would have to come first. "Yeah, yeah. I forgot again. But I'm pretty sure I could take down Homer Garrity with one hand tied behind my back. In fact, I'd like to see that little Hobbit try to—"

"I can't believe you."

"Oops. Gimli is a dwarf. Don't be such a purist."

"I'm not talking about Homer Garrity, and you know it."

"You mean the door? I said I was sorry. It's not that big of a —" My extremities numbed when I took in the high color in his cheeks. "What's wrong?"

Scoffing, he looked away from me and scratched the side of his neck, near his hairline. Then he repeated, "'What's wrong?' Hm. I don't know where to even start. I guess we can start with your innocent act, which you can drop right now, because I'm not buying it."

I jumped to my feet. "Well, it's not an act, because I have no clue what you're talking about."

His eyes met mine. I wished they'd go back to staring at

the seventies metal credenza.

"Who'd you tell first? Horty? Bobby? Lena? Or was it someone here at the shop?" His nostrils flared. "You know what? It doesn't matter. Because it's all over town now. So who cares who you told first? The point is, you told. I thought I could trust you."

With his breakfast concert still so fresh in my mind, I shook my head, confused by such a strong reaction to something that petty getting out. "What? I didn't tell anyone. And if I did, who cares?"

"Who cares?!"

"Yes!" I stepped around him to lead the way to the server room. "Since when do you care about looking silly?"

Staying right where he was, he jammed his hands on his hips. "How can you minimize this? This is not about looking silly. This is about... my *life*. I invited you into my home and confided in you. I trusted you, and you blabbed about it all over town."

"I've been here all day. There's been no blabbing, especially not about your horrible taste in music." I pointed at him. "And another thing, you need to calm down. Maybe listen to less of that stuff and play fewer shoot-'em-up games. Because they're turning you into an angry asshole."

"What the hell are you talking about?"

"What the hell are *you* talking about?"

"I'm talking about Vel. And Larry. And me. And how the only other living person in the world who knew about it was *you*. Until now. Now *everyone* knows."

I reached behind me for the desk chair and fell into it. "W-what?"

"Yeah. I'm sure you thought it was idle chit-chat. Or maybe you didn't mean to say it; it slipped out while you were getting your hair colored."

"Hey!"

"However it happened, you didn't have the guts to give me a heads up. To tell me, 'Hey, Eric. I screwed up. I may have leaked that tiny detail about Vel being your mom and her and Larry having an affair, which pre-dated his sainted wife's death and produced a child—you—who Larry then adopted. Oops. My fucking bad.'"

"For one thing, this is my natural hair color, thank you very much. For another, like my hair, I'm honest, not fake. I haven't told a single soul a single word of your stupid family secret, no matter how cruel it is that your parents forced you to keep it all these years. It's not my secret to tell, so I've kept my promise to you. *For* you." Amazed I could say all that with so little saliva in my mouth, I licked my lips.

"Whatever. I don't believe you."

"Well, that sucks!"

"I want to believe you, but I can't. Because there's no other explanation. Nobody else knows. And I can't imagine it's a coincidence that the truth has stayed hidden all these years, until I tell one person: you. Just own up to it, so I can get on with my pathetic life."

"I'm not going to admit to something I didn't do!"

He snorted. "You're so stubborn. I don't know why I thought you'd cop to being wrong. About anything. Ever."

"I'd confess if I had anything to confess. But I don't. So screw you!"

"Oh, I've been screwed all right. And you know what? Screw *you!* Now I know why Vel never confided in you; she knew she couldn't trust you."

Before I could say anything else, he stormed from the building. On his way out, in harmony with the bell, he shouted, "And lock the damn door!"

CHAPTER TWENTY-SIX

MY FIRST INCLINATION was to go back to his house, pack all of my stuff, and leave before he got home from the visitation for another of Morris's dearly departed souls. But my pride balked at that urge. Because I had done nothing wrong. And I was going to prove it to him.

Plus, I had nowhere else to go. Hortense's house was too small to accommodate a semi-permanent guest. Now that peak foliage season was over, some rooms have opened up at area B&Bs and motels, but back when I'd first been evicted from my house and was looking for somewhere temporary to stay, Eric had told me one place has bedbugs, another was popular with an unsavory local element, and still others didn't allow pets. Sure, I could have left Buster at Eric's (my host wasn't furious at the cat or accusing *him* of telling anyone the big secret, although that would be more logical than accusing *me*) and head for one of those pet-free lodgings. But no! I wasn't going anywhere until he listened to reason… and we figured out who was responsible. Together.

My number one suspect was Cath. She and Aunt Vel had been close. Maybe Vel ad confided in her protégé. Did it sting that my aunt might have told Cath and not me? Absolutely. But that was beside the point. Larry definitely wouldn't have told anyone; Eric hadn't told anyone but me; and I'd never spoken a word about it to anyone but Eric, not even to Shelly. And absolutely nobody in this town. Even if I'd taken up talking in my sleep, there'd been nobody in bed with me—unfortunately—to hear any ramblings. Eric could shove his accusation where the sun didn't shine.

As angry and hurt as I was that he would believe the worst of me, though, I did understand where he was coming from. What else was he supposed to think? Logic was telling him it could *only* have been me. He must have thought it was more possible that I would leak the truth than that Aunt Vel had at some point before she died. He didn't know me well enough to know I'd never betray his confidence. Ever. And although we'd spent a lot of time together, he wasn't with me 24/7, so he didn't have proof of my innocence. Nor did he have faith in me.

That was what hurt the most. Because without realizing it, over the past few months, I'd put all of my trust in him, something I'd never been able to do with anyone other than Aunt Vel. And I would never have doubted his intentions. Knowing that conviction wasn't reciprocated was more than disappointing; it was devastating.

But I wouldn't hide out in my room like some guilty person. Because I wasn't. I was innocent. I was his ally in this, whether or not he liked it. And he might be angry now and not thinking clearly—because how could you think when everyone in town was staring at you and whispering about you, and your whole family was upset with you, for one reason or another?—but I'd make him see I wasn't the enemy here.

Having recovered somewhat from the shock of Eric's irate

accusation, I retreated to his house, where I planned to wait for him to cool down and come home. Instead of packing my bags, I unpacked my art supplies, spread them out on the sun room table, and started drawing. Only graphite and high bond paper this time; no easel required.

My illustrations typically featured one woman at a time, a woman who was strong and exuded independence, confidence, and self-acceptance. I *never* drew men. My art was feminist. Not in an angry, man-hating way (because that's not feminism; that's sexism), but in a girl-power, seek-strength-from-within way.

Today, I made an exception. This drawing was for one person's eyes.

Since I was working on a relatively small sheet of paper, turned sideways, my strokes were short and fast. Within minutes, the seemingly random lines took the shape of two people, one much taller than the other, sitting side-by-side in Adirondack chairs under a pine tree. They were looking straight ahead at a sun dipping into the lake like a giant cookie into a massive bowl of milk, but their hands were linked between their chairs.

I added a few tufts of dark hair to the beefier arm on the right, then a rolled-back shirtsleeve. He also received a neat cap of hair on his head, all of which we could see, plus the back of two crescent-shaped ears, a small section of smooth neck, and, to the lower right, his arm and elbow resting, fully relaxed, on the board that served as the chair's armrest. Through the gaps in the seat back, the outline of his broad shoulders tapered down to a slightly narrower waist. The toes of his shoes and the tips of his knees peeked from either side of his chair, indicative of his spread-legged position.

The female on the left received a more delicate arm, her wrist encircled with a simple bracelet. Only the crown of her head showed above the high back of the chair, but her unruly tendrils were blowing in the direction of her companion, tickling his ear. Through her chair slats, we glimpsed her shoulders, back, and upper arm and elbow as she rested her free hand in her lap. Her heels were perched on the front edge of her seat, because she was sitting with her knees drawn up toward her chest pressing inward on each other.

Since this was a view from behind, I didn't show either of their faces, but in my mind they were definitely smiling, likely recovering from laughter at something funny—or bizarre— the man had said.

Now for the words. While I was pondering what to write in the sparkling water above their heads, I tapped my pencil against my lips, then smudged a few lines on the picture here and there with the pads of my fingers to create shadows for dimension. On the trees flanking them, I added more detail to the bark and the needles. Then more sparkles in the water. Then...

I reached for the fine-tipped black pen I used for the text placeholders on my sketches. Normally, I uploaded the illustration and replaced my less attractive handwriting with Aunt Vel's flowing script, which had become part of my brand. But this would have to be final. I'd have to know exactly what I was going to say, to position it perfectly. In my own hand. And I'd have to get it right the first time. No boo-boos. No second chances.

No pressure.

∼

But Eric never came home.

At some point close to dawn, I fell asleep on the couch, my

black-smudged hands folded lightly over the drawing on my midriff.

I woke in the sun-drenched living room, blinking furiously to get my bearings. The first thing that came into focus was the vacation picture of Eric, Hortense, and Bobby. I turned my head on my stiff neck to look at the clock, but the light streaming through the large windows had already told me it was late morning, nearing early afternoon.

I groaned and sat up, rolling the miraculously un-crumpled drawing into a loose scroll I tucked into the front pouch of my hoodie. Buster sauntered into the room and shot me a sassy yowl that perfectly communicated his dissatisfaction with my sloth.

"Dude, I'm so sorry," I muttered through a mouth full of thick saliva. "Why didn't you wake me sooner?" I rose, dismayed by how old and decrepit I felt. Obviously, I'd reached an age where a real mattress was required each night.

In the tidy kitchen, Buster's dish sat empty. I filled it and refreshed his water before shuffling up the stairs. The furious crunching behind me made me feel worse, but I reminded myself the stout Maine coon could stand to skip a few meals here and there, and one late breakfast wasn't going to kill him. He had most likely been sunning himself and didn't think a thing of it. If he'd truly been hungry, he would have let me know.

The second floor sat silent and empty. I ventured into Eric's room, somewhere I'd never visited before. Not once. Even today, I only took one step over the threshold, feeling decidedly like a trespasser.

His bed was neatly made (somewhat of a surprise, to be honest), and the room was immaculate. The only sign of regular occupancy was the lingering scent of daily showers and shaves wafting from the connecting bathroom. No shoes next to the bed; no piles of dirty clothes. It was masculine chic, like something from an interior decorating magazine. Black wood furniture. Chocolate brown comforter. Silver-framed photos gleaming on the dresser, smiling faces beaming from them. Aunt Vel and Larry. Lena and Hiram. Hortense. Bobby, Jill, and their new baby, Nicholas. Me.

My breath caught in my throat. From the doorway, I stared at the familiar picture, the same one that had sat on Aunt Vel's mantle. I hadn't even noticed it had disappeared. It was a black-and-white portrait for the university's course catalog and website. I'd ordered extras to give to family when it turned out better than I'd expected. The photographer was funny, railing about selling out with corporate photography to pay the bills. I'd told her about my illustrations and recommended some sales sites to her for her commercial work. Girl power. Our conversation had relaxed me and resulted in something that looked less like an institutional mugshot and more like a candid pic taken by a friend.

Now, I considered what it meant that Eric had inherited (or stolen) that photo and placed it on his dresser with the others. Not a goofy snapshot stuck lazily to the fridge with a bottle-cap magnet. Formal. Framed. Positioned precisely in relation to the others. Visible every single day while he dressed for work or undressed for bed. Part of the group. Part of the family.

All last night, I'd resisted tracking him down, because I'd felt I had no right to know his whereabouts. Despite what everyone thought, I wasn't his girlfriend. I wasn't family, either. I was merely a houseguest. A houseguest he suspected of gossiping behind his back.

But you didn't keep a picture of a lodger who meant nothing to you on your dresser. And when someone cared about you enough to have a framed photo of you and to tell you to lock the shop door, despite being furious with you, you didn't sit idly by when he was hurt and could be in trouble.

Closing my eyes, I swallowed my rising worry. He was a grown man, after all, so of course he was fine. This wasn't a movie where the enraged character drove off in a huff and skidded off the road into a tree. Real-life anger rarely resulted in anything that dramatic. No, when a normal person (and for the sake of argument, we'd say that was what Eric was) was upset, he went somewhere to lick his wounds.

A vision of a melting woman at the end of a dock flashed behind my closed lids, followed by block-lettered words: "You can drink to drown your problems, but problems are good swimmers." I gasped and looked around me, almost surprised I was still standing in Eric's bedroom instead of in Vel's living room all those months ago, where he'd found me drunk and humiliated and dumped.

I hissed several curse words at myself. Racing down the hall to my room, I grabbed my purse from the floor next to the bed and dug through it until I found my phone. No surprise that I hadn't missed any calls. Shelly was too busy with Dom; Mom was too busy with... herself; and the only other people who regularly call me were a) dead or b) dead pissed at me.

I dialed Eric's number first, on the chance he'd answer reflexively, or at least text me that he was okay after he screened my call.

No to both.

I called Hortense, but her phone went straight to voice mail, so I rushed to the window and pulled back the blinds, hoping I could see her house from this vantage point. I couldn't. Well, I could see a chimney and some of the roof and gutters. And a dog running around in the yard. But no driveway or cars or other clues as to what was going on over there. Larry's house wasn't visible at all from Eric's (which was interesting, since it was probably visible from space).

Not that I'd have ventured over there, anyway. The elder Mulligan and I weren't exactly BFFs, considering... everything. I'd had a pretty bad attitude toward him, in fact, since Eric shared the whole story of his and Vel's relationship. It had nothing to do with the morality—or lack thereof—of the situation, either. It had everything to do with the impact of his actions on his only son.

Since the elder Mulligan had never made it a point to reach out to me, either, I assumed Eric had told him I knew the whole story, and Larry, intuiting my feelings for him, was avoiding me. And that was fine with me. Aunt Vel hadn't gotten to defend herself to me, so why should he? I didn't want to hear his lame excuses. Regardless, we had never exchanged digits. Normally, that wouldn't have been be a problem. This morning, it would have been nice if I could have consulted him about how best to find his son, though.

Who was I kidding? If he shared Eric's belief that I was the one who could have spilled his precious secret, he wouldn't answer my calls, either.

Well, there was nothing for it. I was going to have to put some legwork into this. That was what a dutiful "girlfriend" would do anyway, so it wouldn't raise any eyebrows if I made my search public.

The question was, where should I look first?

CHAPTER TWENTY-SEVEN

WHEN I COULD FULLY SEE Hortense's house, as I was driving past it, I spied two cars in her driveway, neither of which was Eric's. One belonged, predictably, to Hortense. The other—Cath's hatchback hybrid—did catch my eye—and I almost dropped everything to go over there and confront her, to expose her for the gossiping jerk she was, but finding Eric was my top priority, so I drove past, continuing on my way toward Larry's for my next drive-by. Which was also a bust. If Eric had spent the night there, he'd since left.

Next I gave Hortense's cell another try. She answered this time, sounding overly bright, but she had no idea where Eric is. Then she said, "Uncle Larry's called an emergency meeting at the funeral home at three. But, uh… if you do see Eric before then, could you have him call me? I need to talk to him, and I'd like to do it without everyone else around. Before the meeting."

"Keep trying his cell. I doubt he's going to answer any calls from me, considering he thinks I'm the traitor in this drama." I interpreted her silence as an uncomfortable acknowledgment of her own similar conclusion and said, "Which I'm not. I want you to know that."

"I— No, I— I never thought—"

"It's okay. Everyone does. Whatever. I can't care about that now. I need to find Eric."

Hortense said nothing to that, so with sleep deprivation adding more of an edge to my tone than usual, I say, "Tell Cath I said hi. I'll text you an update later," and hung up in the middle of my name breathlessly coming through the phone.

Although The Poole Table wouldn't be open for another couple of hours, I drove past, looking for Eric's car out back. My shoulders slumped, and I breathed for the first time in what felt like minutes when I didn't see it. The thought of him falling off the wagon because of something he thought I'd done nauseated me, and with each place I passed that could have been his haven and didn't appear to have been, I' became more and more sure I'd find him sleeping off the alcohol in his car. The fact that he wasn't at The Poole Table didn't completely ease my mind, though; he could have been locked in a jail cell... or lying in a hospital bed... or a ditch... or the Mulligan basement.

My stomach lurched and twisted again.

No.

No, no, no.

He wouldn't have done that. Maybe he'd have thrown away years of sobriety, if the urge to drink were too great to resist, but he wouldn't have gotten behind the wheel of his car afterward. He'd dealt with the result of that too many times. Even if he didn't care about his own life, he wouldn't put others' lives at risk. That wasn't Eric. I knew Eric.

You thought you knew Aunt Vel, too. Knew her your whole life, in fact. And look how much you didn't know, how much you had wrong. Who's to say you know this guy, someone you only met five months ago?

Faith.

The drawing in my hoodie echoed that word. Picturing the couple on the paper, I could nearly feel the pressure of Eric's hand against mine.

Faith.

I continued down Main Street, slowing as I approached Mulligan Funeral Home. Sunday funerals and visitations were rare, although they did happen once in a while. Today was not one of those days. The hearses and limos were tucked into their garage stalls, out of sight. The parking lot sat empty except for the transport SUVs.

Pulling into the blacktop lot and sliding the Volvo wagon between two crisp white stripes, I left the car idling and draped myself over the steering wheel, muttering to myself, "Think. Think, think, think. You're Eric. What do you do to decompress? Play video games? Listen to screamo? Split wood? Read? Where do you go?"

I pictured the places away from his house he frequented regularly in his free time, especially Sundays. Church was the first place that popped to mind, but considering everything going on, I didn't think he'd put himself further in the spotlight by going today. Anyway, services were over by now. The secondhand bookstore, where he bought his sci-fi paperbacks, was my next idea. But they were closed on Sundays.

Paperbacks. Solitude. Nature.

I shoved myself away from the steering wheel and pulled the column shifter into "drive," my tires squealing as I turned a tight donut toward the lot's exit. Less than two minutes later, I crunched to a halt in the small gravel parking area next to the trailhead leading to the falls. Eric's car wasn't there, either, but I refused to let that bust my theory. If he had been too drunk to drive, he might have abandoned his vehicle somewhere and walked here.

With a final check that the drawing was snug in its pouch, I jumped from the car. Jogging down the path kept me warm against the biting autumn breeze and carried me faster to my destination than walking would have. Still, it seemed to take forever for me to arrive at Eric's reading bench.

I stared at its emptiness, crestfallen that my brilliant brainstorm had been wrong. Panting, I stood with my hands on my hips and stared at the trail where it disappeared into the golden wood. Then, as I was deciding to make the trek up the hill to check the bridge over the falls, frosty, slippery trails be damned, snapping twigs and rustling leaves to my left captured my attention. I whirled on the noise, ready to defend myself from the critter—or murderer—who had decided to join me on the path.

Eric shook his head at my fight-ready posture. "Gonna take down Sasquatch with the self-defense moves you learned at the Y?"

Too choked to voice a reply—witty or otherwise—I simply relaxed my stance and concentrated on not flinging myself at him. Instead, I studied him. He was still wearing the dress shirt, pants, and shoes he'd been wearing yesterday when he confronted me at Velvet, but the jacket and tie had been given the heave-ho. The shirt looked wrinkled and slept-in, the sleeves rolled to mid-forearm. His face sported a healthy growth that would take some guys several days to achieve. His hair fell across his forehead, like it sometimes did after he'd been playing video games and running his hands through it for a few hours.

"What are you doing?" I asked, looking over his shoulder in the direction from which he came.

"Just now? Taking a whiz. Right before I had to pee?

Thinking about stuff. What am I doing in general, with my life? I have no idea."

"Where'd you stay last night?"

He walked over to the bench, shooting a bemused glance at me on his way past. "On the couch in my office. At the funeral home."

"With the dead people?"

"We only have one guest right now."

I shivered, which made him roll his eyes.

"He was quiet."

"You could have come home. I waited up for you as long as I could. I—" My hands found the scroll in my pocket, but I stopped before taking it out and showing it to him. Suddenly, there in his presence, I was shy about what I'd drawn, what I'd felt while I was drawing it, and I was terrified of his reaction. Doodles would have to wait, as long as he still thought I was behind the gossip.

I cleared my throat. "I wish you had come home. I was worried."

"That was kind of the point." He chuckled at himself. "I knew you would be. But I was mad at you and wanted you to… suffer." Wincing, he said, "I'm sorry. That was immature. And mean."

"No, I… I get it. Since you think I'm the one who did all this. But I didn't. I swear. Eric, I don't— I've thought about it all night, and the only person it could have been was—"

"It was Horty."

I blinked at him, trying to make sense of his matter-of-fact statement.

He patted the bench next to him. "C'mere. Take a load off. You know"—he pointed a finger at his face and traced a circle in the air in front of it—"you're a bit of a mess."

I slapped my palms to my cheeks, and he shifted his focus

to my hands.

"Oh. Your hands, too. What happened?"

Rubbing my face against my sleeve, I said, "Drawing. I was drawing."

"In a coal mine? With a charcoal briquette?"

In spite of my embarrassment, I laughed. "No. In the sun room. With graphite."

"This is the most bizarre game of Clue ever."

I scrubbed my hands against my black leggings but quickly gave up. It was no use. Only a shower was going to get me clean. "Speaking of mysteries, you said Hortense is responsible? How? Who told *her*? It wasn't me!"

He sighed, stretched out his legs, and laced his fingers behind his head. "The Massachusetts Department of Vital Records did. She was researching her family tree, and she got a bright idea: 'I know! I'll trace Eric's birth parents for his thirtieth birthday! Surprise!'" He mimicked my buggy eyes. "Right? Well, her heart was in the right place, I guess. But her research yielded a puzzling—then shocking—result when she saw two extremely familiar names on my birth certificate."

"Holy crap."

"What are the flipping chances, right?"

He waited while that sank in for me, and as soon as it did, I asked, "Aunt Vel named Larry on your birth certificate? But surely, Gayle saw that document at some time, right? Others too. You have to flash that thing around a few times in your life for... stuff. Driver's license, voter registration, school enrollment..."

He shook his head. "It wasn't until right before I graduated college that we had it amended. It was the only thing I asked for, for graduation. I figured by then it was safe. Anything I need to do from here on out that requires it... I can go to Portland. Or whatever."

"Oh."

He dropped his arms. "The point is, what twenty-something takes up genealogy? That's a sign there's literally *nothing* to do around here."

I laughed and, without thinking, took his hand. "Oh, Eric. That's horrible luck."

He seemed surprised to find his hand in mine at first, but he relaxed his palm against mine, then gave me a reassuring squeeze. "Maybe. Or maybe the opposite." When I waited for him to explain, he shook his head. "I don't know yet. It seems like a mess right now, but in a way, I'm relieved it's out. No more hiding. No more lying. No more pretending to be something I'm not. In fact, before I found out Horty was the source of the leak, I was already thinking of how to thank *you* for putting an end to this... this... flimflammery."

That delightfully fancy word almost made me want to take credit for this whole thing, but I wasn't quite ready to joke about it, so I asked, "But how did it get from her to... the entire town?"

"The way she tells it, she panicked. She wasn't sure *I* knew, so she didn't want to confront me about it. She was going to talk to Dad, but she wanted to get some advice about how to broach the subject. It had to be someone close to the family but not quite a member of the family." He snorted. "She said she *almost* told *you,* but she didn't want to be the one to break the traumatic news that your boyfriend was your cousin."

I dropped my head back and groaned toward the branches above us.

"She knows we're not *really* cousins, by the way, but still."

"So, who did she tell?"

"Jake."

"Ah. Pillow talk. Then Jake told...?"

"His mom and sisters."

"And that's all it took. They told someone, who told someone, who told someone…"

"Yep."

"I take it this means you finally answered Hortense's calls and got her side of it?"

"Yeah, but I already knew. Aunt Lena filled me in this morning when she found me sleeping in my office." He assumed a higher pitch and said in a near whisper, "'Now, Eric… Nobody meant to hurt anyone. You didn't mean to hurt us by keeping such a huge secret all these years, and Horty didn't mean to hurt you by discovering it the way she did. We're all going to put the best construction on it and forgive one another and love each other the same way we've loved each other all these years.'"

I paused a second to picture that conversation, with small-but-mighty Lena stating the facts in her soothing way, smoothing ruffled feathers, making sure diplomacy would win the day. In my vision, she held him the whole time, too, like a mother consoling a child who comes home from school with a failing grade or a story about a crush who doesn't return his feelings. Lena would make all of this right. She'd be the strong core that kept the rest of the family upright through whatever blows were to come.

And that was comforting, but if I was following everything Eric had been saying and correctly understanding the sequence of events, I had to acknowledge… "Wait a minute. You knew it wasn't my fault, but you still didn't come home? Or text me? Or anything?"

"I haven't known for *that* long. Aunt Lena told me a couple of hours ago, and I came over here to think about it. To figure out how to apologize to you. To figure out what all this means and what I do next. Then Horty called, and I had to reassure her I'm not mad at her and listen to her lecture *me* about lying to her all these years."

"Oh."

"I feel bad that you were worried. But by the time I knew the truth, I figured an hour or two more wouldn't matter. I had to wrap my head around everything."

Instead of pointing out that *I* had told him the truth—at least the part of it I knew—yesterday in my office, and he'd chosen not to believe it when it came from *me*, I swallowed my hurt and said, "Okay. So… did you figure out all of those things?"

He drew up his knees, placed his feet flat in front of him, and turned slightly to face me. "No. I especially have no idea how to apologize to you for what I said. For what I thought. I *knew* you wouldn't tell anyone. But because I didn't see any other possibility, I assumed I'd been wrong about you. And when you denied it… I figured you were covering your ass, afraid to tell me the truth."

I clamped my jaw against the aching near my ears and in my throat as the tears built in my sinuses. With a tight smile, I choked out, "I wish you'd thought more of me, that's all."

"I did! I do!" He closed his eyes. "That's why I was so enraged. It was the only logical answer, and it sucked, and it hurt, and I was blind to anything else."

"Aunt Vel was rash like that, too. And stubborn. Once she got an idea in her head, forget it."

"I guess I get that from her, then." He pressed his fingertips into his eye sockets and took a shuddering breath.

"You're exhausted." His pale complexion, slack posture, and shaky hands supported my rather obvious hypothesis.

"I didn't sleep worth a damn. I'm ashamed of myself, and I'm so sorry, Whitney."

Wrapping my dirty fingers around his wrists, I pulled on

his hands. "Hey."

He blinked down at me, his normally playful, sparkling eyes dull and bloodshot.

"Enough."

"Yeah?"

"Yes." I wrapped my arms around his shoulders and gave him an awkward side hug. "I love ya, ya big galoot. I'm just glad you're okay. And sober. And safe. And sober."

Turning into my embrace, he laughed and kissed the top of my head and hugged me back. "You thought I was on a bender, eh?"

"Maybe. I didn't know what to think. I wouldn't have blamed you, that's for sure." The sketch in my pouch crinkled and popped between us as I hugged him tighter, holding on as if my life depended on it.

After a few minutes, as if by silent agreement, we separated to the accompaniment of a few final sniffles, then smiled nervously at each other.

He patted the front of my hoodie. "Whatcha got in there, huh?"

I blushed. "Nothing. Just… nothing. Something I drew last night while I was waiting for you to come home."

Wiggling his fingers at me, he said, "Let's see it."

"I don't know." I put my hands in the pouch and wrapped them around the scroll, popping its dents to return its shape to a smooth cylinder.

"I want to see what got you so"—he looked me up and down again—"streaked."

"If you're going to joke about it, forget it."

"Fine. I'm serious. Please. I need to see something nice. I'm assuming it's nice. If it says, 'Go blow yourself, Eric,' maybe I'm okay not knowing. Although I'd understand that sentiment."

"It's nice. But you're eerily close on the message." Before I could lose my nerve, I produced the stiff paper and unrolled it for him, bending it back to flatten it, then holding it up for him to see.

"Wow. I'm hairy. I'm assuming that's me?"

I nodded.

He read the text and laughed. "Nice. Way to make me eat my words there."

I turned the paper around so I could see it, as if I weren't already aware of what I'd written. *Screw the facts. Have faith* stared back at me. I pursed my lips.

He took the drawing from me. "It's your best work yet."

"Yeah?"

"It is. And I want it for always."

"It's yours."

"I'm glad we agree." After rolling it into its portable scroll, he stood and pulled me from the bench with his free hand. "Let's go home. We should clean up and get something to eat before we have to be back at the funeral home at three."

I gulped. "'We'? I have to be there, too?"

"You're part of the family, right? Like it or not."

"Well…"

"I'd like you to be there. Please."

More bravely than I felt, I promised, "Then I will be."

"Great. Drive me to my car?" He gestured for me to walk next to him on the path, which was still wide enough for double occupancy this close to the trailhead.

"Where exactly is that, anyway? I've been looking all over for it."

"Hidden in one of the garage stalls at work."

I slapped his shoulder as he pretended to shrink away from me. "Sneaky jerk."

CHAPTER TWENTY-EIGHT

THE MEETING WAS every bit as awkward and horrible as I'd imagined it would be. Barely contained anger, hurt, and frustration dripped from every question that flew back and forth as the Mulligans, Doolans, and I, the lone Faelhaber family representative, tried to sort through the details of the past thirty years. Jake was there to face up to his part of the drama, too. I suspected he was shocked he wasn't fired during the course of the meeting, but the leaking of the truth to the rest of the town seemed to be pretty low on the list of concerns at that point. Hortense was the most conflicted, waffling from deeply apologetic to accusatory on a minute-by-minute basis. But Larry took the most heat.

I almost started to feel sorry for the guy by the end of the meeting.

Almost.

Because I took my share of flak, too. How long had I known? What, exactly, was my relationship with Eric, in light of this? Blah, blah, blah. I held my own without throwing either of the Mulligans under the hearse. Fortunately, since I'd never lied—only omitted and/or neglected to correct people's assumptions—I didn't have too much apologizing to do. In fact, Eric begged my forgiveness for not telling me sooner and for asking me to keep silent about it. Larry agreed with him.

I glanced nervously at Hortense while accepting their apologies, and I was relieved when she smiled warmly back at me and mouthed, *"It's okay."*

I'd keep telling myself that as I broke all this news to my own family… whenever I summoned the nerve to do that.

The meeting ended with Larry giving a speech that sounded suspiciously rehearsed; more polished than any eulogy he'd ever delivered. It wouldn't have surprised me if he'd been practicing it for the better part of thirty years, in fact, waiting to be exposed. Whether he had planned to confess it all himself at some time or figured his son would tattle on him—inadvertently as a young child or more willfully as a rebellious teenager or drunk adult—I guess we'd never know. But he wasn't speaking off the cuff, that was for sure. His statement resembled every *mea culpa* declaration given by every politician caught in an illegal or immoral act since the beginning of time. Maybe a bit more sincere, given it was delivered to family, but still the words of a cornered man, words that wouldn't have been spoken had they not been forced from him.

Everyone hugged it out before we dispersed, but it was obvious things wouldn't be the same in the family business for a long time… possibly ever.

Afterward, as Eric drove us back to his place, the lack of jokes coming from his side of the car made me so uneasy that I finally blurted near the end of the journey, "Well, that was dead serious."

The grunt I received in reply indicated I should have left the death puns to him, so I muttered what felt like the one millionth apology of the day and looked off to the blazing treetops in the distance.

Neither of us made it much past sundown before retreating to our beds after a silent late afternoon and early evening with both of us buried in our own ruminations. When I woke the next morning to get ready for work, Eric's bedroom door was still firmly closed, and the house seemed stuck on pause. For only the second time since coming to stay here, and for the second day in a row, it fell to me to make the coffee and feed the cat. Not that I minded. But it felt weird, knowing Eric was physically present yet inaccessible in every other way.

I left, still not having seen him and unsure if I should check on him before I went. In the end, I didn't. He was an adult, and I wasn't his mother. Or his sister. Or his cousin, even. I *was* his friend, but friends knew when to back off. Knowing he wasn't stewing about me helped me give him that space. He'd come around when he was ready.

The last thing I wanted to deal with after the weekend I'd survived, though, was a Monday morning bitch session courtesy of Cath, so it was all I could do not to audibly react when I discovered her waiting for me in my office. What she could possibly have had to complain about was beyond me. The email inbox for incoming and pending jobs was working even better than I'd hoped. The last time I'd checked, though, it was as orange as the local trees. Maybe she was here to complain about being overloaded. If that was the case, I'd remind her she could take on as many—or few—jobs as she wanted; I was perfectly capable of leveling the rest of the workload, and her co-workers were equally able to do their share.

With a terse, "Good morning," I took my time removing my jacket and hanging it and my purse on the coat tree behind my desk. By the time I turned to face her, I'd figured out how to arrange my face into some semblance of a smile. Somewhat. I hoped. Probably not, though. It felt pretty grimace-y, akin to the expression that never failed to freak out Eric. *Good. Maybe I'll scare her away.*

Setting my travel mug on the corner of my desk, I asked, "What can I do for you this morning?" and lowered myself to my chair.

She immediately stood and closed the door, then strode back to her own seat across the desk from me. "I heard the big Mulligan family secret broke this weekend," she began, leaning forward conspiratorially.

My temper flared. Honestly, I'd rather have listened to her gripe about her co-workers or the sluggish network or a cranky piece of equipment or my shitty leadership skills than dish with her about this. "You and everyone else. You didn't have to close the door. It's hardly a secret now."

"Right. Well, out of respect for Vel, not to mention Hortense, who's one of my best friends and who's been traumatized by this whole thing, I don't feel like talking about it so everyone can hear us."

Chastened somewhat, I gestured for her to continue.

"I've had my suspicions for years, but I never asked Vel about it—or talked to anyone else about it, either."

Aaaand... annoyed again. "Good for you. I'm sure my aunt appreciated that." Knowing it was rude but not caring at this point, I woke up my computer and logged in to the system, checking email and generally getting situated, hoping Cath would get the message and leave.

But she didn't. In fact, she leaned back in her chair and stared into space, like she and I were sharing a moment. While I was choosing my words to more obviously evict her, she sighed and said, "I wish Vel had confided in me. I bet it was an enormous burden, hiding something like that, something that... that... integral to your life."

My earlier snappy eviction died on my lips as I considered that, something I'd pondered many times since Eric told me the truth. Hadn't I? Surely I had. Surely I hadn't made this all about me. Or even Eric. But I was ashamed to admit to myself that while I might have acknowledged my aunt's struggle with this, my sympathy hadn't been as strong as it could have been. I'd been angrier at her for the effect this had had on Eric—and for not trusting me with her secret.

Cath shook her head. "Imagine not being able to fully show how proud you are of your own kid; how much you love him. That must have sucked."

I swallowed thickly.

"Especially a guy like Eric, someone who gives you so many reasons to be proud. And to think, people thought she and he were..." She focused on my face and widened her eyes. "Not that I ever did. I knew that wasn't the case. Like I said, I recognized her in him. I could see he was her son. Maybe I never put the biological connection together, but I knew in her heart, she was his mother." Looking down at her hands in her lap, she muttered, "It was similar to how she treated me. I always thought she, Eric, and I would have made a nice family."

Normally, I'd have been touched by a declaration like that. I'd have felt pity for her, if nothing else. But for some reason— call it exhaustion, discomfort, whatever—it pissed me off today. Hard-core pissed me off. Like I wanted to crawl across the desk and claw her face.

Before I could wonder at that strange, unkind impulse, she slapped her palms against the wooden arms of her chair and said, "Anyway. Silly fantasy, right? Maybe it makes more sense why he never got close to anyone around here until you came along, though. Too risky."

"Well, he's fair game now, so have at 'im, Cath," I said with an accompanying tetchy click of my mouse button as I close the shared email account.

She paused halfway between sitting and standing, then perched on the edge of her seat. "What?"

I faced her more fully, resting my arms on my desk and folding my hands together in front of me. "I've been trying to tell you for months that nothing is going on between Eric and me, and now you know I was telling the truth. Because he's my... c-cousin."

She pulled her chin back and narrowed her eyes at me. "No, he's not."

"Practically."

"Not even practically."

I sighed, not in the mood to have this tired conversation with yet another person, especially since I didn't believe my own side of the argument enough anymore to hold it. "Whatever. The point is, everyone knows the big secret now, so he can get close to whomever he wants."

Bitterly, she said, "Which... is still you."

"Listen, I have a ton of work to do," I lied, "and so do you, judging by all of the orange in the pending jobs inbox—which reminds me, you shouldn't hoard so many projects. Let some of the others take on a few of those, okay?"

She stood, and I entertained the hope she was going to leave, but she dashed that when she remained standing in front of my desk, towering over me. "Eric's never been interested in me that way. Or any way. You said it yourself."

"I shouldn't have. It wasn't my place."

"But you were right. And it's obvious. He's never been interested in anyone in this town like that. Until now." She inhaled deeply, as if bracing herself to say something that might truly cause physical pain. "I'm sorry I let my jealousy get the best of me. None of this is your fault. You didn't kill Vel, and you can't help who falls in love with you. I've known Eric my whole life, and as much as I hate to admit it, he's come alive since he met you. You make him happy. And that's all I've ever wanted for him. Does it suck that I was never the one to accomplish that? Yeah. It does. But it's been obvious our whole lives that I was never going to be the one to make him happy."

"Sucks for him, too, right? Because it would be seriously hinky, even for an eccentric like him, to get involved with his mother's niece. As it is, because of everyone's stubborn assumptions up till now, we're dealing with some who think we were intimate before finding out the truth." I shivered, pretending it was with revulsion but more because I'd had to block out one of the naughtiest, definitely not-safe-for-work mental images of Eric and me together.

"Who cares what anyone thinks? The fact is, you and Eric aren't related in any way, shape, or form. And you'd be idiots to let all of this other stuff complicate how you feel about each other. Stop over-thinking it."

I snorted.

Now it was her turn to look like she was about to claw off my face. "Those 'stubborn assumptions'? They weren't formed in a vacuum. They came about because people watched the two of you together. They saw that spark, that mutual admiration and respect. So stop pretending you don't love him, too, because it's obvious you do, and it's starting to piss me off that you think it's something to be ashamed of or embarrassed about. You're one of the luckiest people in the world, and if you can't appreciate that…"

I concentrated my attention on the wood grain in the

desktop. She stared down at the industrial carpet under her feet. Neither of us said anything, and I doubted I was alone in holding my breath while we tried to figure out how to end this awkward exchange.

Finally, she strode to the door. "I *do* have a bunch of work to do." Fingers against the handle, she turned, her face blazing. "I only want him to be happy. And so did Vel. And she'd want you to be happy, too. That's all that matters when you love someone."

Without waiting for the response I was unable to give, she exited the room, leaving me more dumbfounded than any other time since moving to this town. And that was saying something.

When everyone else was occupied with lunch, either in the break room or off-site at The Lobster Shack, I closed my office door for the second time that day and sat down behind my desk, staring at the contacts entry on my cell phone screen. Mom and Shelly were waiting for me to call them. In fact, Mom had reluctantly agreed to sit in Shelly's dungeon of an office in the basement of the museum for what I called "a very important conversation." Telling them everything over the phone wasn't my first choice, but waiting until Thanksgiving was out of the question, and I couldn't get down to Boston before then. Since they weren't ever going to come up here to visit me, I had no choice.

I tapped the screen to connect me to Shelly's work number, imagining the phone lighting up on her desk and Mom saying something snide about my forthcoming proclamation.

Before the two of them could monopolize the conversation with relatively frivolous talk about their Black Friday strategy up and down Boylston Street more than a month from now, I announced without preamble, "Aunt Vel has a son here in Morris."

Silence.

More silence.

So much silence I checked my phone to make sure we were still connected and said, "Hello?"

Mom sighed. "That doesn't surprise me much at all, actually. I'm more surprised he wasn't included in her will and that he hasn't come to us for money since then. Or is that how you found out? He approached you for money?"

"He doesn't need our money."

"Who are his people, then?" she inquired, as if we were discussing a pedigreed dog or horse she was considering purchasing.

"He's Eric Mulligan. And his dad is Larry Mulligan."

Shelly giggled. "Oh… that makes sense now."

"Mulligan, Mulligan…" Mom muttered, trying to place the name.

"The funeral home people," Shelly helpfully provided.

"The undertaker? Vel and the *undertaker*? The tall, handsome guy who delivered her eulogy?"

"Uh, yes. I suppose. Larry."

"And… and… their son is the strange one who came over to talk to us? And blurted things about incest and being in the basement with the bodies most of the time?"

"Yes. That's Eric."

"Oh, my. Priceless."

"Right?" Shelly interjected. "Weirdo with a capital 'W.'"

"He's not!" I objected.

Mom simply laughed harder.

"Stop it! This isn't funny. It's… it's been stressful for the family up here to find out about this. It's been stressful for *me*."

That sobered Mom slightly, but there was still plenty of mirth in her voice when she said, "You? Why would it be stressful for you?"

Before I could answer, Shelly replied, "Because Whit's got the hots for Eric. Talk about incest! It's like he was predicting the future."

I twitched in my chair and huffed, "I don't have the hots—"

"Ooooh! Someone's awfully defensive."

"Methinks she doth protest too much."

Refusing to say anything else until they stopped their immature heckling, I clenched my jaw and tapped my fingers on the desk.

Shelly giggled. "We've pissed her off good now. She's doing that finger-drumming thing."

"I bet she's grinding her teeth, too. Now, Whitney, what have I told you about that?" Mom said, suddenly much more serious. "It makes you look like a bulldog. And those wrinkles in your forehead... You'll look like an antique laundry implement before you're forty."

I sighed and slumped onto my desk, resting my head on my arms while the two of them discussed which of my stress-coping mechanisms would age me most quickly. They were arguing about the validity of the theory that jogging is hard on one's reproductive organs when I sat up and said, "Enough!"

Their immediate silence provided all the opening I needed. "If I seem tense, it might be because I've been up here all alone for half a year, learning a new business, adjusting to a new life, and finding out in the process that Aunt Vel had a whole life none of us knew about. A life that included a son, our... cousin."

"He's not really—" Shelly said.

"Shut. Up."

"Bulldog," Mom muttered.

"As for my feelings for Eric..." I took a deep breath, remembering what Cath said across the desk from me only hours ago. "I do love him. Very much. He's been asked to keep the most basic parts of his identity secret his whole life, and somehow, the worst it's done to him is make him... quirky. Someone else might have used it as an excuse to be mean or bitter or a serial killer. But he's not. He's... amazing. And he's been the only person I could depend on. Maybe he's not family by blood, but he's been more supportive than you guys have been."

They spouted their usual excuses, talking over each other and trying to appease me with promises of shopping excursions and female bonding over the upcoming holidays.

"Save it," I snapped after a few seconds.

Shelly, her voice full of pout, said, "A guy will do anything when he's trying to get into your pants, Whit."

Before I could blow up at her, Mom rushed to interject, "Now, now. Your sister has a point."

Since she was the master of noncommittal double-speak, I didn't know which sister she was talking to or about. She probably didn't either. Both of us waited for a clarification that never came.

Finally, she continued, "I don't know the protocol here! What are we supposed to do? Do we reach out to him and host some awkward 'Welcome to the Family' get-together? Or do we wait until he approaches us?"

"I don't know, Mom. Nobody knows. We're all making it up as we go along."

"I could send him a fruit basket."

Shelly made a garbled noise. "Whatever. I say we all

continue on as before. Invite him to Thanksgiving if you absolutely feel the need to assimilate him. But can we not make it a big deal? Talk about uncomfortable."

"You'll tell everyone else?" I checked with Mom.

"Sure. Lord knows what our little sister told him about *us*."

On the verge of hyperventilating from exasperation, I sighed again. "I don't think she bad-mouthed us to him. If anything, she painted us in a better light than we deserved."

"I highly doubt that. Maybe you, her precious favorite, but not the rest of us. Otherwise, she would have found a way to include us in his life while he was growing up. After all, we're a world away from that backwater. Bringing him here for visits wouldn't have threatened her precious secret." She cleared her throat. "Well, what's done is done. Let him know he's welcome to join us for Thanksgiving. Having a newcomer around might break up the usual monotony of political arguments."

In that case, I couldn't wait to extend the invitation.

CHAPTER TWENTY-NINE

AS I WAS LEAVING Velvet for the evening, I notice everyone was still hard at work across the street. The parking lot was full, and as I drove past, I could see in my rear view mirror an ambulance backed up to the receiving bay. I assumed that meant I'd have the house to myself this evening.

Therefore, I was alarmed, at first, to hear a deep voice above me as I climbed the stairs to my room to change into something more comfortable. Until I recognized it as Eric's voice. My insides flitted, my steps felt lighter, and my cheeks lifted so high on my face that I could see them while still looking straight ahead.

Buster greeted me at the top of the stairs like a harried nanny reporting on a naughty child.

"What's your problem?" I asked between meows. "Has he been listening to that 'music' again? I know, it's awful, but it's *his* house. He's allowed to be home and do whatever he wants here."

Down the hall we went, and I pause on my way past Eric's gaming room. Holding onto the door frame, I removed my heels and sank to my normal height. "Hey," I said to my hoodie-and-flannel-pants-wearing roomie. "Uh… what's up?"

He bashed his thumbs against the vibrating controller in his hands and replied distractedly, "Hey— Oh, what the frigging heck, PigSooie2000? I told you to cover me! … Yeah, well you did a crappy job of it. Hang on … I gotta respawn … No! Stay right where you are, you moron. It'll just take a— Oh my gosh! You're useless!" He glanced at me and chucked the controller away. "Hey listen, buddy, I gotta go. … No, my mom's not telling me to turn off my game. But it was good playing with you. I hope that broken leg heals up fast." He laughed at his playmate's reply. "All right. Fair enough, I guess. I'll check for you next time I'm on here, if you promise not to hose me, like you did just now …. 'Kay. See ya."

He stripped off his headset and flattened his hair. "What?" he said to my bemused smirk.

"'PigSooie2000'?"

"The kid's gamer tag. Some middle schooler in Arkansas. Laid up with a broken leg and milking it for all it's worth."

"And, uh, what's your excuse for being home when there's obviously a visitation or funeral tonight, not to mention a dead person being delivered to Mulligan as we speak?"

He stood and stretched his arms over his head, showing off a patch of fuzzy belly when his shirt rode up. "There is? Nobody called me."

"I would think you'd already be there and wouldn't need to be called. Since, you know, it's a Monday, and you work there."

Shrugging, he said, "I took some vacation time."

"I see."

"I needed a few days away from everyone's staring. Time to decompress, you know? I thought staying home and killing zombies would help, but it only reminded me that I'm surrounded by dead people all day in real life, with my dad being the worst of them, because he doesn't realize how dead he is. Inside." He thumped his chest, and I tried not to laugh at his melodrama.

His serious façade cracked. "You know what I mean, though."

"He's still mad at you?"

The darkness returned to his eyes. "Yes. And for what? For being born? I'm not the one who told the whole town his precious secret. And so what if I had been? It was time for us to stop lying, stop hiding. Half the people involved are dead. And guess what we've found out? Folks around here don't care. Or if they do, it's typical morbid curiosity, like you'd expect with any juicy gossip."

He was right. Seemed like everyone was taking it more in stride than I'd thought they would. Most of them were probably trying to collect on bets they made years ago that a Mulligan was banging Vel. Didn't matter that they'd had the wrong one.

He took a quick breath and stood with his back against the brightly lit TV, which was flashing the words "You're Dead" in dripping blood. "You know what all this reinforces? Life's too damn short."

"Absolutely."

Looking down at his feet, he scratched his eyebrow with his thumbnail. "That's why I'm finally leaving the business. Dad's already pissed at me, anyway, so might as well." His head lifted, jaw set. "And you know what? Screw him. Look what merely existing has done for him." He thought about that a second. "Actually, he's done all right for himself. But that's because he likes what he does. If you can believe that. But *I* don't like it. I'm not draining another body. Ever again.

And the only thing I'm ever putting in an oven is food. Now I have to tell *him* that."

My butt hit the wall, which I leaned against for support. "That's great, Eric. I'm… I'm happy for you. This has been a long time coming."

"Now seems like the perfect time to maybe—I don't know —get away from here for a while. Do some things I want to do."

"Like?"

He unplugged his headset and coiled the cord around the band connecting the two earpieces. After setting them on the desk, he turned off the console and the television, plunging the room into darkness so I could no longer read his expression. "Like getting my degree in Game Development."

"As in, going back to college?"

"Yeah. Sort of. There's this school in Florida that specializes in gaming degrees. Highly rated. It's not a traditional college you would have heard about, but it's one of the biggest recruiting grounds for top game developers."

He continued talking into the dim room, but one word kept echoing through my skull: *Florida. Florida. Florida.*

"I realize we're coming up on the busiest time of year at the funeral home. But Dad's going to have to figure out how to manage without me eventually. No time like the present. There's always going to be some reason to keep me here. And I… I can't do this anymore."

I shook my head. "No. No, you shouldn't have to, if you don't want to. Nothing's keeping you here."

He chuckled. "I wouldn't say *that*. I haven't forgotten about patching up the network at Velvet."

"Don't worry about that." I backed into the hallway. "You've been stuck here, stifled, for too long. You should definitely…" I continued reversing, wishing the government's safety czars required humans to make that annoying beeping sound so it would drown out the shakiness in my voice. "Anyway, Florida sounds great. You should totally do that. I need to, uh, change my clothes, and—" While gesticulating, I lost my grip on one of my shoes and it tumbled to the floor, its spike heel barely missing my big toe. I scrambled to pick it up, still backing toward my room.

Eric followed me into the hallway. "Whitney—"

My foot met fur, which resulted in exactly the type of noise you'd expect from a trod-on cat.

"The cat's behind you," Eric finished, wincing and half-covering his eyes as Buster flung himself away from me and into the wall at the end of the hallway.

"Sorry," I muttered to the animal or Eric or the wall or myself. Or all of us. Or no one. I didn't know who I was saying it to. I only knew that I was sorry. Very sorry.

Without another word, I disappeared into my room and closed the door with my elbow. I dropped my shoes with a clunk and, numb, lurched toward the bed, where I flung myself face down. Guilt slammed against my breastbone as I realized I was no better than Larry, no better than Aunt Vel, only thinking of myself, wishing Eric would stay here, although he couldn't achieve the life he wanted by doing that.

I *didn't* want him to remain at a job he hated, though. Or continue his part in running a family business that didn't interest him. I wanted him to be happy, no matter what that meant or where that took him. Even if it was hundreds of miles away from me.

Hundreds? More like a thousand, I bet.

To complete my misery, I pulled my phone from my pocket and Googled it. Thirteen hundred miles from Morris to the Florida state line. Right. Great. *Glad I looked that up.*

I tossed my phone toward my pillows and heaved myself

from the mattress. As I changed from office clothes to jeans, a t-shirt, and my favorite wrap cardigan, I focused on the positive. Eric deserved this. He'd make a great video game designer or developer or whatever. More importantly, that life would make him happy. Listening to him for one minute with that kid from Arkansas—or anyone on the other end of that headset, for that matter—was all the proof anyone would need. He loved gaming and how it brought people together, how it distracted people from their problems.

And he'd love Florida. He hated winter. Well, mostly because of all the dead people. But he wasn't fond of the weather, either. It remained to be seen how "hot and humid" would work with all that body hair, but... whatever. He'd figure it out. It wasn't like he had to stay there after he completed his degree. He could go anywhere in the country— the world!—he wanted to go. Well, probably. I didn't know exactly how that worked. But surely, in a job that technological, you could telecommute.

The point is, he'd found his ticket out of *here*. Finally.

Good for him.

Sitting on the end of the bed, I slid on a pair of fuzzy socks and took a deep breath. Straightening, I looked into the mirror above the dresser a few feet in front of me. This was good. No, this was *great*.

Someone simply needed to deliver the memo to my heart, and fast. I couldn't hide in there forever, trying to convince myself.

~

Fortunately, Eric's enthusiasm was plenty contagious. He was excited enough for both of us. As he should have been. After dinner, while I sprawled lazily on the floor in front of the fire, he paced the living room, revealing more details about his plans for the future. If he thought it was odd that all I could do was alternate, "Good for you!" and "It'll be great!" and "You deserve this!" and "How exciting!" like a motivational pull-string doll, he didn't call me on it. Honestly, he was probably too happy to notice.

Eventually, he halted in the middle of the room and grinned down at me. "Thanks for listening. It'll be easier to say all this to Dad now that I have it straight in my head."

"No problem."

He snapped his fingers and blinked. "Oh my gosh! I've been going on and on about video game school and finding myself, like a nerdy teenager, and I almost forgot you talked to your family today about... everything. How'd that go?"

"It was just my mom and Shelly. My uncles couldn't make the call. Which was okay. It's better if Mom tells them."

Without me. Then she and her siblings could make their snarky asides about how they'd always known Vel was a fruit-cake and blah, blah, blah. Of course, I didn't say that to Eric. Eventually, he might want a relationship with them, and I didn't want to make it any more awkward than it was already going to be. I stopped there and merely smiled tightly.

"And?"

I shrugged. "They were shocked, of course. Well..." *Confession time.* "I'd already told Shelly about the money Aunt Vel gave you." At his chagrined expression, I said, "I'm sorry! I had to tell someone, though. And it was before I knew the whole story."

As if on second thought, he didn't care, he waved off my apology. "And your mom?"

I stared into space, remembering back to the silence, followed by the laughter and all of the teasing about my feelings for Eric. My eyes welled, but I impatiently blinked away

325

the tears and smiled brightly. "A Thanksgiving dinner invitation might be in the works. And, uh, possibly mail-order fruit."

He chuckled and winced. "It's weird, isn't it?"

"A little. But not as uncommon as we think. People give up kids for adoption all the time. And those kids reconnect with their birth parents—and extended families—all the time, too. This is just... unexpected on a few different levels, that's all."

"They weren't mad, though?" he asked, lowering himself to the floor next to me.

I adjusted to a sitting position and picked at the fuzzy rug under us. "No. Nobody's angry. Yet. Until they find out about that money."

I meant it as a joke but immediately realized my mistake at mentioning it again when the shadow passed over his face.

"Kidding," I said, patting his knee. "They'd buy booze with it or piss it away on the stock market. It's much safer with you, funding your continuing education."

He opened his mouth, then quickly closed it.

"What?" I prompted.

He shook his head. "Nothing. Uh... I was just going to say, I might not be ready to meet everyone at Thanksgiving."

"That's okay."

"But I'm glad there are no hard feelings... so far. That's more than I can say for my side of the family."

I reached for his hand. "I'm sorry."

He flipped our hands over and rubbed his thumb along my knuckles. Suddenly, the heat spreading through me had nothing to do with the fire next to us (although that wasn't helping things).

Barely keeping my focus on the conversation, I said, "Lena doesn't seem mad."

"She's the peacekeeper. Or she's trying to be. Things are...

tense between my dad, Horty, and Jake. And Bobby, for some reason. He's worried about the business, but what are people going to do to boycott us? Stop dying? Maybe Dad's not going to be reelected as coroner, but in the grand scheme of things, who cares?"

"And you're not mad at Hortense?"

"No. I already told her not to worry about it. Hell, I should be thanking her. I hear mail-order fruit is a classy gift." He dropped my hand and stared into the fire, then closed his eyes. "I just want everyone to be happy," he said quietly, wistfully. "Is that too much to ask?"

"No, it's not," I said. Then I realized with a sinking heart... it might be.

CHAPTER THIRTY

SIX WEEKS LATER, I was busy faking my way through every day, recapturing that "cheery" reputation Aunt Vel had perpetuated when she'd talked about me, while Eric prepared for his big move to Florida. Oh, excuse me. "Temporary relocation" was what he was calling it. (Ha! Sound familiar?) I went along with that publicly, but privately, I'd taken to thinking of it as "the end of the world." Sometimes, if I was feeling particularly optimistic, I mentally referred to it as, "the saddest day of my life."

As far as the rest of the town—and my mom and sister—knew, I was happy as could be, though. Sure, I fell into bed exhausted every night and cried myself to sleep more often than not, but nobody needed to know about that. That was just… pathetic.

Today, I was extra fake-bubbly, because I was preparing for my long weekend away for Thanksgiving. This meant being stopped every three feet as I ran my post-work errands.

"Yes, it'll be wonderful to catch up with family and friends in Boston!"

"No, Eric's not coming with me; he's too busy packing. But

he's generously offered to keep an eye on the cat and Velvet and my home renovations. What a great guy, huh?"

"What, this sweater? Why thank you! It's one of my favorites, too."

"No, my house won't be ready for a while. But that's no biggie, since I'll be house-sitting for Eric while he's away. Everything works out, right?"

"Yep. He leaves Monday. Exciting! Florida! Must be nice to be escaping right before the winter weather hits. Speaking of weather, I'd better get moving before this storm arrives. I hear sleet's in the forecast. Brrrr!"

Parked in one of the angled spots on Main Street in front of the funeral home, I rubbed my aching cheeks.

A few more days. I can do this.

Never mind that I was sure he was going to fall in love with Florida—and probably someone *in* Florida, someone with unnaturally colored hair (purple, I was thinking) and an aptitude for all the parts of game design he didn't want to or know how to do. They'd become this amazing game-designing duo and travel the world, hosting conferences, where people would pay big money to hear their tips and tricks for making the most addictive, best-selling games. They'd sign autographs and joke about how they couldn't believe they were such rock stars, doing what they loved with the one they loved.

Because once he got a taste of the world away from here, why would he ever come back? I'd been out there. I knew what it was like.

I also knew what it was like to leave a place that didn't hold any happiness for you anymore. I'd been in denial about that for a long time, but now I realized Boston had been that place for me. I wouldn't go back there for all the money in the world. That part of my life was over. The door had been shut. Most of the time, I was not only okay with that, I was glad. And I rarely thought of it. Sure, there were a few big-city conveniences I missed, but Morris was my home now, for better or worse.

Still haven't gotten the nerve to tell anyone else that, not even my sister and mother, but... one obstacle at a time.

In a few more weeks—fingers crossed—my house would be ready for me to move back in. Or at least move in the furniture, including the few pieces from Boston still in storage. Then Eric would return from Florida for a while (I hoped), and I could settle there, too, and see about building that permanent life I've chosen up here. Before I'd had all the facts, granted, but... not *that* much had changed. I'd still rather run Velvet than research communication styles and endlessly argue theory with a bunch of eggheads.

And so what if Eric might not be here? I hadn't moved here for him. I'd moved here for me. Quitting my job in Boston and withdrawing from my graduate studies wasn't relevant to what' was going on in his life, so why bother him with the details? He was busy enough with his own plans. Plans that were separate from mine, like mine were separate from his.

Well, sort of. Like I'd told every one of the more than four thousand residents in this town, I was house-sitting for him while he was away, so that had become part of my plans. And I'd be taking him to the airport in less than a week. If I could get past that... it would all be okay.

I had to admit, with that looming, it was going to be difficult to maintain a cheerful, thankful attitude during my family's holiday dinner, especially since Eric—and my permanent relocation to Maine (once I finally disclosed it)—would be major topics of discussion.

There was no use dwelling on that now, though. Worrying

about it wasn't going to change anything. The best thing to do was get home before the freezing rain hit.

I was about to turn the key in the ignition when movement through my windshield caught my eye. Eric. Walking into Mulligan Funeral Home. For the first time in weeks. Through the front door. Like a guest.

He looked up and glanced around as he pulled on the handle, then paused when he saw me. He smiled and nodded once. Dropping the handle, he shot me a small, uncertain wave.

I waved back and said, "Hi," out loud, like a dummy. He could barely see me from that distance, much less hear me in a closed car.

But it was like he *could* hear me, because he ducked his head against the cold wind already flecked with the occasional raindrop and trotted down the path to the sidewalk. I cranked my window down and dragged out my trusty smile once more.

"Hey, roomie!" I said. "Whatcha doin'?"

He squinted into the spitting precipitation and tucked his hands into his coat pockets as he leaned closer to the window. "Figured I'd put it off long enough and would come down here to get my stuff. Do the walk of shame with my box of personal effects. I wonder if Dad'll make Jake escort me from the premises."

"Oh, come on. It won't be that bad."

With a conceding head tilt, he said, "You're right. This will be downright pleasant compared to Thanksgiving."

"You're welcome to come to Boston with me. The Faelhaber clan is dying to meet you."

He groaned at the pun I pretended was intentional and for his benefit, then said, "Come in with me?" and looked over at the brick colonial. I hesitated, so he pleaded, "Please? They like you so much more than me right now."

"I don't know about that."

"What are you talking about? You and Horty are practically besties."

Unbuckling my seatbelt, I sighed and waited for him to move back so I could open the car door. "Fine. If you'll stop talking like a teenage girl, I'll go inside with you." As we made our way up the walk and under the protective overhang, I said, "You're going to discover nobody's as upset with you as you think they are."

"Hm."

"Including your dad. The new guys seem to be working out okay. Everyone misses you and wishes you'd stop hanging out alone at home in your underwear, playing video games all the time with Buster."

He pulled his chin back as he held the door open for me to let me enter the building first. "What?!"

I shrugged. "I may have embellished a bit when your relatives asked me what you've been up to."

"Uh, thanks."

Inside, we wiped our feet on the all-weather mat and grinned at each other like morons. "Serves you right for hiding from everyone like a big coward."

"People stare. It's uncomfortable."

"Well, they ask *me* uncomfortable questions. I'd take staring any day."

"Anyway, I'm not hiding. I've been busy, fixing the network at Velvet—"

"Thank you. And you're doing a fine job of it. At night. When nobody's there. You big coward."

"During the day, I've been getting the house ready for

winter, since I won't be around to tend to that stuff as it crops up."

"Yeah, yeah." I took a step in the direction of the hallway that led to the offices, but he snagged my elbow and I boomeranged back, colliding with his chest. "Hey, there."

He transferred his hands to my upper arms. "Sorry. But…" His face came closer to mine as he lowered his voice. "Thanks for being the go-between so often lately."

"It's not a big—"

"It means a lot, though. It's not easy smiling in the face of everyone's open stares and nosy questions. And I don't know what I'd do without you being here to reassure Horty and Lena that I'm okay and just need my space, even if you do lie to them and make me sound like a miserable sack of dog turds."

"You're welcome. Maybe if you'd man up and talk to them yourself, you wouldn't have to worry about the version they're getting from me."

"You're right. I'll be better."

"Nice of you to agree to that, five days before you skip town."

He let go of me and led the way toward the office. "Hey, better late than never, right? You want to see the cooler while we're here?"

I rushed to catch up to his long strides. "No!"

"Aw, come on. I'll check to make sure there aren't any gruesome cases first, but you should see it at least once."

"I'm okay with the mental images I already have, thanks."

Hortense greeted us at the door. "I thought I heard familiar voices," she said, pulling Eric roughly to her and smashing her ear against his chest, a rapturous smile on her face. "Aw, Cuz. I've missed you so much!"

He chuckled nervously and nodded at Lena, who ended

her phone call, stood, and circled her desk to meet us in the middle of the room. "Oh, you don't have to lie," he said, patting her back. "I heard one of the new guys is a real looker. Knows how to talk in complete sentences to living people, too, which has to be a huge improvement."

"Neither of them writes obits. I have to do all the print shop business myself now."

I rolled my eyes at her. "Such a hardship."

Lena, seeing her daughter wasn't going to let go of Eric any time soon, joined the hug to make it a threesome. Craning her neck to look up at him, she said, "It's not the same without you."

"What do you do with all the extra time in your day, now that you don't have to go behind me, apologizing for the stupid, awkward things I say in front of guests?"

She slapped his chest. "You!"

Bobby emerged from his office, took one look at the group hug, and disappears again.

"Bobby's happy to see you, too," I quipped.

"He's crankier than usual," Lena stage-whispered. "Nicholas keeps him and Jill up during the night."

"Babies do that, I've heard," Eric said. "Now, uh, this is nice and all, but…" He flapped his arms. "Can we save some hugging for later? Maybe Thanksgiving?"

"You're coming?" Hortense asked hopefully, as she took a tiny step backward to give her cousin some breathing room.

Lena clapped her hands when he nodded and answered, "Of course. I'm in charge of pumpkin pies. And I provide the entertainment, although it's usually unintentional."

"We thought maybe this year…" Hortense glanced at me. "Well, we weren't sure. Whitney said you weren't going to Boston with her, but we hadn't heard if you were going to spend the day alone or…"

"Alone? No. How am I going to eat until I'm sick if I stay home with Buster? And who's going to push back from the table, rub his stomach, and say, 'Huffuhffuhfuhfuhfuh,' like I do? You think I'm going to leave that tradition up to Bobby? Or Jake? They won't get it right." He waved both hands toward Bobby's office.

Laughing, Lena returned to her desk, but Hortense remained in front of Eric, smiling adoringly up at him, her hands on her hips. "I'm so glad you're back."

"Oh, I'm not back," he said firmly. "No, ma'am. I did hear some of my stuff was getting in the way of the new guys, though, so... Where are they, anyway?"

"Had a middle-of-the-night call at the nursing home, so they left early. They've been gone for a while."

"Takes two guys to do the job I used to do, huh? Don't think I haven't noticed that."

"Larry hasn't been around much either," Lena said, sifting through the mail.

"Oh."

"But that's okay. He's a grump, anyway."

"I wouldn't know. He won't answer my calls," Eric said casually. "Anyway. Did you guys already box up my Super Mario action figures, or did you leave them up so the new guys could enjoy them? I hope they didn't get used to them."

Hortense crossed to a closet and opened it. Among the usual pens, pencils, paper reams, and envelopes sat a medium-sized box on a high shelf. She stood on her tiptoes to reach it but couldn't. Eric stepped around her and lifted it over her head.

"I got it, Shorty Horty."

She laughed as she closed the closet door and turned to face him again. "You haven't called me that in forever!"

"I miss it."

One hand on her hip, she asked, "Are you sure you want to reinstate childhood nicknames, Jelly Junk?"

"Whatever. That one's more embarrassing for the person saying it."

"You have a point."

He tapped the top of his box. "Well… I guess this is it."

I turned to give them some privacy while he rushed on, "Well, not *it*. I mean, I'll see you tomorrow at dinner. And for the rest of our lives. But, you know… not around *here* much. I hope not, anyway. Because this place isn't where normal people spend much time. Not voluntarily, anyway. And I'm a normal person now. I guess."

"Never," Hortense said, giving his arm another squeeze. "Promise me that."

"I don't think I have a choice. Speaking of promises, I promised Whitney a tour of the fridge downstairs, so…"

I whirled on the room. "What? No! I said I *didn't* want to see it."

Winking at Hortense, Eric asked, "Any interesting cases we should know about first?"

"No!" I said again, laughing but stifling an irrational panic, like he was somehow going to get me down there against my will, possibly with hypnosis… or sheer physical strength.

Hortense piped up with, "Eric used to take dates down there. 'I'll show you my bodies if you show me yours.'"

"Hey, that line worked! Once. She was weird, though."

"Ya think?" I muttered. "But seriously. I don't want to go down there. Ever."

He shrugged and adjusted the box in his arms. "All right. Your loss."

"I'll find a way to cope."

"The only one down there now is Mrs. Glossner," Hortense said. "She was the nursing home pickup."

"Aw, Mrs. Glossner died?" Eric's jaw dropped. "Man…" He turned to me. "She was my second grade teacher. Super-sweet lady. She used to let me bum cigarettes from her at The Poole Table."

"When you were a kid?!"

"No!" He rolled his eyes at me. "When I was a drunk and used to hang out at The Poole Table."

Lena tutted from her desk. "Eric! I didn't know you used to smoke."

"I only did it occasionally. But I stopped even before I got sober. Seeing your first set of black lungs will cure you of a cigarette addiction in a hurry." He stared into space and shook his head. "Dang. Mrs. Glossner."

"She was old, Eric," Hortense said.

"Yeah, but…"

"And she could barely breathe."

He snapped out of his reverie. "When's her funeral? Friday? Saturday?"

Hortense rooted around in some papers on her desk and came up with a manila folder, which she opened. Clipped to the inside of the cover was a form she skimmed before answering, "Saturday. Visitation is Friday evening."

"I'll be there. Man. Mrs. Glossner." He clicked his tongue, then blinked at me. "Okay, now that I'm completely depressed, let's go."

"Are you going to be okay?" I said, once we were alone again in the vestibule, before we pushed through the doors into the cold, wet evening. My tone was light, but there was plenty of sincerity in the question too.

He waved off my concern. "Of course. Everybody dies, right? It's what you do with life when you're alive that counts. Mrs. Glossner had a good run."

I nodded. "Sounds like it."

"And one positive in the whole thing..."

"What's that?"

"I didn't have to see her naked. Or drain her. Or any of that. I can pay my respects without knowing about every mole and wrinkle on the lady."

I stared at him.

He shifted the box to his other side. "I will tell you one thing, though. I'll be judging these new guys pretty hard on this one. They better get it right on Mrs. Glossner. No crazy makeup or weird facial expressions. No glue over-spill on the eyelids. These guys better bring their A-game."

Still, all I could do was gape, so he smiled uncertainly and asked, "What?"

"You are so bizarre."

"I'm being serious!"

"That's what makes it even more disturbing."

No, what made it more disturbing was that his rant had only served to underscore how much I loved him.

I blinked and swallowed back my emotions, though, and held open the door for him. "Come on, dork. Let's hope the roads haven't started to freeze. I don't want to go to the basement with you, dead or alive."

CHAPTER THIRTY-ONE

WE MADE it back to Eric's safely, and I made it to Boston for Thanksgiving with no problems. I ate a ton of food (although probably not as much as Eric did) and thought of him huffing at the table when I felt like I couldn't eat another bite. I'd missed him.

When my aunts and uncles pumped me for information about this new nephew of theirs, I talked so long and so enthusiastically about him that Shelly started shooting me wide-eyed looks across the table. So I shut up. But he came up again in conversation later, while everyone was nursing their after-dinner cocktails, so I held court for another half hour, describing everything he'd done to repair and optimize the network at Velvet, saving me thousands in upgrade costs.

"Sounds like you two have become close... friends," Uncle Kevin said, with a suggestive eyebrow wiggle.

"That's one way to put it," Shelly muttered into her martini.

I clammed up after that. Nobody understood. Or maybe they understood too well.

Today, instead of the usual Black Friday shenanigans with

Shelly and Mom, I'd opted to visit my old haunts one more time. You know, to make sure I was doing the right thing.

I started at the coffee shop where James and I used to spend lazy Saturday mornings, people-watching and planning the rest of our day (on kid-free weekends, of course). On this occasion, I sat at a table, sipping espresso and sneaking glances at the couple occupying "our" sofa. Did James and I ever look that happy? I couldn't remember objectively enough to know if we had ever been truly happy, though. All of my pleasant memories had been tainted by that final phone call. Now, all I could recall was him dictating our plans or informing me of how busy he was going to be, too busy to "entertain" me.

I left as soon as my tiny cup of caffeine was gone. It wasn't the same. *I* wasn't the same. Despite suspecting my whole day would be full of similar experiences, however, I trudged on with my tour. If nothing else, I needed the closure.

Plus, not everywhere would hold memories of James. I was a strong, independent... Well, you get it. I'd spent plenty of time here by myself... and enjoyed it. I could get lost for hours in an art supply shop. So I visited my favorite one next and stocked up on large, high-bond sketch pads and a new set of charcoal sticks. Remembering the look on Eric's face when he was trying to clue me in to my dirty face on the bench next to the trail made me grin like a goober at the checkout.

The clerk smiled and said, "There's nothing like new supplies, is there? So much possibility!"

I nodded and pretended like my purchases and their potential were my primary source of joy.

Since my apartment wasn't my apartment anymore, and stopping by unannounced wasn't my thing, I skipped a farewell to the place I'd called home for the first few years of my adulthood.

My final stop was the university. More than a setting, it was a physical manifestation of a dream, a goal I'd had for so long that working to attain it had become second nature; a habit. I'd stopped questioning whether it was what I actually wanted. Communication—or at least the study of it—had been my life. And I was going to be a source of information and knowledge for others who sought to make it their lives. They would do likewise. And on and on and on. I was to be a member of an exclusive club of scholars dedicated to shedding light on one of the most basic components to any successful civilization. Campus was the backdrop to this mission, but it was more than a mere background. It was the vehicle through which the ideas flowed.

Thousands of hours I'd spent in the library, researching, writing, chasing down evidence to support my hypotheses. I also graded undergraduates' papers there. And took the occasional nap in the private study nooks, between lectures. To all appearances, I was the intrepid, tireless leader of every group project or presentation I'd ever been assigned. It was me who always said, "One more hour, folks. We're almost there!" Then after everyone else dispersed, I stayed for many more "one more hour"s to type up our work and tie it all together.

Now, standing amongst the shelves in the nearly deserted place on a holiday weekend, my memories felt like a story I'd been told so many times that I'd internalized it and cast myself as the protagonist. But I marveled at her tenacity and wondered what could possibly have been her motivation. For the first time, it seemed so obvious: Don't ever allow yourself to rely on others for anything. Not success, not food or shelter, and definitely not happiness. Be the sole provider for all your own needs. Then, when someone exits your life, you can mourn their loss, but the project as a whole won't collapse.

Strength.

Independence.

They were synonymous.

The only constant in your life was you.

As if to bust this hypothesis, Pearl, one of the university's long-time librarians, waved at me on my way past the circulation desk toward the doors.

"Whitney?"

I circled back and leaned on her counter. "Well, look at you, working on a holiday weekend. Some things never change."

"It's quiet here on days like this. Only the die-hards are hanging around. And they're so self-sufficient, they could have the run of the place without any of us worrying about them." She pushed a cart of books to be shelved to a spot out of the way and motioned for me to join her behind the desk, in a spare chair.

I waved off her invitation. "Can't stay long. I'm here as a visitor."

"How have you been? *Where* have you been?"

I chuckled. "Running a print shop in Maine. Morris, Maine."

"Never heard of it."

"I'd be shocked if you had."

"Was this a 'bucket list' thing? I didn't realize you were interested in… that."

"I got interested in a hurry, after my aunt left it to me in her will."

She frowned. "Now, this sounds familiar. I had heard you'd lost someone close to you. I'm sorry."

"Thanks. It's been an interesting few months."

"I bet. And now you're back?"

I shook my head. "Only to say goodbye." Her startled expression made me laugh. "I know, it's kind of morbid, but…

this place was important to me. To be honest, I came here today because I knew it'd be empty, so I wouldn't embarrass myself if I started blubbering in the stacks."

"And did you? You know, moisture isn't good for books."

Digging my hands into my coat pockets, I shrugged. "I've been surprisingly stoic."

"Do you like Maine, then?"

"I love it. Another surprise."

She spread her hands. "There you have it, then. You've found a new sanctuary. No need for this place."

"Yeah... I suppose you're right."

I asked about her family and downloaded some juicy staff gossip (the librarians know all, trust me) but stopped her before she had a chance to dish about James. I'd rather not know. Then I said goodbye like I'd be in here tomorrow as usual. No need for protracted, melodramatic displays. This place wasn't going anywhere. And if I knew Pearl at all, she wasn't either.

Back outside, I blinked into the autumn sun and inhaled the crisp air that could have been the scent of academia if it were a candle. It made me nostalgic for school supplies and new clothes.

While I was debating whether to stop by the Student Union for one more slice of cardboard pizza before heading back to my car and Mom's house, I spotted him. Hurried as usual, despite there being nothing to rush to or from on the day after a holiday, he was striding across the quad, straight toward me, his head down, his eyes glued to his feet, like always. He'd once explained to me, "They're like a metronome. I always walk to the beat of whatever song is in my head, and nothing around me is more interesting than that." Judging by his speed today, his internal DJ had dialed up something peppy. A Sousa march, perhaps.

My first instinct was to duck behind something, anything, but there wasn't anywhere to hide. It was about as wide open here as it could possibly be, and I was in the middle of the openness, not on the fringe, near any trees.

"Shit," I mumbled, feeling like a squirrel in the middle of a highway. Indecision rooted me to the sidewalk, where I stood, stuck, praying that he'd stay focused on his feet until he passed me. Unfortunately, the presence of anyone else on the quad on such a slow day garnered a rare upward glance. When he looked up and saw me, he missed a beat, probably the first one since he'd learned how to keep time with a baton. But the falter in his otherwise confident gait was so subtle that anyone not as familiar with him would likely have failed to notice. I noticed.

"Oh, my gosh. Whitney," he said, breathless, as he stopped in front of me.

"James. I— Well, this is some luck running into you."

Horrible luck.

His furrowed brow told me he agreed with my silent addition. "Yeah. Wow. I, uh…"

"You look busy."

"I am. You know how it goes. Might only be Thanksgiving for everyone else, but for me that means there's just a few weeks before Christmas everything. The madrigals are caroling in full period costume this year, can you believe it?"

"Whose brilliant idea was that?"

He blinked rapidly. "Mine."

"Oh. When you said, 'Can you believe it?' I thought you… Never mind."

"I meant it was a huge win for me. I've been lobbying for it for years. You know this."

"No. No, I don't remember you ever mentioning it."

"You must not have been listening. Which isn't surprising,

come to think of it, but…" He smiled tightly. "Anyway. It was a tradition for decades. Then the sixties came along, and nobody cared about tradition anymore, and the university saw it as a chance to save some money—the costumes are incredibly expensive to maintain, as you can imagine."

"I can only imagine."

He inhaled as if to continue, then stopped short. "Right."

"Right. You were saying?"

"Never mind. I can tell you're not interested."

"I am!"

"No." He chuckled and looked down at his metronome feet. Hands on his hips, he said, "This is good. Really good."

"What's good?"

"Whenever I second-guess whether I was right to end things with you, I need to keep this conversation in mind. Because it's a perfect example of why we didn't work."

In spite of my outrage, I managed a coughing laugh. "Oh, do enlighten, Maestro."

His head snapped up at my (to him) uncharacteristic retort, but rather than chasten him, it seemed to embolden him. "Your work was of utmost importance, but you had no interest at all in mine."

"That's not true." *Yes, it is, but…* "I always listened to what you said. I always cared, because you cared."

"That's not the same, though."

"Well, I couldn't help that it wasn't my favorite subject."

"You could have hidden it better. But no. You became an annoying parrot every time we discussed my work."

"Excuse me? Annoying parrot?"

"You're doing it now. 'I can only imagine.' 'Annoying parrot?' You know, I was only making conversation to make it less awkward that I came across you in a place you have no business being, unless you were *trying* to run into me."

"Now hang on a minute."

"I'm sure it's been hard, Whit, but you have to move on. I have. You chose Maine, and that hurt at first, but I've come to realize it was for the best. I needed more than an echo chamber. I needed someone as passionate about my passions as I am."

"Good luck with that. All of the whack-job composers died from syphilis hundreds of years ago. Real people in the real, modern world have greater concerns than what some STD-addled alcoholic intended by slowing down the last measure of an insufferably boring symphony. Here's a theory: he fell asleep, and his pen trailed off the paper."

"You're proving my point. This is exactly why it didn't work with you."

"Maybe *you* didn't work with me. Or maybe I just didn't like conversing in song lyrics half the time."

"Mona doesn't mind."

I swallowed loudly. "Mona? Mona Delong?"

He smirked. "Yes."

"Orchestra director Mona Delong? The Mona Delong you bitched incessantly to me about before every joint concert, because she was so scattered and unprepared and... and... *that* Mona?"

He shifted to his other foot. "Yes. Well, it turns out maybe I was unfair about certain quirks of hers."

"Quirks. Oh, I'm sure."

"Listen, I didn't want to say anything. I never *would* have, if you hadn't forced me to. But my point is, she and I are a good match; you and I weren't."

"Obviously."

"And when you find someone else, you'll see that I'm right."

I lifted my chin. "Maybe I have. Found someone else, that is."

He smiled indulgently at me. "Oh, Whit... Well, good. Good for you. I'm sure he's... something."

"He *is* real!"

"I didn't say he wasn't. Someone you met at the print shop? Burly, Maine lumberjack with inky hands?"

"No. He looks good in flannel, knows how to swing an ax, and can grow a beard—unlike *someone* I know—but no to all the other stuff."

"Great. Honestly, Whit, I have to go." He passed me on the path and backed away.

I mirrored his movements, backing in the opposite direction. "I do, too. Because he's expecting me back."

"Waiting for you in his cabin, is he? Well, I wish you all the luck and happiness in the forest."

"And I hope you and Mona make snore-inducing music together."

He turned his back to me and flipped a dismissive wave over his shoulder. "Have a nice life."

"Likewise," I shouted at him, then muttered under my breath, "you pompous little ass."

I wanted to be home. And I didn't want to have only one measly evening before saying goodbye to my best friend. Therefore, I'd come back a day earlier than planned.

Home. That was what Eric's house had become for me. *Bad, I know.*

To privately atone for that sin, I took a detour on my way through town to check on the house I actually did own and stood in the drywall dust, trying to imagine how it was going to look and all the ways it would be mine by the end of this never-ending renovation. But the only thing I could picture was the final invoice from the contractor and how it was going to take me forever to pay off the loan I'd have to procure to finance this disaster.

"Pull it together, Whitney," I muttered out loud repeatedly on my way out of town toward the Mulligan compound. For the rest of the weekend, I was determined to do a fine job of living in the moment. Or putting on a good show of it.

That started with eating the Thanksgiving leftovers Eric had brought home from Lena and Hiram's.

"The woman will never stop forcing food on me, like the neglected little kid she once thought I was," he said across the butcher block, where we were perched on stools, updating each other on our respective holidays.

"So… things weren't weird? Everyone in the Mulligan/Doolan clan is back to normal?"

"We run a funeral home. We've never been normal."

"Right. But everyone's playing nice again? Forgiveness all around?"

He shrugged and regarded the mashed-potato Popsicle he'd made on his fork, then dropped it to his plate. "I guess. We avoided the topic at all costs yesterday, so I guess that means we're done with it… for now."

"Maybe that's for the best. You gonna eat those potatoes?"

He passed the fork across the counter to me. "Go for it."

I did, and he laughed when I ate them straight from the utensil, licking them like ice cream. Keeping my eyes on the tater treat, I said with studied casualness, "I ran into James yesterday."

"Leave it to you to run into the one person you were avoiding in a city the size of Boston."

"It's not a huge city. Six hundred thousand people or so.

But I greatly narrowed the odds by wandering on his turf."

"You went on campus?"

"Yeah." When he groaned at my nostalgic stunt, I defended myself. "I wanted to see it one more time!"

"Sounds like you were punished for that."

"It was fine. Sort of. He's still an ass, and he thinks I have a made-up boyfriend, but…"

"What?!" He slapped the counter between us. "How did he get that impression?"

I pointed my tatersicle at him. "It's not funny. I panicked, all right? He was yammering on and on about sticking his conductor's baton in the university's orchestra director…"

"Whoa, whoa, whoa… Tell me he *didn't* say that."

"Not in so many words, but he did make it clear she's his soul mate, and I never was, which would have been fine, because I've been over him for a long time, but… Then he had to get all condescending and, 'You'll see what I mean when you find someone new,' so I… told him I had someone new. But he didn't believe me for a second."

"Who *is* this mystery guy?"

I refocused on the shrinking glob of potatoes on the fork. "A lumbersexual, apparently."

He stroked his three-day growth. "I see. Anyone I know?"

"Considering it's nobody I know," I lied, "then no."

He sighed. "Well, who cares what that douchemuffin thinks?"

"I don't. That's why it's so dumb that I said what I did." I twirled the fork against my tongue. "Smug bastard implied I was there on campus because I was trying to run into him. As if! I nearly dug a hole in the quad with my bare hands to crawl into and avoid him when I did see him."

"The ground's rock hard by this time of the year."

I shot him a dirty look.

"Just saying."

"Well, the good news is, I won't be missing Boston. Even at the university library, all I could think was how I wished I were here. In Morris," I quickly clarified.

He smiled gently. "That's good. I'm glad you're staying. How did your mom and sister take the news?"

"Like I'd told them I was marrying God and moving to a convent in the Alps."

"They took it better than you thought they would, then. Excellent."

"They think I've lost my mind. But there's nothing there for me anymore. Everything I care about is here."

A few months ago, a realization like that would have sent me running for bleach and a mop. Now, it filled me with a contentment that was so unfamiliar I almost couldn't place it. Almost.

Movement from outside the window drew my attention to my right. I focused on the fading gray light on the other side of the panes. "Did you see that? I thought I saw a snowflake."

He shook his head but watched with me for a while until we saw another one. And another. Then a bunch. He grinned. "We weren't supposed to get snow this weekend, as far as I knew."

"Right? Geez, I'm glad I came home early. This stuff looks like it means business."

Standing, he came around the island and took my hand. "Come on."

"Where are we—" The fork fell to my plate with a clang as I allowed myself to be dragged out the back door onto the flagstone patio. In my socks. Fortunately, the stones were still moderately dry, but with these huge, fluffy flakes, that wasn't going to be the case for long.

Eric tilted his head back toward the sky, catching the snow

on his lashes and cheeks. I did the same, delighting at how quickly the precipitation accumulated on my face and tickled my nose. After only a few seconds, watching the swirling snowflakes against the dark gray sky with no other objects as anchoring frames of reference made me dizzy, and I staggered back a step.

Eric grabbed my hand.

"Whoa there, drunky."

"I'm not drunk!" I laughed as he drew me closer.

"Right. It's the flagstones."

"It's the snow."

"You tell yourself whatever you need to tell yourself."

Considering I'd only drunk half a glass of wine with my dinner, I didn't bother defending myself. Instead, I cuddled up to his chest—for warmth and balance, of course—and closed my eyes while the snow fell onto my head like kisses from Heaven.

But he felt too good, and he smelled even better, so I stepped away after less than a minute. Venturing farther onto the patio, I leaned on a cluster of boulders and stared up at the sky again. "I've never been a fan of snow," I admitted.

Following a few seconds' pause, Eric's voice came from right behind my shoulder. "No? Me neither."

"It creates chaos. Traffic jams and accidents, power outages…"

"Death."

"That, too. It's messy. I don't like messy."

He chuckled. "No, you don't."

"But this…" I sighed as I regarded the quickly disappearing grass not shielded by the pines. "This is beautiful."

"It is," he agreed, but when I looked at him, he wasn't watching the snow at all. He was staring at me.

I blushed and cleared my throat. "Anyway, so you're not

going to miss this in Florida, huh?"

He surveyed the surroundings, then turned to face me again. "Not the snow, no. But I'm definitely going to miss—"

A flash of fur flew between us.

"Buster!" Eric ran after the cat. In a patch of snow-covered grass, he skidded and landed on his butt but quickly regained his feet, calling for and cursing at the escaped feline.

I remained on the patio, covering my mouth to stifle my loudest giggles but doing a horrible job of it.

Eric's laugh echoed in the cold yard. "Buster, you son of a — When I catch you, I'm turning you into a fur coat."

"Smallest fur coat ever!" I yelled.

"A scarf, then. Or a stole. Is that a thing? Get back here! Buster!"

"Let him go! He'll be fine! But you're going to kill yourself," I said, as he proved my point by skidding once more. The cat stared at him from a safe distance, underneath a far pine. Eric shook his fist at him but returned to the patio.

When he arrived in front of me, I smiled up into his face. "You're insane."

"He's an inside cat."

"He won't go far. He's just testing the boundaries, seeing what's out there, what he might have been missing all these years." I gently wiped snow from Eric's cheeks. "But he'll come back. Right?"

Mouth slack, chest heaving, he nodded.

"C'mon. It's freezing out here, and you're all wet from falling down. Why don't we go inside, and you can show me how to play one of those shoot-'em-up games you love so much."

With a final glance back at Buster, we retreated into the warm, dry house. I hoped I was right about both of my adventurers.

CHAPTER THIRTY-TWO

BUSTER CAME BACK (his food dish was inside, after all), and not only did I learn how to play that video game, I didn't want to stop playing for basic things like eating and sleeping. Only after Eric threatened to unplug the console and drag me from the room Sunday night did I relent, on the condition that he set me up with my own gamer tag the next morning.

True to his word, he did exactly that after gathering the last of his things in his carry-on bag. He didn't even tease me —too much—when I chose the name "Chomp-Sky." Which was a bit disappointing, to be honest. I'd thought long and hard about the perfect, groan-worthy tag to make him laugh before his departure.

But he merely snorted and rolled his eyes, then said, "Good one, Nerdicus Maximus," a relatively subdued reaction for him.

After putting in the final information to make my tag official, he turned off the console and the television, spun to face me, and looking miserable, opened his mouth. But despite the large intake of breath that generally precedes an important proclamation, he said nothing.

"What is it? Are you worried I'm going to break your precious game system? I'll be gentle, I promise. Much easier on it than you are when you're bashing away at it, yelling at some faceless person half a world away."

"I'm not worried about that."

"And I'll set a timer to remind me to eat and sleep and use the bathroom. Walk around. I know you worry about death by video game."

That prompted a tiny smile, followed by a wry lift of his eyebrows and a fake lecture about online gamer etiquette, but it was obvious by his distracted delivery that his heart wasn't in it.

"I promise not to abuse strangers—particularly minors—on the headset. Now, if you find a way to connect and play with me from down in Florida—which would be awesome, by the way, and we should totally figure out how to make that happen—all bets are off. I'll yell obscenities at you all night long."

Surely that would elicit an attempt at sexual innuendo, no matter how weak… but no.

"We'll see. I, uh, don't know how much time I'll have for playing games. Although… I could justify it and call it 'research.'" He shouldered his duffel bag and sighed. "Let's go. I'm nervous about what last night's weather is going to mean for my flight. My text alerts say everything's running on time, but you know how that goes. I hate air travel."

"It'll be fine. But if it makes you feel better to get there earlier than planned, we can leave now." It didn't matter that I felt cheated of these final minutes. They were only minutes. We were only delaying the inevitable. Best to rip off the bandage as quickly as possible. A hairy guy like Eric would know that.

Speaking of hairy guys, there was one waiting for us on

the porch when we left the house. No, not Sasquatch—although I could have sworn I saw him the other night, in the trees between here and Hortense's place—but Larry.

He stepped back and shuffled his feet on the stone floor. "I didn't realize... I thought you had a few hours before your flight."

"I do. I want to get there early."

"Good thinking. Sensible."

I turned my back on the men and pretended I wasn't there while I locked the door. I would have offered to wait in the car, but I didn't want to interrupt them (and I was dying to hear what they were saying), so I remained still to give them the illusion of privacy.

Larry took control. "Listen, son. I'm sorry we haven't talked much since you left the business."

"You're mad. I get it."

"I'm not mad."

"Okay, disappointed. Whatever."

"Not disappointed, either. Will you let me talk?" After that snap, he took a deep, shuddering breath. "You know, I deal with other people's feelings all the time. Grief, mostly. But for some reason, it's always been hard to discuss feelings with you. Feelings are intense sometimes. I wanted to protect you from that."

Oh, gosh. Never mind. Get me out of here. Too personal.

I edged toward the porch steps, cursing the uneven flagstones when I stumbled and had to clutch the rail, bringing attention to myself.

Larry gently touched my elbow. "You don't have to go. It's okay that you hear this. I feel like I owe you an explanation, too."

"No, you—"

"Yes, I do. Stay. Please."

That hypnotic undertaker's voice did its usual trick, soothing me into submission. I did wish Eric would invite his dad inside so we wouldn't have to talk on the cold porch, but one look at Eric's face and I could tell he wasn't in a hospitable mood.

He propped his rolling suitcase next to his foot and crossed his arms over his chest. "Go on."

"Right. Where was I?"

While Larry regained his train of thought, I exchanged a glance with Eric. He rolled his eyes and mouthed, *"Sorry."*

I replied soundlessly, *"Be nice."*

Larry, oblivious to our silent exchange, cleared his throat. "As I was saying, I didn't want to burden you with my woes. I know we asked a lot of you to keep the secret, but we did think it was for the best."

"For me or for you two?"

"For all of us."

"Hmm."

"And now... Am I sad that you're not continuing the Mulligan family tradition and staying with the family business? Yes. But not because *you* disappoint me. I'm going to miss you, that's all." His voice broke, so I linked my arm through his. He surprised me by grabbing my hand and squeezing it.

Eric merely gaped at the two of us. Frankly, I didn't blame him. It had been instinctual to comfort the emotional man standing next to me, but now it felt weird. At the same time, it felt good.

While I was analyzing this complex experience, Eric said, "I'll be back. I'm not going to stay down there or anything."

Larry sniffled, his voice stronger. "I know. I know. And I'm glad you're going. This is going to be a good thing. You should pursue your own dreams. I had no idea, though, that you wanted this. I wish you'd told me a long time ago."

"I didn't know either. I only knew I didn't like working with dead people."

"It's not for everyone, I guess."

Uh... for most people?

With a final pat, the senior Mulligan let go of my hand and said in rush, as if he were pulling off that proverbial bandage, "Before you left, I wanted you to know that I'm proud of you. I'm happy for you. But I've been sad for myself, which is why I've distanced myself. It was nice for things to be somewhat back to normal at Thanksgiving, though. That's when I realized I needed to tell you what I'm feeling, as uncomfortable as this is."

"Well, it's cold out here," Eric said.

"Yeah. That's what it must be." He clapped a hand on Eric's shoulder. "Good luck, son. You'll be great, I'm sure."

I grabbed the rolling suitcase and hefted it down the porch steps, quite sure, no matter the men's objections, that I didn't want to be up there anymore. There was going to be some awkward, back-thumping guy hug next, and... ugh. I lugged the luggage to the car and hoisted it into the back seat. In my peripheral vision, I was surprised to witness a real, lasting embrace. No thumping. No blushing. No foot-shifting. Just a father and son, finally connecting, through separation.

I blinked back my own emotions before Eric joined me on the driveway with a brave smile. Larry waved at us from the porch, then honked into a handkerchief when he thought we were too busy getting into the vehicle to notice. But I noticed. And I was sure Eric, as preoccupied as he was with throwing his duffel bag on top of the suitcase in the back, noticed too. A message doesn't need to be acknowledged to be fully received.

On the way to the airport, I spewed a relentless stream of words I couldn't seem to stem, terrified of silences longer than those required for me to breathe between sentences. Or sentence-like utterances. Mostly random observations, flung like candy at a parade.

"Are you excited? You must be excited. And nervous. But you shouldn't be. Because you'll be great. And everyone will love you. You're so funny. Oh, look. They got more snow here than we did. And it stuck. Huh. I'm cool with that, though. At least it's not on the roads. I don't drive well on snow. It looks pretty on the grass and trees, though. Ooh! Look at the icicles on those rocks!"

He nodded and "Mmm"ed like a patient parent with a precocious pre-school prattler, but even his most disinterested reactions didn't deter me. I kept talking. And talking. And talking. Because if I stopped talking, I might cry.

But too soon, we arrived at the airport, and there was nothing more for me to say except the worst word in the world. I eased the old Volvo into a parking space and shoved the column shifter all the way up. We'd agreed last night while staring straight ahead at the TV, dodging bullets, that it would make more sense to say our goodbyes in the parking lot, so I wasn't planning to accompany him inside the terminal.

I rested my hands in my lap and stared at them, blinking back tears.

"Well..." he began. "Here we are."

I managed a, "Yep!"

From the corner of my eye, I watched him wrap his hand around the door handle and pull, but before he shoved against the door to release himself from the vehicle, he stopped and turned to me. "Whitney, I want to thank you. For making all of this possible. If it weren't for you, I'd still be hanging out with stiffs." I tried to wave off the credit, but he persisted. "No. Really. Your illustrations may be about girl power, but they spoke to me."

I laughed through my sniffles and pushed on his shoulder. "Get out."

He laughed back. "Okay, seriously. I'm being serious now."

"Not possible."

"Yes, it is. You know it is." He licked his lips. "You've changed my life. Vel said you would."

"It was nice of her to give *you* a heads up. She didn't warn me at all about you."

He shrugged. "She loved surprises."

"Well, I love *you*, Eric Mulligan."

No. I did not just say that.

I blushed. "Uh… you know what I mean. I love ya, Cous—"

His lips collided with mine, cutting off that last, horrible word. I leaned across the center console to get closer to him as we devour each other's mouths. The already steamy windows became still more opaque. The car rocked under us as we shifted and writhed. I shoved up on the armrest between us so it was no longer an impediment. Into his lap I went, grinding against him until he moaned and pushed me away.

"What's…? I'm sorry," I said, pushing my hair back from my face. "I… I…" I moved to return to the driver's seat, but he held me with his hands around my waist.

"No. Please, please, please, don't say you're sorry."

I touched my nose to his and closed my eyes. "Oh, gosh. This is a horrible time to tell you this, but I do love you. And maybe you don't love me… like that. Maybe you only love me like a cousin, but—"

"Uh, my goodbye with Horty wasn't anything like this. Just so you know."

"Oh, good."

He tilted my chin up a bit, so I opened my eyes. "Call me old fashioned, but I don't want to make out with you in a car —my mother's car—at the airport. I mean, I do. But I don't. If that makes any sense."

"No, I get it. I agree. I got carried away, that's all. Again." I rested my head on his shoulder, my forehead against the pulse in his neck. "I wasn't going to tell you. I was going to let you get on that plane and go to that school and relive your college days the way they should have been the first time, but…"

He chuckled. "I seriously doubt it's going to be like that. Much less booze, that's for sure. Gamers have nothing on aspiring undertakers in the partying department."

I brushed off his attempts to joke away the moment. "You know what I'm saying, though. This time, you'll be learning something you want to learn. I'm so happy for you."

"I am, too. I'd be happier if I could stay here and do it, though."

"But you can't. And you have to go."

"Do I?"

"Yes. I'll be here when you get back."

Eric glanced at the clock in the dashboard and cleared his throat. "Well, uh, thanks for the case of bon voyage blue balls, but…"

I pushed away from him and giggled down at his lap. "If it makes you feel any better, I'll be going home quite frustrated, too."

"Be gentle with my shower walls." His wink turned into blinks when I slapped repeatedly at his chest. He seized my wrist. "Hey. C'mere."

I snuggled close to him again and kissed him gently,

tenderly this time, hoping this memory would sustain me for the next several weeks. But it only deepened the sadness and longing, so I ended the kiss and busied myself finger-combing his mussed hair. "Off to school with you, young man. Make me proud."

He opened his door and we both climbed out, looking around ourselves like a couple of teenagers up to no good. He pulled his large rolling suitcase and duffel bag from the back seat.

Oh, gosh. This is happening. And I'm not going to hold onto my emotions until he's gone. I'm going to lose it right here in the parking lot. And he's going to feel bad on his big day. I'm a selfish, horrible person.

"Now remember," he said. "When you're splitting wood, wear the safety goggles. And keep your arms straight. Let the ax do the work."

He'd split enough wood in the past few weeks to keep the fireplace and wood stove going all winter and then some, but I saluted his silly instructions. "Yes, sir."

"And you keep that print shop door locked when you're working alone there, Missy."

"Okay! I'll try to remember."

"There is no try, there is only do." He shouldered his duffel bag and edged closer to me. "And Whitney?"

"Yes?"

His eyes roamed my face as if he were trying to memorize it, then he said, "I love you too."

I rolled my eyes. "Oh. Good. I was worried, because you hadn't said it yet."

"And one more thing."

"Yes?"

"When I'm 'thinking,' I don't picture Reese Witherspoon. I picture you."

Taking hold of the front of his coat, I laughed into his chest. "Creepy."

"You know you love it."

"Oddly enough, I do."

With one final kiss to my forehead, he backed away and grabbed his suitcase handle. As I was rounding the front of the car to reclaim the driver's side, he took a few steps toward the concourse, then turned so he was backing away from me and yelled into the snow-speckled wind, "See you... whenever!"

"Call me when you land and get settled!" I shouted back.

"We'll see! I may be too busy partying with my new girlfriend!"

I shot him a middle finger.

He pretended to catch it, like it was a precious blown kiss. "Thanks!"

Something told me romance wasn't going to be our strong suit as a couple.

I was okay with that.

CHAPTER THIRTY-THREE

THE DAY BEFORE CHRISTMAS EVE, I was standing in the middle of my sparkling (yet still empty), mold-free house, bucket in hand, having completed a major cleaning binge to keep my mind off spending my first Christmas without Aunt Vel.

She loved this time of year. No, she didn't go crazy with the decorations or start listening to Christmas music the day after Halloween or anything extreme like that. But she embodied the spirit of the season, and she delighted in the fact that even the scroogiest of Scrooges made more of an effort to be kind at this time of year. It might only manifest itself in dropping some money in a red kettle on the way in or out of a store, but the smallest goodwill offerings add up when spread over an entire population. And generosity is contagious. When someone does something unexpectedly nice for you, you feel beholden to keep the streak alive.

So far this year, though, no matter how hard I'd tried, I hadn't been able to muster that spirit, that bubbling, burbling, just-under-the-surface holiday joy. Of course I was still faking it. But there were too many missing elements for me to really feel it. I was still living in a guest room in someone else's house, so I didn't feel comfortable putting up a tree, much less tackling a roof line like Eric's to hang lights. Anyway, who would I be decorating for? Vel was gone. Eric wasn't there. Buster would probably try to eat the pine needles and get sick. No, I figured it was best to keep plugging along like nothing was different, biding my time until I could get to a place that felt familiar.

Boston was going to be my salvation. I'd planned to pass the next couple of days there with family. Unfortunately, we were expecting more snow on top of what we already had, and since the first thirty minutes of my two-hour drive was a two-lane highway wasn't not exactly straight and flat, those plans might have to get abandoned. White-knuckle driving wasn't my favorite.

Larry and the Doolans (which sounded like a Bluegrass band) had graciously invited me to celebrate the holiday with them, as the newest honorary member of the family, but it wouldn't be as much fun without Eric. Although he had a week off from classes, he'd decided to stay in Florida to take advantage of the quiet and work on his first big project, a basic game design due in less than three weeks.

I was disappointed by his decision, but I acted like it was no big deal. After all, I had plenty to keep me busy. He wasn't the only one working hard. It wasn't like I was sitting around doing nothing, waiting for a guy to dictate the direction of my life. Business at Velvet was going well, and my house was finally move-in ready. A few more weeks was totally surviv-able. Buster and I were doing fine. We were strong, indepen-dent... beings. Most days.

As I was admiring the results of my scrubbing in the cozy Cape Cod, the day's mail whispered through the slot in the front door and landed with a slap on the wooden floor. I peeled off my rubber gloves, dropping them into the bucket with the other cleaning supplies and setting it all down next to the front door. Among the junk mail and bills was an envelope bearing the name of the contractor who'd renovated this place.

"That was fast," I muttered. "Don't be shy." Then again, it would be good to have a definite figure to give Niles, so he'd be able to advise me how best to pay for this. Worst case scenario: putting up the house as collateral and taking out a big loan at the bank. Best case scenario: I had enough money in the bank to cover it. Unfortunately, I already knew that wasn't the case, since the contractor had provided me with an estimate before starting work, and it contained more zeroes than I saw each week when I check my account balance. But a girl could dream, right?

Cringing, I tore off one end of the envelope and slid the neatly folded invoice from it. With one eye closed, I flattened the sheet of paper and looked sideways at it, hoping that would make the astounding figure easier to absorb. Instead, three stamped red words greeted me.

PAID IN FULL

Scrawled under that was a sloppy "thank you" from the contractor.

My breath quickening, I stared at the total: $49,653.

My first-grade rounding skills told me that was suspiciously close to a figure that had entered more than a few debates between a certain guy and myself over the past few months.

I texted him with shaking fingers.

You know anything about a fully paid contractor's bill of nearly $50K?

Within seconds, he replied, *Maybe. Depends on how a strong, independent woman feels about that.*

Honestly, I felt like one of the luckiest people on the planet. But I had a reputation to uphold. I tapped back, albeit with a huge grin on my face, *She hates it.*

There are a few ways she can pay me back.

She *definitely* can't agree to those terms. Gross!

I was talking about house sitting, perv.

That is NOT an equal trade.

Equality is overrated.

Not a good argument for this audience.

Fine. Then she can pay me back with no interest, instead of paying back a stupid bank.

I contemplated that for a few seconds. It satisfied the pride test, so I replied, *Deal.*

I hit "send," but immediately composed and sent my next message. *And I'll tack on that other stuff for free.*

Cool. Gotta go "think" now.

While I was thumbing my next zippy retort—a humdinger about splitting wood, maybe—the door behind me creaked open. Spinning, I blushed at being caught texting innuendos with my boyfriend and wondered who was entering my house without knocking. It took my eyes forever to communicate to my brain what—or who—I was seeing. When I did, I nearly dropped my phone. I did drop the invoice.

Eric grinned at me. "That's right. Stomp on that thing and forget all about it."

"W-what are you doing here?" I asked, while shoving my phone into my deep sweater pocket.

"Just wanted to say, 'Merry Christmas.' And drop off this present." He lifted an all-too-familiar heart-speckled gift bag. "I didn't get it into the mail in time, so I thought I'd fly it up here in person."

With one step from him and another from me, we were chest-to-chest. I hopped into his embrace and buried my face in his neck. He held me with my feet a few inches off the floor. The bag tapped against my shoulder blade.

After a tight, prolonged hug, I pulled back from him and lowered my feet to the ground, and although he loosened his hold on me, he didn't let go. I looked up into his face, a face I'd missed enough that it sometimes caused physical pain.

"You're so tan!" I said, when I couldn't think of anything else that wouldn't make me cry.

"It's sunny down there. All the time. When it's not pouring rain. There's, like, no in between."

"I— I wasn't expecting to see you for another two weeks, at least."

"What's wrong? Needed more notice before I came home? Did you trash my house?"

"No! You said you had a project to do, though. You—" I scowled at him. "You *lied* to me!"

"I did *not!* I do have a project to do. And I did plan to work on it during the break. But... I couldn't concentrate on it. So I changed my mind. Do you want me to leave?"

"No! But why didn't you tell me? I would have picked you up from the airport and... and... planned a nice dinner and..." I patted my hair. "I would have taken a shower."

He nudged my nose with his. "You want to take one now? Test out the new walls?"

The shock of seeing him so unexpectedly finally caught up to me, and I sank to the stairs.

With a wince, he set the gift bag by the door and followed me. "Right. Creepy. Sorry. Plenty of time for that later. Maybe. I don't want to assume. I was just spitballing."

I smiled up at him as he settled next to me on the step. "I'm so glad to see you. And—other than the tan—you haven't changed a bit. You're still gloriously awkward and funny and... You didn't meet any purple-haired gaming goddesses down there, did you?"

He looked toward his forehead and pretends to think about it. "Not purple-haired..." He grabbed my hands. "We talk every day. Why would I be different than I was when we talked yesterday?"

I shook my head and admitted, "I don't know. It... it's weird to have you right here, where I can touch you." I bumped knees with him. "Ten minutes ago, I was bleaching everything in this place to within an inch of its life, trying not to think too much about Christmas and how much I miss Aunt Vel... and you. But now you're here."

"I miss her too," he said, pulling me closer with an arm around my shoulders. "That's part of why I originally planned to stay down there. If I spent the holiday alone, it wouldn't feel like the holiday, and it wouldn't be as obvious what's missing this year. But it didn't quite work out how I'd thought. I still missed her, and I was lonely for you." He stared into space for a few seconds, then blinked and surveyed the empty space. "The place looks great." Gesturing to the living room through the open French doors, he said, "Remember that scraggly tree she put up every year?"

"Oh, my gosh, yes! It was awful. It's the only artificial tree I've ever seen shed more than a real one."

"That stupid thing was almost as old as me. But she wouldn't replace it. Or let me cut down a real one for her."

"No way! Tradition!" I said in the same tone she always used.

"Yeah. Tradition." After a few beats of silence, he took a deep breath. "Well, after last year, when I came over to take it down for her, and she was already sick, had gotten that horrible prognosis the week before Christmas, she said, 'I guess you can save yourself the trouble of lugging that thing to the attic. Put it by the curb. I won't need it anymore, and I know you hate it.'"

He stopped, but suspecting he wasn't done, I said nothing.

He tapped his heels a few times, jiggling his legs. "Anyway. I, uh, had been begging her for years to get rid of that damn thing, but when she gave me permission... I... I didn't want to do it. I dragged it from the living room without an argument, but I stood here at the bottom of the stairs for a while, trying to decide if I was going to take it out the front door or put it back in the attic."

I hadn't been in the attic in the months I'd lived here, nor thought about Christmas. I hadn't been planning to stay that long, for one thing. Was it possible...?

"I carried it upstairs. In the hallway, under the pull-down stairs, I threw it onto the floor and stared at it some more. Then I got the box from the attic and tossed it down the ladder. While I squeezed the bendable branches to collapse them and get the stupid thing to fit in the box, plastic needles fell everywhere. They stuck to my clothes and covered the hallway rug. I wrestled that thing into its box and pushed it up the ladder ahead of me. It wasn't until I was vacuuming the hallway that I realized I was crying. Bawling. Like a little kid. Snot and tears and yawning frowny face... the whole shebang."

"Oh, Eric..."

"She had to have heard me, down here on the couch, weak and shivering under some blankets. But when I came down-stairs after putting away the vacuum and composing myself in the bathroom, she didn't say a word. We never spoke about it. She pointed to the other boxes of Christmas decorations that needed to go back in storage, and it was like every other year." He sniffed matter-of-factly. "She called and told you she was sick the next day."

I pondered that timeline and wondered for the millionth time at all of the things that had happened in this house, in this town, in her life, that I never could have fathomed. When Aunt Vel didn't make the trip to Boston last year, we had all figured it was the usual: too busy with the print shop to travel. My plan had been to ring in the new year with her, like I often did when we couldn't spend Christmas Day together. Her call had changed everything, not just my New Year arrangements.

Now, without warning, I shot to my feet and trotted up the stairs, pulling him behind me.

"Are we going to test the shower walls?" he asked. "It's the responsible thing to do, you know. Or is this because you feel sorry for me and don't want me to be sad? Either way, I'm cool with it. I've never been too proud to turn down pity sex."

In the hallway upstairs, I opened the linen closet and pulled out the wooden rod with the metal hook on the end, then threaded the hook through the loop on the attic access panel above us.

"What are you doing?" he asked, bemused, while I struggled to achieve the proper leverage to open the panel and extend the collapsible stairs. He reached out to help. "It's up there, I promise."

"I believe you. And we're going to put it up."

"We are?"

"Yep."

"In this empty house?" he said to my disappearing form, as I climbed the ladder/steps.

"Yep!" I shouted down. Not far from the top of the ladder rested the long, rectangular box with "Christmas Tree" written on the side in sloppy, cursive magic marker. I slid it across the plywood boards and held it at one end, easing it through the opening. "Here it comes!" I warned.

"I got it," I heard from below, so I let go of the box and looked around for the containers of Christmas ornaments.

An hour later, we linked arms in front of a fully trimmed, patchy fake fir, which stood proudly in the empty living room in its usual place, framed by the front window. It had never looked better.

"We're burning this thing after this year, though, right?" Eric checked, toeing a pile of fake needles at our feet.

"Absolutely." I turned to face him and stood on my tiptoes to reach his lips.

Instead of kissing me, he disappointed me by stepping away. He returned a few seconds later with the heart-covered gift bag, which he nestled on top of the skirt under the tree. Back at my side, he admired our handiwork. "There. Now it's perfect."

I squeezed his hand. "Can't wait to open it."

"It's not your real present, you know. Just some silly trinkets from Florida."

"Yeah, my real present is standing right here." I made a second attempt at the kiss I'd tried to start before he got distracted.

He obliged this time. At the end of the first long kiss, he smiled against my lips. "Something tells me Vel got exactly what she wanted for Christmas this year."

"I did, too. Now, let's go test out that shower."

ACKNOWLEDGMENTS

Thanks to family and friends who supported me through the writing of this book, one of many writing ideas spawned during a routine commute that took me past a funeral home but that was a bit more difficult to execute than I originally imagined. Thanks for putting up with my death puns and my half-giggled stories about how awkward one imaginary person could be. I know you're tempted to reach for your phone and call the white coats when I get like that, so I appreciate your resisting that impulse and waiting me out.

Beta readers Erin Baker, Kaley Stewart, Lynda G., Hans Campbell, Heather McCoubrey, Karen Richmond, Elizabeth Jenkins, and Natasha Walsh did their usual bang-up job on their test reads of the first final draft of the book, resulting in a longer, less superficial story than the one I originally handed them. Much longer. If you like big books, you can thank them. If you don't, blame me for being verbose. Special shout-out to Heather, whose insider knowledge of Maine made a big difference in several parts of the book, and Hans, whose explanation of tax law helped with one particular section of dialogue. Thanks to all of you for your time, attention, and diligence to my stories while carrying on your own busy lives.

Thanks, too, to the most understanding, flexible, talented, and hard-working editors and publishers in the biz, Dorothy Zemach and Maggie Sokolik of Wayzgoose Press. This edition is a bit different than the original I published in 2016. Dorothy encouraged me to focus on my current work and took care of everything; all I had to do was review the changes. I can't tell you what a relief it was. So thanks to the best publishers EVER for doing the heavy lifting.

In one of my odder thanks, I'd like to acknowledge the undertakers of this world. Morticians and funeral home directors tend to be joked about or stereotyped, but in our times of grief, they're there for us to take care of the things we'd rather not or simply *can't* do. They spend all day every day among mourners. Death doesn't take a weekend. And they treat our loved ones with respect as we say our final goodbyes. In the process of writing this book, I learned a lot about mortician sciences, yet I only scratched the surface of the industry, one that is rapidly evolving in modern times. For the purposes of my story, a romantic comedy, I took a lighter view and stuck closer to outsiders' preconceived notions of working with the dead. However, these professionals take their responsibilities seriously and provide an invaluable service. It's not sexy; it's not glamorous. It's downright thankless sometimes. So maybe next time you're at a funeral, take a minute to hug a funeral home staff member. Or not. That might be weird. Nodding your appreciation may be sufficient.

Finally, thanks to you, loyal reader, for continuing to return every time I birth a new book. Thanks for "ooh"ing and "aah"ing over my baby and for telling others how cute it is. Your support is amazing. It takes a village, right? Happy reading!

The *Secret Keeper* series:

- *The Secret Keeper* (Book 1)
- *The Secret Keeper Confined* (Book 2)
- *The Secret Keeper Up All Night* (Book 3)
- *The Secret Keeper Holds On* (Book 4)
- *The Secret Keeper Lets Go* (Book 5)
- *The Secret Keeper Fulfilled* (Book 6)

The *Underdog* series:

- *Out of My League* (Book 1)
- *Rookie of the Year* (Book 2)
- *Opportunity Knox* (Book 3)
- *Ready or Knox* (Book 4)

The *Nurse Nate* series:

- *Let's Be Frank* (Book 1)
- *Let's Be Real* (Book 2)
- *Let's Be Friends* (Book 3)

Stand-alone novels:

- *Daydreamer*
- *The Family Plot*
- *Plain Jayne*
- *Quiet, Please!*